Bones Beneath Our Feet

Michael Schein

B&H Bennett & Hastings Publishing

Contents

IV
Treason & Surrender
(March 11 – November 14, 1856)

V
Justice & Mercy
(November 15, 1856 – February 19, 1858)

Author's Note

What follows is fiction, deeply rooted in fact. The essential story and many of the principal characters and details are historically accurate, but I have altered events, created and omitted characters, and shortened a few time periods for dramatic effect.

I dedicate this work to my wife Carol, my daughters, Ava and Nellie, and my son-in-law, Tristan. I also dedicate it to the pioneers and the natives of *Whulge*. Throughout I have asked myself, *could we the living have done better?*

Map of Washington Territory, 1854

At night when the streets of your cities and villages are silent and you think them deserted, they will throng with the returning hosts that once filled them and still love this beautiful land. The white man will never be alone. Let him be just and deal kindly with my people, for the dead are not powerless.

Chief Se-alth

The dead have their own tasks.

Rainer Maria Rilke

I

Tenalquot

1815 – 1849

Chapter One
The Boy Listened

1

The boy listened with his ear against the door for the sound of his mother's breathing. He didn't dare to peek inside, for fear of inciting fresh rage. He didn't dare to leave her, having seen before the effects of this deep melancholia. His father was out in the fields, and besides, what use was he? It was Father's fault that Mother was in this condition. Hadn't Father held the reins that terrible night two years before when the carriage overturned and Mother struck her head and the blood was unstoppable?

Mother, oh dear Mother, how I miss you!

She was right there, behind the white door, but the haggard thing filling Mother's bedclothes was a cruel caricature of the mother of Isaac's memory. How he clung to the image of an industrious, loving and cheerful woman, ready to solve any problem, heal any hurt. But at nine it is hard to hold on to the memories of a seven year old. Which was the true mother, which the imagined?

"No! NO!! You can't fool me – I know what you're up to!" came the guttural cry from within the closed chamber. That was the real mother now, alternately sullen and apoplectic. Isaac heard a crash from within, the sound of breaking china. Swallowing hard, he tried the door. It was locked.

Moans like lava streamed from behind the door. Isaac pushed his shoulder against the barrier, but it would not budge. "NO – POISON!" his mother cried. Furniture scraped, then clunked against the door. Desperate, Isaac ran to fetch the stove ax, then flew back up the stairs, sisters in pursuit. Little Oliver, the toddler, exploded in tears. And where was that no-good servant Amy, whose job it was to care for their mother?

From inside the room came an eerie sound: sobs, interspersed with brittle sing-song, "Hannah Cummings, Cummings and Goings, Goings and Cummings, Hannah my dear!" Then more sobs, so violent they degenerated into clutching gasps for breath. "Goodbye Hannah, Daddy's a Deacon, Deacon of Dying, Going to God."

"Oh Isaac," cried sister Elizabeth, "do something, quick!" as she too tried the door, but it would not budge. "Mother!" called the sisters in unison.

"Children, is that you?" came a voice from within, not quite their mother. A pause. "Children?" A very taut voice.

"Yes, Mother," replied Isaac, trying to stay calm. "Would you let us in, please?" Another pause, a long one, the children barely daring to breathe.

"SAVE YOURSELVES!" Glass shattering. Isaac swung the ax with a strength he'd never known, splitting the door from top to bottom. Isaac and his sisters joined together to thrust away the remnants of white splinters and the rolltop desk jammed up tight. Scrambling through, Isaac was horrified to find his mother straddling the window casement, blood oozing from a dozen cuts inflicted by the jagged glass. In a single bound he was across the room as she pushed off with her trailing foot. He was just able to grab her arm as she fell, pinioning his legs against the moldings. She looked back into his eyes, no sign of recognition in her hateful gaze. "Be gone, ye creature of Satan!" she hissed, but he would not be gone. Though he feared to dislodge her shoulder he pulled for all he was worth. The months of barely pecking at her plate made her light, and he reeled her in like some strange sea creature, who flopped onto the glass-strewn floor, bleeding and unconscious.

Isaac Ingalls Stevens lay down beside his mother, heedless of the glass, trembling head to toe. His sisters stood silent, mouths agape; his little brother wailed. His father and Amy appeared at the doorway, blinking, disoriented, disheveled. Isaac shot his father a cold look. He did not permit himself tears until late that night, when he was alone.

2

The boy listened to the alien sounds coming from the stream bed just beyond the cedars. This was his first quest, to retrieve a medicine stick planted by his father next to the dead snag on *She-nah-nam* creek. Flushed with excitement, he had set out bravely, scampering as quickly as legs in their seventh summer could go. But now, creeping on his belly to the point where sheltering boughs brushed the crest of the bank above the dead snag, his quest seemed doomed to failure. With the tremulous caution of a doe, he parted the boughs a hand's width, and gingerly peeked out.

What Leschi saw was beyond all seeing. Ghost-cheeked men with hairy chins crawled along the creek. They smelled of death. Had some demon shape-shifted these creatures from dying wolves?

Leschi let the boughs fall closed, as he considered his next move. Of course he should turn and run back to the safety of the tribe. He remembered well the many times he had been cautioned against the dangers of the forest. The wolf, bear, cougar and wild boar were terrible, but more terrible still were the enchantments: dwarves who could steal a boy's reason; stealthy, quick demons of the forest like *Seatco*, who could enslave a boy in squalor.

To turn back would disgrace his family. To earn a vision quest Leschi must first pass the smaller tests set by his father. Without a vision quest, he could never know his *tamanous* - spirit guide. Without a *tamanous* he would be but a shadow, a nothing, worse than a slave.

Leschi again parted the curtain of cedar boughs. There were as many of the creatures as he had fingers on one hand. They were gutting and skinning otter, the blue-grey viscera disappearing silently in the creek's hungry current. Leschi was afraid. He closed his eyes, conjuring up his father's resonant voice: "Remember this well, children - in fear, there is no wisdom; only death and suffering."

Steeling himself against fear, Leschi studied the grasses waving under the caress of *Laliad*, the wind spirit. He didn't yet know how he would do it. All he knew was that it must be done. Somehow, he would find a way to creep undetected over open ground the length of a longhouse, retrieve the totem, and steal back to safety. *All under the malevolent eyes of the monsters.*

Leschi prayed to his mother for guidance, though she had perished bringing his sister Skai-kai into the world in his second summer. He could no longer picture his mother's face, but she was with him. She was the breeze in the grass, a voice - a clear sweet song washing over the cradleboard as she bent to her work:

> *Spirit dances in the rain, in the wave, in the wind,*
> *Spirit dances in rock and tree, you and me,*
> *Our hearts drum the dance.*

With a clarity before unknown to him, Leschi peered across the expanse of osoberry, horsetail, rushes, cattails, plantain, nettle. *Are we not the People of the River Grass?* asked his father's voice. The grasses beckoned to him, pointing the way. Breathing deep to fill his lungs, Leschi bent low then slipped from hiding to scamper around the edge of the demons' camp. His light copper skin melded with straw-colored stems and ochre-brown blades shifting in the wind. The padding of his bare feet harmonized with the susurrus of the grass. Just short of his goal, Leschi dropped to his belly, still as a fallen log.

The snag was surrounded by a circle of matted straw; no cover for the length of a stone's throw. Leschi could see the talisman, a pointed stick carved with the face of Raven, the trickster, stuck in the ground by the tree. He looked to the creatures, who appeared to be absorbed in their work. He was downwind, and their scent soured his nostrils like the *hamma hamma* -

rotting fish carcasses that littered the beach. He paused to ask the Creator, *Sah-hah-lee Tyee*, to make him invisible. Then he bolted across the open space and grabbed the medicine stick just as one of the monsters gave a cry, followed by a great babble rising behind him as he flew back to the welcoming grasses. Weaving through and back into the cover of the cedar forest, running like the Cayuse ponies whose hooves barely touch the ground, Leschi heard the demon gibberish fade in the distance, and he gave thanks to all the spirits who had guided him through his moment of peril.

That night, safe in the longhouse at Muck Creek, the first rains came. Soon it would be time to follow the salmon upriver for winter. Leschi inhaled the warm smell of cedar logs, woven grasses, skins and dried salmon, wet dogs trotting in and out. Clutching the raven totem close to his heart, he burrowed deep into the mound of sleeping boys under a bearskin blanket. His eyes grew heavy; his breaths merged with the rain and ancient forest and teeming Nisqually River; with the powerful salmon, sweet crab and musky clams; with the blue, salmon, thimble, black, straw, elder, salal, goose, and huckleberries of *Tenalquot*, the Happy Land, the land of more than enough.

3

Isaac Ingalls Stevens stood stiff and proud in his starched cadet's uniform with the bright red stripe running up the sides of grey trousers cuffed twice to keep from bagging, then tucked into spit-shined calf-high riding boots. His sinewy trunk swam a bit within the capacious grey woolen cut-away jacket with its padded shoulders and bright brass buttons. The plumed hat added welcome height to his otherwise diminutive stature; slipping the strap off his chin, he removed it with reluctance. Even after a full day of parading and drilling, a peculiar energy thrummed from Isaac's every pore. Gleaming hazel eyes were set in a head that appeared to belong elsewhere, perhaps on a man who wrestles alligators in a traveling exhibition. Isaac moved about the barracks sharp and smart, always rushing to keep that oversized head balanced on wiry shoulders. As light dimmed in the western sky, he brushed and folded his uniform with immaculate care, then knelt by his mattress to pray.

As always, Isaac first asked for the Lord to watch over his beloved mother Hannah in Heaven, to which she ascended just a few short months after her abortive attempt to fly from the window. Next he asked the Lord to watch over his sisters and his younger brother, back in Andover. Dutifully, though with less enthusiasm, he prayed to God for blessings upon his father, Isaac Sr., and for Amy, his young stepmother, whom Isaac and his siblings had never forgiven for supplanting their mother. Finally, as he had every night for the short time he had been at West Point, Isaac prayed for "that character of proud disdain and patriotic valor which has inspired the great heroes of history, Alexander, Napoleon, Washington, Jackson, and, God be willing, Stevens."

Isaac's meditations were interrupted by laughter and cursing wafting on whiskey fumes from the opposite corner of the barracks, where a knot of cadets clumped around a game of dice. Gambling, drinking and swearing were strictly prohibited, of course, but since DeRussi had replaced Superintendent Thayer, disciplinary standards had steadily declined. It pained Isaac to realize that even his own hero, General Jackson, had contributed to this sorry state of affairs by reinstating dismissed cadets who were mere riff-raff – part of Old Hickory's perpetual but, to Isaac's mind, misguided, battle against "privilege."

"Gentlemen," cried Isaac, his voice bordering on command, "you discredit our service. To your bunks!"

Silas Casey, an Irish upperclassman whose large head was perfectly matched to broad shoulders and muscled arms, rose up to cast a bemused look at the little plebe who fancied himself a Commandant. "Quiet, gentlemen," said Casey, holding his hand up to his ear, "I think we've got mice!" As the gamblers erupted in derisive laughter, Isaac felt a hot flush in his cheeks. Springing from his bunk, he was across the barracks in a flash, nose to Adam's apple with the startled Casey.

"You, Sir, shall retract that insult!" announced Isaac, with an assurance belied by his stature. Casey, towering over the plebe, swayed a bit from the effects of the alcohol. Uncertainty knitted his brow; he wasn't a bad sort, he didn't wish to crush the mouse, only to set him straight as to what's what. Strategically, the battlefield appeared well under control, so Casey took a long pull at the bottle, set it down carefully, and with practiced swiftness grabbed Isaac's nose and twisted, hard, until the little man went down.

Ha-ha, that done, Casey reached for his bottle, but it was gone! The mouse shot through his legs, sprang up from behind and smashed the bottle across the back of Casey's skull. The bigger man tottered in his tracks, licking at a drop of bloody whiskey, a puzzled expression on his face, as the other cadets stepped back to make room for his fall. When it didn't come fast enough, this mouse – no, this feral rodent – leapt up and kicked Casey in the kidneys, causing him to collapse with a hollow wheeze. It took four cadets to pull Stevens off Casey. From that day until the day in 1839 when Isaac Stevens graduated first in his class, no one ever again taunted West Point's littlest cadet.

Chapter Two
Patkanim's Gambit

1

The Scotsman, Dr. William F. Tolmie, hunkered down into his hooded otterskin mackinaw, though it only protected him from falling rain, not the drenching mist that rose up out of the Puget Sound muck and penetrated everything like a swarm of soggy locusts. It was not just the damp that fretted his shaggy chestnut-bearded face this cold October day in 1843; it was the burden of responsibilities. As newly-appointed Hudson's Bay Company Chief Factor for Fort Nisqually, Tolmie was responsible for seven thousand head of cattle, ten thousand sheep, three thousand horses, a Fort with its trading post and vegetable gardens, and a mercurial workforce. A headstrong brew of descendents of Conquistadors, trappers from the beaver dams of wild French Canada, pagan Natives, British prison refuse, American fugitives, and rotund, implacable Sandwich Islanders vexed Tolmie from dawn to dusk to dawn again.

On this day, Dr. Tolmie was concerned with one particularly unfortunate Sandwich Islander, found dead that morning among the company potatoes. Everyone was watching to see what he would do, measuring just what they could get away with.

The 32-year old Tolmie ducked into the trading post, flicked back his hood to reveal a broad, ruddy forehead, and strode to the front of the room. He saw little sign of welcome in the thirty scruffy faces distorted by the capricious light of whale oil lanterns, but that did not deter him.

"I think you know why we're here, gentlemen. A company employee's been killed on company property." He paused for emphasis. "So long as I'm Chief, we will take care of our own." Measuring the effect of this pronouncement, he concluded, "I want any information you have, and I want it right now."

A beefy young American named Jack Blunt spoke up. "I seen the body. Scalped, like a skinned rabbit, ears gone, jest a skull bone an' bloody pulp fer hair, unnerstand me?" His bright blue eyes raked the room. "Bastard *siwash* done it, who else?" he concluded, using the derogatory term which roughly translated to "savages." Others darkly murmured their agreement. "Mebbe we should pay us a call on that village at Muck Creek," he added. Some men started moving towards the doorway.

"Stop right there, gentlemen," commanded Tolmie, the rounded tones of his London-educated vowels carrying the ancient ring of authority. "I've traded these parts on and off since '33, and seen enough scalps in the hands of our own people to know that scalping is proof of precisely nothing." So, the new Chief Factor was no tenderfoot. "Besides, you men know it's the policy of the company to maintain friendly relations with the Natives."

"So yer jest gonna let 'em cut us down, one by one?" Blunt shot back.

"No, I'm just going to save your bollocks and the company's property by making sure we hang the right Indian. We don't want to give the other fifty thousand in these parts any excuse to take revenge on a few hundred white folks." The doctor stared down Blunt.

"I stand with Dr. Tolmie," cried a young Englishman in buckskin, sporting a beard and a long hunting knife in his belt. "I've often traded with the Natives in these parts, and most of them are peaceable enough – if not provoked; right pardner?" he added in a mocking American twang, glaring at Blunt.

Before Blunt could respond, Dr. Tolmie interjected, "Thank-you, Sir, mister –?"

"John Edgar," said the young fellow.

"Mr. Edgar," repeated the doctor. He paused. Seeing that the group was back in hand, Tolmie continued, "Huggins, please show in our guests, there's a good fellow."

"Yes, Sir!" Huggins disappeared into the storeroom, and emerged a moment later with two Indians, one short and bowlegged with the characteristic sloping forehead of the Coastal Salish, but the other tall and erect, with the more rounded head, light complexion, and aquiline nose of a Yakama warrior.

An ominous grumbling arose among the white men. Dr. Tolmie cut them off. "Gentlemen, these two come from the local Nisqually band. Without any offer of reward, and perhaps at some risk to themselves," he glared at Blunt, "they came to me this afternoon, bearing information about this crime." Then, Dr. Tolmie did something that no other white man in the room could do; he turned to the Indians and began conversing, not in the Chinook trading jargon, but in their own native *Whulshootseed* tongue.

The tall Indian then addressed the crowd through Dr. Tolmie, as interpreter. "Greetings, King George Men. I bring you the good wishes of my people, the Nisquallies. As many of you know, I am called Leschi, and this is my brother, Quiemuth. We share your sorrow at the loss of your brother. We, too, have suffered losses at the same hand. We have examined the cuttings on your brother, and have been to the shoreline and seen the marks left by the war canoes. From this we think we know who made this attack."

"And who might that be?" came a question from the crowd. Dr. Tolmie translated.

"It was the work of the Snoqualmies."

"Patkanim's tribe," added Dr. Tolmie, to show he'd done his homework.

"And how do we know it ain't these siwashes, Leschi and his brother, out to throw yer limey noses off the scent?" interjected Blunt, and some of the other men grunted in support.

Dr. Tolmie placed his hand on Leschi's shoulder. "I think I know an honest man when I see one," was all he said. It was the way he stared at Blunt while saying it that turned it to an insult.

"That's good enough for me," said Edgar, and enough of the other men nodded approval to carry the crowd. But as they dispersed, someone grumbled, "I think I know a horse's ass when I see one," followed by *Har! Har! Har!* more like the crack of a whip than a laugh. It was Blunt, no mirth in his eyes.

2

The next morning, Leschi, Quiemuth, and ten painted warriors, led Dr. Tolmie and his musket-wielding force of twenty men, out of the Nisqually reach in two war canoes. They paddled through drenching rain into the narrows, a swift-running choppy passage between the mainland and a peninsula named for old Chief Kitsap, who had guided Captain Vancouver's wind-drinking canoe. "*Me-si-ka-kwass kopa s'kookum chuck?*" laughed Leschi, when he saw a few of the King George men turn green – "Are you afraid of the rough waters?"

Inland they paddled on the Black River with powerful smooth strokes, pausing to sleep one night along sand beaches on the great lake of the Duwamish, which the white man called "Lake Washington." There they dug for freshwater clams and buried them in the sand, wrapped in seaweed atop hot rocks, then feasted on the delicate viscous flesh, hot and fragrant. The next morning, they broke camp and paddled up the Sammamish River into a foreboding wind under a canopy of grey, to half-way up the great expanse of Lake Sammamish. There they hid the canoes and marched east on narrow forest paths until they approached Halalt, the central stronghold of Chief Patkanim of the Snoqualmies. Leschi and Quiemuth led the way to the edge of a clearing across from where the Tolt emptied into the Snoqualmie River, within view of Patkanim's cedar longhouse, but not so near as to alert the sentries guarding the perimeter.

The brothers huddled a few minutes with Dr. Tolmie, and then the white men and Quiemuth hid nearby in a thick spruce grove. The remaining Nisquallies stepped boldly from the edge of the wood. Owl calls of sentries sang across the clearing to the longhouse. War canoes launched almost as quickly as the echoing cries died in the distant hills, and soon Leschi and his ten braves were confronted by Chief Patkanim, his brother Kassas, and thirty warriors. A few were armed with the Hudson's Bay fusee musket that bore the distinctive burnished brass dragon side ornament; the rest were armed with spears, clubs, knives, bows and arrows. Patkanim was dressed in a rag-tag King George suit, a black frock coat over his red flannel shirt, with fringed native buckskin leggings over his bowed legs. His canny eyes darted under a battered top hat adorned with eagle feathers. His weasel-quick smooth face was smeared with vermillion and black paint. In the crook of his arm he cradled his prize, a gleaming British percussion musket.

Patkanim smiled, revealing his perfect white teeth. "Leschi, to what do we owe the honor of this visit?" he inquired in *Whulshootseed*. "Have you come to smoke a pipe with your brother-in-law?"

"Great *Tyee*, nothing would give me more pleasure," responded Leschi evenly, "but first, there is a small matter."

"Yes?" asked Patkanim, mentally calculating Leschi's value when taken alive as his *elita* – slave.

"It seems that one of the King George men was killed the other day, and the King Georges will be looking to our tribe for revenge if we do not bring them the guilty party. I happen to know that it was one of your people. I have come to demand his surrender." Leschi paused, sizing up Patkanim's bemused expression. "I do not ask this for nothing, great *Tyee*," continued Leschi, his flattery intended to maintain the illusion of weakness. "We offer this: ten company blankets for the guilty man."

Patkanim considered the circumstances. He knew well who had done the deed, which he himself had ordered. Quallawort, his loyal brother, had the glory of that kill. Quallawort, so different from his other brother Kassas, who plotted against him even as he stood there by his side.

And now Leschi had come to him carrying the white man's spear. What a fool! These white men were a pestilence upon the land; the sooner they were wiped out, the better. Right now, their numbers were small, their fortifications weak; but in the moons to come, who could tell? The Nisquallies were like old women, always talking peace and friendship, spending their days lolling about the riverbanks, getting fat on salmon and clams. He regretted marrying Leschi's sister, Skai-kai, though she was surely a beauty; what had he gained besides

21

her marriage price? The Nisquallies were worthless as allies against the Haida from the North or the King George men; even worthless as enemies. They were nothing to be feared. Patkanim was ready to order the attack, when …

The blue-grey peregrine falcon, Patkanim's *tamanous*, plummeted from the sky in a clear straight dive, its white breast like a shooting star. The attack was silent but for the crack as it struck its hapless target in mid-air. A *warning*. Patkanim's senses heightened, and suddenly he knew that Leschi was not fool enough to show himself like this without some hidden reinforcement. A trap, and as he cursed to himself, he nonetheless felt a grudging admiration for this one Nisqually.

Still, he was Patkanim, greatest Chief of *Whulge*, the great water. Could he not turn every situation to advantage? Like the falcon, he must be swift and ruthless. Perhaps today was not the day to fight; he would let the white man do his killing.

"Thirty blankets," was Patkanim's response. Surprise filled the eyes of his warriors, but they dared not flinch beside their leader. Leschi watched closely, noting the moment of fear in Kassas' eyes. Skai-kai had informed him that Patkanim suspected Kassas of treachery.

"Twenty," countered Leschi.

"Twenty and two muskets; I have said it," was Patkanim's reply. Leschi nodded tersely. The two men stepped forward to clasp in a firm embrace, sealing the fate of Kassas.

3

Leschi and his braves returned, bearing Kassas trussed up like a pig for the fire, and dropped him at the feet of Dr. Tolmie.

"So, this is the murderer?" asked Tolmie. Leschi said nothing. Tolmie took him by both shoulders. "Thank-you, my friend."

They camped with their prisoner on the shore of Lake Sammamish. Leschi was uneasy. Time and again his eyes met those of Kassas, who bore his captivity stoically. Leschi brought him meat from the fire, and had the guard adjust his restraints so he could eat and rest with a semblance of comfort. The two men spoke as Kassas ate his supper.

Afterwards, Leschi unburdened himself to Quiemuth. "Brother, I cannot rest because Kassas is not the right man. Let's go back and get the real murderer."

Quiemuth had been against going to the King George fort in the first place, but Leschi with his gift for words had moved the council. Now, he had to admit, the plan looked to be a good one. The advantage was theirs; why spoil it?

"Leschi, as the elder I say: you must be practical. What do we care which man Patkanim chooses to throw to the *t'kope tillicum* – the white man? You said we should help the King George men so they would not seek revenge on our own village. That is done. Nothing more is necessary."

"Yes, brother, as usual, your wisdom is greater than mine." Leschi paused. "But what of your heart?"

Quiemuth hid the sting. "My heart keeps me alive, brother," he replied evenly. "So does yours," he added. "See that it does not also get you killed." He chewed thoughtfully at a strip of pemmican. "Now get some sleep. The way is long, there is always another time to be foolish." Quiemuth lay down, wrapped in a tightly woven company blanket, and soon he was breathing evenly.

Leschi could not sleep, so he went to see Dr. Tolmie. He found the doctor smoking his pipe by lantern light, scratching at one of the white man's talking papers with a metal stick. Tolmie looked up. "What is it, my friend?" he asked in *Whulshootseed*.

"*Tyee* doctor," said Leschi, "I do not think this man is the one."

"What?"

"I know Patkanim; I know his tricks. If he gave a man so easily, it is not the right man."

"Well, I am sorry about that Leschi, but I have a responsibility to maintain order at my fort. We have a murder; we have a Chief who has surrendered a suspect; now we must have a *trial*" – he used the English word – "and deal with this in our own way."

"This man," persisted Leschi, "is Kassas, Patkanim's brother. I know him; he is a good man. I have spoken with him. He says he is innocent, and I believe him. But," here Leschi looked away, "he refuses to tell me who is responsible."

"Then it is out of my hands," said the doctor, peremptorily. Seeing Leschi's anguish, he added more softly, "It is out of your hands, too, Leschi. Among our people, we have a tradition: it is called a *trial*." Again, that strange English word. There was no comparable word in Leschi's own language, and the closest Chinook was *pight* – battle.

"A *t-lial?*" Leschi wrestled the unfamiliar consonant.

"*TRI-al*," repeated the doctor. "It is a special kind of council to test whether the man we have accused is guilty or innocent of the murder. It is not for you, or for me, or for Patkanim, or for anyone else to say; that is for the jury to say, at the trial. If this man is not guilty, then the trial will protect him."

"This is good," said Leschi. "This *t-lial* must be strong medicine." Leschi thanked the doctor. They sat together a little longer, smoking and listening, as unseen waves lapped polished stones in the thin starlight. At length, Leschi returned to sleep by his brother, his conscience clear.

Four days later, after the trial, Kassas was pronounced guilty for the murder he did not commit, and hanged by the neck until dead.

Chapter Three
Helping Hands

1

Curse that incompetent orderly, thought Lieutenant Isaac Stevens, as he rode back from the front just south of Mexico City, towards the village of Coyoacan. Hadn't he given strict instructions that he was to be awakened at three a.m. sharp? It mortified him to think that the unwanted two hours of extra sleep had cost him another shot at the history books. While he dozed, General Persifor Smith routed Santa Anna's main force without him.

Stevens' bile rose all the more as he considered his many lost opportunities. He had shared the enthusiasm of his brothers in arms when war with Mexico broke out at last in 1845. "Ain't it glorious!" cried his friend McClellan. It seemed so, until Stevens was left behind because his command of forts protecting the New England and Mid-Atlantic coasts was deemed too important to permit reassignment to Mexico. Border tensions with Great Britain were high; rumors had it that the British fleet might sail any day. Having Stevens at home pleased Mrs. Margaret Stevens and was good for the children – his little man, four-year old Hazard, and his precious baby girl, Virginia – but it didn't suit Isaac. He hadn't chosen a military career for a life of pencil-pushing and nursery duty. He was a man of action, destined for greatness; not like his father who'd failed in business and come running home, tail between his legs, to do nothing but take out his frustration on dear Mother.

Oh, the pain of those years before mobilization in January, 1847. It seemed that all life was but the reaper's grim bluff. In five short years Isaac had lost all four of his sisters to the wracking, bleeding, gasping consumption. Then, on the very eve of their wedding, Meg's father dropped dead in a sudden apoplectic fit.

All this, Stevens could take. He was strong. After the loss of his mother, what could he not endure?

Like dammed water in a tempest, the dreaded memory surged through every crack in his composure: The sweet babble of healthy pink-cheeked Virginia toddling about the parlor after Thanksgiving dinner. The urgent message to attend upon his wife. The bitter cold ride on snow-swept December roads into the north wind off the Maine coast, from Fort Preble to the family home in Bucksport. The grim expression on the doctor's face. Meg's futile attempt at courage. Virginia's glassy stare and strangely arched back. How he'd taken her tiny hand in his, and it was colder than the wind off the Atlantic.

Virginia's death was what he could not endure. It had been a joyless Christmas 1845. For the first time, Isaac began drinking, not cordially, but the kind of serious drinking men use to escape from the world. When not mean drunk, Isaac simply jerked through the motions of each day, a marionette under untrained hands. There are times, however, when life refuses to be set aside. Soon baby Susan was born, followed – at last! – by the call to action.

Seeing him off in Boston, his father had ridiculed the great Mexican campaign as a slaveowner's war for territory, but Isaac knew it was far more than that. It was solidarity with the brave Texians who were fighting for independence; it was Manifest Destiny – the God-given right of a vigorous and growing nation to expand its frontiers and spread the gospel of Protestant Christianity from sea to sea. Mexico's day was past; it was a decadent shell of its former self. "God's great glory," Stevens scolded his father, "is now better served under the banner of the Stars and Stripes." Dissenters like his father, Mr. Emerson, that young Congressman Lincoln from Illinois, and that tax-dodger Thoreau, were just plain fools in Stevens' book. They might mean well, but in the end all they did was give aid and comfort to the enemy.

So Isaac sailed proudly off to Mexico, disembarking in a vast stew of confusion at Brazos Santiago. Everywhere men, supplies and animals, stirred, steamed and congealed like stew in a pot, arguing, laboring, defecating, requisitioning, squandering, drilling, profiteering, building, tearing down. At the heart of it all stood the massive hulk of "Old Fuss and Feathers" himself – General Winfield Scott, veteran of the War of 1812 and Indian campaigns from Florida to the Great Lakes. At six foot four, General Scott towered over the young Lieutenant, who despaired of making an impression on such a giant. Stevens poured every iota of his vast storehouse of frenetic energy into his work. The Engineer Corps outshined its rival, the Quartermaster Corps, and brought order to chaos.

But order is not glory.

Riding through stands of saguaro and crazed Joshua trees, Stevens saw the small village of Coyoacan ahead. Its smattering of squat mud adobe houses nestled for protection under an elegant sandstone church, steeple brushing the sky. Stevens frowned, thinking how close he'd come to glory at Cerro Gordo – hadn't it been he who had surveyed the flanking attack that carried the day? And he who would have held the route over which Santa Anna escaped with his army, had not his cursed chronic hernia burst from too much hard riding over the rough Mexican terrain? Instead the glory went to Twiggs, Lee, Beauregard and McClellan, as he lay like an old woman in the infirmary.

Damn his infirmity, and his father too, for he'd first suffered a hernia while trying to prove to Old Isaac that he could clear an entire field in a single day. True, the General had come by later to offer words of encouragement, but Stevens suspected that all the while the big man was reproaching himself for putting too much faith in a frail little runt.

Stevens clenched his jaw tight. "And now this," he hissed. "No more. I'll show them all!" Galloping to the church, he dismounted and burst through the doors, saber and pistol at the ready. A single old peasant woman, wrapped in a black shawl, knelt before the Madonna, pouring out terrified supplications to God, to the crazed gringo, to anyone who might listen. Ignoring her, Stevens bounded up the winding stone stairs to the belfry, up a shaky ladder into the apex of the steeple. Removing a spyglass from his belt, he surveyed the scene northward to Mexico City. Everywhere he looked, he saw Mexican troops mixed with small pockets of civilians streaming towards the capital in undisciplined retreat. Climbing down, he sped off to report to General Scott, who ordered him and General Twiggs to cut off Santa Anna's retreat. They galloped out of the village of Coyoacan, six thousand men strong, Stevens to the General's immediate right, the stars and stripes crisp against the blue desert sky. The earth shook under the weight of their hooves. Now was the moment of glory!

Twigg's force galloped due north, straight at the heart of the Mexican capital, across the narrow plain between lava beds on the left and Lake Xochimilco on the right. Suddenly, a barrage of shells exploded in their midst, throwing blue-coated bodies and horses about like toys. Up ahead, there loomed a palatial church and convent, heavily fortified with stone walls thirty feet high. Cannon smoke rose from the towering red-brown domes of the Convent of Santa Maria de Churubusco, gleaming fiercely in the hot August sun. Quickly, the American force pulled up and regrouped in broad skirmish lines just beyond range.

Stevens seized the moment in true Andrew Jackson style. "General, I've seen the Mexican forces retreating in disarray. They're demoralized by our victories; it's their Latin nature to flee from a bold attack. I say press the advantage quickly, and not lose our momentum. Let's move batteries in from each flank and the center simultaneously. It'll overwhelm them. And General," Stevens added, "I request permission to lead the central battery."

"It's a bold plan, Lieutenant," replied Twiggs, looking down at Isaac, "but perhaps boldness is what's called for." Stevens exulted; at last his moment had

come. "However, I need you here at the command center. Taylor," he barked
to the tall strapping artillery captain, "you'll command the central attack."

So, there it was again – his plan, some strapping brute tapped to execute
it. Stevens watched helplessly as Taylor's force was deployed. But trouble
developed quickly – the left flank, meant to cover the frontal assault, met stiff
resistance from the Mexicans, pinned down by two cannons and hand to hand
combat at a bridge over a small creek that soon ran bloody. Then the right
flank floundered too, as Mexican troops more determined than Stevens had
expected poured from the convent and engaged them with muskets, pistols
and swords. As Taylor struggled to bring his big guns to bear on the convent
walls, the Mexican artillery concentrated its fire on the attackers, decimating
them in their exposed position.

Reinforcements were needed, so Stevens was at last permitted to gallop
into action. No sooner was the word given than he leapt upon his palomino,
one hand on the reins, the other brandishing a saber so sharp he'd used it to
shave just that morning. The smoke was intoxicating, the cries rising from the
mangled forms of men he'd known and led were but spurs in his own flank,
goading him in a clear-eyed fury. He saw the field in slow motion, sized up
the opportunities, rushed into the breach at the center of the line. Grapeshot
whistled and screamed like *alebrijes* – Aztec demons – but Stevens took no
notice. Seeing the enemy, he whooped and charged, running a man through
the breastbone as he dismounted. His only thought as he looked into his
victim's gloaming eyes was how satisfying it was to kill the enemy. He slashed
and fired and grappled and cursed his way around corpses and prickly pear
cactus until he reached Captain Taylor. A shell burst nearby, spattering them
with earth and viscera, but neither man flinched. They fought side by side for
a desperate hour, until it became clear that the position was hopeless, and even
then Stevens fought on though Taylor ordered the bugler to sound a retreat.

Stevens growled as he thrust again and again, slashing as much at the
gnawing realization that it had been his folly that had led them into hell,
as at the enemy itself. Determined not to lose even one cannon, he shot an
enemy soldier off his horse, grabbed the reins, and bent to hook an unsalvaged
artillery piece to the bridle. Suddenly, Stevens was jolted by the hot splinter of
a ball tearing through his right foot. At the same time, a guttural cry split the
air, though he knew somehow that it was not his own. Falling, Stevens saw his
assailant fall before him, dead from a blue-coat's saber blow that had split his
head and deflected his aim. Stevens grasped the hand that appeared before
his face, and was scooped up onto the mount behind his rescuer. Clinging
to consciousness, Stevens recognized the scar on the back of the head of the

big Irishman from West Point, a scar like a whiskey bottle might make, as the heavily burdened beast strained, stumbled, and then regained his stride, to pull Stevens and Casey from the grisly field

2

The fifty-five year old Negro freedman, Washington Bush, startled awake to find himself surrounded by savage-looking men and women. He reached for his gun, but it was gone. Just then Bush heard his partner, the big Kentuckian Mike Simmons, cry out as he was subdued by two warriors. Bush looked for help to Jim and Martha McAllister, but they too were pinned down, guns out of reach.

So all their struggles had come to this. They'd left Missouri the year before, in 1844. They'd survived the sun-baked plains, the buffalo stampedes, the snows of the Bitterroots, the rapids of the Columbia that tried to drown them as they poled their way from The Dalles on a rickety scow of lashed timbers, weighted down with all their earthly possessions. They'd endured the race hatred that chased them north from the settled part of Oregon territory, making them the first Americans to seek settlement on Peter Puget's Sound. They'd followed the Cowlitz trail recommended to them by the Chief Factor at Fort Vancouver on the Columbia. The Cowlitz River provided a sure path, north and north and north. It led them through dark mountains and trackless forests, past the mouth of the Toutle with its silty glacial wash carried down from a looming volcano. Then it took them further north, between descending hills teeming with wolves, bears, and cougars, until at last they came to the lowland forests. There the river turned eastward, marooning them on its northern elbow, abandoned and uncertain how to proceed.

Soon they found themselves hacking at thorns that tore at their flannels, cursing the dark trees that obscured them from God's view. Early winter rains rotted their toes and stiffened their buckskins. The damp chill gave the younger children the pleurisy; they thought they'd lost the McAllister girl, Ainsley, so flushed and hot was she, yet with a shot of brandy and a kick of mule-stubborn pioneer spirit, she pulled through. They jettisoned half their gear to lighten the load, their food spoiled and waned, until they had to rely on hunting, fishing, and foraging for the few remaining autumn berries and the strange mushrooms that hopefully wouldn't kill them.

Still they stumbled on, stubbornly dragging themselves and their feverish children through the incessant mist, from swamp to knoll to icy stream crossing. Desperately, they clung to their few essentials: axes, adzes, nails, bedrolls, frying pans, cups, silverware, hardtack, flour, salt, lard, seeds, clothing, a bolt of cloth, a faded etching of loved ones left behind, perhaps forever. The men's boots chafed and blistered their feet; the hems of the ladies' dresses drank in the forest's muddy floor. When they slept on boughs laid upon the cold ground, it was the sleep of the dead.

Until this rude awakening. Jim and Martha's boy, Jimmy, leapt up from where he'd been half-concealed in the underbrush, dodged between their captors and sped off into the forest. One of the Indians sprinted after him. "Go Jimmy, go!" cried Martha, but no sooner had the words escaped than she was plagued with second thoughts. What were the chances of an eight-year-old boy alone in that bleak forest? Martha was thankful to see the Indian return a few minutes later with Jimmy slung over his shoulder, kicking and squirming. Jimmy's flailing quieted down, and Quiemuth returned him to his mother, with a smile and a nod.

"*Klahowya*," said the tallest of the Indians, as he held each white man by the shoulder, then slicked his hands down their arms in greeting. Leschi's muscles and the sharp bone-tipped spear in his quiver looked fierce, but his open face beneath a large conical cedar hat was friendly. Most of the Natives were adorned with multiple earrings, nose piercings, black tattoos, hairpieces of *hiqua* shells and bird bones. Leschi wore only a single shell necklace.

At his signal, the women stepped forward with baskets full of dried salmon, berries, nuts, and strange green-white bulbs that were soft and delicious. "*Muck-a-muck*," said Leschi, miming eating. Wordlessly communicating with quick glances, a tentative truce blossomed, allowing the pioneers' hunger to momentarily overshadow their fear.

Speaking the few words of Chinook jargon they shared in common, augmented by hand signals, Leschi was able to communicate that his people wished to provide help. Word had reached the Fort that a party of *t'kope tillicum* – white men – had left Fort Vancouver in early October. When they did not arrive when expected, Dr. Tolmie had sent Leschi and Quiemuth to go in search for them. Leschi and Quiemuth brought their *klootchmen* – wives – so the white women could be cared for in comfort. They brought dry clothes, fresh meat, and horses. Together, they could get to Fort Nisqually in two sleeps.

The Americans huddled. They did not like the way they had been awakened, but had to admit that if they'd reached their guns, killing might have preceded understanding. "They had us in their power," added Washington. "They could have cut our throats, but did not. Here we are, slogging around in circles, and this is what the Good Lord has sent us. Brothers, it is enough for me."

Mike Simmons wasn't so sure, but what choice did he have? He nodded. Jim looked to his wife, Martha, who was Mike's sister. She nodded tersely. "*Mawkit* Injuns," said Jim, using the Scottish slang for "filthy." "I wish I'd ne'er left Kansas City." But he nodded.

"It is *kloshe* - good," announced the black white man. "Leschi, take us here," he added. Brandishing the British map they'd traded for at Fort Vancouver, Bush pointed to where the Little Deschutes River emptied into Budd Inlet. Leschi did not understand the white man's talking paper; he did not see how land could be captured on a piece of paper. At last he was made to understand. They would go to where *chuck* becomes *Whulge* - river disappears into Puget Sound. Leschi smiled and spoke the Indian name for that place, "*Spuck-ulth*," adding, "*Kloshe mamook hunt*." Good hunting.

By dusk the next day, Leschi had guided the pioneers to a place by a waterfall that the Simmons man called "Tumwater." Leschi and his braves helped the settlers build two small cabins to shelter them from the winter storms. Dr. Tolmie sent a supply of food from the Fort to keep them through the first winter, and seeds for a winter planting in the mild weather.

Martha wanted a place of her own, so Jim McAllister took his family on to the Fort. There they enjoyed secure, though cramped, winter lodgings, on the northern bluff overlooking the Nisqually Delta.

When springtime came, Leschi called upon Jim, who now called him *tillicum* - friend, in the Chinook jargon he'd been mastering all winter. Out they rode, from between the glistening chartreuse and red Madronas, blue-green hemlock and Sitka spruce of the bluff, down to the rich stew of the delta, where waves of white-blossoming osoberry and purple camas flowers intertwined with river rushes, luminous skunk cabbages, thickets of willows, dainty stands of Oregon ash, and the majestic black cottonwood. There they paused to watch as flocks of waterfowl numerous as the buffalo of the plains spooked into the air at the sound of their hooves, framing the layered clouds and bright blue patches of sky with winged silhouettes. Upriver about a mile from the Sound, the ground rose into the beginnings of a broad, fertile prairie, softened by a carpet of long grass the color of a Mallard's head, redolent with the nectar of Nootka rose, painted pink and white with red-flowering currant and Queen Anne's lace. "This, my friend," said Leschi, "is our people's council ground. This is where our fathers have gathered since the creation of *Whulge* to settle disputes, to decide on questions of war and peace, to dance, and to talk with the spirit world."

Jim surveyed north over the rich grasses and scattered copses of willows, vine maples, alders and crabapples undulating out to the riverbank. He looked south to see the playful waters of *She-nah-nam* – Medicine Creek – wend their serpentine way to the Nisqually. He looked west and saw the waters of the Sound sparkling beneath the hallucinatory snowy peaks of the Olympic Mountains. He looked east and saw the massive unearthly glaciers of Mount Rainier. This land, thought Jim, was well worth two thousand grueling miles.

"It was here, my friend," continued Leschi, "that our tribe held a great council last summer, to decide whether to treat the white man as friend or foe. Some, including our old Chief's eldest son, Wyamooch, spoke for war. I spoke for peace, and that, my friend, is why your scalp is not dangling from Wyamooch's longhouse on this fine day!" Laughing, with a deft flick at the reins of his Cayuse pony, Leschi galloped away in a display of bravado.

When the tribe gathered for council that summer, they found a large plot of their traditional council grounds staked and fenced along Medicine Creek. When Leschi called upon the McAllisters to ask how one could own *Sah-hah-lee Tyee's* earth itself, Jim just laughed.

"But Leschi," Martha added with a warm smile, taking his big weathered hand in hers, "as a special friend to our family, you will always be a welcome visitor to our humble l'il ole home."

Chapter Four
Owl in Daylight

1

"Father," asked Kwahnesum in a demure whisper, never raising her eyes from the waters of Budd Inlet to view the fledgling white settlement of Tumwater nestled at the mouth of the Little Deschutes, "who is this *Sah-hah-lee Tyee* of the white man, Jesus Christ?" Kwahnesum's long black hair was tightly braided, each braid weighted by a stone. Although traveling by canoe, she sat stock straight under a blanket canopy that hid her soft skin from the sun. Her eyebrows and the hairs of her forehead had been carefully plucked by her personal slave, to accentuate her broad, sloping forehead. At the peak, the scalp where her hair parted was painted bright red. At twelve summers, her budding figure already pressed against the embroidered cotton blouse for which Leschi had traded two fine otter skins at the Fort. A village head man's daughter must be elevated in every particular.

Kwahnesum's cousin, Sluggia, morose son of Leschi's elder sister who had died while birthing him, scowled to hear such a question from a woman. Leschi ignored him. "It was right of you to ask, my daughter," he said, assuring Kwahnesum that this rare display of curiosity had not overstepped the bounds of propriety. "It is told by both the King George and Boston men that there was no greater *Tyee* than Jesus." Leschi bent again and again to paddle a rhythm answered by waves slapping the prow. "I have been with my *tillicums* Tolmie and McAllister to the white man's church. There, the Black Robes sing praises of Jesus and tell stories of his great deeds. They say, my dear, that Jesus is the secret behind the white man's power over the earth and the waters." Leschi looked up at the smoke rising from Mike Simmons' new sawmill. "The white man's religion places God only in the sky, so that the white man can chop up the earth to serve himself. I do not know whether it is good, but it is strong medicine."

"Kwahnesum," said Sara, Leschi's elder wife, whose wizened copper face glinted in the sun, "you should not be bothering the menfolk with silly questions; why does a girl need to know of such things?"

"I do not mind," said Leschi.

"You will confuse her with strong talk," scolded Sara. "I am many summers a married woman, and I do not believe that the white man's medicine comes from Jesus or from any other great spirit."

"Then from where does it come?" asked Leschi. He rested his paddle and turned about in his seat, as droplets dappled the surface in their wake. Behind him, Quiemuth and Sluggia continued to push against the gentle current. "They are teaching our people to bring food up out of the ground wherever we choose to plant –"

"Did we ever go hungry before?" interjected Sara, and the startling whiteness of her oval eyes flashed.

"– they come in canoes grander than any our people could build, powered by the hot breath of fire and water," continued Leschi, trying to steamroll the interruptions –

"Ships that belch smoke and ash and make waves that tip our canoes –"

"– they have given us metal tools, which are hard and lasting and useful; which do not chip and break like bone, and are sharper than stone –"

"So that now," shot back Sara, "the ground is littered with rusty nails for the children to stab themselves on, and get sick –"

"– they have brought us closely woven blankets to keep us warm in the winters –"

"Did you ever go cold before the white man? Did we not survive generations beyond counting? Are not our cedar hats and cloaks better protection against the rains than the soggy woolens of the white man?"

"– our people have more things for their comfort since the coming of the white man –"

"– more things to fight over; less time to honor the spirits of their ancestors –"

"– and the whites have given us work for which we are paid in blankets and bolts of cloth, so that everything need not be woven by hand –"

"– as if you, a man, ever wove a stitch! Did you find your freedom so hard that you must be a slave to the white man?"

"Woman, what do you know?" scowled Leschi.

"Too much, dear husband, too much."

"*Aiieee* –" cried Leschi, as he waved her off with his big hand, then turned to give his second wife, dutiful Ann, a tender stroking.

They traveled the rest of the way in silence to the growing, prosperous farm of Washington Bush. Washington bounded down the river bank and glided his hands down the arms of men and women alike, "slicking them down" in the native greeting.

"Leschi, Quiemuth, my *tillicums*," said Washington in his now-facile Chinook, "I have a present for you." He called to his son and a blond-haired farm hand, who emerged from the barn carrying a gleaming metal plow. "Now you and Quiemuth shall farm your land like real Boston men!" Washington told Leschi, with the delight of a teacher rewarding two precocious pupils. The brothers thanked him with great ceremony.

"It is nothing," replied Washington. "We will never forget what you did for us."

Leschi cast a reproachful glance at Sara, but she was paying little attention to him. Instead, her eye was on Kwahnesum who, in breach of all Nisqually precepts of decency, had risked a sidelong glance at the honey-haired man who had helped bring out the plow. Sara whispered a sharp warning, and Kwahnesum's eyes became ever more firmly fixed on her feet. Sara had a bad feeling about this whitest of all white men, whose eyes trapped the light.

"Folks," said Washington, "I'd like you to meet Charlie Eden. Charlie's from the great state of New York, ain't you, Charlie?"

"Yessir, Mr. Bush," said the young man. He extended a hand to the men, but his eyes were elsewhere. Kwahnesum did not even have to look up; she could feel them sure as she felt the sun on her cheek.

2

Quiemuth and Sluggia returned overland in Washington Bush's wagon, carrying the precious plow back to their longhouse in Yokwa village, where Muck Creek plunges into the Nisqually. Washington sent Charlie Eden along to show them how to fit the harness and carve a smooth furrow without shattering the blade on rocks.

Kwahnesum found herself with Father and Mother and Second Mother, out on the water in the long summer evening. With languid strokes they paddled northward up *Whulge* to visit with Puyallup cousins at *Wollochet*, the village named for its squirting clams. Kwahnesum longed above all else for the day, soon to come, when she could marry and be free to wander without chaperone; it was all she had thought of since she was old enough to weave. Yesterday, the range of breathless dreams ran from marrying a man of her own people to a man of another tribe. In today's light, yesterday's dreams seemed dull as a rain cloud. She couldn't free her mind from the face of that shining *t'kope tillicum* Eden, so like the sun itself. Such men had always seemed unthinkable – to marry one would be like stepping off the edge of the earth! Yes, off the earth into a place of enchantment ... She had glimpsed the Boston women on their way to an evening soiree, in their heavy sparkling gowns. They played in palaces filled with strange music and sorcery. Her father was right – there was powerful medicine in the white man's world, and she wanted to drink it down.

But what of dashing Wyamooch? As the son of their recently departed Chief, he could become an important man. She remembered well the thrill of that night when one of the boards of her sleeping cubby lifted to reveal a pouch of gently softened buckskin filled with red face paint. It was then that she knew he loved her. Did she love him? That was a question she had pondered the long hours as her fingers wove rushes into baskets, or gathered berries in afternoon sun. She had thought so, but now he was just another Nisqually boy. Try as she might to picture his tangled dark locks bedecked by eagle feathers and an otterskin wedding crown, all she could visualize was a shining halo of honey-colored hair.

As it had each warm day since *Sah-hah-lee Tyee* created it, the air above *Whulge* filled with the sweet, haunting songs of the native maidens, the boastful calls and responses of braves, the wistful harmonies of the elders, layer upon layer of prayer and yearning. Looking up, Kwahnesum saw *Ta-co-bet* – "nourishing breast," the mountain the Bostons called Rainier – pinking in the slanted rays of the sun. She felt the cool of the glaciers and the heat of the volcano all at once, as if the mountain itself were at war over her heart.

In the twilight of the long summer night, at last they reached *Wollochet*. Strange, there was no singing in the village, no sound of laughter, no barking of dogs, no fires burning, no dancing, no feasting. On the beach they saw dark piles, as if skins were piled for trading.

"*Mesachie, mesachie, mesachie*," Sara began chanting, as soon as they were close enough to see, "Evil, evil, evil." Ann joined in, and soon the three women were all wailing as they pulled their canoe up among piles of skins that had recently held the life-spirits of their loved ones. There was no sign of attack by an outside enemy; old and young skins alike had simply betrayed their inhabitants, forming crusty, pus-filled lesions from which life leaked away. Everywhere they looked, dead upon dead, and dead dogs and wolves that had tried to feast on the corpses. The stench was overwhelming.

"Go back," commanded Leschi to his women, "go back quickly and take the canoe around the point. I will look for survivors, and meet you there."

"Leschi, please, let us stay with you," begged Sara.

"Go back, woman, before it is too late. And take Kwahnesum."

They left him there alone, amidst death. He stood still, listening long, letting the wind carry to him any sign of life. At last he heard it, a faint whimpering from the longhouse farthest from the beach. Leschi pushed back the elk-skin covering and climbed through the entryway. Before him was an old man, curled in fetal position, holding his gut and whimpering. Pools of vomit surrounded him, but his skin was unmarked by the pox.

Leschi lifted the old man's head gently, wiped his sweaty face, lifted a flask of water to his lips. Slowly, the old man's eyes began to focus. "What is your story, Grandfather?" asked Leschi.

"I am Kul-sass," said the man, with difficulty. Leschi put his ear closer to the man's lips, to catch his faint whisperings. "I was medicine man here. My medicine was no good. Many died, but not me. Others ran away. Not me." The man grimaced as a convulsion wracked his bowels.

"What was the cause of all this?" asked Leschi.

"*T'kope tillicum* – white man. They come, they share our food, they kiss our women. Then they go, and the people get sick with spots."

"But you did not get sick?"

"No, not all. But many." He groaned and choked back bile. "So many ..."

"Now you are dying. Why?" asked Leschi.

Kul-sass looked at Leschi, eyes wet with tears. "What is a medicine man with no spirit? I could not save my people. Each death was me. Without spirit, there is no life." Kul-sass paused, fighting for breath. Leschi had seen this before. No death cap mushroom was more potent than the shaman's curse upon himself. "My son, please do me honor – finish me now."

The medicine man began to mumble prayers too soft and quick for Leschi to discern. When the medicine man's prayers were overcome by wracking cramps that he fought, so he could hold his head up and meet Leschi's eyes, it was time. Leschi stepped back, took down a war club hanging on the wall, and whispered his own prayer: "*Jesus, who died for the white man's sins, this man is your brother too.*" He brought down the club, and the silence afterwards was louder than any howl.

3

Summer passed into autumn. The people lovingly placed the first returning salmon on a bed of ferns, head facing upstream, and spoke the ancient blessings. They cleaned the salmon scout with a special mussel-shell knife, roasted him with great ceremony, and each member of the tribe shared a morsel. Before sundown first salmon's bones were carefully returned to the spot where he was caught, to be reclaimed by his family. Only if salmon scout were handled strictly in accordance with the ancient rituals, would the

Salmon People know they were respected by the People of the River Grass. Then they would not fear to follow, leaping and straining against the current in vast numbers until the second winter moon.

Later, snug in their winter lodgings upriver at Mashel village, the Nisqually people ate the dried salmon and clams. It was the time of weaving, trapping, story-telling, repairing the implements of summer. Soon it was followed by another spring, another summer, another salmon scout, the great wheel spinning, heedless of the worries of any one man.

On a warm April day, the horned owl froze Leschi and Quiemuth in their tracks just outside the massive gates of Fort Nisqually, where they had come to trade their pelts. The low, sonorous, *hooo, hoo-hoo, hooo, hooo,* the second and third notes shorter and quicker than the rest, was often heard from the tops of the towering black cottonwoods scattered about the delta - *but not during the daytime.* The brothers' eyes met; communication was wordless and instantaneous. *Patkanim.*

A recent war council was fresh in Leschi's mind: Patkanim's call for total annihilation of the white man "before it is too late"; the support of the many Chiefs who feared him, until Leschi stood to address the council. "Great Chiefs, hear me well," he had said. "Is *Sah-hah-lee Tyee* so feeble that he made your lands too small? Are not the fields and forests vast, the mountains huge, the waters of *Whulge* deep beyond sounding, the rivers and streams filled with salmon beyond number? Is there not room for all?" In calling for peace, Leschi was supported by the Chiefs of southern *Whulge,* and soon it became clear that Patkanim's strategy had failed. The Snoqualmie Chief's fury knew no bounds; he insulted the recalcitrant guests, spurned their gifts, called Leschi a *t'kope klootchman* - white woman - and swore revenge.

Leschi and Quiemuth ran for the gates of the Fort, which were standing open. A group of men Leschi recognized from Mike Simmons' mill were huddled outside the gates, absorbed in talk. "*Hyak cooley*" -"Quick run" - shouted Leschi, but they did not understand.

"What you siwashes so hot fer?" laughed young Leander Wallace, fresh from the mountains of Virginia. "Superstitious -" was as far as he got; puzzled at his inability to speak, he reached up to feel a shaft protruding from his windpipe. Wallace wavered and fell, as the air about them suddenly filled with the swoosh of arrows. The words *hyak cooley* took on clear meaning to his comrades, who sprinted behind Leschi and Quiemuth towards the gates, pursued by gleeful war whoops and a second fusillade of arrows.

They passed through just as the gates swung shut, and were met by Dr. Tolmie. Together they took the stairs to the top of the battlements three at a time, from which vantage point Leschi could now clearly make out the forces arrayed against them. "I count seven war canoes on the beach below the bluff, *Tyee*," said Leschi, "so, perhaps as many as one hundred warriors." Only about twenty braves were visible below; Patkanim knew better than to expend his main force on a frontal assault.

"Thank-you, Leschi," said the doctor. "I am gratified to hear that we're only outnumbered two-to-one," he added, with a touch of gallows humor.

Firing from the battlements became general, but the smooth bore muskets in the hands of trappers, shepherds and farmers were ineffectual, and none of the attackers fell. The deafening noise and smoke combined with lead balls splattering the ground forced Patkanim's braves to keep their distance. They scampered quickly back into the forest when the fort's two cannon fired, tearing great divots from the earth.

"*Tyee* doctor," said Leschi, "let me and my brother go with a small force of five of your men; we know what to do." The doctor signaled his assent; John Edgar volunteered to lead the men sent with Leschi and Quiemuth. Mounted, they galloped out a momentary crack in the gate under cover of another cannon blast, then swooped away across the upper delta, disappearing into the forest along the banks of Medicine Creek.

As soon as they were out of view, Leschi ordered that they divide: Quiemuth to alert Yokwa village; two white men to alert the Bostons south at Tumwater; two white men northwest to alert the Bostons at the fledgling settlement of Steilacoom. Leschi and Edgar headed down towards the water, where they left their mounts behind at the edge of the forest. Using only hand signals, Leschi led Edgar through a maze of willows, cattails, bracken and interwoven pools. Just as Edgar became disoriented and convinced that they were doubling back upon themselves, they reached a thicket of crabapple and horsetail. Although well covered, not thirty feet away on the beach they could clearly see Patkanim's seven war canoes, lined up gunwale to gunwale.

The canoes were guarded by only two bored braves. Edgar raised his musket, but Leschi held a hand to his lips to signal quiet and pressed the barrel back down towards the ground. Stringing an arrow, Leschi pulled the bow taut and let the shaft fly to where it found its mark, square in the chest of a guard, who fell with a strangled cry. Leaping to his feet, the guard's companion whirled around once and, finding no definite target, ran off into the woods.

"Let him go," commanded Leschi in Chinook. "We want Patkanim to know. Now, quick, make your fire." Edgar dashed from their hiding place and removed the horn of gunpowder Leschi had told him to bring. He spread a line of powder from bow to bow the whole length of the canoes. Sowing hellish seed, he flung handfuls in long lines along the floors of each vessel. Then he struck his flint once, twice, three times, and suddenly the black powder devoured the spark and kissed the sky with a flashing tongue of fire.

By the time they got back to the Fort, Patkanim knew he was trapped. Black smoke billowed up from the beach, blotting the sunset. Overnight, reinforcements arrived from both Tumwater and Steilacoom. Patkanim was not prepared for a long siege. Soon, he sent word that he wished to parley with the *Tyee* doctor. Dr. Tolmie responded that he would see the Snoqualmie Chief, unarmed and accompanied by no more than four men.

Patkanim's eyes flashed when he saw Leschi at Dr. Tolmie's side, but he held his tongue, and smiled. "Dr. Tolmie," he began with a politician's ease, "I must apologize. We came on a trading mission. But it seems that some of my young men learned that Simmons' men had relations with a *klootchman* who belongs to one of them." Patkanim turned his clear gaze on Leschi. "Leschi, ask your nephew, Sluggia - he knows of it." Leschi clenched his fists, but stood mute. Patkanim turned back to Dr. Tolmie. "They sought revenge. Of course, I had no knowledge of this. Regrettable, but it is ever so with young men," he added lightly. "It seems, however, that we are even: a life for a life. And not only even, but this little misunderstanding will profit you, doctor, for we must trade for canoes to return home."

Dr. Tolmie had no need to consult with Leschi or his nephew. One hundred painted warriors did not resemble a trading party. But however absurd the explanation, it was clear that Patkanim wished to go, and gone was exactly where Tolmie wanted him.

Not, however, without setting an example. "Wise *Tyee*," replied Tolmie, matching Patkanim's glibness, "your apology is appreciated. But our people cannot allow an innocent death to go unanswered. Your man was killed in defense of our Fort; ours killed without cause. You wish to trade? For six canoes I will take two of the men from the force that attacked this Fort. And let it be known from this day forth, that any attack upon this Fort will be answered in blood, two to one!"

There was neither anger nor fear on Patkanim's face. He felt kinship with the white man's attachment to vengeance. This was a tribe with which he could do business. He nodded his agreement. "You shall have your men. I have said it."

The next day the gallows at Fort Nisqually disposed of two more pawns in Patkanim's game, one a slave Leschi had traded to him years before for a canoe, the other the inattentive second guard whose life had so recently been spared by Leschi.

II

Solemn Promises,
Broken Promises

Summer, 1849 – October 24, 1855

Chapter Five
Cry of the *Zach-ad*

1

The killing of the Boston man incited fears up and down the Sound. Urgent appeals for protection flew to Washington City, then back to General John Wool, Commander of the Army of the Pacific, in San Francisco. General Wool dispatched Colonel Silas Casey and the men of M Company to the wilds of Northern Oregon Territory, with orders to establish an American fort at Steilacoom. As fifty men in blue uniforms with polished swords and muskets marched in smart formation down the gangplank of the bark Harpooner, it was clear that Patkanim's effort to rid the territory of the white man had backfired. Now the white man was more firmly entrenched than ever in the land of *Whulge*. Behind the infantry came the artillery, rolling guns big as bears that could fell a Doug fir in a single blast.

As a head man of Yokwa, the largest Nisqually village, Leschi kept his finger on the pulse of political relations between the two white tribes, the King George men and the Bostons. He watched with growing unease as the Bostons established their new fort a mile east of Steilacoom village, then plunged right into patrolling while intoxicated, bullying native men, pawing their *klootchmen*, and generally making a nuisance of themselves. Leschi was sorry to hear from his friend Dr. Tolmie, that the Bostons had won the argument between the white tribes, so that eventually all the King George men would have to leave, or pledge fealty to a Great *Tyee* in Washington City. At least Dr. Tolmie and his people planned to stay on a while longer, until they could negotiate fair payment for their lands and holdings.

All the while more and more Bostons arrived, over land from the Columbia, and by sea in the many steamers and barks that plied the Sound, delivering passengers, and departing loaded with fresh-cut trees. Everywhere the Bostons settled, the trees were cut and the stumps burned, so that the air filled with smoke and Leschi's *tamanous*, great *Ta-co-bet* itself, disappeared behind clouds of ash. Soon the little settlement at Tumwater mushroomed into the town of Olympia, fueled by Mike Simmons' sawmill and Washington Bush's great fields of wheat, corn and potatoes, which he generously shared with newly-arriving pioneers. Steilacoom bloomed seven miles northwest of Fort Nisqually from a few shacks into a town of thirty log cabins, a church, a courthouse, a hotel and two stores. It rivaled Olympia in size and influence, with a deep water harbor on the Sound. North of Steilacoom, at the mouth of the Puyallup River, the Bostons founded the town of "Tacoma," named after *Takhoma, Whulshootseed* for "great snowy peak." And north of Tacoma yet another town began to eat away at the forested cliffs of Elliott Bay, in the land of the Duwamish. At first it was called *Duwamps* after the mudflats on which it was situated, but soon that name was changed to "Seattle" in a transliteration of Duwamish Chief Se-alth's name, which the Bostons felt free to alter because it was too hard for them to pronounce. Next thing Leschi knew, the Bostons were claiming all the land from *Whulge* to *Ta-co-bet* and beyond, saying it was all one Territory named for their greatest warrior, Washington.

What could they do? The Nisquallies carried on, speaking tales of old into the wind of the startling new world. Around fires, huddled in longhouses, they told of Raven the trickster, *Doquebulth* the shapeshifter, and *Otlas-Skio*, the paradise of the dead just below the flat earth, where perfumed balmy breezes caress ancestors hunting game-rich prairies, as birdsong springs from their lips and salmon leap straight down their open gullets. Leschi and his people continued their migratory ways, up and down the length of the Nisqually River, from the delta to the Mashel River in the foothills of *Ta-co-bet*. As they had since the land was new, they followed the salmon that strain against ocean and waterfall to return to that one calm pool called home, where they spawn and die. The Nisquallies wandered up as high as the snow line, hunting deer with snares, and digging pits to entrap *schut-whud*, the lusty bear, that they might club him and give thanks to his spirit as he, and perhaps a hunter or two, lay dying in the pit. They dried the meat on cedar racks over the open fires in their longhouses, the salmon diverted by weirs of willow and netted in nettle twine, the clams and oysters dug from the tideflats. They gathered nuts and berries and herbs filled with special magic. They harvested bear grass and cattails to work with cedar bark and roots into baskets and mats, decorated with maidenhair fern stems and cherry bark strips. They made pressed cakes of pemmican out of ground dried fish, mixed with bear fat and dried crushed berries, to survive the winter, and to carry with them on journeys.

But like the mighty Chinook snared in their weirs, every day their lives became more entangled with those of the white man. Leschi saw his cousin Puyallup Betsy courted and wed by John Edgar, the Hudson's Bay Company man who'd fought by his side on the day of Patkanim's attack. Other native women followed suit, until intermarriage became common, and there arose along Muck Creek a whole community of former company men with their native brides living in white-men-style farms, an ill-fitting extension of Yokwa village. The people became accustomed to new luxuries: metal tools, bolts of bright cloth, clocks that chopped the sun and moon into bits, muskets, strange chairs that rocked, pennywhistles and fiddles, bright shiny buttons, canoes that moved without paddling, ribbons, lace curtains, fancy hats, and boxes to store what nobody could use. The young braves spent too many idle hours in Steilacoom, where the tavern-keeper sold them rum and whiskey until they had no more money, and nothing left to trade. Then he kicked them out into the mud, until they could steal something and crawl back to feed their new addiction. Even Leschi's brother-in-law, Stahi, succumbed to the white man's firewater, leaving Sluggia without a father to guide him. Native women came too, seeking Boston husbands but, failing that, finding that they could support their parents by selling their bodies. Meanwhile, the white man's illnesses – measles, smallpox, influenza and syphilis – raged from village to village, crippling and destroying families in their wake.

Leschi could not understand it. The more they drank of the white man's powerful medicine, the more disoriented they became. It was as if the white man's way of life were itself a kind of liquor, and the whole world was becoming drunk. The liquor tasted fine going down, but it was slow poison. It was killing the life his ancestors had passed down a thousand times, the life that he, as a tribal leader, was charged with preserving. And still the white man came, more and more, over the mountains and by the sea, too many to fight even if he'd wanted to. Leschi began to despair for his people.

On a raw day of the last autumn moon, Leschi was brooding on these intractable problems when his good friend and strongest supporter on the council, Wahoolit, came to share his bear kill and a pipe. "I bring news, my *Tyee*," said Wahoolit, his hawk-like features glistening with reflected firelight.

"Good news, I hope, my friend?" asked Leschi, whose face now betrayed the burden of cares.

"News," answered Wahoolit, a man who betrayed little. "Mike Simmons came to me at my longhouse on Yelm Prairie, to say that the Bostons are sending a great Chief all the way from Washington City to Olympia, to lead their tribe. He says this Chief has been given power by the white *Tyee* of *Tyees* to protect our lands and our way of life. The Chief who is coming here has called a treaty council and potlach for all the tribes of *Whulge*, to be held on the day of the birth of their *Sah-hah-lee Tyee*, Jesus. At this council, a treaty will be made to ensure that all the tribes shall have lands upon which we can hunt and fish, and live in peace with the Bostons for all time. Simmons promises that many fine gifts will be distributed."

It was as if a weight had been lifted from Leschi's shoulders. "Can this be true?" he asked, floating to his feet and into a grateful embrace with Wahoolit, tears flowing down his cheeks. Together they sat and smoked, blowing the smoke at the fire that burned bright and warmed them through. "Who is this great *Tyee?*" asked Leschi.

An ember exploded with a crack. "He is called Stevens," said Wahoolit.

2

On the twentieth consecutive day of drizzle, a blustery Saturday, November 25, 1854, tidings arrived to brighten the gloom: Governor Isaac I. Stevens' much-anticipated arrival in Olympia was to be that very day. Plans that had been nurtured over the long dark weeks were instantly set in motion, as Lizzie Simmons, Martha McAllister and Isobel Bush, rallied the ladies of Steilacoom and Olympia to bake and roast and decorate, while dispatching elder sons on splattering hooves in all directions to spread the news. By mid-afternoon, the ladies had bedecked the tables at Olympia's finest – and only – hotel, the Washington, with red-white-and-blue bunting. Then they loaded these tables down with rashers of beef, whole sides of roast mutton and pork, heaping plates of venison steaks, steaming bowls of creamed-to-perfection corn, mashed potatoes, baked yams, apple pies and jellied fools. The air buzzed with excitement as the newest American Territory's finest citizens preened, horse-traded, laughed, and speculated on the new Governor.

"Tell us, Mr. Mason, what is he like?" asked the gregarious Mary Slaughter, doe-eyed wife of the dashing mutton-chopped young Lieutenant Will Slaughter of Fort Steilacoom, who stood silent, erect and brass-buttoned by her side. Mrs. Slaughter pressed her delicate white hand upon the soft, slightly pudgy fingers of the studious Mr. Mason, who had been selected by Stevens himself to serve as Territorial Secretary, and therefore Acting Governor.

Pushing up his gold-rimmed spectacles and flicking his long auburn hair back with an affected toss of his head, Charles H. Mason smiled that winning boyish smile of his. "I am afraid, my dear Mrs. Slaughter, that I cannot illuminate you on this subject, any more than could anyone present *heah* today." Though a native of Rhode Island, Secretary Mason spoke as a Boston Brahmin. "Although Governor Stevens befriended my brother, regrettably I was away at *Hahvard* during this time, and did not myself meet the man. But I am assured that he is a tower of strength; just the sort of decisive fellow we need out here."

"And a military man," interjected Mrs. Mary Ann Conklin, eyeing Lieutenant Slaughter's stiff bearing from beneath a cascade of bright red ringlets. "I do so love military men!" she cooed, eliciting a blush from both Slaughter and Mason. Mrs. Conklin unleashed the unladylike cackle so familiar to the guests at her large and especially hospitable "boarding house," located a stone's throw from Yesler's sawmill in Seattle. In polite company, if mentioned at all, Mrs. Conklin's house was known as "Mother Mary's," or simply "that House," but to soldiers and sailors throughout the Pacific, it was "Mother Damnable's."

"Dear Mrs. Conklin," asked the innocent Mrs. Slaughter, "whenever shall we meet your absent husband, that sea Captain we've heard so much about? Was he in any sort of service?"

"Aye, there was a serviceable man," cried Mrs. Conklin, lustily, "but his primary service to me now is being lost at sea!" *Cackle-cackle*. Poor Mrs. Slaughter blinked blankly.

"A true public service," interjected a middle-aged upright dandy with receding salt and pepper hair slicked into a high pompadour. As he spoke, he slid his arm around Mrs. Conklin's Rubenesque waist, his merry open face beaming from broad forehead to prominent chin, where the merest suggestion of a beard outlined his jaw. Gently lifting the hem of Mrs. Conklin's hoop skirts with the tip of his pearl-handled cane, David Swinton Maynard, known to everyone as "Doc" Maynard, repeated with emphasis: "A true public service."

Arthur Armstrong Denny, the teetotaler by Doc's side, frowned at this display. "Doctor Maynard, if you please," interjected Mr. Denny, "show some respect." Mr. Denny glanced at his pocket watch for the fifteenth time that hour.

Doc shrugged an exasperated shrug at Mrs. Conklin, who winked back at him. "Thank-you, Mr. Denny," she pronounced with exaggerated stuffiness, "it is gratifying to find a gentleman in the house." She curtsied low before him, giving him such a grand view down her overstuffed bodice, that his little protruding ears took on the hue of the pink-lipped singing scallops found in abundance on the Duwamish mud flats. Again, he consulted his pocket watch.

The guest of honor was late, not by minutes, but by hours. "A toast," Jack Blunt called out loud and clear, the buttons of his frock coat straining as he held up his glass. "Though he ain't here yet, we oughta drink a toast to the man who's gonna put us on the map. His Honor, Isaac Stevens!"

Everyone raised their glasses and drank as they shifted about impatiently. The drizzle had turned to hard rain, the light was fading, and the food beginning to congeal. People's stomachs churned and their tongues loosened as they drank and waited. A lone traveler in a slouch hat and drenched muddy buckskin asked what the commotion was about. Told that all the important people in the Territory were gathered to await the arrival of the Governor, he was content to go around back to the kitchen for his meal. Indians huddled outside, wrapped in their blankets. The livery stable worked overtime, tending the wagons and a few fancy carriages.

"We need to deal with the Indian question first," Secretary Mason was explaining to a crowd that now included Dr. Tolmie, Charlie Eden and his jumpy friend, Tony Rabbeson, a pock-marked trapper and miner. "Our instructions are to consolidate them as much as possible, as far as possible away from civilized settlements. Perhaps we could put them all across the mountains."

"Excuse me, Mr. Secretary, but that hardly seems humane," chimed in Dr. Tolmie. "These people are adapted to life in a temperate climate, where the salmon and shellfish are plentiful. How could they survive across the mountains?"

"Oh, we would feed them, of course," replied Mason, his quick intellect earnestly wrapping itself around this fascinating technical problem. "We could ship over some hardtack and beans, until they get their own farms established. Maybe they could dig irrigation channels. And they could do some hunting," he added, "like Judge Lander and I did when we came over the Naches Pass with the Sargeant train last year. We ate wolf meat you know – pretty gamey stuff!" Mason puffed out his chest, trying to look rough and tough, but he only looked more cherubic.

"I don't know, Mr. Mason," said Tony Rabbeson, and for a moment Dr. Tolmie thought he had an ally. "It'll cost a lot to feed 'em. What's the point of keepin' 'em alive, anyhow, just so's they kin take our scalps?" Rabbeson elbowed Charlie and laughed without smiling. Charlie joined in nervously, while the dripping buckskinned stranger who'd slipped in from the kitchen nodded, and raised his whiskey to Rabbeson.

Washington Bush pulled Charlie aside. "I'm sorry to hear you laughing at the plight of these poor creatures. You know as well as I do that there are some very fine Indians. How about our friend Mr. Leschi and his brother?"

"Yeah, I s'pose so, Mr. Bush, I don't mean no offense, Sir." Out of the corner of his eye he glanced at Tony, hoping he wasn't listening. He had Tony to thank for the money he'd brought back from the California gold mines, but the truth was he was tired of taking orders from Tony. Tired of following him around. The last few months Charlie'd been thinking of settling down, but women were scarce.

White women, anyway. Over the years, since that first day at Bush's farm, he'd caught the occasional glimpse of Kwahnesum. Lately, she'd begun to inhabit his dreams day and night. Course, they'd barely spoken, but who needs a woman who talks all the time, anyhow? Other men were marrying Indians; why not him? He'd heard that the Natives make good brides – obedient and hardworking, they know their place, and were grateful for what you could give them. Heck, he'd be doing her a big favor lifting her out of the savage life, giving her a plank floor under her feet and some nice clothes. Why not?

"To tell you the truth, Mr. B-bush," he said, stuttering a bit as his pale cheeks flushed, "I've kinda taken a shine to Leschi's daughter, Kwahnesum. Do you think she'd have me?"

"Why Charlie," said Washington, a smile dawning across his face, "that would be wonderful." He clapped his muscular arm around the young man's shoulders. "Yes, I think it could be done. She is the daughter of an important man, so it won't be easy. Isobel!" he called, and the three huddled, whispered, and even laughed a bit over the next half hour.

Meanwhile, across the room, a white-haired, distinguished gentleman confided, "My friends, I'm afraid the news isn't all good," to the small coterie gathered about him. It was Chief Judge Edward Lander, the same fellow mentioned by Mr. Mason. Judge Lander was enjoying a cigar with Frank Clark, a sharp-eyed lawyer from Tacoma who was used to being the smartest fellow in the room, and Benjamin Frank Shaw, a young hat-on-a-stick of a man, who wore his unruly red beard half way to his navel. "You know," continued Judge Lander, "the new Governor's delayed because he has been surveying the northern route for the transcontinental railroad?"

"Yes indeedie," chirped Shaw. "Sounds like a great idea to me!"

"I agree," said Judge Lander, "but poorly executed. Point is, my brother Fred was part of Stevens' surveying party, and he got so fed up with Stevens and his high-handed ways that he declared he'd never serve under him again, under any circumstances." The Judge shook his head. "I mean, that's what he says – 'Under any circumstances.' Period."

"Why not?" asked Frank Clark, who was always looking for leverage.

"Because Stevens is so cocksure that he's the smartest man in the room that he doesn't listen to anybody." Frank Clark blanched a bit; competition was coming!

"Not always the smartest," chimed in the little stranger in buckskin, popping up between the Judge and the lawyer, "but I do try to stay a step ahead by the use of strategy." Stevens looked from man to man to man as the meaning began to register and their eyes grew wide. "Besides, your brother need not apply, Judge Lander; in my administration, I want men who will carry out orders, not look for reasons not to."

As word ricocheted about the room that the great and powerful Governor Stevens was one and the same with the muddy little runt of a wrangler who had mingled incognito for nearly an hour, gathering intelligence on everyone's unguarded opinion of him, half the room flared with swallowed fury while the other half swooned in admiration, and yet a third half found itself in both camps simultaneously. The ladies surrounded the dashing if diminutive Governor, took his hat to reveal a full head of wavy black hair atop that curiously oversized head, and led him to the front of the great table. All the famished, astonished, and somewhat inebriated guests arrayed themselves before the Governor as quickly as the general pandemonium would allow.

Putting up a brave front, Chief Judge Lander clinked his glass with a spoon, until all had quieted down. "Ladies and Gentlemen, as most of you in this room will know, I hail originally from the Commonwealth of Massachusetts, where I obtained my law degree from Harvard, practiced law for a number of years, and then got the benighted idea into my head that by going as far west as possible, I might get rich, or at least have some fun." A few polite scattered laughs from people who shared that idea, but perhaps weren't yet willing to poke fun at it. "I was selected to welcome our new Governor based on our kinship, in that he, too, is a son of Massachusetts." Polite applause. The Judge took the opportunity to steal a glance at the enigmatic man who had so rudely appeared amongst them, and found that he did not seem to be paying any attention, but was instead whispering something to his Territorial Secretary, Mr. Mason.

"Long ago, while still in Massachusetts, I had the honor of meeting Isaac Stevens," explained the Judge, pausing to permit quizzical expressions to form on the faces of those to whom he'd told the contrary. "Not the son," he added with a smile, "but the father." At this, suddenly the son was paying rapt attention. "If there be truth to the saying that the acorn never falls far from the oak, then there is no doubt in my mind that we are blessed to have such a man appointed to lead us, for Isaac Sr. was known to me as a man of the very highest social ideals. He was a devout Unitarian, who cared deeply about the common man, fought against injustice in any form, and condemned special privilege in favor of the American ideals of equality and democracy." Stronger applause. "My friends, my neighbors, my fellow Washingtonians, I give you our first Governor, Isaac I. Stevens." Everyone rose and applauded.

The little man stood, then bounded onto his chair and took in the applause, smiling and raising both fists, turning this way and that, embracing each and every person with the magnetism of his hazel eyes. When at last the applause and cheers died, he affected a humble countenance. "I thank you,

Judge Lander, for those fond reminiscences of that dear man, my father, may he rest in peace." Again the applause rang out, this time mixed with tears in the eyes of some of the ladies. Stevens alertly did not miss the advantage. "And I wish to thank the ladies for this great and welcoming feast, for I know from experience that no fine meal is prepared without the dutiful attentions of the weaker sex." He had them now; they swooned in their seats. "On behalf of myself, and my beloved wife Meg, who is even now bravely making the long voyage up from Panama with our four children, I say again, God bless you." And when he said it, they felt blessed.

"Brave pioneers of the northwestern wilderness, it is to you that the great eye of Providence now turns. Judge Lander jokes about riches." *He was listening?* "It is no joke. Stand by me, and riches shall be ours, as we open all the resources of this great land to usefulness, as God intended." Powerful applause.

"But something more important than riches awaits us –" they leaned forward in their seats; what could it be? – "Destiny! My friends, we stand today on the brink of the greatest expansion of civilization in America's short but glorious history. We are the chosen vanguard, selected by Divine Providence to spread the gospel of Jesus Christ to the savages, and to bring the countless blessings of civilized life to the shores of the Pacific, and beyond. Will there be hardships? Of course there will! But I say – bring – them – on!" he roared, pumping his fist with each word, and most of the room stood and roared in answer, "*Bring them on! Bring them on! Bring them on!*"

"Will we prevail?"

"YES!" they whooped, giddy for the first time in years.

"People of Washington Territory, from your determined hands a Christian Democratic Empire will rise on the ashes of the savage way of life. Together, we will lay the foundation of a glorious and powerful new age of civilization that we can proudly pass on to our children, and their children, and their children, all in the best and greatest cause for which men live and die: the cause of freedom."

The clouds over their hearts parted, and the sun was named Stevens.

3

The brothers were loading their canoe when Washington and Isobel Bush arrived on horseback. "Leschi," called Washington, wobbling down the bank as he tried to get his old legs back under him after the half-day's ride, "I'm glad I caught you. Where are you off to?"

"We're going fishing," replied Leschi.

"Well," said Washington with a grin, "you may have already caught a big one. You remember Charlie, that fellow who used to work for me?" Leschi looked blank. "You know, Charlie Eden, the blond feller?"

"Oh yes," said Leschi, "the man with golden hair."

"That's not all that's golden about him," said Washington, with a chuckle. "He just got back from California with his pal Tony Rabbeson, and they had a pretty good *strike*." He used the English word.

"What is a *strike*?" asked Leschi.

"*Pil chikamin* – gold!"

Leschi himself had found a vein of the yellow metal that the Bostons cherished in a cave on the side of *Ta-co-bet*, but had never revealed his find for fear of drawing Bostons to his *tamanous*. What was Charlie Eden's gold to him? Sara, who had come down to listen in, was scowling.

"Now, I just saw Charlie the other day, at the dinner for the new Governor," Washington was saying. "He's lonely, wants to settle down, stake himself a claim, begin farming. He says to me, 'Washington, what do you think about Leschi's daughter, Kwahnesum?' I said, 'well, she is a Head Man's daughter, but if you're respectful, and make a good offer, I don't see why not.'" Here he paused, beaming broadly, like he'd just given away the bride. "I mean, it's no mystery, the way she looks at him, if you don't mind my saying so."

"It is the sweetest thing, Sara," added Isobel, giving Sara's hand a little squeeze. Sara pulled away.

Washington glanced nervously at Sara. "He makes a doozy of an offer for her hand, folks. Listen to this: he offers ten good horses with saddles, twenty blankets, five bolts of wool and five of cotton, a hundred brass buttons, ten rifles with ammunition, a canoe, and $50 in gold! Isn't that generous?"

"Husband," said Sara, "I will talk to you now."

Leschi, astonished as much by the bride price as the identity of the potential son-in-law, held up his hand. "There is something I must know first. Washington, I have known you now nine summers since I led you from the forest. You have proven yourself a true friend. You have taught us to farm, and given us a fine plow. You have shown us the love of Jesus, whom we have made our own *tamanous*. So tell me, what of this man, *Challie* Eden? Will he stand by Kwahnesum, protect her, and never beat her?"

"I believe so, Leschi. If not, he'll have me to deal with," pledged Washington.

"Husband," insisted Sara. "A family council is needed."

"I say when a family council is needed," objected Leschi, but when he saw the look on Sara's face he added, "and that time is now. Little Brother, Little Sister," said Leschi to the family servants, using the customary diminutive for native slaves, "tend to our guests while we are in council."

"Leschi," objected Washington, firmly, "I have told you this before. I never will take a thing from slaves." His eyes softened to gently take in the servants. "No offense intended, my friends," he said. Then he and Isobel briefly dipped their canteens and watered their horses in Muck Creek, before heading back downriver.

Leschi's family sat in a circle on mats on the swept dirt floor of the longhouse, a rare late autumn sun illuminating the openings over the two fire pits. Around them were cattail mats covering the walls for warmth, and over them, the skins of *schutwhud* long since eaten, the hides of elk with their antlers, and great slabs of drying salmon as long as a man is tall. For a long time they held hands, rocked, sang songs, and asked the spirits of their ancestors for guidance. At last, as the clouds above turned purple, Leschi nodded to Sara, who was more than ready.

"Hear me well, my *Tyee*, my husband, my friend. For three tens of summers I have filled your bowl, swept your lodge, tended your wounds, heard your sorrows. In that time, we have not always seen eye to eye, it is true, but I have supported you. You are a wise man, but even wise men do foolish things. I have held my tongue, as befits a Nisqually woman. But I am also the daughter of a Puyallup Chief. I have seen much in my life, and now, when so much is at stake, I cannot be silent. I love our daughter – our daughter, for it was I who gave birth to her. But I would sooner see her dead than married to a *mesachie t'kope tillicum* like that man Eden. There; I have said it."

Stunned silence as the powerful words hung in the air. Then Quiemuth spoke: "Sister, how can you know this man Eden's heart, that you call him evil?"

"I have heard the *zach-ad*, the spirit of the swamp that cries out at night, and portends death. The *zach-ad* has sent a warning. Would you ignore it?"

The tense silence was broken at last by the saturnine Sluggia, at eighteen only a single summer older than Kwahnesum. "Uncle, I too oppose this union. The white men come and take all our best women. Where are young men like me to find *klootchmen*? They like our women because they are obedient. The white women do not obey, but chatter like the mockingbird, always scolding. And the white women do not want our men. So, if you as a *Tyee* set this example, what will be left for our tribe? We will soon be of mixed blood, and there will be nothing left of our people."

Again, the silence, displaced at last with soft singing as the light faded. Quietly, Ann moved about the longhouse, lighting the torches. Then Leschi turned to his father, Sennatco. "What say you to our *tillicum* Bush's proposal?" he asked.

His father's forehead furrowed in deep concentration. "Without the tribe, my son, there is nothing. That is my word."

"Yes," replied Leschi, "that is so. That has been my fear, day and night, since the coming of the Bostons, like ants upon the ground. Thank you, Father." Then Leschi extracted a long clay pipe, stuffed it with tobacco, lit it and took a long drag. There was one whose destiny was most entwined in this conference, who had said nothing. Though she would burst, Kwahnesum was forbidden by custom from speaking unless asked.

"Kwahnesum," said Leschi kindly, "you know the traditions. It is not for you to choose a husband; that choice belongs to me, your father and master." Kwahnesum held her shining face open and expectant, her heart betrayed only in by the flutter in her throat. "But, little daughter, it pleases me to know your wishes in this matter." Sara gasped, struggling to hold her tongue. Sluggia stomped away to the far corner of the longhouse. Leschi ignored them. "What do you say about this *Challie* Eden, who would take you not only from your father, as is a husband's right, but from your world? Speak, little one," he encouraged.

"I love him, Father –"

"Love!" cried Sara. "What does she know –"

"SILENCE, woman!" commanded Leschi. "You have spoken well. Do not make your words small in weight by adding to their number." He nodded gently to Kwahnesum.

"I know, Father, that I am young, and that I have much to learn. But there was a time last summer when I was near the Fort with Second Mother. There were some company men who were insulting to us. One of them tried to touch me." Cries of anger circled the fire. "Mr. Eden protected me, isn't that right, Second Mother?"

"I could have done the same," Sluggia called out from across the room, before Ann could respond.

"Yes, dear cousin, I know; but it was Char – Mr. Eden," she corrected, "who challenged the man, who backed down. It was very gallant."

"Kwahnesum," said Leschi, "there is more to marriage than one gallant gesture. Life is long –"

"—especially with certain men!" exclaimed Sara –

"—and men quickly tire of what they once cherished."

"I will guard against that, Father," said Kwahnesum. "You have made me special. Please Father, I love him, I only want to be with him. If I cannot, I fear the *zach-ad* has called for me, for I must surely die!"

Brow furrowed, Leschi passed the pipe to Quiemuth. "Speak, my brother. It is always your wise counsel that I save for last."

Quiemuth's round face, broad nose, and stocky shoulders folded in around his full wide mouth, as he plumbed his own depths. Leaning in to the fire, his face glowed so that, for a moment, it seemed that he warmed it, and not the other way around. At last, he began to speak. "I have been with this man, Eden, when Washington Bush gave us the plow. Although pale as the sun, he is a man under a cloud; I cannot tell whether he is worthy." He looked Leschi directly in the eye. "But this is not a question only of our Kwahnesum. It is a question, also, of our tribe, our survival. When Old Laghlet grew too old to govern and his son Wyamooch was found wanting, a great burden descended upon us, brother. The council asked us to serve as head men at a time like no time in memory. There are no stories to guide us. We can only be guided by the spirits, and by our hearts." He paused to draw on the pipe, and the smoke came out black against the fire.

"Remember, brother, as we brought Kassas in, you once suggested I had no heart? That was not true; it was simply that you thought heart required protection of the one; I thought it required protection of the many. Now, as then, my heart tells me the same thing. Our tribe cannot stand against the power and numbers of the white man. We will need all the white allies we can get – including this man Eden – if we are to make our peace with the white man, and survive as a tribe.

"You and I, my brother, accepted the charge of the council to lead our tribe. In doing so we said that the tribe is our family. If, for the good of the tribe, you must risk your own daughter, so be it." Quiemuth passed the pipe back to his brother, and settled back against Moonya, who sat behind him in a first wife's place. There was no second wife. Though it was his right, Quiemuth never sought further after winning Moonya.

Silence settled so thick it seemed to impede breathing. Long Leschi sat, considering his options. The pipe went cold in his hand. At last, he spoke.

"Sluggia, come here." Sluggia had no choice but to rejoin the family circle. Leschi looked into the delicate ovals of his eyes, and saw there the sadness of his own elder sister. "Sluggia, I love you as if you were my own. Your words have wisdom, but they do not move my heart. Long have we intermarried with other tribes, yet still we are the Nisquallies, the People of the River Grass.

Your own dear mother, my elder sister, married your Puyallup father, Stahi."
Sluggia scowled at the mention of his father, but said nothing. "My own little
sister, Skai-kai, has long been married to Patkanim of the Snoqualmies, and
lives with them. It has not been easy on her, but Father thought it would help
protect our tribe, and I believe he was right.

"The Bostons are but another tribe. Yes, they are great and powerful,
but that makes it even more important to build alliances. When the council
was considering asking your uncles to serve as village head men, what was
said against us? That we were not true Nisquallies, because our mother
was Klickitat, the granddaughter of the Yakama Chief, Ye-ow-wich. But
we are Nisquallies. No matter who we marry, so long as our people honor
their ancestors and live beside our river, we will still be the Nisquallies. If
Kwahnesum does her job as a mother, raising her children to know the ways
of our people, then they too shall be Nisquallies, and there is no power on
earth that can change that."

Leschi paused, then turned towards Sara, took her face in his hands, and
kissed her broad nose. She held stiff, eyes averted, but a few tears betrayed her.

"Sara, my *Tyee*, my *klootchman*, my friend. For three tens of summers you
have filled my bowl, swept my lodge, tended my wounds, heard my sorrows.
I have brought you game, fish, ponies, a beautiful daughter, and built your
longhouses. I have tried to lighten your sorrows, although I know that I have
caused more than I ever soothed. I am not wise enough to know who is right
about the character of the man Eden. I have heard Kwahnesum's expressions
of love, which are sincere, I am sure, but I know well how easily a youthful
heart can be deceived. I have also heard your words, wise Sara, saying this
man is *mesachie t'kope tillicum*, though I know well how a mother *schut-whud*
will protect her cub." Here, Leschi stopped, as if rethinking the whole matter.
He began to sing, and his singing went on for a long while as he asked his
tamanous for guidance.

"Five summers ago I rejected Patkanim's call for a great war against the
white man. I do not know what will become of us now that we have chosen to
live in peace with them. But *Sah-hah-lee Tyee* did not bring us to *illahee tobcadad*
– land of the war spirit. When our ancestors were in need, when they were
suffering and afraid, the Creator guided them to *Tenalquot* – the Happy Land.
Our only path is friendship. This has ever been the path of the Nisquallies.
We are not a warlike tribe. We have survived a thousand generations among
warlike tribes by being the last to take up arms. We choose parley over battle,
trust over fear. This is what Kwahnesum asks us to do today. This choice has
brought us to a moment in which the great *Tyee* Stevens wishes to make peace

with our people and assure us our lands forever, and in which a wealthy Boston offers honorable sums to marry our daughter. We have peace, we have honor, we have our river, we have our way of life. I am content."

Leschi turned to his trembling daughter. "Kwahnesum, I give you my blessing." She knelt in thanks before him, as Sara sobbed softly. Outside, night had fallen. A lone wolf could be heard, sounding its hollow cry.

4

Margaret Lyman Hazard Stevens, daughter of the late Benjamin Hazard, Esquire, of Providence, Rhode Island, flower of two centuries of New England aristocrats, raven-haired beauty with skin like the pink-white snowberry blossom, stepped demurely from puddle to muck, doing her best to avoid the manure stew which passed for the public thoroughfare in the Washington Territorial Capitol. Under the watchful eyes of the town ladies, she maintained a dignified smile though her stomach clenched with each *squench-squench-squench* of her inadequate boots. Then she laid eyes on the ramshackle one-story warehouse with attached shed, rented by the Governor to serve as both gubernatorial mansion, and office of the Territorial Government.

God is punishing me, thought Meg, *for my discontented nature*. Always the one to mock convention, to seek adventure, now look what she'd reaped. First, there was yellow fever for herself and Sue and Maude, and even baby Kate, while crossing Panama (but not for her dear son Hazard, thank God!). Then they'd endured that ghastly carriage on the steamer up from San Francisco, with every sailor leering at her night and day. Next was the canoe trip up the Cowlitz, between wolves and wild savages, to the so-called "inn" of U.B. Warbass, known as "Hardbreads" to all the snot-bearded gnarled roustabouts sleeping six to a bed, the kind of men who give the fleas fleas. Finally, the overland trip through forests so dark that no sun would ever reach the earth even if it had not rained day and night the whole way. All that, dragging sick and whining children and, more terrifying still, children so sick they could whine no longer, just to reach this godforsaken shack stinking of unwashed men and rotting clams, perched on the edge of a cold, slate-grey sea. As the wife of the Governor, Meg turned once more before ducking down under the low rough-hewn doorway, waved to the onlookers, and smiled.

Ohhhh, at last she collapsed in Isaac's arms. His kisses were genuine and her tears were like the Puget Sound rain, inexhaustible. "There, there, buck up, my Meg," cooed Isaac, stroking her face, guiding her away from the prying eyes of his staff, into their private quarters. He set her up by the warm Franklin stove, making sure she had strong coffee and a wool shawl, and worked quickly with that thrumming energy she'd grown to admire, to build up the fire and be sure that the children were snug in dry bedclothes. Seeing the yellow pallor of poor, listless Maude, Isaac sent for the doctor immediately. Knowing that at last she could lay down her burden, Meg fell into a deep and dreamless sleep.

Doc Maynard, still enjoying the remnants of the Governor's welcoming party, staggered in, shaking the alcoholic fog from his brain. He looked at the little girl's eyes and saw yellow where he wished he'd seen white, listened to her labored breathing, felt her burning forehead and fluttering pulse. She turned her head to retch, but nothing remained to come up. Doc Maynard held her tiny face in his hands until she settled back into a fitful unconsciousness. Then he stepped away and shook his lowered head.

"Governor," he whispered, "you probably heard what happened in New Orleans last year. Eight thousand they lost to the yellow fever – eight thousand! I don't know how she made it this far. Do you believe in God?"

"Of course," said Isaac.

"Then pray."

"I will, Doc," said Isaac, rolling up his sleeves, "but I've learned from bitter experience that sometimes God needs a little help. What can I do?"

"Do?" echoed Doc blankly. "We don't really have any medicines that'll fight this thing. All I can say is that she needs to get some fluid in her, in some way that she can keep it in her, and then she needs her fever brought down, and if all that happens, then she might be ready for a little nutrition to give her body the strength to fight it off." Doc looked Isaac in the eye. "It'll take round the clock care, Governor, but the chances are, well ... "

"Just write out what I'm to do," snapped Stevens, blinking back visions of Virginia's glassy stare. So Doc jotted out some instructions, and handed them over.

"Thanks, Doc." Maynard stood there expectantly. "What do I owe you?" added Stevens.

"Oh, no charge, Governor." Doc Maynard cleared his throat. "'Course, they do need a Justice of the Peace and Clerk for the new Court up there in Seattle."

"You a Democrat, Doc?"

"Absolutely," slurred the candidate.

"Right; tell Mr. Mason you're the man."

"Thank-you, Governor," said Doc. Bending down, he gave the little girl a quick kiss on her hot, dry forehead, then stood on wobbly legs, blinked the mist from his eyes, and grasped Stevens' hand with both of his own. "Good luck to you, Governor."

Following the instructions, Isaac took an eyedropper from a tincture of iodine, washed it carefully, brewed some peppermint tea, and sat by Maude's bedside all the night through. Each time her eyes lolled open, he fed her drops of the sweet elixir, to calm her tummy and re-hydrate her. Gently, drop by drop, her nausea abated. Then he bathed her in tepid water to bring down the fever a few degrees. Meg awoke, and took the other children out to explore their new home. Mason came by with urgent bulletins about preparations for the treaty council, but Stevens just shooed him away. Boiling up a beef shank with salt and *allium cernuum*, the wild nodding onion known to calm flatulence, Stevens made a digestible and nutritious broth for his daughter, which he served her over the next twenty-four hours at the rate of several spoonfuls each waking hour. Then he grated carrots and beets to a soft mush, to which he added melted butter and rare lemon juice purchased dear off a trading bark from Southern California, and fed it to her bite by bite, to flush the toxins from her liver. Gradually, he added other tonics and foods recommended by Doc's instructions, as the yellow faded from her eyes, and the pallor from her countenance. A week later Maude was sitting up, alert and chirpy. Her father gratefully kissed her bright alabaster cheek, returned her to her mother's care, and turned back to affairs of State.

Meg managed without Isaac that week, as she had learned so well to do over thirteen years married to a military man and public servant. As the shock of her new surroundings subsided, she began to enjoy the attention and deference shown her by the townspeople. It was a mere matter of days before she had arranged suitable household service, including a nanny to watch the children, thus freeing herself for the social obligations attendant on her position. She was most pleased to find that not all the men of Washington Territory were flea lorries like the men at Hardbreads. In fact, the moon-faced gentleman, Mr. Mason, who hailed from Providence like herself, was extremely pleasant company. She thought it most gallant of Mr. Mason to volunteer to escort her about town, to make introductions.

"Such a busy man," Meg confided in her newfound friends, Mary Slaughter and Lizzie Simmons, "and yet he makes time for a lady. How kind."

How kind, indeed. Lizzie was perhaps too tactful to say anything, except in confidence to Mary, but there did seem to be a particular lightness to the young bachelor's step when in the presence of his boss's snowberry wife. "Well," replied Mary, "they are both well bred; it can be aught but friendship, and the tendency of two kindred spirits to bond in wayward circumstances."

For such was the kindness of Mary's heart that she always looked to the best for the elevated members of society.

Within two weeks of her arrival, Meg let it be known that the present quarters were decidedly temporary. She convened the best surveyor, carpenter and mason (perhaps second-best for that) within the county on the top of a hill overlooking Budd Inlet, to plan the Governor's mansion. Cost, of course, was no object; surely funds could be found within the Territorial budget to ensure that the Governor had quarters commensurate with his dignity. Aside from the longhouses of the Natives, which remarkably were crafted of split planks, not rough-hewn logs, this was to be the first finished lumber two-story house in Thurston County. It would rival – dare she even think it! – Mother Damnable's commodious guest house in Seattle.

There was only one small problem with Meg's vision of a new home. It was the same problem that plagued every eager pioneer, who endured so much hardship and toil for the right to claim their acreage in this wilderness. It was the question of legal title; just a technicality, really, the kind of thing governments are instituted among civilized men to secure. As 1854 faded towards Christmas, and Meg was busy planning how best to get her family into their new home, the Governor and his treaty commissioners huddled day and night, busily planning how best to relieve the Natives of their lands.

When at last they had the treaty draft to their liking, the Governor looked around the room at his team of treaty commissioners: Indian Agent Mike Simmons, Interpreter Benjamin Frank Shaw, Secretary Charles Mason, Surveyor George Gibbs, and Lieutenant Will Slaughter of the U.S. Army. "Gentlemen, you understand, there will be plenty of talk, but no negotiations. I don't need to tell you that each of us has a lot riding on the success of these treaties. Why, we figure that once title is cleared up, all our land will triple in value within a few short years. Triple in value," he added for emphasis.

No repetition was necessary. Mike Simmons, who'd been buying up parcels all around Olympia, had a particularly firm grasp of the economics behind his public service.

"Do you think you can get the Indians to sign this thing?" asked Stevens.

Everyone looked to Shaw, who was fluent in many *Whulshootseed* dialects and Chinook, and was therefore tapped to serve as interpreter. "Don't worry, Governor," pledged the hat on a stick with a glint in his eye. "I could get these Indians to sign their own death warrant."

Chapter Six
Polaklie Illahee

1

Just below the rocky slough where *She-nah-nam* – Medicine Creek – emerges from wooded hills to coil its way towards *Whulge's* briny oblivion, like a snake with its head in a snare, the great dead snag of Leschi's youthful first quest stands alone, stark against the backdrop of the Nisqually Delta. All around this snag, grasses and low shrubs dot the broad earthen floor on both sides of the creek's undulating scrawl. The walls of cedar, hemlock, spruce, fir, and distant shining mountains, hold up a ceiling of tumbling clouds. It is as majestic a meeting hall as any back in Washington City. To this spot the tribes of the South Sound were summoned on Christmas Eve, 1854, for the first great treaty council with the new Governor.

Leschi and Quiemuth came downriver by canoe to the spot, with Sluggia, Quiemuth's son George, and their wives. Upon arrival, the women built *wikiups* for shelter, covering them with cedar bark and boughs against the winter rains, and fronting them with fire pits to repel the chill. Leschi was proud to see the numbers of his people, and of the neighboring tribes, pouring in to the council grounds. All the many Nisqually villages were represented, as well as Puyallups, Klickitats, Tulalips, Duwamish, and Squaxons. Necklaces of speckled *hiqua*, bear claw, and mother-of-pearl, added a festive air to the momentous gathering. Swimming their ponies across *She-nah-nam*, the people were like a plentiful run of Chinook, shimmering in midday mist.

A man the size of a bear rose up out of the fog to clasp Leschi to his breast. "Cousin, it is good to see you again," boomed Kanasket, Chief of the Klickitats, a band of Yakamas that had been forced by war over the mountains from the east, into the rugged highlands of the upper Green and White Rivers. Leschi remembered fondly Kanasket's annual summer visits to the Nisqually Delta. Even when testing themselves against one another in the hot blood of youth, Kanasket had never used his enormous strength to intimidate. Conscious of his strength, he was slow to take offense, even slower to anger. He was also one of the few Natives for whom Leschi had to look up to meet his eyes, and when he did so on this day he found uncharacteristic lines of worry.

"My friend," said Leschi, "it pleases me greatly to see you again. I hope your belly is full, and your village peaceful."

Kanasket grasped each of Leschi's forearms and held him fast. "These are strange times, cousin, strange times," he muttered, shaking his head.

"There have been many changes brought by the white man," replied Leschi. "Their ways are different from ours. But," he added, "ways are only ways. It is heart that matters. Are their hearts so different?"

Kanasket looked long at his dear friend. "Let us hope not," he said at last.

"It is true," acknowledged Leschi, eyeing the small crowd gathering to hear the two *Tyees*, "that we have all felt the encroachments of the Bostons on our lands. But this council is proof that the Boston *Tyee* has heard of our troubles, and wishes to make amends. Now he will tell us, for all time, what land belongs to the Indian, and what land belongs to the white man."

"There was a time, not many summers ago, when you would not have known what it means to own the earth itself," chided Kanasket. He was a simple man, who took change hard.

"We do not claim it as our own like the white man, or write it on a talking paper," agreed Leschi, "but we have always known what land our tribes could hunt and fish, and where our villages and summer camps could stand. Your own fathers learned the hard way what it means to lose your land – not at the hand of the Bostons, but of the Cayuse."

"It is true," replied Kanasket.

"The Bostons could perhaps destroy us all, yet they choose instead to offer gifts and talk peace," said Leschi. "This council is a chance for your tribe to once again have a place it can call its own. I think we should listen with open minds."

"Yes," agreed Kanasket. "As usual, cousin, you speak with wisdom." His face relaxed into its more accustomed calm, and he smiled. "Besides, I have heard that you might soon have a Boston son-in-law. Is this true?"

"It is," confirmed Leschi, beaming with pride, and he accepted the congratulations of Kanasket and the old Duwamish Chief Se-alth.

But the Suquamish Chief, Kitsap, a barrel-chested youngster with a scar across his left cheek, was not in a congratulatory mood. "So tell me, Leschi," he asked, "will you be getting any special reward for giving away the land of our ancestors to your new tribe?"

Leschi tasted anger's bile, though he had no desire to fight this hot-blooded young man. Everyone knew well that the Duwamish warrior who'd left his mark on Kitsap's cheek now dwelled in *Otlas-Skio*. But it would not do for Leschi to let the insult pass. "Perhaps you did not hear me, young pup," he barked, head held high. "I said we should listen with open minds, not that we should give away our lands. This I pledge above all else: My people shall have land enough to live. Without that, there can be no treaty."

2

As the early dusk of Christmas Eve fell over the treaty grounds, a commotion arose at the western bank of the rain-swollen creek. It was the Governor and his entourage, canoeing up from the steamer *Major Tompkins*, that had whisked them from Olympia to the delta in only two hours. Moving with the efficiency of ants, the Bostons unloaded mountains of supplies, setting up two large white canvas tents, each the size of hunting camps. On tables that had been constructed for this purpose, they piled great platters of beef, mutton, venison, elk, goose, duck and salmon, along with carrots and potatoes, all still steaming from the shipboard ovens.

The Governor quickly disappeared into a tent, but Leschi was gratified to see his old friend Mike Simmons emerge through the darkening air, his formerly flame-red beard now tangled with grey. Though Mike was strong as ever, Leschi noticed the creeping paunch around his middle, a sign not merely of age but of new-found prosperity. "Mike Simmons!" he called, and Mike came right over and extended a big, calloused hand.

"Leschi! *Klahowya?*" was all Mike could say, his Chinook being somewhat limited, "*Klahowya? klahowya?*" – "How are you? how are you?" – and he pulled Leschi in to his chest and pounded him on the back.

"*Muck-a-muck?*" asked Leschi, hungrily eyeing the mounds of food.

"*Wake*" – "No" – answered Mike, shaking his head and waving Ben Shaw over to interpret. "Before we feast," he began, his drawl clipped by Shaw's Northern chirp, "there is much to do. Since the first day we met, I have always wanted to repay the favor you did us, Leschi. Now, I can do so. I am joined with the greatest *Tyee* in the West, Isaac Stevens. It pleases him to use his power to help the Indians, and this pleases me too, because of our long friendship." After pausing to allow Shaw to interpret his words, Mike held up a paper covered in ornate black scrawls. "This, Leschi, is an important paper that I have gotten for you. It is a commission signed by the Governor himself, appointing you as one of the Chiefs of the Nisquallies. With this paper, the Great Father in Washington City will recognize you as a big man with the power to sign a treaty for all of your tribe. This paper is strong medicine; guard it carefully, and keep it always safe." Mike held out the paper to Leschi, who took it proudly, and displayed it about for his family and tribesmen to see.

"Quiemuth," called Mike, and Quiemuth stepped forward. Speaking through Shaw, Mike bestowed upon him with equal ceremony, another commission as a Chief of the Nisquallies. Quiemuth held it out from his face, as if it might bite. The paper felt dry, a thing of death. It had no scent. He had no place to keep such a totem; he handed it to Moonya with instructions to place it between two mats, roll it up, put it inside a bearskin pouch, and carry it straight to the medicine man to be examined for evil *tamanous*.

Mike distributed several more commissions to other Nisqually head men, including John Hiton of Olympia, and Wahoolit of Yelm Prairie. To Leschi's dismay, Mike also handed a commission to Wyamooch, who glowed with pleasure at the recognition denied by his own tribe.

Then Mike held up another even larger paper. "This paper," he said through Shaw, "contains on it the outline of *Whulge*, all the land from the ocean to the tops of the Cascade Mountains, and from the Columbia River to the tip of Vancouver's Island. For reference, we've drawn the principal lakes and rivers, as best as we could do it. Using these pencils that I will give you –" and he held up sticks, pointed like small black-tipped arrows – "the Governor orders the Chiefs to draw out the full area of land which has been claimed by your tribe in the past. This is not the land you will get when we make our treaty, but the lands you now claim, including the lands you will sell to us so that all of us, and our children, may forever live together in peace. Do you understand?"

Leschi nodded though his head was spinning, for it would not do for a great *Tyee* to betray any sign of weakness. Mike handed over the paper with an eager flash of his green eyes. "*Kloshe, kloshe*," he said without Shaw's aid – "Good, good." Leschi, Quiemuth, and their fellow Chiefs spread the large map on a table furnished by Simmons, and huddled by the light of the Bostons' oil lanterns. The paper was filled with squiggly black lines, but no matter how long they discussed it, they could not fathom how this paper related to their river with its still pools, narrow rapids, broad rocky crossings and meanderings. They and their ancestors wandered far and wide, as did the people of the neighboring tribes; what were they to say about the overlap in their lands? And what of the places where only spirits could go – if they were to mark those down upon the white man's talking paper, would the spirits be angered? They stared and stared but could not see *Ta-co-bet's* shimmering snowfields on the paper, or the soft limbs of the red alder glowing in late autumn sunshine, or the splashing smaller creeks like Muck and Tanwax and Ohop, or the spike and bright yellow spathe of the skunk cabbage in spring, or the quiet marshes where the great blue heron stands still as death, waiting for the silver flash of a fish, or even *Laliad,* spirit of the wind, which every fool knows is everywhere.

When Mike returned but a short time later, he was annoyed to find that they had marked nothing on their paper. Pulling a watch from his pocket he exploded with a long string of angry words. Shaw sought in vain a translation for "hour," then whittled it down to one bland question: "It has been an *hour* – what have you been doing?"

Insulted, Leschi tried to explain. "This *oow* of which you speak, it is nothing. We have wandered this land since *Whulge* was new."

Mike just scowled, and grabbed the map away. "Tell me, what is the farthest south your people range?"

"To the *Skookumchuk,*" replied Leschi, referring to the fast-running river that flows into the land of the Chehalis.

"And the furthest north?"

"The *T'kope,*" replied Leschi, referring to the river that joins the Puyallup, then empties into Commencement Bay by the growing town of Tacoma.

"OK," said Mike. "And we'll assume you go all the way from Sound to mountains – right?" No answer. So he made two big slashes on the talking paper. "There, that wasn't so hard, was it?" he asked with an unfriendly grin. "Now you can *muck-a-muck,*" he added as an afterthought. Gathering up the pencils and the map, he rushed off to the next table, where the Puyallups stood puzzling over their own strange talking paper, to do the same for them.

The Nisquallies shuffled off to the feasting tables, but the food was cold.

3

Christmas Day, 1854, did not dawn crystalline and bright on Medicine Creek; some say it did not dawn at all. It was one of those Pacific Northwest winter mornings in which the transition from night to day is imperceptible, a mere exchange of gloom for gloom, one wet, consumptive breath following another. It was dark, and then it was less dark. The lone raven perched on a dripping limb of the snag gradually adjusted its eye to a startling tableau below: seven hundred painted and bejeweled Natives gathered in concentric arcs before two glowing white tents. The Chiefs stood tall as their bowlegged statures would allow, in breeches and tunics of cedar, trimmed with whistling marmot and cougar, majestic in bearskin cloaks, gripping Hudson's Bay fusee muskets and bone-tipped spears by their sides. Their faces were painted black and ochre beneath otterskin caps, brightened by white eagle and indigo mallard feathers. In a display of wealth, the Chiefs' necks were laden with string upon string of rare *hiqua* necklaces.

Facing the Natives sat the treaty commissioners, snug under a canopy in stiff-backed fir chairs at document-strewn tables, brandishing steel quills in the place of muskets and spears. Lieutenant Slaughter wore his full dress uniform, red-striped pants smart over spit-shined boots. Shaw, a veteran of General Zachary Taylor's campaign from Palo Alto to Buena Vista, was also in uniform, gold braid on his shoulder pining for a bit of light to reflect. The Harvard men, Charles Mason and surveyor George Gibbs, wore proper black woolen frock coats, with high starched collars and black cravats smartly pinned at the throat. Mike Simmons represented the pioneer spirit, in fringed buckskin under a big black woolen greatcoat with brass buttons.

One empty seat waited at the very heart of this assemblage, directly in front of the point where the towering treaty snag, like some grey and malevolent wizard, was calling down buckets of torrential rain. At last two small vibrant figures emerged from the tent. It was the Governor, accompanied by his twelve-year-old son Hazard, who stood off to the side between soldiers and members of the Governor's staff as his father strode to the center table. The Governor was wearing a dark frock coat over a red flannel shirt, with baggy woolen trousers tucked into his scuffed boots "California style," and his trademark insouciant felt slouch hat angled on his head. As usual, a clay pipe was tucked neatly into the hatband. Two sharp points protruded beneath the hat: Stevens' nose and his neatly trimmed goatee, giving him at first the appearance of Punch from Punch and Judy. Rather than sitting, the Governor mounted the chair to survey the Chiefs with eyes that danced and burned like lightning. They saw his power, and some were afraid.

Stevens began to speak in a clear high voice, and although Shaw had already demonstrated facility with *Whulshootseed*, he interpreted in the clumsy Chinook trading jargon with its limited vocabulary. Leschi was surprised, but Shaw knew what he was doing: following the Governor's strict instructions.

"Today is Christmas, a special day for the white man because Jesus Christ, the son of God, was born this day," he began. "And this particular Christmas is extra special, because it is a day of peace and friendship between your people and mine for all time to come. You are about to be paid for your lands." Leschi smiled and relaxed upon hearing this news affirmed by the great man himself, thinking that it was indeed, as his friend Mike Simmons had said, *kloshe*.

"The Great Father in Washington City has sent me today to treat with you concerning payment. The Great Father lives far off beyond the mountains. He has many children, too many for him to keep track of by himself, so he sent me here to watch out for them. My people and I have studied your wants and your needs, and because I feel much for you, I went to the Great Father and told him what we have seen here of your hardships, of the white settlements on your lands and the quarrels that have arisen, of the diseases you catch from the white man. The Great Father took pity on his children, and he has sent me here today to make a treaty for your benefit."

"Leschi," whispered Kitsap, "I am no child. I am a man. What about you?" Leschi shifted uneasily, but said nothing.

"The Great Father wishes you to have homes, pasture for your horses and fishing places. He wishes you to learn to farm, and for your children to go to a good school. He wants me to make a bargain with you, in which you will sell your lands, and in return be provided with all these things. My commissioners will explain to you the terms of the treaty. If it is good you will sign it, and I will send it to the Great Father. I think he will be pleased with it and say it is good. If he does, it will be a fixed bargain, and payment will be made. If he wants changes he will say so, and then if you agree it will be a fixed bargain and payment will be made." This was confusing and especially hard to follow in Chinook, but each time he spoke of payment Stevens waved his hand toward the many tables heaped high with furs, blankets, necklaces, bolts of calico and lace, bales of brightly-colored ribbons, crates of shiny axes, shovels, hammers, pitchforks and knives, saddles, bridles, harnesses, plows and harrows. The Indians looked longingly at the tables, but they were guarded by soldiers holding rifles.

Kitsap leaned over and whispered to Leschi, "Look carefully, fellow *Tyee*. There is everything we could want on that table, except for the guns needed to keep the white man from stealing it all back again." Leschi nodded; the point was not lost on him.

The Governor turned the proceedings over to Secretary Mason, who did his best to bore everyone into submission by a long recital of what he called "irrevocable covenants and conditions between the treating *paahties*," which Shaw translated as *skookum mahkook kwahnesum* – "strong bargain forever." What was this? Leschi did not understand. No two tribes had ever made a treaty that could not be changed later. Did not the great cedars themselves grow old and eventually fall? Everything changes. How could men make something that could not change? Something outside the great wheel of life?

Mason continued: "The Indians will retain the right to take fish at all usual and accustomed grounds and stations in common with all citizens of the Territory, together with the privilege of hunting, gathering roots and berries, and pasturing their horses on open and unclaimed lands." Well, thought

Leschi, that is very good. *Sah-hah-lee Tyee* made the earth big enough for all, and *Doquebuth* stocked the streams to bursting; there could never come a time when there was not enough land or fish for all.

"Indians will be prohibited from using or selling firewater on the reservations," continued Mason, which pleased Leschi, "and they will also be barred from keeping or trading in slaves," which did not seem right to Leschi. Had they not always done so? Hadn't Washington Bush admitted to him that the *Tyee* of *Tyees* in Washington City protected his own peoples' right to own slaves in many of the lands controlled by the Bostons? Besides, without slaves, who would do their hardest, dirtiest labor? Toilet pits could not be filled by free members of the tribe, even women. They would be soiled irrevocably, so the spirits would not help them into the afterworld.

"The Government can deduct each year from its payments for your lands, the value of any property stolen by Indians," continued Mason. Leschi frowned. Treating them as criminals dishonored them. In unscrupulous hands, could this not prevent them from receiving any payment at all? Leschi was becoming concerned.

Young Hazard Stevens grew bored with the lengthy recitation of legalisms, and ran off with Quiemuth's son George and the other Indian boys, to explore down by the creek. Mason droned on and on, still never really getting to the point of what it was that they had come to hear. Finally, he turned to Mike Simmons. "Mr. Simmons will now explain the lands set aside for you, and the payments to be made. Mike?"

There was Leschi's good friend, the man he'd rescued like a helpless bear cub now grown full to grizzly, ready to repay the debt. Only the words were not adding up; perhaps it was the jargon. The Nisquallies were to be paid a lot of money – Mike called it "$32,500." Leschi did not know what that was; such numbers were unfamiliar to him. They were to be paid that money over twenty years. He knew "years" – it meant a cycle of seasons, what his people called "summers," and "twenty" was two tens. But at the beginning they would get $3,250, and then in other years different amounts, until at the end they would get $1,000. Was that more or less? And was it more or less than $32,500? What were these numbers? Was it as many as the salmon that they were to give up? As many as the trees in the forests they were to sell? He knew what his people could do with a salmon or a red cedar, but what could they do with $32,500?

"You will not be paid, of course, until the Great Father in Washington ratifies the treaty." The word was translated – *tumtum kunamokst* – agree. If the Great *Tyee* Stevens says it is good, is it not a bargain? Or has he not the power we were told that he had? Leschi did not understand. How could the White *Tyee* of *Tyees* in Washington City, who had never visited their land, never looked them in the eye or seen how they live, know what is best for them?

"You will not be paid in cash, but in the equivalent value in goods, selected at the discretion of the Government." There was no word for "Government," so Shaw simply substituted *Boston lalang* – "Boston Tribe." Leschi's head began to swim. They would be paid, but not yet, and then not paid. How would the Bostons know better than they how to spend their dollars?

"The President retains the authority," continued Mike – which Shaw translated as *skookum*, this time meaning "power" instead of "strong" – "when the interests of the Territory may require, to relocate your reservation to another location which, in his sole discretion, is suitable for your purposes." Speaking quickly to keep up, Shaw first rendered "another location" as *polaklie illahee*, then paused and thought for a minute, before correcting it to *huloima illahee*. A murmur of dismay was audible from the gathered Natives. Despite the correction, the damage was done: Shaw had spoken the name of the land of perpetual blackness, a frigid land where the streams run foul and a single sting of an insect is fatal.

"Silence!" commanded Stevens, "allow Mr. Simmons to finish." And Simmons proceeded to the most important part, explaining in detail exactly where the various reservations for the tribes were to be located. Leschi listened intently as Simmons pointed behind them to the rocky wooded bluff that dropped to the sea from high cliffs, comprised of what he called "1,280 acres of prime forest land."

"This high land by the Sound," said Leschi's friend Mike Simmons, uttering simple words that slashed like bear claws, "shall be the reservation for the Nisqually people."

Even the gulls fell silent.

Simmons asked if there were any questions. Leschi's stomach felt as if he'd been punched hard. He closed his eyes and transported himself back to the rim of *Ta-co-bet* from which he drew a powerful angry breath of flame. "Would you move all of your people there," he cried, jerking his thumb over his shoulder towards the inhospitable bluff, "foresaking *Tenalquot* to live on a tiny, rocky, wooded cliff, *Govenol Stevens?*" Leschi spit out the name in English, his black eyes like coals startling the little Governor, who had not expected to be addressed directly and by name.

"Questions for *me*, Leschi," hissed Simmons through Shaw, but Stevens was already standing, pushing Simmons aside.

"Translate it," commanded Stevens, and Shaw did so. Stevens leaned over to his commissioners. "Who is this impudent *siwash?*" he demanded.

"Leschi, sir. One of the Nisqually Chiefs," replied Mason. "Dr. Tolmie vouches for him; says he's been a good friend to the whites."

"You believe that limey weasel?" muttered Stevens. "Simmons, you seem to be acquainted with this so-called Chief. Is he a troublemaker?"

Mike paused only half a beat. "Yes, suh."

"What do we know about him – I mean, to his disadvantage?"

"Well, Gov'nor, the varmit's only half-Nisqually. His ma was Klickitat. A lot of his people ain't too comfortable with that; them Klickitats got themselves chased over to this-here side of the mountains, and the Nisquallies think the Klickitats're trying to take over their lands." Stevens smiled and nodded. Mike had done his job well.

Stevens turned to face the Indians once again. Everyone was tense, waiting to see how he would respond to the challenge. The Governor just smiled blandly at Leschi. "If I were in your position, Mr. Leschi, charged with looking out for the best interests of the *Nisquallies*," he said with extra emphasis, "I would move my people to that safe and secure ridge, and be grateful for the opportunity."

"We are grateful, great *Tyee*," responded Leschi cooly, straining to rein in his temper. "We are grateful every day when we rise, and we see the trees and sky, and the fish jumping in the river, like our ancestors before us. You say there is a Great Father in a place called Washington City, who feels pity for his children. We are not grateful for that. We are men, like yourselves. We ask for respect, not pity. We have come here as men, to make a treaty with other men."

"We have made you our offer, Leschi, because we want your people to be cared for," replied Stevens. "But you must realize, you can no longer care for yourselves in a land governed by the United States of America. A people who cannot care for themselves are like children. Be thankful that you have a Father in Washington City who really does care for the best interests of all his children, and who will treat you with justice and mercy. Now, we will all take a break to enjoy the great feast that I, as your host, have prepared for you, my honored guests. As you eat, consider well what we offer to you – peaceful homes on a protected reservation, all the usual fishing, hunting and gathering that you have always done, plus the means to learn the white man's way of life. There will be no changes to our offer. If it is good, sign the treaty; if it is not, do not. But I warn you," and here his voice grew hard, "there will be consequences for any tribe that does not sign." The row of soldiers brandishing rifles made it unnecessary to elaborate. Stevens smiled. "Now, eat well. Enjoy the blessings that only come from peace."

4

Leschi cursed himself for speaking in anger. There was something about the Governor's arrogant calm that vexed him. It wasn't what he said, though that was bad enough. It was the way he said it, like he was swatting at a fly, and the outcome was both predetermined, and of no real consequence.

There was more. Leschi was forced to admit that the Governor's words stung because there was some truth to them. Indeed, Leschi himself had begun to think and act like a dependent child ever since he first marveled at the white man's powers. All these months, even for years, he had been looking forward to the day when the white man would solve the tribe's problems for them, tell them where to live, how to get by. What a fool he had been! And this was the result: crumbs from the white man's table.

Now Leschi sat in council with his people, deciding whether to accept those crumbs. "Leschi has dishonored us," said Wyamooch, hatchet-faced son of the old Chief. "It was said that I was too wild to lead our people, but who is the wild one now?"

"And what would you have us do?" snapped Quiemuth, coming to his brother's defense. "Shall we sell our land so the Bostons can ship us all away to *polackie illahee*?"

John Hiton, head man of the Olympia village, spoke up. "I agree with Leschi that this forested bluff is no good, but insulting our host is not going to get us anywhere. I am ready to sign this treaty, because it grants us the right to fish and forage on our traditional lands. Even if we must move our villages, at least we can still wander the river."

"For how long?" asked Wahoolit. "Soon the white man will enclose everything with his fences, and claim all the land with his talking papers."

"You may be right, Wahoolit," answered Wyamooch. "There was a time when I urged that we join Patkanim in war. Remember that it was Leschi and Quiemuth who disagreed. Now it is too late; the white man is too strong. You see now that you should have listened to me." Wyamooch stood, and walked over to Leschi, who was seated by the fire, eating. "Am I right, Leschi?" he said, his voice full of challenge.

Leschi rose. "Until this man Stevens came, the white man was our friend. I stand by the decision not to attack a friend. Besides, even had we taken your advice, Wyamooch, do you think that would have been the end of it?

The white man is like the berry on the thornbush; you may take your fill and your hands will run red and bloody, but always, more come. Had we attacked them, we would all be dead today."

"Then we must sign this treaty," said John Hiton.

"No," said Leschi. "We must find another way. How can we sign a treaty that takes away our home?"

"You heard the white *Tyee* – no bargaining!" roared Wyamooch. "You will lead us to war and destruction."

"'No bargaining' is just what you or I would say to bring down the price," said Leschi. "If this man Stevens is not a madman, he will give us a little more if he sees we stand united."

"That would be good, Leschi," said John Hiton, "but I must warn you, if you fail, I will sign without you for my village." He lowered his head in his hands, showing the stumps where his two outer fingers had been cut off by a Haida invader many summers ago. "I am sorry."

"The Nisqually people need new *Tyees*, John," said Wyamooch. "*Tyees* that are true Nisquallies, not half-breeds." He glared at Leschi, then looked to John Hiton. "I'll sign too!"

"This is the fruit of Stevens," said Leschi, "Nisqually turning on Nisqually." Leschi looked around the council fire, taking in each man, one by one. "You know me, you know my brother, you know my father, and my father's father. I for one will never sign a paper that gives away all the land of the Nisquallies except for one useless rock. I would rather die than sign such a paper."

Soon after Leschi spoke these words, the Governor's people made special payments to a few particularly helpful Natives, who fanned out across the broad floodplain, whispering of the strange conference between Leschi and his cousin, Chief Kanasket of the Klickitats. "Can you believe it," they said in hushed tones, "we actually heard Leschi saying that he would lead his people into war rather than sign the treaty, while at the same time urging Kanasket to sign it." Was this not obviously a plot to trick the Nisquallies? Leschi wanted them to miss out on the Governor's generous offer, while his mother's people, the Klickitats, would get all the riches that rightfully belong to the Nisquallies. Or so it was whispered, from forked tongue to trembling ear.

5

The mid-day *muck-a-muck* boosted the spirits of many, but not Leschi. He knew he had to find some other way to approach this inscrutable white *Tyee*, but it was difficult to read him. The Governor might really believe that he was their savior; at the least, he seemed untroubled by his complete ignorance of their true situation. Perhaps if he were better informed, thought Leschi ...

Leschi's reveries were broken by the arrival of Jim McAllister, who had tramped down from his home just a few hundred yards upland. Jim had proven his worth when trapping up in Canada, where he'd found a half-starved Similkameen boy who'd been held as a slave by the Haidas, staked to his master's grave. This was the Haida custom, to ensure that the slave could go on serving his master in *Otlas-Skio*, land of the dead. Jim rescued the little boy, Clipwalen. The McAllisters kept the boy as a house servant, and treated him kindly. Many local Indians thought Jim was a fool for interfering, but Leschi admired him for it.

Over the years, Jim had gained a pretty serviceable familiarity with *Whulshootseed.* "Leschi," he said, "yer a sight for sore eyes, Laddie. And, I hear, a real troublemaker," but Jim chuckled, as if to say he knew it wasn't so. "What's this, then? Haven't we always got along pretty good?"

"Yes," said Leschi, "until Stevens we did. What drives this man?"

"Same thing that drives us all, I'd say," Jim mused. "He wants what he wants. Difference is, he knows how to get it." Jim paused. "You want my advice?"

"Yes, please," said Leschi.

"I think you'd better do a *midgie* o' fence mending with that there Governor of ours, sign where he tells you to sign, and thank him for his trouble, 'cause let me tell you, he ain't the type you cross and live to tell of it." Jim dropped his chin and looked Leschi long and hard out the tops of his eyes, right through his raised bushy eyebrows, before trotting off to get a slap on the back from Mike Simmons.

Leschi was weighing these words as the commissioners marched out of their tent, Stevens in the lead. The others sat, but Stevens remained standing, the slight flush to his cheeks betraying his preferred lunchtime tonic. "We will now hear from the Chiefs, with any questions or words that they would like to speak. After that, we will set out the treaty for signing. Once it is signed, the gifts will be distributed." Stevens motioned again towards the heavily laden tables.

Leschi rose, and all eyes turned upon him. "*Tyee* Stevens," he said, "I must apologize. I did not mean to sound ungrateful this morning. I am grateful to you, and to the Great Chief in Washington City, for the offer you make here today." Stevens waited, sensing that there would be more.

"You said this morning that we could no longer care for ourselves in a land governed by your people. There is some wisdom to your words. I know that our people's numbers have dwindled even as your people have grown numerous as the gulls overhead. I know that there have been conflicts between our people. Some say we must adapt, or perish. I have said it myself. But, upon sober reflection, I see that this is wrong. If we adapt too much, we perish.

"It is for this reason that we must have enough land to maintain our traditional way of life. We do not need your pity, we do not need to be cared for like children; all we need is a small part of the land along the river that is already ours, and then our fate is in our hands." Leschi paused, and seeing little softening in Stevens' stony eyes, he stepped to within arm's length of the Governor to make his final appeal, man to man.

"Great *Tyee*, you know little of us, so I will tell you. We do not live in one place like the white man; we migrate like the salmon. There is nothing we can do with that bluff behind us. We cannot fish it; it is dry. We cannot farm it; it is too rocky. We cannot hunt it; it is too barren. We cannot roam it; it is too small. We cannot build our villages, it is too wooded, and if we clear it, it will be too exposed. We cannot honor our river and the salmon upon it; it has no river and no salmon to honor. We cannot honor our ancestors there; their spirits dwell forever along the river.

"Great *Tyee*, you also know little of how my family has been a friend to your people, so I will tell you that also. Without my help, and my brother's help, there would be no white man here today for you to lead." He saw amusement pool in Stevens' eyes. "No, mighty Stevens, do not laugh! It was we who brought Snoqualmie murderers to your *t-lial*. We faced down Patkanim at his council when he wanted to declare war on all white men, back when your people were few and weak. We defended Fort Nisqually against Patkanim's attack. We saved your Mike Simmons and this man here, Jim McAllister, and their families, when they were lost and starving in the forest. We fed many pioneers who would have starved their first winter without our help. We gave horses and labor and guides to help your settlers build the road over the Naches Pass that your Mr. Mason traveled to get here." Mason's pursing lips confirmed it. "Now, I am asked to give my daughter in marriage to a Boston man, Eden. I have consented in the spirit of friendship and peace. But friendship is a two-way path, my brother.

"What we ask is nothing to you, but it is everything to us. We do not ask to sit in your councils. We do not ask to live in your towns, marry your women, drink your firewater, ride on your steamships, work in your mills, or shop in your stores. We do not ask to keep even more than one in every hundred parts of the lands our ancestors have held since before the beginning of time. All we ask, Great *Tyee*, is that we be allowed to keep some land along our river, just enough to support our accustomed way of life."

Stevens glared at Leschi, but still he said nothing. *What kind of man is this?* thought Leschi, but he forged ahead. "This I ask, *Govenol* Stevens, in the name of the justice and mercy of which you speak. It is what any people must demand, or surrender their claim to be a people; it is what any wise *Tyee* must grant, or surrender his claim to be a leader. Give us just this, and I will proudly sign your paper."

Nawitka, nawitka, nawitka – "Yes, yes, yes!" cried voices all around the treaty ground, and the combination of the power of Leschi's words and his strong square jaw towering over Stevens, needled the little man's herniated gut.

"Nisqually people," said the Governor, speaking right past Leschi, "this man Leschi speaks well enough, but for whom does he speak? Is it for the Nisquallies, or for the Klickitats?"

There was muttering all about, until Kanasket arose. "Silence!" he demanded. "The Klickitats speak for themselves."

Wyamooch rose, the Governor's dollars jingling softly in the pouch at his belt. "Yes, Kanasket, we thought you'd say so." Kanasket just glowered at him, but said nothing. "Consider well what Leschi is asking us to do, my people," said Wyamooch. "He wants us to give up fishing rights and hunting and gathering rights that assure us everything we have ever had, just because he is too old and tired to clear a few trees!"

"This is madness!" cried Leschi, "it is not the trees."

"Then what is it?" Wyamooch goaded. "Or perhaps I should ask your cousin, Kanasket?" But Kanasket, the simple giant, was bewildered, bewilderment that was read by many as duplicity.

Delighted with the turmoil in the Nisqually ranks, the Governor pressed home the advantage. "Leschi misunderstands what we are here to do today. I have extended to you the offer of the Great Father in Washington City. The terms I have offered may even be too generous, because I feel warm in my heart for you, and wish to protect you. You may sign or not sign, that is your choice, but I want to make clear: you will never see a better offer than this. If you do not sign, you may lose everything. Consider well the pain of war against the white man, with his big guns. Consider well all the gifts you will receive, and the secure lands promised to you forever, if you do sign. Consider well how you would feel, Nisqually people, to be the only ones left with nothing, as other tribes like the Puyallups and the Klickitats enjoy the fruits of our generosity, and you are reduced to begging for bitter scraps!"

"Hear me!" cried Leschi, and he stepped nose to nose with the Governor, so close that he could smell the whiskey on Stevens' breath. Lieutenant Slaughter rose, hand on the hilt of his sword, but Stevens waved him off. Leschi abruptly turned his back on the Governor, blotting him out with his height. "Fellow Nisquallies, People of the River Grass, hear me! I am for peace; it is this man Stevens who talks of war. He is clever, and would deceive you into quarreling among yourselves. He offers only a tiny piece of useless land on which no one could live, and says that even that can be taken away whenever he chooses, so we can be shipped off to *polackie illahee*. He says that we are children, and that we cannot even bargain for enough land to live on." He spun again to face Stevens, and the clash of their wills lit the gloom between them. "For the last time, I say to you, *Tyee* Stevens – give us but a small piece of the river that bears our name, and we shall be the Bostons' friends forever. We do not want war."

The Governor pictured his hero, Andy Jackson, who stared down the United States Supreme Court itself rather than give in to the demands of savages. "The Great Father does not bargain with his children," said Stevens, spitting each word like bloodied teeth.

"Then this is what I think of your treaty!" cried Leschi, turning so all could see as he held up the precious commission signed by the Governor, and tore it into little pieces, which he proceeded to stamp into the rich Nisqually earth under his feet. From *Otlas-Skio* beneath the ground, the fingers of ancestors eagerly clawed at the fragments.

All watched in silence while Leschi and Quiemuth gathered their families, and as many Nisquallies as would follow, and disappeared into the mist. The Governor whispered a few words to Mike Simmons, who grabbed Jim McAllister and the treaty and went chasing after them. Wahoolit stood, gathered his family, and marched off in solidarity. The young Suquamish hot-head, Kitsap, walked off as well. But that was all. Other Nisquallies, and all the other tribes represented, just stood watching, paralyzed by a web of fear and suspicion. They began muttering among themselves, unsure which way the wind would take them.

Stevens nodded to Chief Se-alth, the old and respected leader who, as a child, had greeted Vancouver's ships. His people, the Duwamish, were lobbying for good lands on the Black River, and had an interest in currying the Governor's favor. Seeing that Se-alth was about to speak, the assemblage fell quiet.

"Great *Tyee*," he began, addressing Stevens, "you must excuse our brother Leschi. He fears what he does not understand, and indeed, we all find it difficult to understand the ways of the white man with his talking papers and reservations. To us the remains of our ancestors are sacred and their resting place is hallowed ground. You wander far from the graves of your ancestors and seemingly without regret. Your dead cease to love you and the land of their birth as soon as they pass the portals of the tomb and wander away beyond the stars. They are soon forgotten and never return. Our dead never forget this beautiful world that gave them being.

"Day and night cannot dwell together. The red man has ever fled the approach of the white man, as the morning mist flees before the sun. However, your proposition seems fair, and I think that my people will accept it, and will retire to the reservation you offer them. Then we will dwell apart in peace, for the words of the Great White Chief speak to my people out of dense darkness."

Stevens began to smile and step forward, but Chief Se-alth stopped him with his outstretched weathered palm. "It matters little where we pass the remnant of our days," continued the great Chief. "They will not be many. A few more winters, and not one of the descendants of the mighty hosts that once moved over this broad land or lived in happy homes, protected by the Great Spirit, will remain to mourn over the graves of a people once more powerful and hopeful than yours. But why should I mourn at the untimely fate of my people? Tribe follows tribe, nation follows nation, like the waves of the sea. It is the order of things, and regret is useless. Your time of decay may be distant, but it will surely come, for even the white man whose God walked and talked with him as friend to friend, cannot be exempt from the common destiny. We may be brothers after all. We will see." And the old Chief smiled an ominous smile, so that Stevens sat down, and the other commissioners fidgeted in their seats.

"Every part of this soil is sacred in the eyes of my people," declared Chief Se-alth with deep feeling, his voice cracking, so that the people leaned in to catch each word, their hands cupped to their ears. "Every hillside, every valley, every plain and grove, has been hallowed by some sad or happy event in days long vanished. Even the rocks, which seem to be dumb, thrill with memories of stirring events in the lives of my people, and the very dirt upon which you now stand responds more lovingly to our footsteps than yours, because it is rich with the blood of our ancestors. And when the last red man shall have perished, and the memory of my tribe and all the coastal tribes shall have become a myth among the white men, these shores will swarm with the invisible dead of our tribes. When your children's children think themselves alone in the field, the store, the shop, upon the highway, or in the silence of the pathless woods, they will not be alone. At night when the streets of your cities are silent and you think them deserted, they will throng with the returning hosts that once filled them and still love this beautiful land. The white man will never be alone. Let him be just and deal kindly with my people, for the dead are not powerless."

With these words hanging heavier than the deep fog upon the delta, Simmons and McAllister returned, Simmons holding up the Treaty in triumph. Lo and behold! By the names "Leschi" and "Quiemuth" there were two big X's, witnessed by Mike, Jim, and the Governor's boy, Hazard. "We spoke to Leschi as old friends, privately," explained Mike through an interpreter, "and he came around. You remember him saying that he was for peace? Well, we warned him that not to sign would mean war, and that seemed to be what did it. He told me to tell all his people to do what you think is best, but that he does not want war."

Simmons laid the treaty before Wyamooch, who made his mark with a flourish. Wyamooch handed the pen to John Hiton, who could barely grip it, but he managed to make a shaky "X". Soon the other Chiefs trudged forward, one by one, to add their marks. Finally, when only a few hold-outs were left, Simmons went from man to man, whispering of favors for each one who signed, saying that these other Chiefs will get hatfuls of money, and won't you feel like a fool to be left out? By the time that fateful day's darkness deepened imperceptibly into night, the treaty of Medicine Creek, providing that Leschi's people were to give up an area two-thirds the size of Rhode Island in exchange for 1,280 acres of rocky bluff, and $32,500 in goods paid over twenty years, was fully executed. Then the furs, blankets, necklaces, crates of shiny axes, shovels, hammers, pitchforks and knives, saddles, bridles, harnesses, plows and harrows, were all packed snug in their crates, and each Indian still present received a signing bonus of a few yards of calico, some black strap molasses, and a pinch of tobacco for the men.

Chapter Seven
The War Canoe

1

The Governor's tireless correspondence trumpeted the success of the Medicine Creek Treaty far and wide. He wrote to his friend President Franklin Pierce, whose election Stevens' stump speeches had helped secure. He wrote to his younger brother, who was still farming the old family estate, and could profit from the elder brother's example of gumption. Seated late at night at his writing desk in the anteroom to their bedroom, Isaac dipped his nib once more to pen a sober warning to General John E. Wool, Commander of the Army of the Pacific, stationed at the San Francisco Presidio. "The Coastal Indians are a docile and superstitious lot," he wrote, "and for the most part easily controlled. However, there are one or two bad apples in the barrel. I think a show of force may be helpful when the time comes to relocate them to their reservations." Drawing on his West Point training, Stevens then proceeding to detail the technical requirements of the force needed, which he set at four hundred men.

Isaac was just launching into an exposition of his Mexican War exploits, when he was distracted by tender fingers kneading the cramped muscles of his neck and shoulders. "Come to bed, Ingy," cooed Meg in his ear, nuzzling him with little kisses, switching playfully from side to side as he tried to shoo her away.

"Just one more –" Isaac said, but her hands were playing down his chest, her dark tresses falling over his face, her breasts pressing at the nape of his neck. As the blood rushed from brain to groin, he lost all ability to concentrate.

"Oh, how I've missed you, my darling, my Governor," Meg whispered. "Come," she coaxed, smiling and leading him by the hand from the writing desk to their bed, dropping her nightgown to reveal by moonlight her milky-hued breasts and belly, the dark tangle of her pubis. "I've got something better than that cold ink pot for your dipping pleasure," she teased. Saber unsheathed, Stevens nonetheless took a moment to fold and lay his shirt and trousers carefully over the bedstead. Meg delighted in knocking them helter-skelter while in the thrall of an otherwise heedless passion.

Within minutes of exploding inside her, Isaac was snoring softly in the moonlight. Look at him, thought Meg, so sweet lying there in bliss, that boyish wispy growth on smooth cheeks. Hard to believe the young man who'd read

Keats with such feeling, then pushed her home in the sleigh from the reading society meeting, was tonight the white *Tyee* of all the savages on the Sound. She had favored *Ode to a Nightingale*, but he preferred the *Two Sonnets on Fame*, though he seemed more to embody than profit from them. She could still hear his high clear voice wrapped around Keats' metered diphthongs:

How fever'd is the man, who cannot look
Upon his mortal days with temperate blood,
Who vexes all the leaves of his life's book,
And robs his fair name of its maidenhood ...

How fever'd, indeed. If only Isaac's father had lived to see what his son had achieved: the Governorship, a fine family, control over the local tribes, the beginnings of a University, a library, a common school system, the adoration of the people. Perhaps, thought Meg, perhaps at last, this will be enough. Meg stroked Isaac's blue-white brow and the wavy black hair falling about the pillow. Lord knows, it hasn't been easy, what with his tirades. Ingy could learn a thing or two about self-restraint from dear Mr. Mason.

Meg permitted her thoughts to stray to Charles, as her hand lingered in her husband's hair. Charles was handsome and attentive. Of course, he was too much of a gentleman to cross the line without any clear sign of encouragement from her. Should she give a signal? She smiled, then shook her head. No, she'd better not. In her position, she could ill afford the gossip. Besides, though Charles was gentle in a way Ingy couldn't even imagine, there was a reason that Isaac was Governor, while Charles played second fiddle. God, she did love the way Isaac could fill the room like a rooster, dominating men twice his size. She loved the fighter in him, even if it sometimes meant getting bruised herself. That happened only after he'd hit the bottle first, which wasn't really him, was it?

Oh Lord, prayed Meg, silently moving her lips, *let him find happiness here. Let him find peace somewhere other than in that cursed bottle.*

Meg closed her eyes to sleep, but moonlight through the windowpanes pulled like exotic music, making her restless. She got up to draw the curtains, pausing to look out over the beach to the moon-capped waves breaking gently on dunes, extending in the distance to the Nisqually village abutting Olympia. The view was wild and achingly beautiful, the bleached driftwood scattered like bones of ancient giants, but it only reminded her that they were living too close to the power and stink of this untamed fjord. She feared the Sound; death could come too quickly into or out of it. She worried for the children every day, trembling at imagined war canoes crashing ashore. Construction would soon begin on the new house on the hill, but it was too slow to suit her. With a sharp tug, she pulled the curtains closed and returned to bed, chilled through.

Meg was just beginning to warm and doze when she heard the sound – the mournful *ooooaaaaiiii* of the Indian song. *Blast!* she thought, *there go the heathens again.* Once they started singing to the moon there was no stopping them; sometimes they went all night. She tried to shut out the sound by covering her head with the pillow, but the dissonance of the many voices had a penetrating quality that reached through walls, windows, curtains and feathers, entering through the vestigial tail at the base of the spine. *Such melancholy must be a sin, couldn't they just shut up? People have to get some rest. Unlike the savages, we have work to do tomorrow.*

"Ingy, Ingy dear, wake up," said Meg.

"Hmmmmmm." Just an extension of his snore.

"Ingy? Ingy, please, don't you hear that?"

"Mmmmmmm."

"ISAAC!" He jumped up and reached for his gun.

"It's those blessed *siwash* again," said Meg. "I mean, listen to them! I can't get a wink of sleep with them carrying on like this. 'nisqually' must be Indian for 'People who howl like banshees.' Please, Ingy, please do something."

Isaac put down his gun, dragged on an overcoat, his slouch hat, and a pair of boots. Out in the shed he picked up a club the size of a buffalo's thigh bone. Meg watched from the window as he tramped across the beach to the Nisqually village. Pushing aside women seated on the outer perimeter of the circle, Isaac stomped to the center by the fire, where men in red and black paint were dancing. Silence fell.

"*Mitwhit!*" ordered the Governor – "Stand up!" Everybody stood. Repeatedly smacking the club against his palm, the stump-legged Governor circled the ring, staring each and every celebrant in the eye. In broken Chinook, he got his message across. "Any man, woman or child who opens their mouth to sing, I will knock down with this club." Stunned silence, as Stevens circled the fire several times, patting the club against his hand with a soft *tick, tick, tick.* "Good – now, sleep!" And he stood his ground until all the Indians had dispersed.

That was the last night of the Nisqually songs, a music so ancient and familiar that *Whulge* still echoes it back to the empty shore in the wail and moan of its storm surge.

2

Leschi and his family canoed up the Nisqually to Muck Creek, where they got ponies and packed winter supplies for the retreat to Mashel Village, but they could not outrun ill fate. Sara got hotter and hotter until the chills of the cold-sick wracked her body, and she could not go on. Leschi called the medicine man, who donned his robes and danced with his wooden rattle over Sara's mat as the people of Yokwa village pounded with sticks on the walls and roof of their longhouse. The medicine man could not visualize the spirit tormenting her. "It is a strange wraith," he said, "sent by a Boston sorcerer, beyond my spirit's powers." He shook his head, eyes downcast. "I am sorry, there is nothing I can do."

So Leschi sent the family to Mashel, except for Kwahnesum, who stayed to help him care for Sara. Ann protested, but he was firm; she must care for his father, Sennatco, whose many summers weighted each step. Ann donned a cheerful face like an ill-fitting mask, and knelt to kiss Sara goodbye. "I will see you soon, and together we will coil baskets for the winter moon," she whispered. Sara reached up to brush Ann's brittle smile. "First Wife," Sara replied, passing the honorific and with it all the household burdens. "Our husband will need great care in this time of danger." Ann rushed from the chamber, holding back her tears until she crossed the threshold.

Day became night became day as Leschi hovered, holding Sara's head in his lap, wiping her brow with cool water, building the fire, offering her small sips of broth. Each new day he felt her once-strong frame lighten for the long journey to her new home. *At least she is going to a land Stevens cannot steal,* thought Leschi bitterly.

On the seventh night, Leschi and Kwahnesum sat by Sara's mat as she dozed fitfully, struggling to draw each wet breath. Tenderly, Leschi took Sara's worn hand in his, and pressed it to his cheek. Her eyes opened, and focused upon her husband and daughter with a clarity that had been absent for two suns. She tried to speak, but could not. Kwahnesum held water to her lips, and she drank.

"Kwahnesum," Sara whispered, "take this." She fumbled at her pouch for a moment, until Leschi saw what she was after. He helped her remove the sharp knife of flaked obsidian, with inlaid mother-of-pearl handle, that had been a wedding gift from her father, the Puyallup Chief. Sara presented the knife to Kwahnesum. "Waterbird," she said, referring to her daughter's *tamanous*, "in these times, you may need to fight." Kwahnesum began to cry. "Don't," said

Sara, "your father needs you." *And I need you*, thought Kwahnesum, kissing her mother's cheek.

Then Sara turned to her husband. "Great *Tyee*," she managed to breathe the words, "at the council, I was proud to be your *klootchman*." Their eyes met. "That basket," she said at last, indicating with the merest flick of her eyes. Leschi fetched the basket, and found within a necklace of tortoise shell and bear teeth. "Wise and strong," Sara whispered as he put it on. "Don't get fat head," she added, smiling.

Again, Leschi took Sara's hand, startled by its cold transparency. They sat in silence for a time. "Sing," she sighed. So Leschi and Kwahnesum sang, not just sad songs, but songs of love and youth, songs from the fields and forests that Sara loved, songs that brought the red-flowering currant and bright fireweed into bloom in the gloom of the longhouse, and called to mind the happy summer song of the meadowlark. Seeing her tiring, they closed with her favorite:

> Spirit dances in the rain, in the wave, in the wind,
> Spirit dances in rock and tree, you and me,
> Our hearts drum the dance.

Leschi felt Sara's fingers touch back, as she smiled and faded almost to sleep. Eyes closed, she whispered one phrase more: "Do not fear." Whether it was advice or merely a report on the state of her own heart, Leschi was not sure, as he watched her go deeper, and deeper, until with a small flutter, she was gone.

They washed and wrapped the body in mats Sara herself had woven from the Nisqually river grasses. Loosening a plank from the side of the longhouse, they slipped the body out. To take it by the door was unthinkable. If they had, Sara would remember the way back in and return to take one of her family with her to the land of the dead.

With help from a few other villagers who had not yet departed for winter quarters, they gently arranged Sara's body, crouched in a painted canoe, hands clasped about her knees. They placed her favorite periwinkle necklace around her neck, and gave her blankets and food for the journey to *Otlas-Skio*. Then they killed the canoe by boring a hole in it, and killed the blankets by tearing each one, so they could go with her to the land of the dead.

At last they were ready for the long, mournful march to the graveyard, where many tens of burial canoes hung from the trees. Each step of the way, their wails rose up to startle the winter birds. They placed Sara in a broad deodar, then went to the river to purify themselves with stones and branches. After a thorough cleansing, they returned to their house to fast for five days as Sara made her journey, keening day and night for their lost mother and wife, their cries echoing off the empty longhouses of the deserted summer village. Finally, exhausted, they rested quietly, ate a little more each day, until they were ready to follow their diminished family upriver, to winter lodgings.

3

Now was the time of unquiet in Leschi's soul. Had not Sara heard the cry of the *zach-ad? Oh, my first and best wife! Did it sing only for you? Or are more to come? Did it cry for the whole of our people, the People of the River Grass no more?*

Leschi stayed shut in his longhouse at Mashel, deep in mourning. Dutiful Ann brought him fresh food and took it away uneaten, but always brought more. The men kept their distance on the rare occasions when he emerged to bathe, scouring his body with rough branches. Leschi refused to join in the games, the dances, the storytelling, the work of repairing nets and weirs, tools and weapons, the preparations for the next turn of the great wheel.

Kwahnesum, too, felt her world crumbling. Just a month before, she had been the daughter of a powerful *Tyee*, pledged to the rich Boston man she had worshipped from afar. Now, she had lost First Mother, and, she feared, any chance of marrying Charlie Eden. After the way her father had insulted the Boston *Tyee*, what white man would have her? How could he have done this, with her wedding planned for that very spring? But perhaps it was not too late; perhaps if they could make peace, then she could have her cozy white woman's cabin, with the honey-haired Charlie.

Kwahnesum's anger overshadowed her concern for her father. She wanted him well, but only because instinctively she knew that her price depended on his strength. She went to her Uncle Quiemuth, begging him to intervene. "Do you not think it pains me too, to see him like this, my child?" replied Quiemuth. "I love him more than myself. But there are times when a man must find his own way. Be patient."

So they were patient, steady as the rain that dripped through the glowing lichens and ferns clinging to the branches of lugubrious firs and red cedars. They were patient as the winter clouds slipped by, and gradually the light began to lengthen towards spring. At last, on a cold day in which fresh snow dressed the boughs and forest paths in finery, Leschi emerged from their longhouse wearing the necklace Sara had given him. "Quiemuth," he said, "we must assemble as many wise men from as many tribes as we can, to consider best how to proceed."

"You would go to war?" asked Quiemuth.

"Is it a country I can choose to visit or not?" asked Leschi, a wan smile on his face. "I will stay home, if I am left one. But there are times when war comes to us."

Quiemuth nodded, his face grim.

"We should learn all we can," continued Leschi. "We must forge alliances for war even as we try to keep the peace. We must stand ready to defend our homes."

"I will send word," said Quiemuth. The brothers embraced, and he mounted and rode off.

"Oh, Father," cried Kwahnesum, seeing him up and about, "I was so worried," and she ran to kneel before him. Leschi kissed the vermillion-painted crown of her head. Kwahnesum and Ann brought him a feast of fresh-killed deer, roasted camas bulbs, and *charlaque* – a paste of dried berries and salmon roe – with *kalse* – a liquor made from sunflower roots. He ate and drank heartily, being careful not to show his teeth. As he ate, Kwahnesum chattered on, her mellifluous voice jumping from subject to subject, until it worked its way backwards like a rufous-sided towhee kicking at underbrush, to the question of making peace with the Bostons. "I am frightened for you, Father," she implored, "frightened for all of us. Please, find a way to make peace."

Leschi saw again that his daughter's and the tribe's fate were intertwined. "I will try, my daughter," he said. She kissed him, then brought him his pipe filled with roasted *kinnikinnick* leaves. As he smoked the intoxicating herb and watched the sun break through to ignite the melting snow, so beautiful in its passing, he felt his *tamanous*, the mountain, calling him.

With a sudden rush of energy Leschi set off to climb the peak behind the village, up into deeper snow, where the large firs and cedars give way to mountain hemlock, Sitka spruce, and the fresh-scented blue-green noble firs. After an hour of vigorous climbing, he took the rocky summit. From there he could see the entire expanse of the Nisqually lands. He faced the cool wind flowing in from the direction of *Whulge*, and saw the river he knew with his eyes shut twisting its way through forests below *Tenalquot* prairie, to Muck Creek, to the delta, and into the light-capped waters. Then he turned to the mountain, the nourishing breast of his people, towering in the spirit-filled air, glacier upon glacier, spawning the Nisqually, the Mashel, the Puyallup. *Ta-co-bet*, lifeblood of tribe upon tribe. With humility, he knelt and opened himself to the mountain, praying for the wisdom to act rightly in this time of crisis.

When he looked up, Leschi saw a strange cloud rise up out of *Ta-co-bet's* crater, its sharp bright edges clearly defining the shape of a great war canoe, launching from mountain to sky.

Chapter Eight
Captain Eden

1

Johnny King's maw didn't want him out here by the edge of the forest 'cause it was dangerous, she said, but heck, he didn't see what all the fuss was about. So right now, while she was busy with his step-paw 'n Cooper, the hired man, plantin' row after row of them stupid fruit saplings, he was gonna take Georgie-Porgie out fer a real Injun bear hunt. Georgie was only five, not seven like him, so he was kinda a baby, but least he bit his lip and didn't cry too much, 'cause he liked bein' around Johnny. Georgie had the same last name as Johnny but he warn't his brother. Johnny let him know that he'd kilt his own real brother back on th' wagon train when he caught him stealin' the tail he himself had cut right off a live rattler. After hearin' this, 'course, Georgie did jest whatever Johnny said, which he'd better if he didn't want a whuppin'.

Georgie lived up 'bout a half mile along the White River with his maw 'n paw. Johnny liked sneakin' through the forest path up to their place, past the Brannan's, without makin' a sound, Injun style. He snuck up behind Georgie, and coulda cut his throat then 'n there if'n Georgie's maw hadn't seen him and hollar'd out loud 'nuff to spook a rock, "Well, Johnny King, good to see you boy, how're your folks holdin' up?" So then he couldn't jest up'n murder Georgie; he had to talk a bit and eat some biscuits with honeysuckle jam, which warn't all that bad.

Then he and Georgie went down by the river, "but not right up to it" warned Mrs. King, an' he got out the piece of charcoal he'd snuck from the fire pit, an' they painted their faces all black like the Injun Nelson told 'em. Then they broke off some sticks and whittled 'em down to pointed spears, and went bear huntin'. An' jest when they had a great big woolly one in their sights, an' they were downwind jest right so's they could smell its stink and it couldn't smell them, they lifted their spears and –

"Johhhhhnnnnnniiiieeeeee!"

Fer cryin' peepers! Ain't it jest like a maw to scare the critter away! Next thing he knows he's bein' led by the ear back out to the King's clearin', an' his maw and Georgie's maw are goin' on and on 'bout how're they ever gonna keep these boys from gettin' themself's kilt in this cantankerosterous wilderness, and Georgie's maw hollers as they're leavin', "Hey, Eliza, why don't you an' Harvey come on back up here fer dinner tonight, an' bring that sweet little girl a yers, and th' baby." Now Johnny knows that the rest of the day and th' whole night too are ruined, what with his maw bein' sore, an' all his chores a-waitin', and then dinner at th' Kings. It'll be *talk talk talk* like there warn't no tomorrow, all 'bout how cute his half-sister Becky is, and how sweet that little lumpa vomit his baby half-brother Tom is, an' he knows he jest knows if'n his real paw and his older brother hadn't gone an' died on 'em from th' cholera half-way cross the plains, things woulda been a whole lot better'n this.

2

Three days after Leschi saw the war canoe in the sky, Nisqually, Suquamish, Duwamish and Kickitat, gathered in council at Mashel village. Before conferring, they smoked *kinnikinnick* leaves from a long clay pipe draped in feathers, carried hand to hand by John Hiton's pretty young daughter, Mary. When they had finished smoking, Mary retreated on soft moccasins to stand outside the circle, where Ann, Moonya and Kwahnesum glared at her.

Then Leschi spoke. "My friends, you have heard my words already at the Treaty council. I know many of you signed that treaty –"

"As did you," rudely interrupted Wyamooch.

"What?"

"Mike Simmons displayed the paper with your mark, and said you told him above all else, you did not want war."

Leschi shot up like sparks from a bonfire. "And you believed him?" he bellowed. "You believed that I would sign away our river? Never!"

"Well, it doesn't really matter," Wyamooch replied with a smirk. "It is done a thousand times over, and no force on earth can undo it. Your leadership has failed us, Leschi, and it is time for you to step aside."

"How can we have failed," replied Leschi, "when no battle has yet been fought? Have they packed up the river in their steamship and taken it away?" No one answered. "All right, then. So long as water flows through the Nisqually, we will stay by its side."

"But you yourself said we cannot fight the white man," said Kanasket.

"We will start no war," said Leschi. "But neither will we go willingly to *polacklie illahee*. We will remain peacefully upon the lands of our ancestors, and force the white man to be the aggressor if he has the stomach for it. I think Stevens will find that there are many Bostons who will not join him in such a fight. Remember, it is harder to destroy the great cedar that stands immobile, than the shallow-rooted plantain that scrambles all over the seaside bluffs."

"The Bostons cut down plenty of cedars," snorted Wyamooch. "I say if we are to go to war, we go to war now and against every white man on *Whulge*. There is no sense in sitting on the river, waiting to be wiped out."

"What do you say?" asked Leschi. Each man was polled; each spoke his anger and his fears. At last it was settled.

"We will go down the river as we always have," said Leschi. "We shall live peacefully on our lands as we always have. We will do nothing to provoke anger. We will use our white friendships to try to move this *tillicum kopa wake tumtum* – man with no heart – Stevens." They laughed at the Chief's mocking use of Chinook jargon.

"But meanwhile," cautioned Kitsap, "we must be ready for war." And so it was decided that Kanasket and Kitsap would cross the mountains to confer with the Yakama chief, Kamiakan, to see if he could send help.

"One more thing," said Leschi, who was not oblivious to the plea written on Kwahnesum's face. "My daughter is pledged to a Boston man, *Challie* Eden. I thought, after the treaty council, that it could never happen, that Sara's curse was upon it. But on further reflection, I think we need Bostons on our side more now than ever. And we may need the rifles he has pledged as part of the bride price. I would let the wedding go forward. What do you say?"

Over Sluggia's protestations, the rest agreed.

"It is good," said Leschi, and he rose, ending the council. Ann and Kwahnesum both moved to offer him refreshment, but Mary Hiton darted in front like a lithe salamander. As Leschi dipped into the bowl of sweet yam, their eyes met, and she did not turn away.

3

Charlie worked the auger meticulously, twisting and straining at the wrist-sized bit, dwarfed by the massive six-foot diameter trunk. His friend, Abram Benton Moses, whom Charlie called "Ben", shook aside curly brown locks as he pressed and grunted at the pommel, forcing the drill into the heart of the tree. Jim McAllister was a hundred feet away, stripping branches from trees already felled. Sweating mightily despite the cool April breeze, Charlie and Ben stood back to survey their hour's work. Two neatly drilled holes angled into the Douglas fir's trunk, meeting at the core. "OK, *khaver* –" which Charlie had learned was Jew-talk for 'buddy', "now for the fun!" Ben expertly scraped black pitch into the holes, pressing it deep inside with a stick, over and over, until the tunnels were lined all the way from core to bark. Taking two red hot pokers from the brushfire Jim had fed with branches, Ben lit the pitch and stepped back, listening appreciatively to the hiss of fueled combustion. "Now we let the fire do our work for us," he said, and they moved on to the next tree.

That was ten down, about forty more to go, then dressing, stumpage, and planking, before Charlie would be ready to build. Fortunately, he had friends like Ben and his brother Jackson Moses, Tony Rabbeson, and Jim McAllister, to help him out. Working together from sunup to sundown, they'd have it cleared in a week, trees dressed and planked the next week, the house framed the week after, and the whole thing finished by summer. They'd haul the extras down to the river, where they could be rafted to a steamer at Commencement Bay. Then Charlie would be sitting pretty in a whitewashed, framed, home-sweet-home, on a rise overlooking the confluence of the Stuck and Puyallup Rivers, his pink-purple sunset view eight miles out to Puget Sound and the Olympics.

Why was there hollowness to Charlie's labor? Could it be because, when he'd claimed this choice land, it was with visions of an Indian princess? He'd wanted to make a real home.

He remembered his snug New York home back East, cared for by his doting mother, God rest her soul. He'd felt bad about leaving her, but what could a feller do? Besides, she had the old man, though he had to wonder, was that comfort or curse? The image of his stepfather with his hatred of landlords, bosses, micks, kikes and bankers, and the explosive snap of his belt, brought back all the reasons he'd left. He'd told himself it was for adventure, but deep down he knew it was a search for comfort, security, the home of childhood. Adventure just sounds better.

Too bad things had gone wrong. Tony'd been ribbing him pretty hard about marrying this *siwash* girl, and then her father had gone and stirred up a hornets' nest. Suddenly, marrying into that family didn't look so great. True, the old Chief had come around and signed the treaty, so maybe it was all right. If he could rescue that pretty little gal from being herded into the reservation with the rest of her kind, well, she oughta just about worship him. He could see her dancing for him on a fire lit knoll, shadows playing at the ring of trees, lifting her blouse slowly, slowly, 'til he could see first her smooth flat belly, then the swell where the breasts rise out of the rib cage, then –

"LOOKOUT!" and Charlie was hit hard from the side by Ben's flying tackle as a two hundred fifty foot trunk thundered to the ground where he'd been standing, dreaming the day away. Scraped and whipped by boughs, they picked themselves up, dusted themselves off, and began to laugh and laugh like nothing in the whole world was ever so funny as just being alive one more second.

Jim ran over. "You two *dafties* gotta watch what you're doin'," he cried, shaking all over, and he pulled out a dirty rag and mopped his bright red forehead. "You near scared me to death!"

"Well, you are a lucky cuss-ass, Charlie Eden!" hollered Tony Rabbeson, trotting up the path from the direction of the little settlement dubbed *Puyallup*, after the people with more than enough. "Not only do you not get kilt fer bein' stupid, but you get to meet one of my most special friends, all in one day." Tony smiled his chilly smile. "C'mon, we got us an important meetin' back down to Fort Steilacoom."

"Who is it, that Mother Damnable you been talkin' 'bout?" laughed Charlie, still brushing off the debris.

"You'll see," snapped Tony. That was clearly all he was going to say about it.

"Heck, Tony, that's a good ten miles," protested Charlie. Tony just glared at him. "OK, OK," said Charlie, "c'mon guys."

"Not them," Tony barked. He didn't cotton to Jews, and it was clear from the way Ben glared back that the feeling was mutual. "This friend o' mine wants to talk to you, alone." He spit from horseback for emphasis.

Charlie looked to Ben and Jim, apology in his eyes. "That's fine," said Ben. "You go ahead. Jackson's 'sposed ta be along soon, and the three of us'll have fun droppin' trees on each other for a few more hours." Charlie still stalled. "I'll see you tomorrow, at my brother's place, for that Seder we talked about, ok?"

"Yeah," Charlie whispered. Tony scowled.

"Go ahead, Laddie," urged Jim, so Charlie untied his horse, and rode off with Tony on the Military Road to the Fort.

Fort Steilacoom wasn't a fortified structure, but just a collection of log cabins up on a flat plain about a mile inland from the village and Sound. Charlie and Tony were waved in by uniformed sentries at the perimeter of the parade grounds, and directed to a ramshackle elongated cabin with an open covered porch, tucked under a spreading Sitka spruce. Two men, one compact, the other big and fat, sat tilted back against the cabin front, hats down over their eyes, apparently asleep. Charlie was about to walk right on by them into the cabin, when the compact fellow pushed back his slouch hat, revealing a large head and quick, hazel eyes. "Is this the young man you mentioned to me, Tony?" he asked.

"Yes, Sir, Governor," replied Tony, and Charlie nearly fainted. He'd heard of Stevens, of course. Stevens was all anybody talked about, as the tireless Governor sewed up near all the territory west of the Bitterroots, making one treaty after another. But he never expected this little flannel-shirted wrangler to turn out to be the man himself.

The fat fellow pushed his hat back, and stood. Charlie knew him, what was his name? Bond, Bunt, Blunt! That's it, Jack Blunt. He'd rode with Blunt some years back, scouting for the Naches road. "Well, shit, boy, I ain't no ghost, though you're 'bout white as one!" He laughed – *har! har! har!* "Yessir, Gov'nor, this here's the boy, though he ain't no boy no more. Lookin' good, l'il buddy," said Blunt, slapping him on the back. "Life in the Wild West agrees with ya!" *Har! har! har!*

"Y-your Honor, I-I'm ..." *Damn.*

Stevens eyed him with amusement. "Sorry, son, didn't mean to scare you. I'm sure you can understand that there are times when affairs of State are best conducted with a little privacy, right?"

"Y-yes Sir, Mr. Governor, Sir," said Charlie. *Affairs of State? What did he know about affairs of State?* And then an awful feeling gnawed its way from his stomach to his brain: *This couldn't have anything to do with that Injun girl, could it?*

As if reading his mind, Stevens said, "All right, well Charlie, don't worry about a thing. You aren't in any trouble, far from it. Let's just pull up a few more chairs and we'll have us a meeting, OK?" So two more chairs were fetched, and then Blunt handed the Governor a piece of paper, which he held up before Charlie.

"Charlie," said Stevens, "you know what this is?" Charlie shook his head, still trying to uncleave his tongue from the roof of his mouth. "This is a commission appointing a fellow named Charlie Eden as Captain of Company A of the Washington Territorial Volunteers."

Stevens saw the look of astonishment on Charlie's face, but held up his hand to forestall any questions. "We gotta be ready to protect our way of life, son," said the Governor. "We've decided to raise up some volunteers." Stevens bitterly recalled General Wool's response to his letter. Wool had dismissed the Governor's request for troops out of hand. He warned Stevens – had the temerity to lecture him – against goading the Indians into hostilities by mistreatment. General Wool hadn't changed much since he'd been court-martialed for taking the Cherokee side when the Army relocated them out of Georgia.

The Governor leaned towards Charlie. "General Wool and his lap dog, Colonel Casey, don't see the threat that I saw quite plainly while parleying with the savages. They say we oughta just back off, and confine ourselves to a few little towns, and sneak around trying not to make trouble. Now, the way I see it, God brought us here for a reason, and it sure wasn't to live like savages. For one thing, it would do away with that nice house you're building up on the Puyallup plateau, not to mention hundreds of other settlements all over our Territory. So, the long and the short of it is, the regular Army isn't going to be defending us, and we've got to do it ourselves. Are you with me, son?"

Did that mean, "do you understand," or "are you on my side?" Charlie didn't dare ask. "Yes, Sir," he mumbled. "But why me? I mean, I don't know much 'bout soldiering –"

"Colonel Blunt here –" at hearing the title Blunt stuck out his chest until he looked like a grouse puffing for its mate, "– recommended you, young fellow, based on your service up in the Naches pass. That's good enough for me." The Governor held out the commission, so what could Charlie do but take it, and there were handshakes and congratulations all around.

"But, what should I do?" asked Charlie.

"Captain," said Blunt, and Charlie liked the sound of it, "we're gonna hold off recruitin' for now, while we get our officers in place. You'll get your orders when we're ready." Then Blunt pulled himself up and sucked in his gut. "Dis – missed!" he barked, and Charlie involuntarily snapped to attention and whipped off a salute, which was returned. But as he turned and marched off the porch, the Governor called to him.

"One more thing, Captain!" Charlie turned back to look up at the little man smiling down at him from the porch. "It's all right to marry that girl, Leschi's daughter." Charlie's cheeks burned beet red. So they knew about that. "Just keep your eyes and ears open, you know what I mean, and if anything comes up, you report to me personally, got it?"

What could Charlie say? This was the Governor, his Commander in Chief. "Yes Sir!" Captain Eden saluted again and marched off, feeling in his soul like a buck private.

Chapter Nine
The Wedding

1

As the cottonwood released seeds to drift like snowflakes upon the early summer air, the time had come to tie the bond between the Nisqually and Boston tribes. The wedding was planned for three days and two nights, as befitted the daughter of a Chief. But this was not the way of the Bostons, so they were permitted to delay their arrival to the day of the final ceremony.

On the first day, a thunder of hooves tore up the grasslands as thirty Cayuse ponies galloped down from the east, bearing Leschi's formidable cousin Owhi, son of Chief Kamiakan. With him were Kitsap and Kanasket, returning from their mission as emissaries. Dugout cedar canoes, festooned with fireweed, bright purple lupines, and fluttering ribbons from the company trading post, spilled dear friends from neighboring tribes, *klootchmen*, children, parents, cousins, nephews, aunts and uncles.

By evening the feasting and games were in full swing. Leschi, proud papa, paraded from bonfire to bonfire, plain Ann on one arm, beautiful young Mary on the other. At the camp of the Yakamas, beside a blazing cedar pyre over which roasted alder planked slabs of salmon as long as a man is tall, young men from many tribes were engaged in games of skill and strength. They strained at tug of war with a thin cedar pole, exhibited quickness and sureness of aim in the hoop-and-spear game, showed off their strength in wrestling, and their speed in foot-racing.

"A fine feast," complimented Owhi, "worthy of your Yakama blood." For the first time since he'd grown to adulthood, Leschi had a chance to assess the elder son of Chief Kamiakan. Unquestionably he was strong, but there was a rough, brash edge about him. Was it reckless pride, or simply youth? Leschi would wait to draw his conclusions.

"You are too kind," replied Leschi modestly.

"Never," said Owhi. "Kitsap and Kanasket have told us of your troubles. We too have troubles caused by the white man. The devil Stevens travels everywhere, making treaties to steal our land. Old men like my father sign these treaties," he said, the blood rising to his face. "White men come to dig into the earth with picks and shovels. The way they leer at our sisters would turn your stomach if you could see it," he said angrily, his eyes fixed on the winsome Mary. "They spread diseases, and give our warriors firewater to make them stupid. How can we live with such a people?" Suddenly realizing that he was there to celebrate the marriage of Leschi's daughter to one of those people, Owhi added, "Perhaps it is different here on the coast. You have your own ways; you have always had plenty to eat, without having to hunt for survival. But for us, the time has come when we must fight, or perish."

"It is not so different," said Leschi, sadly. "Still, we try to find another way."

"Try as you will; I say you will be driven to war by these devils," cried Owhi. "Like you, my father, Kamiakan, is slow to admit that war is inevitable. Nevertheless, he sends me to say that if you must fight, we will stand with you. Unless I am pinned down fighting to save my own homeland, I will come with braves and muskets, Leschi, you have my pledge." He pounded his chest, and held forth his hand.

"Thank-you, brother, and give my thanks to Chief Kamiakan," replied Leschi, returning the gesture and clasping the young warrior in a tight embrace. Leschi was moved by Owhi's fervor.

Remembering his manners, Owhi added, "I thank you again, great Chief, for this wedding feast."

"Oh, this little thing," said Leschi, waving his arm across a field piled high with delicacies. "This is nothing."

At Leschi's signal, everyone gathered in eager anticipation of the potlatch ritual. Quiemuth stepped forward and embraced his brother, and then together they sang an epic song that told of their tribe's origins in the hot lands, the long march led by the sacred mink to the Yakama country, the dispute with ocean, and the reward of *Tenalquot*. Then they picked out two slaves to help the tribal men carry a massive canoe as long as four men are tall, filled to overflowing with furs, *hiqua* necklaces, carved paddles, blankets, and bags of dried clams strung on kelp twine.

Winyea, one of the two slaves, felt that he could have hoisted the canoe single-handedly, so great was his joy at being chosen by Leschi. The beneficence of the potlatch ceremony required that Leschi free any slave chosen for this honor. Though he was now permitted to return home, Winyea decided at that moment that he would always stand by Leschi's side.

"Brothers," cried Leschi, "this I do for the glory of the Nisqually People!" He clapped his hands and the brimming canoe was hoisted up onto cedar stakes across the bonfire. The flames shot up to embrace the gift of canoe and contents, exploding in a shimmer of sparks lighting the night air. All games came to a halt, as young and old alike watched wealth beyond their imagining disappear into smoke and ash, the flames stitching face to face to face across the broad prairie.

With a joyous whoop, John Hiton bounded into the ring. This was the signal for all the Nisqually men to join in a wedding dance to honor their Chief. Even taciturn Wahoolit joined in. Drums appeared and began sounding a cacophony echoed by the trees ringing the prairie, deepened in resonance by the spirits of ancestors, climbing out of the ground to join the wedding dance. Painted masks of raven, owl, eagle, bear and frog, melded to ecstatic faces, transforming the dancers into spirits of forest and sky. The dance pulsed, blissful and reverent, celebratory and harmonious, its wildness anchored deep to the core of this river basin that held them like the arms of a mother to her flowing breast.

Across the firepit Leschi saw two who were not dancing. Wyamooch and Sluggia stood together, sullen-cheeked, arms crossed over their painted chests. Great chunks of burned canoe and loot cascaded down, showering the dancers with ash, as embers glowered like the eyes of these two truculent warriors. This insult Leschi could not let pass. But as the dancing reached its climax, Leschi was distracted by fingers hidden in shadow softly exploring his neck and shoulders, down his spine and beyond. He was hard, and wanted the young minx who'd clawed her way into his life suddenly at this most desperate time, a time fit for passion. Together Leschi and Mary melted into the spreading boughs of fir circling the inferno, and soon their cries of ecstasy joined the cries of the fire-lit dancers.

2

Leschi arose late the next morning feeling more refreshed than he had in months. After bathing in Muck Creek he found Quiemuth at breakfast. As soon as they'd gotten out of Moonya's earshot, Leschi told his brother about his newfound love for Mary.

"She is fickle," warned Quiemuth, "a cup of water that, left untended, will vanish into air." But still, what harm could it do? Leschi needed to put Sara's death behind him, and this could be just the medicine to dispel melancholy. Quiemuth gave his blessing to the proposed union. Together, they went out to mingle with the many guests who were reviving themselves after the first night of revelry.

In an aspen copse above the prairie, they saw a line of Nisquallies kneeling behind a canoe paddle, forming a vee-shape like migrating geese with the opposing line of Yakamas. This was the formation for gambling. Leschi could see staked to the ground the prizes: many strings of glass and ceramic beads, and a pile of cheap iron knives, on the Yakama side; smoked salmon, mussel-shell cutting tools, and strings of dried clams, on the Nisqually side. As they got closer, Leschi saw the chosen tricksters, Sluggia for the Nisquallies, and Owhi for the Yakamas. From the predominance of counting sticks stuck in the ground on the Nisqually side, it was clear that these men had been up all night gambling, and that the Nisquallies were only one stick away from victory.

Sluggia showed the two bone cylinders to Owhi, the Woman smooth and unmarked except at the tips, the Man identically marked at the tips, but also dotted around the circumference with three little black bands. Owhi glowered intently as his opponent's fingers closed around game pieces. Without warning, Sluggia's chosen drummer, Wyamooch, split the sky with a wild patter of staccato beats, and the Nisqually team began singing and beating the paddle, logs, one another's backs, and their own cheeks and chests with sticks, to distract Owhi, as Sluggia writhed and spun like a man possessed. Sluggia's hands flashed like crazed minnows up and down and behind and all around, exchanging the game pieces from hand to practiced hand quick as the striking snake, again and again until no man could tell what was where or how it got there.

The drum beat faster and faster, as the Nisquallies chanted the chant sung by Deer who gambled with fierce Wolf and won:

> *I am going to run*
> *Between your legs*
> *So fast you'll think*
> *It was the wind*
> *I've already gone*
> *And you're waiting*
> *Ha! ha! I'm back*
> *And gone again.*

At "between your legs" Sluggia passed the pieces between his legs, and at "Ha! ha!" he spun. With one last ear-splitting roll the drumming stopped, the team fell silent, and Sluggia froze, his closed fists extended to his opponent. Owhi's task was to choose the hand holding Woman. After many intense whispered consultations, and a fierce study of Sluggia's impassive face, Owhi pointed to Sluggia's left hand. The fingers twitched as though holding something alive, then opened to disclose the dappled bands of the Man – a final loss for the Yakamas!

While everyone was watching the left hand open, Leschi was already studying the right. Owhi, torn by defeat, demanded to see the other bone.

Sluggia opened his right hand, and held up the prized Woman bone with its unmarked middle. Owhi held her for a moment, then dropped her in the dirt dejectedly. Whooping with exaltation, Sluggia took the last counting stick, and the Nisquallies jumped up to claim the precious Yakama stake.

"*Halt!*" commanded Leschi, his five quick strides barely beating Wyamooch to the Woman piece in the dirt. The celebration choked off just as it was beginning. Leschi stood nose to nose with Sluggia. "Nephew, show me the Man." Sluggia tried to turn away but Leschi grabbed one arm and spun him back. "Will you show it, or must I?"

Sluggia's desperate look appealed to Quiemuth, who said, "Do as your uncle says."

Staring daggers at Leschi with his dead sister's eyes, Sluggia held up the Man, with its dotted middle, then tried to turn away. Leschi was too quick; he snatched the piece from Sluggia's hand, then held up the Man in his left, the Woman in his right, for all to see. But wait - now it was the Woman in his left, the Man in his right, and then again the Man in his left, the Woman in his right, as by magic Man became Woman, Woman became Man. The Yakamas had been cheated by trick bones, expertly crafted to telescope from Man to Woman, and back again, with the slightest pressure on just the right spot.

Leschi pushed Sluggia down upon one knee. "You have dishonored your tribe," he thundered. "You will beg forgiveness of our brother, Owhi, and offer him your service for one full moon. The stake is forfeit to the Yakamas. I have said it."

Sluggia was left alone on one knee in dirt made muddy by his tears, as he swore to himself over and over that never, ever, would he forgive his uncle for this unbearable humiliation.

3

The long trip south on a ship that swallows trees in its boiler belly and spits steam was astonishing enough, but now Patkanim could not believe the evidence of his senses. Bobbing in the harbor before him was a forest of masts, thick as any Pacific Northwest stand of Douglas fir. Beyond it lay a village that went on forever, wood, brick and stone lodges, warehouses, hotels, gambling dens, theaters, saloons, and beached abandoned sailing vessels, piled one upon another to the smoky horizon atop Telegraph Hill, where a stone tower capped the whole seething mess.

Tony Rabbeson threw his arm around Patkanim's frock-coated shoulders. "There she be, Chief," he said, "San-Fran-Cisco, one juicy whore of a city, and she's all ours!" So it wasn't just a tale told to frighten their people, this *San Francisco*. The Bostons' giant paradise was real, and you didn't even have to die to see it. San Francisco was all Patkanim had heard about for several years, as he patiently learned English from the sea captains sailing past his summer lodge on Whidbey's Island. San Francisco, they'd told him, where one Doug fir is worth a thousand bucks, a city growing so big so fast that they build thirty new buildings a day, a place so rough they drink in five hundred different bars, gamble in a thousand dens, commit seven murders a week, and lynch twice that number.

"You heard of th' gold standard fer money?" asked Tony. "Here you wipe yer ass with gold, and they're on the whiskey 'n pussy standard!" He might have been joking, but he so rarely smiled that it was hard to tell.

Everything about San Francisco that Patkanim had heard was so far beyond his experience, that it was impossible to tell where the truth left off and fantasy began. That was why Patkanim had decided he had to see this wonder for himself. If it really existed, and was as big as they all said, then he knew it would be impossible to defeat the Bostons. What was it to kill ten tens of Bostons, or even twice that number, if they had a city from which they could send more men than anyone could possibly kill? If there really was a San Francisco, Patkanim knew whose side he wanted to be on. So he insisted on one special condition to the treaty Stevens handed him: send him down to San Francisco for a week. Well, here he was, and here it was, the thrilling stink wrapping itself about them like – well, Tony had said it best, like whore's thighs.

As they disembarked, Tony grabbed that great big wicker cage of stray cats he'd hauled down from Portland, and set them out on the wharf. Patkanim had thought him crazy, but when Tony promised him five dollars a cat, he'd personally caught fifteen himself. Within minutes a crowd had gathered to check out the newly arrived goods from the ship. Before Patkanim could take in the vista of unbelievable abundance stacked against glass-windowed warehouses towering three stories high, Tony had sold all twenty-five hissing critters to the denizens of this rat-gnawed paradise for ten dollars apiece.

Then they plunged into the amazing streets, swept along through muck and manure by crowds of Chinamen, Mexicans, grubby miners, bar girls, pompadoured gentlemen, and crinoline-and-lace ladies. Out front of a general store, they saw a great stack of prospecting pans, next to which was a sign: $2 ea. "Get out," said Tony. "Them pans useta go fer ten cents." The proprietor emerged, and scooped up a shovelful of dirt right out of the street. Patkanim and Tony joined the crowd to watch him carefully wash out the dirt in one of his pans. There, at the bottom of the pan – GOLD! – plain as day, sparkling in the June sunshine. Within minutes the entire stock of pans was sold out, and men were down on their knees, digging up the street. Patkanim would have bought one, had Tony not pulled him aside. "Don't be a rube," he said. "I seen that trick before, when Charlie and me was down here. The feller planted that gold dust last night."

Fortunately the Governor had given Tony enough of an expense account so they could afford the hundred-dollar-a-night Oriental Hotel, with plenty left over for amusement. Prominently displayed in the ornate lobby was a garish poster:

> War! War! War!
> The celabrated Bull-killing Bear
> GENERALL SCOTT
> will fite a Bull on Saturday the 9th inst. at 6 PM
> at Hall of Comparitive Ovashuns
> PUBLICK is corduly invited

Tony insisted they attend this great cultural event. When they arrived, they found themselves on the grounds of the E. Clampus Vitus Society, a fraternal order the nature of which was obscure even to a well-traveled rascal such as Mr. Rabbeson. It was not long before they made the acquaintance of a stout gentleman wearing a red union suit glittering with tin-can badges, who was pleased to explain the society to a real Indian Chief.

"Greetings, fellow Chief," he intoned with excessive solemnity. "I am Edwin H. Van Decor, Noble Grand Humbug of the San Francisco Lodge, order of E. Clampus Vitus, at your service." As he bowed, his tin-can badges jingled and flashed. "We are an ancient order, dating back to 4004 B.C., dedicated to the comforting of orphans and widows, especially," he cleared his throat and gave a lascivious appraisal of a particularly shapely young lady, "the latter." *Wink, wink,* broad grin.

Mr. Van Decor led the two visitors to a box overlooking a fenced amphitheater. In the center was a grizzly bear, firmly staked to the ground with a chain attached to his collar. The agitated beast stood on his hind legs, displaying his full bulk in a show of menace. He snarled and pawed at the ground, digging a hole from which to defend himself. Men with muzzle-loading rifles stood about the ring, keeping a watchful eye on the bear. Patkanim felt a pang of disgust. Such a magnificent animal should be treated with respect. The bear's spirit was huge; Patkanim could feel it pressing at his own chest from a ship's length away. Yet the Bostons seemed not to feel it; they gambled and smoked and drank their whiskey, delighting not in the grizzly's power, but its subjugation.

What followed was the most incomprehensible procession Patkanim had ever witnessed. A gaggle of Clampers – for such they were called – in identical red union suits, bedecked by tin-can medals, led a hoop-skirted billy goat wearing a gold necklace and a top hat around the outer ring of the arena. They were careful to keep well away from the bear, so the goat did not bolt. They carried flags made of hoop skirts of all colors, a giant musket with a two-inch bore labeled, "Blunderbusket," and the sacred seven-foot long Sword of Justice and Mercy. All around the arena they saluted their fellow Clampers by raising their thumbs to their ears, wiggling fingers, and chanting the Clamper motto, *Quia Credo Absurdium*, which Mr. Van Decor translated as, "I Believe because it is Absurd." Having completed three such circuits around the ring, the marchers came to a halt before the box occupied by Tony, Patkanim, and Mr. Van Decor, the latter of whom stood.

"Clampatriarch and Roisteruos Scutis, you have done well," shouted Mr. Van Decor.

"Damn you, Noble Grand Humbug," replied the two he'd addressed, bowing their heads in unison.

"Give me the Sword of Justice and Mercy," commanded the Grand Humbug.

"Never!" they cried, and they did.

"Bring me the poor defenseless goat."

"Over our grandmothers' graves!" they protested, and they led the goat before him.

Mr. Van Decor raised the huge sword over the goat's head. "Brother Clampers, shall I smite him?" cried the Humbug.

"No!" came the roar from the assembled Clampers. With a mighty blow, he split the goat's top hat and head, and the poor creature's bloody brains ran hot on the ground.

"Let the games begin!" commanded Van Decor, as the goat convulsed his last. "Watch closely," he said to his guests. "A perfectly wild, young Spanish-born bull, will now be released into the ring. His horns are of natural length, not sawed off."

The gleam in the Humbug's eye was reflected in Tony's craggy face, as a young bull emerged from the cage in which he'd been held, paused and pawed the ground, then charged straight at the chained grizzly. The grizzly pivoted in a dark blur and the horns glanced off his side, the bull's neck exposed as it twisted to gore upward into the bear's tender gut. The bear lunged spinning, striking for the neck, but caught the bull's nose instead, and they stood there locked for a desperate interval, their powerful muscles rippling as they tore up the gritty battlefield. At last, the bull literally ripped his own nose away, gushing blood over the path of his retreat. He circled for a few moments in a daze, then charged again, but this time the bear made short work of him, raking aside the onslaught with his razor claws and clamping huge jaws down over the back of the bull's neck, forcing him to a dirty death, pressed to earth.

"That's the way they do it," said Mr. Van Decor. "If the bull gets the bear up, he'll win, but once the bear gets the bull down, its all over for him. Take a letter, Roisteruos Scutis," he hollered to one of the Clampers who'd accompanied the goat to his doom. Roisteruos Scrutis produced an extravagant striped feather quill, that wriggled as he wrote, and began to take dictation on his starched cuff. "Dear Wall Street bigwigs: You may hereafter call upward trending markets bull markets, downward trending markets bear markets. Yours in Ridiculousity, Noble Grand Humbug, et cetera, et cetera."

Van Decor turned back to his guests. "Gentlemen, this is all very thirsty work. Please, do me the honor of accompanying me to one of San Francisco's most genteel establishments."

Though Patkanim barely understood a word uttered by this incomprehensible man, he knew they'd just been invited out drinking. Off they went to John Henry Brown's Saloon, an opulent palace with bullet holes in the floor. There, pretty ladies with painted faces danced to strange music played on a box of bones, kicking up their heels so far you could almost glimpse their *cootchies*.

A drunken miner stood up on the bar and announced he was going to ride his horse right in through the plate-glass window that was as long as a war canoe and as tall as two men.

"You do that," warned Mr. Brown from behind his handlebar mustache, "and it will be the most expensive bloody ride you've ever taken."

"How much?" asked the miner.

"One thousand dollars."

The miner tossed him a sack of gold. "Keep the change, Mr. Limey, and buy a round fer the house!" he hollered, as he staggered outside. Everyone cheered, but no one expected to see him back again.

White-gowned senoritas sat on the bar puffing *cigaritas*, their midnight locks styled in cascading ringlets. Suitors plied them with fifty dollar bottles of brandy deliberately overspilled into tiny wineglasses, which they quaffed in dainty, self-satisfied sips.

The piano player stopped his plinking, and the dancing girls made a quick exit. The lanterns in the hall were dimmed, as men scurried to illuminate the stage with lime flairs. A massively muscled bald-headed impresario emerged from the wings. "Ladies, Gentlemen, an' th' rest o' you scallywags!" he cried. "John Henry Brown's is proud to present, all the way from Barcelona via Bavaria, that internationally famous entertainer of the crown princes of Europe, Miss Lola Montez!" Wild cheers, foot stomping and the sound of beer steins smashing down on the tables greeted the alleged Spaniard, Miss Montez. Her enticing flash of emerald behind a black veil betrayed her cheap Limerick birth, even as the pancake makeup papered over the worry lines from being run out of Austria for bigamy, and from throwing her fourth husband down a flight of stairs after catching him *in flagrante delicto* with the floozy she'd called her lady in waiting. Still, as she hovered amidst the faux silken cobwebs in her low cut gown, the four extra appendages of her arachnid costume vibrating about her ever so slightly, Lola Montez already held the crowd entranced by her famous *Bailar de la Arafia* - the Spider Dance.

A flamenco guitar cut the air as Lola tensed, then flung her arms over her head, releasing a spray of wire spiders into the air as she began to beat out the rhythm on six-inch silver spike heels. She spun and the skirt of her dress flew off, revealing a leotard with a black widow of cloth and wires attached to her rear. She wiggled lasciviously against a male dancer, who paid for his liberties in gruesome mock death.

"Watch this then," said Van Decor, who obviously was a regular. The leotard vanished in a sudden upward swipe of Lola's hand, leaving only the veil and three cotton gauze spiders adhered strategically to Lola's otherwise nude torso. The limelight dimmed, the music moaned its sultriest trills, as Lola carefully reached up to remove the veil and the little velvet cap to which it was attached. Patkanim was astonished to see Lola shake four live tarantulas from the cap onto the stage. The great hairy critters landed scuttling in all directions, causing a few tough broncos to blanch despite themselves. They needn't have feared; in a sudden final explosion of guitar and murderous staccato heels, Lola smashed each of the fleeing arachnids into the floorboards. The crowd stomped and whooped and shot their guns into the floor in approval, as Miss Montez took bow after bow amid the littered corpses, her breasts hanging heavy with every fresh curtain call.

"So tell me, Chief," said Van Decor, when the noise had died down, "what brings you to our 'burg?"

Before Patkanim could even figure out the question, Tony chimed in. "Chief here is a big man in Washington Territory. He's a guest of the Gov'nor."

"Big man, huh?" said Van Decor, in that way of his, both serious and mocking. "Big man oughta have a little lady, right?" He made a sign to Mr. Brown, and within a minute three beauties sauntered up to their table. "Which one do you fancy, Chief?" asked Van Decor. "They're all bona fide widows, and I reckon maybe that one's an orphan to boot," and he pointed at the blonde wearing a threadbare bustier over a plain muslin dress. Patkanim smiled agreeably. He wouldn't mind a little *tikegh* with this white woman; the shame would be her's and her family's, not his. He reached out his hand and slid it across her rump. She slid right into it, no resistance whatsoever. But just as Patkanim closed his eyes to receive her wet kiss, he heard an ominous click. His eyes opened on the barrel of a gun where warm breasts should have been.

The man squinting at him from behind the six-shooter was just a hat over a beard, with hair sprouting out his ears, but he had that pistol sighted right square on the center of Patkanim's chest, hammer cocked. His hawk-nosed buddy was covering Tony and Mr. Van Decor. The music and dancers stopped, cards were laid down, the din silenced. It was time for the other main attraction.

Obeying a jerk of the barrel, the girls skittered away. "I don't like Injuns," the squinter announced. "I 'specially don't like 'em pawin' up th' white girls," he added. "How 'bout yew, Jed?"

"Me neither," the hawk-nosed fellow divulged.

"Hey Chief," said the squinter, motioning toward the floor, "step out there where I kin see ya." Patkanim had seen these revolver guns before – they spit plenty of bullets. He had a knife in his belt and a derringer up his sleeve, but he knew the one-shot wonder was no match for the six-shooter. Slowly, watching carefully for any opening, Patkanim glided to the center of the floor.

"We come over on th' train, Chief, in '52, me 'n my wife," said the squinter, referring to a wagon train. "Out ta Chimney Rock we got us ambushed by redskins. Kilt my wife. That's why I'm gonna kill you, Chief. I jest wanted you to know that."

"Yeah, well, don't let me pee on yer campfire, mister," said Tony, his tone flat and his gaze even, "but them there Injuns was Flatheads. This here's a Snoqualmie from up t' Washington Territory. He warn't anywhere's within a thousand miles of Chimney Rock."

"What are you, some kinda Injun lover?" spat the gunman with a sideways glance, but that was just the break needed as Patkanim jumped to the side so the first shot went wide, smack into the belly of the naked lady painted up behind the bar. If there was a second shot no one heard it, because right then a mounted rider crashed through the plate glass window whooping and hollering, and galloped around the room trampling tables and chairs as Tony and Patkanim high-tailed it out of there.

Early the next morning, they were on the first ship they could find headed north. Patkanim was thankful he'd survived his visit. His last view of San Francisco caught through the morning fog was of two men hanging by the neck from the crow's nest of a vessel. "What is that sign around their necks?" he asked Tony. "Cattle rustler?"

Tony peered into the fog. "Nope," he replied. "Cat rustler."

Patkanim swore to himself that he would never again make war against the *pelton tamanous* – demented spirits – of the sprawling Boston empire.

4

On the third morning of celebration, a glorious summer day that the Bostons called a Saturday in June, 1855, the marriage ceremony was held. It was attended by hundreds of Natives from a half-dozen tribes, as well as the mixed families from Muck Creek, and many King George and Boston men from up and down the Sound. Jim and Martha McAllister made the upriver slog with their whole brood in tow: two boys including Jimmy, who was now taller than his father, and three girls including Ainsley, now a strawberry-blonde princess riding side-saddle in a green and white checked gingham dress. To Leschi's delight, Dr. Tolmie himself came up from Fort Nisqually, in the company of his sturdy no-nonsense wife Jane, daughter of the Chief Factor at Victoria. Dr. and Mrs. Tolmie were accompanied by a wiry Puyallup farmer named Ezra Meeker, and his wife and two young children. Even Doc Maynard showed up with his new bride, Catherine, all the way from Seattle.

Kwahnesum was hidden deep in the longhouse, guarded by elder women, fasting in silence and darkness. She would be brought out only at the last minute; it would not do to risk sullying her just before the great event.

The groom made his appearance mid-morning by canoe, accompanied by Washington and Isobel Bush, and Ben and Jackson Moses. Tony had been invited, but declined. Under Isabel's watchful eye, Ben and Jackson carried a large crate up to the site of the feast. Leschi was happy to discover inside the very first butter-cream frosted triple-layer chocolate cake the Nisquallies had ever seen, miraculously intact. "It's a plot to make your warriors fat," warned Washington, but Leschi, fearless and jovial, devoured two slices on the spot.

"My friend," said Washington, throwing his big arm over the Chief's broad shoulders, "I am so sorry about Sara."

Leschi winced to hear her name spoken. It was not right to speak the name of one of the dead; it could summon her back, and a spirit called against its will was a dangerous thing. Leschi forgave Washington, who did not know their ways, and thanked him for his concern.

"But I was overjoyed when I heard that the wedding was going forward," continued Washington. "You had Isobel and me worried there for a bit, when we heard that you'd told the Governor your people would rather go to war than to the reservation."

"I did not say we would go to war," replied Leschi. "These are false rumors."

"Good, that's good, I'm relieved to hear it."

"But, Washington," continued Leschi, "have you seen the *cultus illahee*" – inferior land – "to which the Governor would send my people?"

Washington looked to the ground and pursed his lips. "Yes, Leschi, I've seen it, and I agree that it's no good. You have to be patient with the white man – and here, I speak as a *klale tillicum*" – black man. "Like you, my family came very close to losing all our land just this past year."

Leschi reprimanded himself. So wrapped up had he been in his own problems, that he had not even noticed his friend's. "I didn't know," he said. "I am sorry that I was not there to help you, Washington –"

"Don't fret a minute, Leschi. I know that if there's anything you can do, all I've got to do is ask. But this wasn't something you could fix."

"What happened?"

"Remember I told you about slavery, how the *klale tillicum* doesn't have the same rights as the *t'kope tillicum?*" Leschi nodded. "The same bad laws that forced us to come up here in the first place, were put into effect north of the Columbia when Washington became a Territory. Under those laws, no black man or his wife could claim their acreage under the Donation Lands Act. So, even though Isobel and I got here first, and have worked our land from dawn to dusk every day but the Sabbath – and some of those, truth be told – suddenly we were just squatters on unclaimed land."

Leschi's jaw clenched. The white man's laws seemed well suited to turn wrong into right.

"You know how we've been feeding the newly arrived pioneers all these years; you think I'm just a nice fellow, huh?"

"You're a very good man, Washington."

"Yeah, well, a nigger like me gotta be twice as good or twice as bad just to get by. I ain't much good at bad, so ..."

"What is this word, '*nigger*'?"

"It's like *siwash*, only for *klale tillicum*." Leschi nodded grimly.

"I've got so many friends in this Territory," continued Washington, "so many families that wouldn't have made it through the winter if it wasn't for me, that they got together and passed a special law granting us our land." Washington smiled. "That's the ticket for you, too, Leschi. *Siwash* and *nigger* – we gotta use our brains, my friend, not our guns. You be patient, you kiss their *kimta* –" rear end "– and in the end you get what you want."

"I don't know," said Leschi, shaking his head. "Maybe that is the answer."

"No 'maybe' about it," warned Washington. "You can't fight them, Leschi. They'll crush you."

On this ominous note, the time had come for the ceremony. First, all the bride gifts were gathered: not the promised ten, but twenty fine quarter horses corralled together, the blankets neatly folded and stacked, the wool and cotton bolts and brass buttons laid over the blankets, a beautiful fresh-dug cedar canoe placed in front, the saddles lined up against its side, ten Hudson's Bay muskets, with shot, polished and gleaming, and five stacks of gold coins laid carefully at the center. Kwahnesum was led forth from the longhouse, covered from head to toe in veils of softened cedar bark, so that no human form could be detected. A gentle mare was led out from among the horses into the midst of the piled treasure, and Kwahnesum was hoisted onto her back. Then, one by one, the veils were removed, revealing at last Kwahnesum's elegant aquiline nose and high forehead, dark curled lashes under plucked brows, eyes pellucid and quick with excitement. She wore only the softest calf-length doeskin gown, with bright-colored beads worked into the bodice, belted with slick coral-and-gold snakeskin. In deference to her Boston husband-to-be, Kwahnesum had replaced the traditional otter-skin crown with a white ribbon headdress, trimmed in white and pink lace rosettes. From beneath the headdress, her raven tresses dressed in Queen Anne's lace tumbled down across her breast. Moonstone earrings glowed from her lobes; her throat was adorned with a glistening *hiqua* and mother-of-pearl necklace that was a wedding gift from Ann.

Charlie, smart in a stiff white shirt with black tie and frock coat, puffed out his chest, astonished by his good fortune. If his father could see him now! A man of means astride a stallion, a Captain consulted by the Governor, he waited across the field as Leschi had instructed, ready to take the most beautiful Indian princess in the Territory as his bride. Nisqually braves danced and sang in a circle around the piled treasure and the mounted bride. Then the signal was given, and Charlie dug his spurs into the stallion's powerful barrel. "Yaaahhhh!" he cried, galloping across the prairie under wheeling blue sky and cotton clouds, all the new fresh earth of this paradise rising up to reveal its mysteries. "YAAAHHH!" he cried again and again, as the warriors parted to grant him his right. He swooped by and lifted the girl by her tiny starved waist. She was light as the wind as she swung her legs over the stallion's croup and snuggled just behind his saddle, leaning into his back with her arms around his chest. The warriors held up their muskets and whooped and ran alongside, as he delivered Kwahnesum to where Leschi, Quiemuth, and old Sennatco sat, impassive, at the head of the feasting blankets. There, Charlie dismounted, catching Kwahnesum as she slipped down off the horse. As he had been taught in the weeks leading to the wedding, Charlie knelt with his bride-to-be before her father.

"Great – Chief," said Charlie, in his halting *Whulshootseed*, "I – I – come to – to ask your – daughter." Then, switching to Chinook, with which he was more comfortable, "I come to ask permission for the hand of your daughter in marriage. I will stay with her and give her children and fight and die for her, and if she dies before me I will dress her and launch her on the voyage to *Otlas-Skio*. For this honor I have brought you gifts." Charlie proceeded nervously to detail the bride gifts in halting Chinook.

Leschi rose, Dr. Tolmie serving as interpreter. Charlie marveled to see just how big and powerful his prospective father-in-law was. "My son," Leschi began warmly, but his smile was cold, "we of the Nisqually welcome you and all our Boston and King George friends on this great occasion. We are honored by your presence here. As you may know, my family is connected to many tribes. My grandfather was chief of the Yakamas. My first wife's father was Chief of the Puyallups. My sister is married to the Snoqualmie Chief. I have cousins and uncles among the Klickitat, the Yakamas, the Puyallups, the Squaxons and the Skokomish." Leschi impaled Charlie on the shaft of a sudden dark stare. "In all these connections with other tribes, with other peoples, we have never yet found it necessary to remind the groom of his bargain." Charlie felt his stomach clench. Of course Leschi would notice the switch; he'd told Tony over and over, but Tony said it would be fine if he threw in a few extra horses.

"The Bostons are a strange tribe, but men are men," continued Leschi evenly. "When a man tells me he will give me a rifle that shoots straight and far, but instead he gives me a musket, it means that he fears me. Do you fear me, my son?"

Charlie stood, knees knocking confirmation, and suddenly the ceremonial warriors with their muskets did not appear festive, but very threatening. Leschi waited patiently for a response. "N-no, Sir," Charlie lied, his ears burning, the stiff collar cutting into his neck as he gulped for air.

"Then would you please explain to me why you broke your solemn promise to bring me ten rifles, with ammunition?"

Governor's orders, Tony'd said, but of course Charlie couldn't say so here without violating his oath of secrecy. "I'm sorry, great *Tyee*, but they're in short supply right now. I couldn't get any. I-I brought muskets and ten extra horses instead – worth more than rifles."

"I have plenty of muskets, plenty of horses, but not plenty of rifles," said Leschi simply. "You have broken your word to me, Mr. Eden. The wedding is off!"

"No, Father, NO!" screamed Kwahnesum, and Leschi's blow was swift and she fell silenced, as was his right. Quickly, Ann and Moonya helped her up and led her away, muddied and quaking in silent agony, the ribbon headdress torn and dragging off her neck. Charlie just stood stunned as his whole world collapsed before him. His mouth worked to no effect, like a fish thrown in a canoe bottom. Face bright red, he turned to go.

"Stop right there, *Challie* Eden!" commanded Leschi. As Charlie turned back, he saw Leschi's warriors tightening their grip on their muskets. Fear flashed from pale face to pale face. "There is a tradition, *Challie* Eden, among my people. The father of the bride is permitted to set a test for the groom. Only upon completion of the test, may the marriage go forward."

"But, you said it was off!" said Charlie, finding his tongue at last.

"I said it was off; so, I could as easily say it was on again. All you need do is talk to your *Govenol* Stevens for me; tell him we want peace; tell him we must have some land by the river or we cannot live. Find the words to change his heart, so that he gives us back just a little of our land. If you do this, you shall have my daughter, and your bride gifts returned to you, doubled."

Charlie was totally flummoxed. He had been told he could expect a test of physical prowess, such as fetching an eagle's feather from a nest, or wrestling a warrior who, if the bride price was good, was under strict instructions to lose. But this? How was it that his simple desire for a pretty Indian girl had ground him like a stalk of wheat between the millstones of two such foes?

"Great Chief," he said, "I am but a small man. I have no power over the Governor."

"There are no small men," replied Leschi. "There are only men who lack the courage to be big. Now go! Take my stallion!" Charlie did not argue; he mounted and galloped away, grateful to have escaped with his life, unsure what to make of this strange message for the Governor.

"My friends," said Leschi, turning back to the astonished guests, "it is a shame to waste a wedding feast." With a mischievous smile, he looked to Mary by his side, and she met his gaze with hungry eyes. "With John Hiton's permission, this woman Mary shall become my second wife today!"

John Hiton rose. "I have waited long for such a day," he said, tears filling his eyes. "I am honored, Chief Leschi." Leschi remembered well the baby girl – Mary's little sister – that the Haida invader had literally cut from John Hiton's hand, that terrible day so long ago, and it filled him with gladness to see joy again on his old friend's face.

The stunned murmurs of the white men were drowned as the Indians whooped and sang and shot their muskets into the air. The wedding of a Chief! John Hiton accepted Leschi's pledges, and a gift of twenty horses. Then the young bride and the groom, who was old enough to be her father, ate from the same plate and drank from the same cup, while pledging themselves to one another.

Ben Moses and Ezra Meeker broke out their fiddles. At last the white folks opened their stiff collars and did a little whooping of their own, just happy to be alive. "Reminds me of the first time I came after you, my dear," huffed Doc Maynard, kicking up his heels with Catherine. "Your brother chased me off with a shotgun." *Serves you right*, she thought, *proposing to me while still married to that lady back in Ohio!* All cares momentarily forgotten, Dr. Tolmie and Jane, Quiemuth and Moonya, John Edgar and Betsy, and even Wahoolit and Ann, stepped out together, do-si-do-ing with the best of them.

Chapter Ten
Trouble Under Sky World

1

Owhi's band of warriors swept down from the sagebrush-dotted ridge called Umtanum. Dropping into the Wenas Creek valley, their hooves sent up clouds of pink-grey dust across the undulating rocky slope. Henry Matisse, an American miner with more greed than art in his veins, chucked his morning coffee and bolted for his musket. "Wake up, ya bastards!" he screamed at his two partners, still bedrolled under the wagon, "Injuns!" One fellow sat up so fast he whacked his head on the axle, but there was no time to moan as the hoofbeat earthquake gave way to a volley of lead, spraying dirt and splintering the undercarriage.

"Yeeeeeoooooooowwwwww!" cried the third miner, holding an eye mangled by flying splinters. He rolled out and jumped up, one hand staunching the blood, the other sweeping blindly for the Kentucky rifle that had fallen when the volley hit. An arrow through the chest stopped him in mid-sweep, and with a strangled cry he toppled, twitched once, then lay still.

Henry'd gotten a charge into his musket pan and it exploded with a flash of fire and smoke, but his hasty aim was high and the shot wasted. Owhi dismounted on the fly. Swinging his spear with the momentum of his gallop, he knocked Henry's musket clear and laid him flat, leaving a nasty gash through one arm and across the side of his face. The miner who'd whacked his head scurried out, hands in the air, waving a musty brown-white undershirt, crying in English, "Don't shoot, don't shoot, I give up." He was roughly pushed down on top of Henry. Together they cowered in the dirt and stones by the creek, painted Yakama warriors on one side, boulder-strewn rapids on the other.

Owhi glared at them with his fierce, close-set eyes. Then he spoke in Chinook: "*Nesika kahpho kapswalla klootchman.*" Our sister was raped. "*Alta mesika mimoluse.*" Now you die.

"No, we don't know nothing about that," protested Henry in perfect *Shahaptian*, language of the Yakama.

And in *Shahaptian* came the response: "She said it was three white men camped by Wenas Creek, and that she trusted them because one spoke to her sweetly in her own tongue." The man who'd surrendered bolted towards the water, but a shot with the newly captured Kentucky rifle caught him square in the back. He fell with a splash and was carried away.

"Fuckin' *siwash*," cursed Henry, and it was the last thing he said in any language as two braves yanked down on his jaw while two more yanked up. Owhi's long knife sliced out his tongue, leaving him speechless with his head yanked back as he kicked and choked and drowned in his own blood.

Word of the miners' violent deaths soon reached the ears of Indian Agent Andrew Bolon, a red-bearded bear of a man who'd been appointed by Governor Stevens for his fluency in several native languages. Bolon rode solo into Kamiakan's camp on a bright October morning, just a week after the killings, boldly demanding to see the old Chief. Kamiakan, regal in feathered war bonnet trailing over muscled shoulders down to his thickened waist, received Bolon in a warm embrace.

"My friend, Red Bear, to what do we owe the honor of your visit?" asked the Chief, feigning innocence.

"I am investigating the deaths of three miners that occurred down on Wenas Creek," replied Bolon. "I have reports that some of your people were involved."

"My people are many," replied the canny Chief.

"So you can spare one or two in the name of justice," replied Bolon.

"We have come to be friends over the past year," replied Kamiakan. "But what is a year, compared to ties of blood that go back beyond memory? You are a brave man, Bolon, but the line between courage and foolishness is a thin one. It is not safe for you here."

"Chief, there is danger enough for all," warned Bolon. "I am concerned about how the news of this murder will be received by the Governor, and the Army. The white man has a big Army, we have guns that shoot straight and far, and big howitzers that spit thunder and can destroy many men at once." While true, Bolon knew he was stretching for effect. The thinly-scattered Army of the Pacific had only one thousand men from Mexico to Canada, an average of only one soldier for every seven hundred square miles – even if its commanders saw fit to mobilize. Thus far, General Wool had shown no inclination to deploy even the small company stationed in Washington Territory, despite the Governor's repeated promptings.

Bolon pressed his point. "Many of our people believe that the Indians are getting ready for war. Even Great Chiefs can be dragged into war by foolish underlings. Unless you mean war, today is the time to stand for peace. Turn over the suspects, and save your people."

Kamiakan weighed Bolon's words. It was true that his hot-headed elder son Owhi was acting on his own, against his wishes. Bolon did not yet know it, but Kamiakan knew that Owhi and his band had also attacked and killed a party of miners coming across Snoqualmie Pass. Owhi was out of control, and his example was stirring the young men into a frenzy. Perhaps he had been wrong all these years; perhaps his younger son, Moshell, was better suited to rule. But to avoid war, could he sacrifice his own son? He knew that the safety of the tribe came before the life of any one man. The burdens of leadership lay heavy upon Kamiakan's heart.

"Moshell!" ordered Kamiakan. A pudgy youth with mild eyes and long flowing hair sprang forward. "You remember our friend, Red Bear? I grant him safe passage in our lands. Guide him to the Ahtanum Mission. Wait there for me; I will come later with Owhi."

Kamiakan didn't state his purpose, but Moshell could guess. Owhi was to have the honor of killing Red Bear. This, he could not abide. Moshell was jealous of the prestige Owhi was winning by his exploits. It was time for Moshell to win his own fame. Late that night, rather than carrying out his father's orders, Moshell sprang the trap. As his brother warrior slipped up behind Bolon and seized his arms from behind, Moshell sliced his knife deep across Bolon's throat. They danced as Red Bear thrashed and died.

When Kamiakan heard of the cowardly way that his son had murdered the agent to whom he had promised safe passage, he cried in shame, rent his garments, and rubbed ash into his hair. "I have no son but Owhi," he declared.

Word of Bolon's death soon reached Olympia. Secretary Mason summoned J.W. Wiley, pliant publisher of the Territory's only newspaper, the *Pioneer & Democrat*. After a full briefing, Mason leaned across his new mahogany desk, the scent of *hama hama* – rotting fish carcasses – heavy in the air. "I don't need to tell you that this may be a bit of a blessing in disguise. We've never really known what to do with so many Indians, have we?" Mason sat back, pressed his fingers together, and smiled that boyish smile Meg liked so well.

The next morning, a special edition of the *Pioneer & Democrat* spat out the shocking news: KAMIAKAN ON THE WARPATH! MURDER OF INDIAN AGENT! DEATH TO THE YAKAMAS! ALL ABLE-BODIED MEN ORDERED TO REPORT FOR DUTY!

2

Kwahnesum stroked the honey hair on the pillow – *goose-down pillow!* – beside her. Did her father really believe he could hold her back with that raucous display of bravado he'd staged? She'd bided her time, playing the wounded but dutiful daughter, as summer turned towards autumn. It was all a charade; she never intended to return upriver to winter with her tribe.

As the days became weeks, her family's guard dropped, and she was even the subject of solicitude. Not from Mary; oh no, she was cold, jealous of any competition for the Chief's affection. Ann, though nominally First Wife, was reduced to a mere servant, forced to wait upon the royal couple. Kwahnesum's father, blinded by love, or lust, never saw it. Mary was careful only to show her fangs behind his back.

It was no longer her concern, thought Kwahnesum. She lay snug in a lacy cotton nightgown with a wool shawl over her shoulders, watching the grey daylight creep in through the panes – *glass panes!* – in the windows, filtered by thin muslin curtains. She was not interested in the tribe's solicitude; she would have her Boston man, with or without her father's consent.

It was only two suns – no, *days* – since she made her break. The elopement was secretly planned with the help of Sluggia, who had mysteriously transformed into her ally. Sluggia alerted Charlie, who promised to wait for her with his friend Ben Moses and Reverend Bill out on Elk plain, half way between Yokwa village and Puyallup. She rose after the fires were cold and tiptoed out – nothing unusual, just a call of nature, as indeed it was, but of a different sort. Once outside, she quickly slipped into the buckskin jacket and trousers Sluggia had hidden, and ran to the prearranged meeting place in the aspen grove. Her cousin waited with two ponies. Together, they stole away to the north with a friendly salute from Wyamooch, whose night it was to stand sentry.

Kwahnesum shivered as she savored the memory of that star-lit ride! Sluggia had to turn back at the half-way mark, for fear that his complicity might be detected. As Kwahnesum rode alone for the first time in her life, she heard her father's voice, telling the story of the creation of Sky and Stars. Long ago, soon after *Sah-hah-lee Tyee* created the world, the sky was too low. Tall people bumped their heads against it. Wives who were dissatisfied with their husbands climbed trees and escaped to Sky World, but snuck back down at night to get food. The wise men of many tribes came together in council to decide what to do. They decided that all the people and animals had to push up against the sky to lift it higher. Everybody cut long poles from the tallest trees to use for pushing. When the day arrived, the signal was given – *ya-hoh* – which means "lift together." *Ya-hoh!* everybody lifted, *ya-hoh!* first the fish from down in the sea, *ya-hoh!* the snakes who crawled, *ya-hoh!* the animals on four legs, *ya-hoh!* the men who walk upright, and finally, *ya-hoh!* the eagles who fly highest. This pushed sky way up above, higher than any mountain. That night, when the dissatisfied wives awakened, they found themselves too high to climb down, stranded forever in Sky World. Their longing eyes, looking down every night with sadness at the land they left behind, form the stars in the sky.

A moment of fear gripped Kwahnesum, as she rode to her waiting husband. Would she find herself trapped like the women of Sky World, never able to return? As soon as she reached Charlie's honey embrace, she forgot her fears. Why would she ever want to go back? She would never be alone. Her brave forebears, the women of Sky World, were there above Elk plain, to witness her marriage. They would be with her whenever she needed a friend.

The newlyweds had been in bed – *a soft, feather bed!* – ever since that star-light elopement, casting upon one another the intoxicating spell of carnal intimacy. They were both timid at first. Gingerly, she held his member in her hand and guided it into the swollen wetness between her legs. Soon he was emboldened to slide down and taste her. Then did she reach the stars in a single breath! They made love and love and love and slept and made love again, and only after two days and a few sips of water and stale biscuits, did it occur to either of them that they could not survive solely on one another's nectar. Charlie got up and made her a Boston delicacy, bacon and eggs. The eggs were awful, but she ate them anyway.

Then they made love again, and now, here he was, asleep against her *tootosh* – breast – with the grey light of a rainy morning softly illuminating the luxuries of a Boston wife's house. Kwahnesum was happy at last.

A sharp rap at the door shattered Kwahnesum's reveries. Charlie bolted as she pulled the blankets up to cover her nakedness. *Father!* she thought. "Be careful, Charlie!" she cried in Chinook. Charlie was already out of the bedroom, yanking up his trousers and reaching for his gun. A quick glance out the front window, and he relaxed. It was only the familiar pock-marked mug of Tony Rabbeson.

Charlie flung open the door. "Hey, Tony," he said, "c'mon in."

"Shit, what happened to you?" smirked Tony, looking the bleary-eyed Charlie up and down, though he knew quite well. He tried to get a glimpse into the bedroom, but Charlie blocked the view.

"Look, Romeo, I don't wanna be a homewrecker or nothin', but we got us some orders. You gotta get to Olympia tomorrow. Company A is musterin'."

"What?" said Charlie, blankly. The last two days and nights had erased most everything but his name from memory.

"Orders, Bub!" barked Tony. "Or, should I say, Capt'n Bub!" It hit Charlie. "Get scrubbed up, man, you stink! I'll be back in an hour. Be ready to ride."

"For how long?"

"Long as it takes, Capt'n. Yer goin' to Olympia. I'm headed up the Naches with that Jew-boy pal o' yers."

"You 'n Ben joined the reg'lars?"

"I shoulda, pay's better, but Hell no. Gov'nor finally got that slug Casey to send some reg'lar Army boys under Lieutenant Slaughter up the Naches. Gov'nor's ordered a few of us Volunteers to tag along, to make sure them reg'lars don't beg forgiveness from the Noble Savage."

"They weren't savages 'til we came along," objected Charlie.

Tony just glared at him, then spat on the doorstep. "You be ready – one hour, got it, *Captain?*" he replied, turning the honorific into an insult. Charlie nodded solemnly.

How brittle our hold on bliss! Kwahnesum did not understand. A Nisqually woman goes to war with her husband. She keeps him fed and clothed, keeps his weapons clean and tends his wounds. Charlie was firm; she could not go with him. Kwahnesum wailed and clawed at his sleeve, as he tried to reason with her in three languages, none of which spoke to her heart. In the end Charlie just pushed her away, leaving her marooned in dark Sky World, as he marched off to war.

3

On the ride back through Elk Plain, the clouds blotted out the stars, as Kwahnesum dragged herself through rain that clung like fish oil. Carefully skirting Muck Creek, she headed west over familiar paths to the Nisqually Delta, beyond which lay Olympia, and Charlie.

He had told her not to follow, but what was she to do? She had sat alone – alone! – as she had never been before. There was no tribe, no village, no clan of women with flashing hands and playful songs to pass the time. She paced the empty cabin like a caged lioness, her roars echoing unanswered. She tried to use the stove just as she'd seen Charlie do, building the fire inside its cast iron belly, but she lacked the Boston magic and the house had filled with smoke, forcing her out.

Once outside, Kwahnesum began to get her bearings. Under some oak bushes she spotted the broad, dark green leaf, and mottled orange and brown bell-shaped flower, of *charlaque*, which she harvested for the delicate-tasting roots. Adding mushrooms, berries and camas bulbs, she soon had a feast that cleansed her stomach of the sour eggs. Then she rode into the misting rain to find her man.

Her white woman's clothes were heavy and scratchy; they did nothing to protect her. She shed the outer layer which, when wet, was heavier than three baskets of smoked clams, and just as stinky. This left her in woolen bloomers and a flannel petticoat, with the frilly cotton nightgown of her honeymoon ardors tucked in at the waist. She was chilled to the bone by the time she reached the delta, and the thin light was fading. Boldly, she rode up to the McAllister's new two-story plank house, built only fifty yards upland of the original fortified log house. She'd never seen such a grand house – it must have ten rooms down and up. But she was a Boston woman now. Taking a deep breath, she pulled the bobkin to lift the latch, pushed open the heavy pine door without knocking, and marched right into the foyer.

Lila Sue McAllister was justifiably proud of her first real pudding, so she shooed aside the Indian servants in order to enjoy serving it herself. Just as she was about to set it down in front of Papa, the latch lifted with a click, the door burst open, and her favorite little brown pup, Baxter, began to bark and growl. Lila Sue spun around to find herself confronted by a crazed Injun girl in dripping wet white women's underwear. Her recurring nightmare of a massacre had come to life! Lila Sue screamed and dropped her mother's porcelain serving dish, the one with the little blue pictures of promenading ladies in big hoop dresses, and gentlemen with high hats and starched breech-coats, that Ma'd brought all the way from Kentucky in the wagon without it getting so much as a chip – as she'd been told many times before. Now it shattered into a thousand pieces, and Lila Sue was wearing huckleberry pudding all over her brand-new boots with the silver eyes for lacing. She began to cry.

"*Klahowya!*" said Kwahnesum smiling through the wild black hair pasted to her face. As Martha McAllister pulled a pistol and trained it on her, Kwahnesum began to get the feeling that this hadn't been such a good idea. *Wasn't there something white folks did before they entered a lodge,* thought Kwahnesum, *some ritual they performed at the doorway?*

"Baxter, shush!" commanded Martha, lowering the pistol. The little puppy swallowed its most vicious bark in a wounded whimper, as it retreated to Ainsley's skirts. "Lila Sue!" scolded Martha, "you clean that up." Her elder sister stood to provide assistance. "Ainsley!" barked Martha, "your sister kin do it."

Pistol still in hand, Martha strode across the room to inspect, rather than greet, the new arrival. She sniffed, and wrinkled her nose. Kwahnesum's nipples were plastered to the drenched cotton nightgown. Martha shot a sharp, reproachful glare at Jimmy, who was clearly entranced by the Indian Lady Godiva.

"Jimmy, take Mick 'n Mackenzie and git upstairs right now!" she commanded, and Jimmy shoved little brother Mick before him and grabbed his little sister Mackenzie's trembling hand, making sure to lead her on the scenic route.

Pretending that it was all just another unpleasant chore for the defender of the hearth, Big Jim stepped around Lila Sue and the remains of the pudding, to study the dripping apparition. "Why, Martha," he said after a minute, "I do believe we've got us a princess. Isn't this Leschi's girl, Kala - Kala - Kwahnesum, that's it. The lassie who married Charlie last week?"

"What's going on, Mrs. Eden?" Jim asked Kwahnesum, in *Whulshootseed*.

"I am alone," replied Kwahnesum. "My husband has gone to Olympia to fight. I need a place to stay tonight. I need dry clothes, and food. May I stay here? Will you help me, please?"

Jim conveyed her predicament to Martha, who put aside the gun. "Ainsley," she instructed, "take this here young - Lady - into th' kitchen and heat up a bath fer her. Scrub her up real good, and have Mrs. Mommacdish get her some grub too, y'hear?"

"Yes, m'am." Ainsley hustled Kwahnesum to the kitchen, presided over by their cook, a Skykomish woman of matronly dignity.

"You don't know how lucky you are," whispered Ainsley to Kwahnesum in perfect *Whulshootseed* as soon as they were out of earshot. "Last Indian who burst in our front door without knocking, mama shot him with a full load of buckshot in both his legs. Took her three months to nurse him back to health!"

Kwahnesum did know how lucky she was. This angel with hair like strawberries and cream fed her, and drew for her an intoxicating tub of steaming water. Before immersing herself, she paused just long enough to touch herself once and lift her fingers to her lips for a parting taste of Charlie. Then with a sigh she submerged all her cares in the great kettle of *klootchman* soup. Once in, she swore never to bathe in the river again.

Jim and Martha were deep in conversation when they heard a scratching and shuffling at their door - the characteristic sign that an Indian was out there. Damn buggers never could understand knocking! Fortunately, after Kwahnesum's rude surprise, they'd pulled in the bobkin so nobody else could come bursting in unannounced. Jim grabbed his shotgun and nodded. Martha flung open the door and stepped aside. They were both astonished to find Leschi filling the doorway, his great conical cedar hat and cape shedding water in sheets like the receding tide.

"*Klahowya*, Jim McAllister!" boomed Leschi as he strode forward, pushed the shotgun aside, and embraced his friend in a drenching bear hug. Then he did the same to Martha, oblivious to her squirming.

Martha offered to fetch Leschi something to eat, then disappeared quickly into the kitchen, shutting the door firmly behind her. "The men will talk in here," announced Jim, herding Leschi away from the kitchen towards the parlor. It was the opportunity Jimmy was watching for; he slipped outside and dashed furtively to the kitchen window.

Martha leaned down by the steaming kettle just as Kwahnesum was coming up for air, splashing and giggling like a child. "Papa Leschi *highas* –" Father Leschi here – "*kopet* noise!" Silence!

Kwahnesum bolted up and out of the tub, slipped and nearly fell. Ainsley caught her and wrapped her in a towel, shushing her and rubbing her dry, as Mrs. Mommacdish cut a joint of beef for Leschi. Kwahnesum's long, night-sky tresses would never dry quickly. She dropped her towel and bent over the hot stove as Ainsley brushed and brushed. As Martha brought out the beef, she thought she heard a cry from the kitchen window, then dismissed it without investigation.

Leschi ate quickly to be nourished, any enjoyment crushed under the weight of cares. "I cannot thank you properly; my troubles are too many," he said when he finished. "My first wife is dead. My people look to me to save their lands from your *Govenol*, but I cannot even save my own daughter." He did not elaborate. Everyone knew of the elopement.

"Now we have received word from Stevens that the treaty has been accepted by the Great *Tyee* in Washington City, and we are ordered to report to the reservation. He gives us fourteen suns, my friend – fourteen suns to pack up lives lived since before the first eagle flew. After this time, he says that any unemployed Indian not on the reservation is a renegade who can be shot down!" Leschi looked up at Jim, fury in his eyes. "What kind of people are you, Jim McAllister?"

Jim got up and grimly poured himself a scotch. "Laddie," he replied, "doan take it so hard. Just get yourself down to wherever it is the Governor says you oughta, and you'll be fed and given warm clothes. They say that next year they'll be buildin' schools for your *weans* to learn farmin' 'n trades at." He forced a little laugh. "Why, sounds so good after all our hard work, time may come when we'll all want to join you!"

"Tell me something, Jim," said Leschi, rising up and staring right through him, "did you see me sign that treaty?" Jim got real finicky, drank his scotch as his whole head bloomed red, but he didn't say anything. "That's what I thought," said Leschi.

Ainsley helped Kwahnesum into a simple, modest sky-blue muslin dress, and crisp white apron. She helped her lace on leather boots that made Kwahnesum feel like a staked tomato plant. Kwahnesum tiptoed – actually, clomped – to the kitchen door, and cracked it to eavesdrop, just in time to see strawberry-faced Jimmy slip in and up the stairs.

"Word is that the tribes been talkin' about fighting the white man to get their land back –" it was Mr. McAllister's voice "– and that's not just what the Governor says. That's what I hear in the war dances on the prairie. Kin you deny it?"

Her father didn't deny it. "Jim," he said, "I'm going to Olympia to try one more time to talk peace with the *Govenol*. I'm going to ask him for some river bottom."

"He'll never give in."

Leschi brushed aside Jim's bleak view. "I'd like a talking paper from you, Jim, saying you support me. You 'n Martha, you're the first Bostons to settle by our river. If you said you supported me, it would mean a lot." Silence. "I'm asking as a friend, Jim," urged Leschi.

Jim's eyes flitted nervously towards Martha who signaled "No!" with a tight, almost imperceptible shake of her head. "Laddie, what kin I do?" said Jim. "If it were up to me, I'd give you your *hame* by the river, sure enough. But it's out of me hands. He's the Governor; I cain't cross 'im."

"I'm not asking you to cross him, Jim. I am only asking you to tell him what you just told me – that you, the first settler on our land, want us to stay right here, by the river."

"And what if he won't do it?"

Kwahnesum heard a long pause. She saw the angry *tamanous* fill the air, a dark, brooding shape. "Then it is *pight* –" spat Leschi: war. Kwahnesum could not believe her ears. *Her father was going to fight the Bostons?* She hadn't thought he had the nerve. *What would this mean for Charlie? What would it mean for her?* She snuck – plunk, plunk, plunk – into the dining room, to peek into the parlor, where her father stood not four arm lengths away, his back to her.

"No, Leschi," Martha protested, her apron raised to her cheeks, "we're yer *tillicums!*"

Leschi turned to Martha as Kwahnesum stumbled back to the kitchen to avoid being seen. "Then stay in your houses. Any settler who stays at home will be safe. But any settler who takes up arms against us –" and here his head jerked back towards Jim, "will be dealt with as an enemy."

"Then it's true," said Jim, a look of grim determination on his face.

"Jim, dear," drawled Martha, her voice soft but her eyes hard, "perhaps we kin find a way to help our ole friend, after all." Jim looked surprised as Martha took his arm and sidled him over to the writing desk. "'Member, now, honey, this here's the man that helped us out when we was in a pickle." Then she whispered a few quick words in Jim's ear.

"Well, Laddie," said Jim, "it looks like you get your talking paper for the Governor." And he wrote out a short letter, sealed with wax.

Leschi received the paper gratefully. "Thank-you, Jim, Martha. I knew I could count on you." He embraced them both again, with great warmth. "I sincerely hope that it is not too late for peace. If all fails and it does come to war, remember my warning: stay on your farm. Farewell, my *tillicums*." With a tired smile, he kissed Martha, then turned to leave.

At the door, Leschi paused. "Please, one more thing. Ask my daughter, *where is her husband now?*"

4

"Where is your husband now?" taunted Sluggia from the bank of Muck Creek, where Mary bathed in the soft rain of early morn.

"If you are caught he will tear out your eyes, cut off your little dangly root, and feed it to you," said Mary. She stood her full height to face Sluggia, exposing her dripping charms, daring him.

"Not so little," replied Sluggia, peeling aside his breechcloth. He stepped towards her, into the water, then stopped. "Young girl like you, it must get tedious with that old man, who comes once, then rolls over and goes to sleep."

Mary did not deny it. Sluggia took her silence as an invitation to close the remaining distance between them. Concealed behind the rhododendron on the bank, Ann watched in silence.

Chapter Eleven
To the Brink

1

Oh Lordy, them troubles never stop, thought Mrs. Eliza Jones to herself, as she patted at her husband's feverish brow with a damp cloth. She shone a cheery smile at little Becky and Tom, who rubbed the sleepies outa their eyes. Johnny was already up, out fetching water fer porridge. She worried 'bout him out there alone, but as Harvey had said to her back on the train after her first husband and her dear boy Zeke succumbed to the cholera, you gotta live yer life. She knew what he meant; in those five words were wrapped the whole pioneer philosophy. Sure yer scairt, everyone's scairt, but if you just crawl under a log you've had it. You pick yerself up and dust yerself off, and so long as the Good Lord puts breath in yer lungs, by gum you better use it! So she'd married Harvey not two weeks after burying Zeke and his paw. *You gotta live yer life.*

She and Harvey'd taken the advice of a young scarecrow of a pioneer named Ezra Meeker to snap up some of this rich land, lying where the elbows of the White and Green Rivers nearly touched. They'd built their cabin, and she'd sown seeds of larkspur, pansy, and the daffodil bulbs she'd brought all the way from Wisconsin in the pockets of her apron. The gaily-colored flowers brought a touch of home to this wilderness, but Eliza would never get used to dark evergreens that towered two hundred feet overhead. No matter how many you cleared, it was never enough. When storms whipped through the heavy boughs, those impossible trees seemed to mock their puny efforts, crying out, "This is our land, not yours."

Eliza Jones knew that over the last few weeks some of the White River settlers had picked up and moved to Seattle. It was 'cause of the rumors of Indian uprising. She'd been to Seattle; you could smell it a mile before you could see it. That wasn't for her. She and Harvey had worked their fingers raw to make this claim successful. They had eleven head of cattle, nine hogs, and with the help of their new hired man, Enos Cooper, they'd just planted a thousand apple and cherry trees. She couldn't hardly wait to see the patchwork quilt of blossoms and to breathe the heady fragrance next spring. No way she'd run off now, after all they'd done. No sirree, they was stayin' put!

She had the fire going pretty good by the time Johnny came back in with water, and the porridge was bubbling in the pot soon after, when they heard a shuffling and grunting on the front stoop. With her man sick in bed and all the rumors flying, Eliza grabbed Harvey's revolver before opening the door.

"Hey Maw, it's jest Nelson!" cried Johnny, and he ran over to hug th' scraggly-haired Duwamish, who grunted again and lumbered inside. Eliza wrinkled her nose at the musty-smelling coot, but she couldn't help smile, half at Johnny's love for this broken-down old thing, half at her own ridiculous nerves. 'Course it was just old Nelson, maybe fishin' fer some porridge. Nelson was always ready with a little gossip and a strange tale; good enough, he'd keep the children busy.

But as morning wore on, it became clear that this wasn't the same old Nelson they'd come to know so well. He was taciturn, he wouldn't eat, he barely spoke, he didn't play with the little ones, or tell them stories. He just sat there, wrapped in his blanket, and glowered. By noon time, they were walking around him like he was a lump of wood. It made Becky cry. Johnny ran off disgusted. Eliza felt a strange unease. Finally, when the sun beyond the clouds must have passed its zenith, Nelson stood and cleared his throat. Then he spoke – in English! – "Pretty soon Indian be gone, and white man have all land around here!"

Eliza went over to him, pushed back his tangled grey-black hair and touched his cheek. She drew back startled, her hand wet with tears. Nelson held her eyes too long, then rushed from the cabin without another word. All was silent, but for Harvey's labored breathing and the rush of the river. Tommy toddled over. "Mamma up!" he said, tugging at her apron. She shone her cheery smile agin as she lifted her little boy into her arms, and hugged him tight.

2

Leschi had never felt like the Bostons' enemy until this moment. As he trotted into Olympia towards the Governor's office, the ladies of the outlying houses bustled their children indoors, and the men on the boardwalks stopped whatever they were doing just to turn and glare. Olympia, he knew, was the Governor's stronghold. They were riding directly into the jaws of the beast – like that old story his father liked to tell of Coyote tricking the lake monster into swallowing him, then killing him from the inside out.

Leschi had stayed the previous night at Fort Nisqually, where Dr. Tolmie had welcomed him and his tribesmen, Wahoolit and Winyea. Dr. Tolmie had fed them and housed them, filled them in on the latest political news, and given Leschi a good deal on a new beaver coat and felt *vaquero* hat. Leschi had been gratified to learn that the Bostons were divided over the Governor's treatment of his tribe. There were powerful forces, especially in Steilacoom and Seattle, forming to oppose the Governor's warlike policies.

Leschi feared that perhaps he'd been naive to think that three Indians could just ride into town and straighten everything out, as if it were a quarrel over a woman. He was grateful to Dr. Tolmie, who'd volunteered to come along to help with the parley. Without Dr. Tolmie's pink dome bouncing along beside them, there's no telling what the sullen townsmen of Olympia might have done. Even as it was, when they stopped to get a bucket of water by the livery stable, a young tough had thrown Wahoolit into the mud. Fortunately, not everyone in town felt the same way; before Leschi could react, the proprietor of the stable had thrown the n'er-do-well into the same mud hole, and they were able to get on their way, and even laugh it off later.

Now they were "waiting on His Majesty," as Dr. Tolmie put it, in the anteroom to Secretary Mason's office. Who would have thought this dilapidated old fishing shack could house such a warren of offices? Talking papers like snowdrifts wafted from tables to floor. The sight of so many papers made Leschi begin to doubt the power of the one small paper tucked inside his belt. Something so common could not possibly carry the strong medicine he'd hoped for. Perhaps Dr. Tolmie would know.

Dr. Tolmie looked at the paper and shook his head. "Jim McAllister gave you this?" he asked, though Leschi had already plainly explained the circumstances. "He knew you were to show it to the Governor? To support your claim?"

"Yes," confirmed Leschi, "yes."

"'Dear Sir:'" read Dr. Tolmie, translating into *Whulshootseed*. "'The bearer of this letter, Chief Leschi, plans to make war upon us. In the interest of public safety, he should be arrested. Your obedient servant, James McAllister.'" He handed the paper back to Leschi, who grimly tore it to shreds.

"Thank-you, my friend," said Leschi, more in sadness than in anger.

"Secretary Mason will see you now," intoned a young pimply-faced fellow. They were ushered into an office that had increased in grandeur remarkably over the past six months, though it still smelled of fish. Now it was richly carpeted, the walls freshly papered above oak wainscoting. Official portraits were scattered around a gleaming mahogany desk, behind which presided the gold-spectacled, cherubic Territorial Secretary. Behind him was Old Glory with its thirteen stripes and thirty-one stars, and a beefy fellow wearing a revolver.

The Secretary did not rise, but indicated chairs with a wave of his hand. He introduced Colonel Blunt of the Territorial Volunteers, who flashed a cat-and-canary smile at them.

"What can I do for you, gentlemen?" asked Mr. Mason. Dr. Tolmie acted as interpreter.

"We have come to speak directly with *Govenol* Stevens," replied Leschi. "We want him to know our hearts, which are filled with feelings of peace and good will for your people. We want to move to the reservation. But we must have his word that we can have a part of the river bottom."

Secretary Mason flicked back his auburn locks and pressed his fingers together. "The Governor knows you are *heah*, Leschi," he intoned in his best Brahmin. "He instructed me fully in this matter. He says that the treaty is complete and binding. He has no power to renegotiate it."

"I signed no treaty," insisted Leschi.

Mason shrugged, barely missing a beat. "The treaty has been signed by the Chiefs of all the Tribes and the Great Father in Washington City. It has been approved by the Senate, our tribe's greatest council. The Governor says you should come in to the reservation now, and you will be fed and clothed and kept safe all winter." *Wintah.*

Leschi stood, towering over the mahogany desk and the studious man behind it. "I am a Chief," he said. "I do not negotiate through underlings. I want to hear this from Stevens himself."

Blunt's hand dropped to rest on the butt of his pistol. But Mason replied in the bored tone of a clerk addressing a question of road levies. "The Governor is a busy man, Leschi; he has many affairs of State with which to concern himself. There is no ambiguity in his instructions to me. I believe I have conveyed them clearly. Now, if there is nothing else ..." He rose, smiled perfunctorily, and extended his hand.

Faster than anyone could react, the wind off Leschi's spear parted the startled bureaucrat's wavy black locks as the tip drove deep through a star in the flag behind him. Blunt's pistol flew up and then down even quicker, as Wahoolit's spear neatly disarmed him, then pressed him harmlessly back against the wall.

"Since you are such a good message boy," said Leschi, his dark eyes belying the calm in his voice, "tell your *Tyee* that if he wants one more inch of Nisqually land, he will have to pay in blood." Dr. Tolmie stood silent.

"Translate it!" barked Leschi.

"I'd rather not, my friend, for your sake," pleaded Tolmie. "The Bostons have cities with more people than there are trees in the forest. You have only a few hundred warriors. How in God's name can you fight them?"

Softly came Leschi's reply. "How can we not?" His visage was fierce, but there was peace in his breast that had long been absent. "Tell him."

Mason was told.

3

Wednesday, October 24, 1855, dawned clear and unseasonably warm. Only a gentle breeze off the Sound stirred the red-white-and-blue bunting lining Third & Main Streets in Olympia, where Company A was mustering. On the boardwalk, a small brass band honked out a few patriotic tunes. At the head of the column of volunteers, Captain Charles Eden sat tall in the saddle of a new Morgan charger, for which he'd traded his old draft plus a handful of scrip issued to him by the Territory in lieu of cash wages. With a freshly-sewn tan jacket, a blue "WT" sewn on his sleeve, a steel sword in his scabbard, and a new breech-loading rifle holstered against his saddle, Charlie should have been feeling a lot better than he actually felt.

The Volunteer Company had only fallen eight short of its goal of fifty men, though most of the forty-two young men who'd turned out looked to be more familiar with a cow's udder than either a musket or a razor. The wives, children, parents, sisters, aunts, uncles, godparents, neighbors, servants and drinking buddies of all forty-two brave farm boys lined the street on both sides, clapping, cheering and crying. They knew, of course, that the regular Army had finally been persuaded to take the field against the pesky Yakamas. A hundred seasoned regulars were reportedly heading north and west into Yakama country from Fort Dalles on the Columbia, to meet up with fifty men under Lieutenant Slaughter, sent east from Fort Steilacoom, on the Military Road through Naches Pass. But the Washington pioneers were not the kind of folks who sat back and let others do their fighting for them. At least, that was what the Governor and Secretary Mason had been saying to anyone up and down the Sound who would listen, and that's what the *Pioneer & Democrat* claimed every red-blooded American pioneer was saying, so people had begun to figure it must be so, whether they'd actually heard their neighbor say it or not.

Although Charlie knew that it was the greatest honor his Territory could confer to choose him to lead their first Volunteer Company into the field, he was again the reluctant adventurer. He remembered the predawn call to the Governor's office, standing with his Lieutenant, Jim McAllister, at his side, to receive their orders from Colonel Blunt. Blunt had handed Charlie his orders, which he crudely summarized: "Go to Muck Creek, l'il buddy, and bring in Leschi 'n Quiemuth. If they ain't there, you boys have yerself some fun huntin' Injuns and –" here his bright blue eyes merrily pinned Charlie to the wall – "Injun girls." *Har! Har! Har!*

Charlie remembered the unreality of it all, when he stepped outside the Governor's office, the sky just pinking. He'd heard a familiar voice from a side street. The white woman's bonnet did nothing to disguise that coppered face both alien and dear, the high forehead and long straight nose dipping to lips sweet as the buddleia nectar. She'd kissed him, and he didn't want to but he'd kissed her back. Before he knew it, they were down two alleys into the little Nisqually village adjacent to town, where soft fir boughs and doeskin mats awaited them. After they'd made love, he told her everything, saying over and over again, "I'm sorry, Kwahnesum, I'm sorry."

"Take me with you, Charlie," she replied. "If you take me with you, I can help convince him to come in peacefully."

"I'm sorry, Kwahnesum, but I can't."

"What will you do if he resists, Charlie?" she asked. "He is my father, and I am your wife, which makes him your father too. Will you kill him?"

This is what Charlie had tried to push from his mind. He remembered the Governor's final orders. *Alive, if possible, but bring them in.* How could he go to war against his own father-in-law? Charlie risked a glance at Kwahnesum, and she saw his weakness.

"If you catch him, he will make me a widow," she had said. Again she demanded to come along, but he had refused, and she had cursed him in *Whulshootseed*, Chinook and English, as they parted.

Now, with Kwahnesum's words clawing undigested like bad meat, Charlie squirmed in his saddle, trying to play the part of the brave warrior awaiting his Commander in Chief. He had a lot on his mind. He wasn't sure he trusted the two Indian scouts, Stahi, who'd been recommended by a friend of the Governor, and Clipwalen, the Similkameen boy rescued by Jim McAllister. More immediately, Charlie simply prayed to get out of town before he had to answer the call of nature.

The horses were anxious and pawing the dirt. The band was butchering a second rendition of its limited repertoire, when at last Governor Stevens, with Secretary Mason, Indian Agent Mike Simmons, and newspaper publisher J.W. Wiley, arrived at a gallop from three blocks away. Armed only with his pen, Wiley joined the column to report on its glories. That made forty-six men, counting Charlie and two scouts.

Mason presented a recently-mended Old Glory to the Company, which was turned over to young Andrew Laws, their beardless standard-bearer. Then the Governor cleared his throat, ready for the grand send-off.

"Brave Volunteers! Ladies and Gentlemen!" came the Governor's clear high voice, and all eyes turned upon the little frock-coated man with the strict military bearing. Stevens' big head was spinning all about, like a tornado sucking in everything in its wake. Then suddenly it stopped, fixed on Charlie. "Captain Eden, from this day forward Company A shall be known as Eden's Rangers!" Right on cue, Martha and Ainsley McAllister ran from the crowd, bearing a neatly folded banner, which they presented to Charlie. As Charlie held it up it unfurled in the breeze to reveal roiling black clouds against a light blue silk background, from which emerged a silver thunderbolt. At the point of impact with the earth, the words EDEN'S RANGERS spilled forth in bright gold letters.

As the spectators cheered, Ainsley clung to her father's hands, cheeks slick with tears. Martha did the same with young Private Jimmy McAllister, mounted in the column behind his father. Martha kissed her son and husband goodbye, slipping her silk hankie into Jim's breast pocket as he bent down. "Don't fret, me *weans*," said Jim, fighting his emotions. "We'll be fine, won't we laddie?" Jimmy nodded and smiled with all the confidence of youth. "Why," continued his father, "I could drive the whole lot of them Nisquallies into the reservation with me cane, not that any drivin' will be necessary when they see our lads!"

"This is a simple matter of justice," cried the Governor. "We have a treaty, signed by the Chiefs of the Indian Nations. The task set for Eden's Rangers is to enforce that treaty, and to escort the Indians to the reservation." Cheers all around. After allowing them to crest, Stevens modestly held up his hand.

"Brave volunteers, you are the hand of Providence. To you falls the glorious task of doing God's work by opening up our lands to free Americans. By moving the savages to the reservation, where they can be fed and cared for, and taught the ways of civilized society, you are acting with Christian charity and nobility. As soldiers of God, you pave the way for the ever-increasing progress and prosperity of Washington Territory. It is our manifest destiny as Americans and Christians to plant the blessings of civilization from sea to sea. Go forward, soldiers, and do your duty well!"

The band struck up the Star Spangled Banner, and everyone sang along. Swallowing hard, Charlie raised his hand and yelled, "COMPANY HOOOO!" With Jim McAllister at his left proudly carrying the banner of Eden's Rangers, and young Andrew Laws with the Stars and Stripes unfurled on his right, they trotted off with a warm breeze at their backs, to do their duty for God and Country.

A half mile out of town, the column halted while its Captain did his duty in the bushes. Meanwhile, a Cayuse pony bearing a copper-faced beauty, whose dark tresses flowed behind her like grasses in the current of the river bottom, galloped ahead to sound the alarm.

III

The Burial Canoe

October 25, 1855 – March 10, 1856

Chapter Twelve
Blood Spilled in *Tenalquot*

1

The plow stood idle in the half-cut furrow. The fire pits smoldered. Flies buzzed around plates of unfinished food. Clams not turned on the smoking racks blackened on one side, while rotting on the other. Twenty quarter horses fidgeted nervously up on the pasture, tails swatting their rumps. Charlie raised his hand, ordering a halt at the southern edge of the Muck Creek clearing. Over the snorting and muttering of their own mounts, they listened carefully, straining for any sign of an impending ambush.

All seemed quiet, but Charlie was taking no chances. Wordlessly, he ordered dispersal of the column into a center and two flanking forces. Holding their position, he ordered the McAllisters forward to reconnoiter Yokwa village. They went longhouse by longhouse, gingerly poking their muskets first, and then their heads, through the multiple flaps of elk skin covering twisted doorways designed to thwart invaders. Each time Jim pressed through, he felt the hackles rise on his neck, anticipating a blow by some hidden assailant. Each time there was nothing. He came to the last longhouse, the one he knew to be Leschi's.

Leschi had returned home and reported to the council the results of his parley with Mason. Runners were sent to call Nisqually, Puyallup, Duwamish, Klickitat, Suquamish, and any other willing warriors, to gather just south of the White River on Tenalquot Prairie. Leschi was gratified to receive pledges of support from tribal leaders throughout Whulge, who together could put a thousand armed warriors in the field. Quiemuth shook his head, and simply went out to plow the fields. Some young men taunted him, as he prepared the ground for the winter crops. "Would you be like the white man," Quiemuth asked in reply, "fighting over land you do not use?"

Just outside Leschi's dwelling, Jim used hand signals to call his son Jimmy to one side of the entryway. Musket primed and bayonet fixed, Jim flicked back the first layer and pressed ahead. Momentarily disoriented by the darkness, he slashed wildly at the next skin, which tore but did not fall loose. He tried to jump through the opening, but caught his foot and began to fall, just as he glimpsed something lunge and heard a snarl. Jimmy cried, "Look out pa!" Jim heard the explosion of his son's musket, followed by a howl as the dying dog's snout smacked against his side. The acrid smell of burnt powder mixed with the salt smell of blood.

The news had come swift as the first run of Chinooks. First, a messenger from the East. The Yakamas under Chief Kamiakin had won a glorious victory, beating back the troops from Fort Dalles in a battle at Toppenish Creek. The Bostons were not invincible after all! Then Kwahnesum had ridden in. The women of the tribe acted as if she were not there, and the men spit on her, as she deserved. Head held high, she bore all this, insisting that she must have counsel with her father. The Chief emerged from his longhouse, but could not look her in the eye. "You have desecrated the memory of your mother. Your grandfather, Sennatco, went to the woods in shame, howled like a dog for three days taking neither food nor drink, and died. You are dead to me," pronounced Leschi, but his eyes said that it was he who was mortally stricken.

Ears ringing, Jim shook off the bloody dog, and looked around. The thin light through the fire holes showed plainly that Leschi's longhouse was empty like all the others. Jim looked back and saw Jimmy kneeling down, stroking and comforting the dying animal. Jim went over, gently lifted his trembling son, and led him outside. "It's all right," he whispered.

"I din' know," said Jimmy.

"Coulda been anythin' in there. You coulda saved me life."

"Yeah," said Jimmy, still dazed. "Coulda been a little *wean*, too." Or that beautiful girl, the Chief's daughter, thought Jimmy. He'd barely been able to get her out of his mind since that night outside the kitchen window watching the lantern glow off her long neck, dark hair, and beautiful round buttocks.

"Tyee Leschi," replied Kwahnesum, speaking in Chinook like a white woman, "I will mourn for my Grandfather. I have no claim upon your tumtum; that I know. But you have claim upon mine, and so does this people I, I," and here she faltered, reverting to Whulshootseed, "loved – no, love." She took a breath to regain her composure. "I have ridden as fast as possible to warn you that soldiers are coming. Soldiers are coming now, under the command of my husband. Please, you must flee!"

The central body of Eden's rangers thundered across Muck Creek plain, drawn to the musket fire. "Don't let 'em see you like this, me boy," whispered Jim, who turned and waved his arms at the approaching force. "All clear!" he hollered, as Jimmy wiped his eyes and pulled himself together, then joined in, waving and hollering, "all clear." After the explanations, Jimmy took the Dog-Warrior First Class ribbing stoically. He promised himself that he'd be a little slower to pull the trigger next time.

Some said they should stand and fight, but Leschi counseled caution. "We are but one village with a small number of warriors. We are too exposed here, and too near the Boston reinforcements. Our warriors are already gathering at Tenalquot Prairie, in the heart of the land given to us by Sah-hah-lee Tyee. If the white man insists upon a fight, let us fight him there."

Charlie sent Stahi and Clipwalen to scout the perimeter. Soon they returned with news of fresh tracks headed off to the northeast, towards the Puyallup. "Many riders," said Stahi. "Maybe six tens. But they have with them their women, children and elders. We can catch them."

The village hastily packed only the most essential items, and headed deep into the wilderness towards Tenalquot Prairie, the Happy Land. Once Leschi was certain that his people were well under way, he selected a small band of scouts to double back and spy on the Bostons. Though Quiemuth counseled against it, Leschi returned with the scouts. "If the opportunity presents itself, I will speak with Challie Eden," he said. "Perhaps we can stop this before it is too late."

Charlie didn't like it. What had seemed a fairly simple mission was turning into something more complicated. Should he launch a military campaign into the wilds? He was uneasy about the idea of pursuing an entire village into the dense forest. But what was the alternative? To go back to Olympia, tail between his legs, saying that they'd knocked on the door and Leschi wasn't home, so they left a calling card inviting him to tea?

Everyone was looking to Charlie for orders. Especially that snake, J.W. Wiley, the newspaperman. "Let's go, men," he said. "Let's get 'em!" War whoops went up through the entire column. Wiley gave Charlie a small nod of approval.

Leschi and his scouts hid their ponies well, and then crept carefully to the darkest part of the northern boundary of Muck Creek Prairie, next to the sacred burial grounds. There they climbed the firs, and were quickly invisible among the boughs.

"Requisition anything useful from the village," ordered Charlie.

"Yes, Sir!" Though he hadn't intended it, the undisciplined volunteers, flush with an imaginary victory, broke ranks and poured over Yokwa village before anyone could stop them, smashing and looting everything in sight. Soldiers marauded over the plain from end to end, trampling the remaining crops into the ground, slashing at weirs and drying racks with their swords, carrying faggots from house to house, setting everything ablaze. One group of soldiers even stumbled across ancient rotting canoes hanging from the trees, which they cut down and trampled into the earth, mashing their dusty cargo of jewelry, worm-eaten blankets, and skeletons.

Later, after the troops were gone, Leschi and the scouts climbed down out of the trees. With tears in his eyes, Leschi stooped to gather shattered periwinkle shells, mixed with browning autumn leaves, and fragments of bone. Slowly, he closed his fist around the meager handful that was all that was left of First Wife. Leschi squeezed until the sharp edges cut into his flesh, then squeezed harder.

2

Grandfathers, grandmothers, and children notwithstanding, the Nisquallies proved devilishly difficult to catch. Eden's Rangers made little ground before darkness set in that first day. Then the weather turned, the temperature dropped, and a thin rain began to fall. Soon, the forest floor was muddy and slick, the underbrush cold and drenching. All day the Volunteers slogged inland, following the twisting bed of Muck Creek, over Elk Plain to the Puyallup River valley. There they forded the icy river, into which they lost a horse, but fortunately no men. They made camp on the north bank of the Puyallup, and dried what they could over smoky fires eked from soggy logs split open. Whatever they managed to dry was quickly drenched the next morning, crossing the Carbon River.

When at last they reached the Military Road, Charlie sent eight men back to Olympia for supplies and reinforcements. He figured the rest of his Company would sit tight at the nearby home of his big Irish Corporal, Michael Connell, and wait for help. It was a steep climb along the creek bed to the crest of Elhi Hill. From there, they slogged through two heavily timbered swamps littered with underbrush and fallen logs, separated by several miles of boggy clearing, before they finally burst onto Connell's Prairie.

At that moment it seemed as if all their labors were to be rewarded. The afternoon sun peeked through breaking clouds, illuminating dappled copses of silver and noble firs, streaked with red alder, bigleaf maple, and mountain ash. The pastures between the trees shimmered in gold-green waves, as breezes played over a grassland sea. In the foreground was an Indian hunting camp, already cleared by advance scouts, which in better times during summer hunts had been shared by Puyallups and Nisquallies. Connell's claim sat in the distance, a tidy log cabin and barn tucked under a tall cedar, framed by forested saw-toothed hills. Clouds banked above the hills hid Mt. Rainier, but the foothills were breathtaking on their own. Charlie was just starting to relax, nothing more vexing on his mind than whether to sleep in Connell's cabin or barn, when one of his scouts galloped in from the east.

"Indians, Sir, 'bout three miles east of here. Saw 'em fishin' down by the White River."

"How many?" asked Charlie.

"A lot."

"What's that mean, Private?"

"It means a heckuva lot, Capt'n."

"Numbers, Private," cut in Lieutenant McAllister. "Give us numbers."

"I ain't so good with numbers, Lieutenant. But heckuva lot more a them than us."

"Women and children?" asked Charlie.

"I don't think so, Capt'n. But I didn't hang around long enough to check fer tits."

Charlie scowled as he dismissed the worthless scout. This wasn't enough information to act on. Charlie ordered Jim to take a patrol out to survey the Indians' position and strength. "Talk to them if you think it's safe; try to find out their intentions," said Charlie. "Take Connell; he knows this land best. Take the Injun scouts. I want you back by dark," ordered Charlie as firmly as he could. It was already mid-afternoon, and the days were getting shorter.

"Take me too, Father," pleaded Jimmy.

"Sounds good to me, Laddie," said Jim. "You're my good luck charm." The scouting party of three Bostons and two Indians rode off at a brisk canter along the Military Road, towards the White River.

As soon as the road was swallowed by forest, the elation they'd felt on the prairie died. Brooding fir upon fir leaned in, wringing sunlight from the air. Jimmy rode with one hand on the reins, one hand on his musket. Every chatter of a squirrel or woodpecker's *kuk-kuk-kuk* caused him to jump in his saddle, tighten the grip on his weapon. The road, if such a tortured way could be dignified by so civilized a name, was poorly built and even more poorly maintained. From time to time they had to dismount to negotiate fallen timbers, or marshy areas that threatened to suck them in and break a horse's leg. Only Stahi seemed light and eager as they pressed on, and that very eagerness made Jimmy uneasy.

To call it a clearing would be an embellishment; it was a slight pause in the gloom. They'd just come round a gnarl of roots reaching up like devil's fingers, when they saw before them five, no ten, no – many warriors. Painted black and red, they were armed with muskets. Jimmy was ready to fire, but remembered the dog. *Think before firing,* he told himself. That man up there in the big felt hat. It was Leschi, his father's friend. Surely, they were safe with him.

Jimmy watched without comprehension as Stahi peeled off to the side of the trail and dived off his horse. Just as he matched the action to the shock of meaning, he heard the musket's report and the sickening thud of a ball entering his father's chest. Jim McAllister fell back. Jimmy reached out to try to stop the fall but it was dead weight, an empty shell where a moment ago his father had been. Another ball whistled past where his own head had been only a moment before. Jimmy's terrified horse bolted, and he dropped his musket trying to grab the reins. There was another shot, and Jimmy saw blood spurt from Connell's left arm, as they both spun away. Together, Jimmy, Connell, and Clipwalen galloped back into the warren of fallen timbers and slop that passed for a road, clinging tight to their horses' withers.

"Stay off the path! Ambush!" hollared Clipwalen, disappearing into the forest. Jimmy didn't trust him. He and Connell plummeted together along the crude, jumbled road. This time they did not dismount, their frightened horses leaping any obstacle they could not circumnavigate or duck beneath. Behind them, and off to the side along the road, they heard the Indian war whoop, *aaaaaiiiiiiiiiieeeeeeee*, as balls whistled by and thudded into trees. At a gallop, they rounded a corner into a full frontal volley from the trees ahead. There was a cry from Connell as another ball found its mark, and then Jimmy was alone, galloping on and on into the clearing at last, only his fury and the pungent odor of his own shit in his trousers telling him, *you're still alive, you're still alive*, but so numb with shame and bitter regret that what did it matter?

3

At the report of gunfire, Charlie turned towards Mr. Wiley and cried, "My God! Our boys are dead!" With that, all tentativeness left Captain Eden. Acting with calm assurance, he spit out order after order, marshalling his forces in the Indian camp, fortifying and supplying it with weapons, ammunition, food and water, secreting the horses at several different locations. Jimmy came flying out of the woods and would never have stopped had two men not chased him down. Then Clipwalen emerged on foot, not from the path but from a tangle of brush along a swampy area. Charlie got the news from Clipwalen, who appeared to be genuinely distraught. "Mrs. McAllister told me to look after him. How can I face her now?" he cried.

They all hunkered down inside the camp to await the siege, peering out of the few small chinks they'd hastily cut between planked timbers. Jimmy was collapsed in the back corner, shaking but silent. He had cleaned himself, but there were no spare trousers so he was given a cedar-bark loincloth found in the camp. Clipwalen wrapped him in a blanket.

"Hold your fire 'til there's a few braves within range," Charlie ordered. They didn't have long to wait. Within minutes the first warrior poked his head gingerly out of the brush to the east. Dusk was falling, and the dim visage of his painted face aroused ancient fears of the unknown savage. The Volunteers did their best to breathe softly, though their hearts pounded in their ears. Young Andrew Laws felt his knees knocking together. He prayed he wouldn't wet himself. Then another warrior appeared, and another, so that three crept through the thin light to within about sixty yards, not an easy shot, but one that could be made with a musket.

Andrew was as surprised as anyone when the weapon in his hands discharged and the report bruised his shoulder. He must've tightened his trigger finger without realizing it. His shot harmlessly sprayed dirt thirty yards short of the exposed warriors, who turned on their heels to run just as the entire company loosed a withering fusillade. A bullet from Charlie's breech-loading rifle met its intended mark, and with a cry one warrior fell. The other two never broke stride until they disappeared into the brush by the woods.

A few men scowled at Andrew, who cringed. Charlie just walked the length of the line and said, "nice shootin', men." The words were barely out of his mouth when a volley from the brush slammed into the wall of the longhouse. Then another and another. It was unnerving at first, but soon the men trapped inside began to relax as it became apparent that the Indians' arms were useless at that range against their own solid construction. After the exchange of several more rounds, firing became sporadic, as both sides elected to conserve powder and shot. Soon darkness fell, and clouds rolled back in to hide the moon.

"Look, men, we're trapped and outnumbered," whispered Charlie. "I need a volunteer to try to make it back to the Fort for help. I can't say you're gonna live to tell the tale, but then maybe it beats being holed up here."

"I'll go," came a voice from the back, and they all turned to look at half-naked Jimmy.

"Jimmy –" began Charlie.

"I said I'll go!" snapped Jimmy. "I'm already dressed Injun, you paint me up and I'll crawl right through them buggers." Still, some men balked at entrusting their lives to this shaky waif.

"I think I earned this shot," Jimmy said, his face drawn with determination. Charlie nodded.

"Me too," said Clipwalen in perfect English.

Jimmy shook his head. He was humiliated that Clipwalen knew how he'd failed his father. Besides, he still didn't trust him. "No," he said, a little too sharply, "I gotta do this myself."

"You speak *Whulshootseed?*" Charlie asked Clipwalen. Reluctantly, Clipwalen nodded in the affirmative. "You stay."

They rubbed Jimmy all over with charcoal from an old fire pit, and even rubbed down his musket barrel to try to cut any telltale glimmer. "Godspeed,"

Charlie whispered, as the near-naked, blackened boy crept out a quick crack in the door under cover of darkest darkness. He slithered off around back on his belly, clutching his musket. Creeping as silently as possible, he felt his way down the slope towards the ravine where they'd tied a group of horses. The moon emerged momentarily. Looking back up the hill, he saw one lone warrior leading away a team of horses. He was mad to shoot the bastard in the back, though it would be suicide. The moon slipped away, and the shot was gone.

So were the horses. Jimmy did not relish the thought of blundering around, looking for horses, but it would take days to get back on foot. Jimmy sat still as possible, and listened. The moon emerged for another moment, and he heard the crack of desultory musket fire in the distance. Then the clouds returned, and with them, near-total darkness. He heard the wolves and owls discussing the strange disturbances on the prairie. Then he heard a crackling in the brush, and tensed, raising his musket as he crouched behind a clump of scrub pines. To fire meant certain death. From between dark trees not thirty feet away, he saw a large, dark shape poke its head out. What was it? A cougar, an Indian, a grizzly?

Jimmy was relieved to hear a whinnying sound, that familiar sweet greeting of a horse who smells man, and thinks she's about to get some oats. It was a stray Morgan mare the Indians had overlooked. She was happy enough to offer her bit to Jimmy, who was overjoyed to take it. He led her away along the perimeter of the Military Road, down Elhi Hill, towards the Puyallup River. At last, he felt safe enough to mount her and ride. There was even a coat in her saddle bags, which Jimmy donned gratefully.

It was dawn by the time Jimmy reached the Puyallup. There was an old Indian by the crossing, standing in the river fishing. Could be that's all he was doing; could be a trap. This time, Jimmy didn't pause to figure which. He shot him dead, then watched as the *siwash* blood make a merry plume in the current.

4

Charlie decided that his men would be better off following Jimmy than waiting to be slaughtered. Two by two, then four by four, they slipped out a slot made by loosening a plank in the back of the camp shed, and crept away into the night, not stopping to rendezvous until early the next morning.

Just after midnight, the sky cleared and the near-full moon bathed *Tenalquot* in milky half-light. All was quiet. When Leschi's men held up shirts on sticks and drew no fire, their hunch that the enemy had escaped was confirmed. Still, they were elated. Kitsap, Wyamooch, and Sluggia galloped to Connell's claim, and set fire to the house and barn. The younger warriors whooped and danced around the blaze. Then Leschi rode up with other tribal elders flanking him.

"Stop this!" ordered Leschi. "Our brother Topitor has fallen this night. It was he who killed the Boston soldier." Leschi paused, a struggle within his breast. Though Topitor pulled the trigger, Leschi knew who had given the command by which his old friend, McAllister, had died. "There will be no dancing, no celebrations! Go, dress the body, give Topitor his due. He has died honorably, and we owe him this."

Ashamed, the revelers did as they were told. After the body was washed, bound in a blanket, and set high in the limb of a fir tree, Kitsap and Wyamooch returned to bragging about what a great victory they had won.

"It has only begun," said Leschi. "More troops will come from the direction of *Whulge*. Get some sleep so you are ready to fight tomorrow."

"Why should we wait for troops to come?" replied Kitsap. "We know where the white man lives. Wherever he lives on our land, now he will die." Many in the war party cheered.

"No!" cried Leschi. "This is not a raid on some little tribal village. This is war. A warrior fights armed men, not women and children."

"Only a woman cries over the death of women," taunted Wyamooch.

"And only a fool pokes at *schut-whud* – the bear – with a stick," retorted Leschi. "The Bostons are many and powerful, but right now they lack the will to fight. So long as the battle is about nothing more than Stevens' stubborn plan to pen us up where no fair-minded man would kennel his dogs, the Bostons will remain divided. But if you attack them in their houses, you will unite them in a fight for survival." Leschi looked at the faces lit by the glow of Connell's burning house. No one dared challenge him further, at least not openly, not yet. "Post sentries covering the road from *Whulge*, and get some rest. We can discuss our strategy more in the morning." Leschi saw the scowl linger on Kitsap's scarred cheek. "You too, Kitsap, and you, Wyamooch," he added, "I will see you at the council tomorrow morning."

But impetuous youth could not wait for the light of day. After most of the men were asleep, a small party of warriors led by Kitsap, Wyamooch, and Sluggia, stole off towards the north by the dim light of a gibbous moon. Nelson, the old Duwamish, could not sleep. Were those wolves he heard in the forest, or beasts of a far more dangerous kind?

Chapter Thirteen
Kaddish

1

Sunday morning. Johnny King, his maw Eliza Jones, his little half-sister Becky, and half-brother Tommy, was eatin' their porridge when they heard that shufflin' and gruntin' by the door that meant Injun. Johnny was kinda mad at Ole Nelson fer the way he'd acted the other day, but what with his step-paw a-bed fer five days with the pleursy there hadn't been much fun lately, so he figured maybe this would be fun at last. Maybe Nelson would take him down to the river and show him how to build a weir, or somethin'. So Johnny and Becky scampered over to the door with Maw, and she opened it, and even though she closed it again quicker than an eagle takes a salmon, Johnny would never forget what he saw if he lived to be a hunnert, or even just eight, which wasn't lookin' too likely right then. It was Ole Nelson who'd grunted, then stepped off to the side, and right behind him by their log shed was a scar-faced Injun Johnny'd never seen before, holding a great big Hudson's Bay fusee musket pointed smack dab at Johnny's maw. This scar-faced Injun was sighting down the barrel with the cock pulled back and his finger on the trigger, an' maybe it was only the surprise of seeing a woman 'stead of a man open the door that made him hesitate just one split second, 'cause soon as the door slammed and Johnny's maw screamed and threw her kids to the floor, that gun went *crack!* A hole splintered in the door right where Maw'd been standing not one second before. Johnny'd shot that kind of musket before, though it was near long as he was tall. They wasn't much fer hittin' what you're aiming at, but at close range that big lead ball packed a nasty wallop.

Johnny wasn't s'pose ta say hell or even think it, but right then all hell broke loose. If a little three-room cabin surrounded by a whole buncha blood-crazed Injuns miles from the nearest town, with only two men countin' his sick step-paw, one woman, two little kids, and one big seven-year-old ain't hell, then what is? Johnny looked out the main window, an' saw what seemed like a thousand of them buggers just rise right up out of the ground, all painted black and red. They was whoopin' their fool heads off and swingin' tomahawks an' shootin' off flintlocks that splintered the walls and made a fearsome racket. Course Becky and Tommy was wailin', like that was gonna do any good, but Mr. Cooper, their hired man, was returning fire with his breech-loading rifle, and then Johnny's maw grabbed his step-paw's five-shooter and emptied it.

Between the two of them, they kilt or winged one or two Injuns, and that gave 'em somethin' to think about, but not nearly enough.

Even a kid like Johnny could tell that the situation was hopeless, but Maw wouldn't give up. She grabbed the children and Johnny too, and shoved 'em into the back bedroom and made 'em lie down in the far back corner, an' then she threw the big feather bed mattress over them. Mr. Cooper was in the doorway of the room firing his rifle quick as he could load it, sweat drippin' off his big forehead, though it was a cool morning, and he was just wearing one raggy shirt. Johnny's step-paw Harvey had dragged hisself out of bed and reloaded the pistol. He was shooting out each of the windows, and there weren't no other weapons, so what more could they do? Balls were flyin' everywhere, and Johnny pulled his head in when he heard one thump right into the mattress. It didn't go through all them feathers, so they was safe for a few minutes anyway. Johnny sat under there in the dark for what seemed like forever, listenin' to Becky and Tommy whimperin', maybe even doin' a little hisself, truth be told, and there was shooting and screamin' from above but it was all muffled and far away, like it was happenin' somewheres else.

Johnny poked his head out for a breath of fresh air, just as he heard a cry: "Oh God, I'm shot!" He saw his step-paw stagger into Maw's arms and she cried, "Oh, Harvey, don't say so!" as the pistol fell from his hand. She opened his shirt, and there was a huge sucking wound near the nipple. As Mr. Cooper covered her with the pistol, Johnny saw Maw help his step-paw back to bed, though she must have known that there was no point in putting a dying man to bed. Johnny pulled his head back under the mattress. Mr. Cooper kept firing and loading, while Maw prayed by the side of Harvey's bed, askin' Jesus to let them and his real paw and Zeke all meet again in Heaven. Johnny heard his step-paw interrupt her prayers to tell Maw he loved her, and that if she loved him she'd forget about him and Jesus right that second and go save herself and the children if she could. Johnny peeked out again, and Maw was just clinging to Step-Paw and shootin' his pistol all together. Step-paw began to cough and choke, and then he was quiet, so Johnny figured him for a goner and pulled his head back under the mattress.

The next thing Johnny heard was Maw and Mr. Cooper talkin' 'bout escape, his maw telling Mr. Cooper to pry off the window stop with an ax, and then he heard her yell "Go now!" Maw screamed, then it was smothered. Johnny set real still and didn't look out. Everythin' got real quiet for a while, and even Tommy knew enough to keep his snivelin' trap shut. When after a while Johnny was just thinking 'bout maybe peekin' out, suddenly the mattress lifted right off of them leaving them blinkin' and trembling and huddled on the floor together, arms over their heads as if that could stop a tomahawk.

When no one kilt them on the spot, Johnny risked looking up. There was Ole Nelson, peering down at them through his scraggly hair. Behind him other Injuns was looting food from the kitchen and clothes from the wardrobe and ammunition and stuff. All the windows was shattered, the furniture broken up, and the walls full of holes. Nelson reached down, his big hand swallowed Johnny's, and Johnny felt hisself being lifted to his feet. "*Halo kwass,*" Nelson whispered – "No afraid." Johnny didn't know what to think. "*Chahko hyak,*" – "Come quick." Was he savin' them, or leadin' them to slaughter? They did as they was told – what choice did they have? They went out past the puddle of blood his step-paw'd left on the floor, then right through the other Injuns in plain sight, and no one paid them any mind. They huddled behind Nelson out there by Maw's little flower patch, as the other Injuns brought out blankets and a few smashed chairs, and jammed 'em under the house. The Injuns placed a torch to 'em, and soon the whole house was ablaze, and Johnny was hot and sweating and shivering all at the same time. Looking in the direction of the Brannans and Kings, Johnny saw smoke risin' there too, any hope of a quick rescue gone on the wind.

While the other Injuns was distracted by the roaring flames, Nelson backed towards the edge of the clearing with the children in tow. Then he knelt down and spoke quickly to Johnny in broken English. "Go Mr. Thomas's," he ordered, referring to their schoolmaster who lived two miles downriver. "Go straight. Some Indians kill you. Not me. Go!"

Johnny didn't need no more urging, and he grabbed up the young'uns an' lit off. Although it was mornin', the woods were dark, the path narrow and hard to follow. Johnny'd never gone the whole way all by hisself, and Little Becky was cryin' a bit too loud. Johnny silenced her by hissing, "Injuns kill – hush!"

Tommy didn't get it; he thought Johnny was playin' some kinda mean trick. "Want Mawwwwww," he bawled, "I'm hungryyyy." No amount of shusshing would shut him up. So Johnny made them both promise to wait real quiet, hidden in a little sink hole in the ground, which he covered over with fir boughs an' called Fort Tommy Jones. Then he went to fetch some food. Creepin' back to their claim, he arrived just in time to see l'il Georgie-Porgie strapped to an Injun pony, being led away howling. Johnny was mad as a hornet; boy oh boy, if he'd just had his paw's five-shooter, he'd a rescued Georgie-Porgie on the spot an' then they'd ride off with the ponies, and he'd save Becky and Tommy and find Maw and Mr. Cooper, and ride right into Seattle with everyone cheering. Yessir!

When he was sure they was gone, Johnny crossed double-quick to the smoulderin' remains of the shed where they stored their taters. Sure enough, some of them taters was roasted from the fire, and he carried them back to his half-brother and sister, wrapped in a singed blanket. They were all starving, their breakfast having been so brutally interrupted, so they made an eager feast of this bounty.

Feeling better, the children took off along the path to Mr. Thomas's, but it soon became clear that l'il Tommy couldn't keep up, so Johnny had to piggy-back him all the long way. At last they arrived. Johnny was sorry to find no one t'home 'cept fer Mr. Thomas's dog, Lucky. Becky and Tommy were too little to unnerstand, so they were just happy to find this cute l'il pup, who jumped and played and yipped as if this was just another great day in the forest, which to him it was. When the children begged Johnny to let them take Lucky along, he refused, an' he brought them both to tears by chasing the poor animal off with a stick. Heck, he hated to do it hisself, but someone had ta be the grownup, and that's what he figured his step-paw woulda done. "If'n we see an Injun and need to hide, that critter'll give us away, sure as can be," he explained, but still they cried and cried and Becky beat at him with her fists and said, "Mawww, I want Mawwww," and Tommy joined in, and it was a long time before they would go anywhere's with him.

Finally, when they would, where was they ta go? It was afternoon now, late October, and a-fore long the sun would be gettin' low and it was already kinda chilly. The nearest settlement was maybe fifteen or twenty miles away, and Johnny sure didn't know how t' get there. So's his feet took him along the familiar paths, and from time to time he called, "Maw! Maw!" or "Cooper! Cooper!" Then suddenly he'd clam up, scairt that he'd alert some passin' Injun, who'd finish 'em off with a big stone club.

They went along this way fer a time, and pretty soon they was back where they'd started, the pull of a home that no longer was, bein' too strong to escape. Then Johnny saw off to the side of the path, some hunnert feet or so from their cabin, something that made his heart stop right there in his chest – it was Maw! Lyin' there in the dirt – Maw! "Mawwwwww!" he cried, running like all get out, tears whipping off by his ears, and the little ones was left in his dust as they all run at her quick as they could. Then Johnny was touchin' her, and she was cold and covered with blood and dirt, but she opened her eyes, smiled, and whispered, "Oh Lord, thank-you, thank-you, I must truly be in heaven now." Johnny kissed her and told her they weren't kilt, that Nelson had rescued them, and now here she was alive too, and they could all go back and live together, and be happy forever.

Maw got a real serious look on her bruised-up face, and that stopped him. "Johnny, you shoulda been gone far from here by now." His face fell at Maw's scoldin'. "Johnny, dear, I love you so," she added tenderly, but the serious look was still there. "I know this is hard, but you are my little man right now, so you gotta do jest exactly what I say, right?"

"Sure, Maw, anything," said Johnny, not even beginning to imagine what that might be.

"I cain't live, Johnny, I'm hurt too bad –"

"No, Maw –"

"Yes, Johnny. Now listen to me." She coughed, and drew breath with difficulty. "You're gonna have to go without me."

Johnny's whole body went numb, so cold it froze his tears. Becky and Tommy just cried on Maw's other side, nuzzling up to her blood-stained apron.

Those trees, those damn trees. Straining, Maw drew a breath. "You take your brother and sister and follow the river back up to Thomas's –"

"He ain't there, Maw."

"Then follow the White River all the way up, jest keep goin' to the Duwamish if you have to, 'til you find someone to help you."

"But Maw," said Johnny. How could he leave her lyin' there?

"Johnny, I want you to remember what I'm gonna say now, and I want you to tell it to Becky and Tommy when they're older."

After a reluctant pause, Johnny said, "Yeah, Maw?"

"You kids never be scairt, ok?" Johnny looked away. "OK? Look at me, Johnny." He looked. "You never be scairt, hear me?" Johnny nodded. "After what happened, you could live your whole lives bein' scairt, but I don't want that. You gotta live yer life, not run from it." She coughed again, more a gurgle like a stopped drain, but then somehow she found the breath to go on. "Whenever you start feelin' scairt, remember: I love you, and that don't never die. I'll be watchin' you, each one of you, and if you start feelin' scairt you kin talk to me, ok? And whenever you talk to me, I'll send you a sign to show I hear you, and I'm watchin' out fer you, and then everythin' will be all right. You unnerstand?"

Now Johnny was crying, he couldn't help it, he just was. "Yeah, Maw."

"Now, go," she said. It seemed she was letting go of her own life right along with them.

"Up, Mawww," said Tommy, reaching out, trying to lift her limp arm to place it around his back.

She mustered the strength to open her eyes again. "Mamma cain't right now, Tommy. What I want you to do, each of you, is give your maw a kiss, and then Johnny is gonna take you on a long walk in the woods, and you do just what Johnny sez, and you'll be safe. OK?" Eliza Jones savored a last kiss from each one of her children. As they stood to go, she shut out the dark trees and imagined that her children were trees, a bright forest of children growing to love this land. Nothing hurt more than this final parting, not that scar-faced Injun's roughness between her legs, not the lead ball in her gut or the blows to her head and breast. Still, she knew there was one last thing she had to do before she could let go. With her last flicker of life she gave her children a parting gift, the gift of her familiar cheery smile. Her little ones smiled back, and then they were gone. Eliza closed her eyes, and at last those damned trees were gone too.

2

The first survivors straggled into Seattle around ten o'clock that night, piled together in two canoes coming down the Duwamish. They told horrific tales of Indians gone mad, firing wildly into doorways as they made their escape, of the sounds of gunfire and desperate shrieks from neighboring claims. Charlie Salitat, a friendly, broad-faced Duwamish, known and well liked by everyone, volunteered to join the latter-day Paul Reveres sent out to sound the alarm. Within twenty-four hours, the American community from Bellingham to Tumwater was in a panic. Claims that had been the object of back-breaking dawn to dusk labor for years, were abandoned in hours. Wagons ground their way through the boggy earth of the hinterlands, towards the strongholds of Fort Steilacoom, Olympia or Seattle, piled with clocks, beds, linens, frightened cats, tables and chairs, plows, muskets with powder and shot, cooking utensils, flour and lard, a wicker coop of squawking chickens, squabbling relatives, and braying children. Behind them paraded the mule, hog, pig, cow, sheep, turkey and goat, plus a few hound dogs. Everywhere, settlers were building tall narrow blockhouses, with tiny chinks for their gun barrels to peek out, in bluster and terror. At the Fort, Colonel Casey put his troops out of their garrison to make room for the women and children. Soon the garrison was packed from wall to wall with all the stuff that the wagons had carried, and no invading force of Indians could possibly have done a better job immobilizing the Army.

Into this frenzy rode Jimmy McAllister, bearing news of the death of his father and Connell, which spread like measles and wasn't near as welcome. He'd ridden all day October 28, before collapsing for four hours. He was off again before dawn, and arrived at outlying settlements early the 29th, just as rumors of the massacre began to fly. The two reports, repeated and embellished, made it sound as if merciless savages had risen throughout the Territory in a coordinated attack, killing hundreds of white men, women, and children.

As soon as Jimmy galloped out of the forest into the clearing by his home, he wished he hadn't. His mother was at the door in an instant, waving and smiling. Jimmy would rather cut out his own tongue than break the terrible news to her. There was no need to speak; Martha read his face the moment he came into focus. "I'm sorry Ma," was all he said, but she shook off his words as her eyes turned hard.

"Leschi!" Martha cursed, then dropped to the floor in a dead faint.

3

Johnny'd carried and dragged Becky and Tommy all the way back to Thomas's and even a few miles further on by nightfall. They felt pretty bleak by the time they burrowed down under a blanket of fir boughs, squinched together for warmth and comfort, their bellies churnin'. They'd eaten a little duck potato, the tuber the Indians called *wapato*, which Maw had shown Johnny how to find, but they had no way of makin' a fire. It was tough and bitter when raw, so that didn't work out too good. They was shiverin' and whimperin', and finally it was only exhaustion that quieted Tommy and Becky in time for them not to be heard by the Injun walking down the path in the moonlight. He didn't seem like a bad sort – he had on a reg'lar shirt an' trousers and leather boots. He was maybe a little older than Johnny's step-paw, and his face wasn't painted, and he warn't carryin' no musket, though who knows what he had up his sleeve. Johnny knew they wouldn't last much longer out there all alone, so he decided to risk it.

Real quiet, he let the Injun pass so's not to tip him to where Becky and Tommy slept, just in case. Then Johnny snuck out onto the path and gave a short whistle. The Injun spun about and drew a pistol, and Johnny's heart near stopped right then, but soon as the Injun could see what was what he laughed, and put the pistol back. "You gave me a start there, young fella," he said, and though Johnny couldn't unnerstand the words, he sure unnerstood the tone. It was friendly, and *thank-you Jesus* as Maw always said, *we're saved!*

Johnny roused Becky and Tommy, who was scairt at first but soon got over it. The Injun took Johnny by the hand, Becky took Johnny's hand, and Tommy took Becky's, and that's how they walked to the Injun's camp. His *klootchman* fed them tasty soft-boiled wapato, baked salmon, and dried berries, and they slept on puffy warm blankets. Then the Injun took them by canoe up to where the White and Black Rivers mixed into the Duwamish, and by the end of the next day they were handed over safe and well fed, to Doc Maynard in Seattle.

Johnny never got that Injun's name, but one thing he always remembered about him was his hand, how good it had felt, even though it was missing two fingers.

4

There was no council the morning after the first battle of *Tenalquot* Prairie. Leschi awoke to the news that young warriors had defied his orders, and gone on a raiding party against White River settlers. When the sun stood half-way up *Ta-co-bet*, the warriors returned, with blood-crusted hair and a small Boston prisoner. They thundered through the camp, raising muskets, fists, and cries in exaltation. Wyamooch galloped straight at Leschi, pulling up at the last moment, his pony's clattering hooves spraying the unflinching Chief with dirt. Grabbing little George King by the hair, Wyamooch lifted the boy's head off his horse's rump. "Since you care so for the white man, Leschi," declared Wyamooch, "I have brought you a slave." A quick flash of knife blade cut the cord that bound Georgie, who tumbled at Leschi's feet with a muffled cry. There he lay, curled up, very still.

Leschi was angry, but what had happened could not be undone. *Seatco*, demon of dark forces, had been loosed. He himself had sown the seeds. Who was he to turn his back on the harvest?

"I accept your present, young warrior, with one condition – this boy shall not be a slave, but a warrior like you. If he combines your strength with what you lack – wisdom – then he shall be a Chief some day." Wyamooch glared at Leschi. "You make war against women and little children and think that makes you a big man?" Leschi said, returning the glare. "I will teach you what it takes to be a big man. You who have killed this boy's father will raise him like a son, show him the ways of our people!" Wyamooch said nothing as he rode off.

Kitsap was not so timid. Dismounting, he challenged Leschi face to face. "Why should we follow you, old man?" he taunted. "What great victory have you brought us?" There were eighty warriors and as many again of women, children, and elders, gathered about on the prairie, watching intently, wondering, *who will be our leader?* Kitsap's challenge stirred murmurings of discontent. People were scared. The brash young men of action offered a clear plan they could understand – kill all the whites.

"You think you have brought us a victory?" thundered Leschi, his profile sharp against looming *Ta-co-bet* on the horizon. "Foolish child! Do we have our land? Have you forgotten why we fight? It is not so Bostons die, but so we can live. If you think it is us or them, you are thinking like Stevens. Such madness can only lead to reprisals against our own women and children. Thanks to you, our people are less secure, not more. We are further from our real goal. Is that your 'victory'? A few more such victories, and all will be lost!"

Leschi turned to address his people. "Now that our young men have made this a war of extermination, troops will arrive very soon. We must maintain round the clock sentries on the road from *Whulge*. Children, elders, and those women not needed here to support their warriors, should immediately go upriver to the Green River stronghold of our brother, Kanaskat. All able-bodied fighting men who are not yet here, must answer our call – send messengers to all our brothers. Now, more than ever, the red man must stand united."

Then Leschi turned back to face Kitsap. "I am not so old that I could not kill you on the spot." Kitsap tensed, his hand on his spear. "But unlike you, I am old enough to know better. Your recklessness is born of a righteous rage against the white man for stealing our land. Your people need you, my brother. Stevens would rather we were divided; divided we are weak. United, we can win this war." Leschi paused, as Kitsap wavered. "If you stay," warned Leschi, "you will follow my command. There can only be one Chief in time of war." His dark eyes bore into Kitsap, but they were caring, the eyes of a father disciplining an unruly son.

Kitsap's grip on his spear relaxed. He nodded, the two men embraced, and the cheers of the people echoed across *Tenalquot*, rising into the thin air of *Ta-co-bet's* eternal snow.

5

They didn't come from *Whulge*, they came down out of the mountains at a gallop, seven crazed soldiers. They burst from the trees onto a smattering of unsuspecting braves and their *klootchmen*, who were milling about a cooking pit by the remains of Connell's house. The harelipped British surgeon, Matthew P. Burns, reached past the broad spotted breast of his prize Appaloosa, King

William, yanked Winyea's pistol right out of his belt, and poured the powder from the pan back down in Winyea's face. "Look here," lisped Dr. Burns to the small squad of express riders detailed by Lieutenant Slaughter to carry military dispatches back to the Fort, "I've got the drop on Chief Lethi. I'm gonna turn him into a good Indian – *memaloothe* him here and now, right o?"

Tony Rabbeson nodded eagerly, even though he suspected that this young fellow wasn't Leschi, but Ben Moses intervened. "Y'know, doc, that might not be too smart, seeing as there are only seven of us, and Lord knows how many of them hereabouts."

Joseph Miles, a nervous lawyer from Olympia who was regretting his rash decision to volunteer, agreed. Eyes darting hither and yon, he whispered under his breath, "Confound it, Dr. Burns, you'll get us all killed!"

"Bollockths to the lot o' you!" cried the bitter doctor, drawing his pistol. With a flick of his whip William Tidd disarmed the rash physician, saving poor Winyea. Tidd donned a smile for show, and spoke in Chinook, "Please excuse our hot-headed friend. We come in friendship, and wish you well."

A scar-faced Indian stepped up. His concern was not so much these seven; they could be taken. It was the greater force that might be coming up behind. "Friendship is good," he said, stalling for time. "We are peaceful Indians."

Tidd played along. Though the prickling hairs at the nape of his neck urged, *flee! flee!* instead he turned his smile on a particularly fat *klootchman*, and calmly traded some jerky for a pair of moccasins. "Wait'll I show these to the Lieutenant," he said in Chinook, glancing meaningfully back towards foothills that loomed cold in the afternoon mist. "We're the advance for a large force that was planning to camp at Connell's," Tidd added, turning again towards the Indians. "What happened here?" He nodded casually towards the blackened ruins.

"We don't know anything about that," said the scar-faced Indian. "We're just here to tend our winter stock."

Tidd nodded, satisfied with the exchange of lies. "*Klahowya tillicums!*" he said. The express riders started off with false nonchalance down the narrow dirt Military Road, moving quickly from walk to canter to gallop, flinching at the vividly imagined shot in the back. The broad exposed prairie whizzed past, as each man made a silent inventory of life to that point, too often coming up short. Entering a swampy thicket of brush, menacing fir trees swallowed them up, seven pale, trembling morsels.

Tony Rabbeson saw the flash an instant before he heard the shots. It came from across a small dank clearing beyond the right shoulder of Ben Moses up ahead, followed by a strangled cry from behind. As Tony's mount spun in fear, he struggled to get off a return volley into the whirling panorama of mist, smoke, moss-encrusted logs, Joseph Miles' gnarled fingers reaching up from the lagoon, Indian shadows melting back into the forest, rotting tree trunks, Miles' gushing neck wound, rich layers of fir needles shading from yellow to green to purple to black. Ahead, Ben Moses was already crouched forward in a hard gallop; behind, Miles staggered to his feet, his fingers still probing upward in search of a helping hand. Tony sheathed his smoking musket, put his head down, and dug his heels hard into his terrified mount, just as another musket blast thundered through the swamp.

Abram Benton Moses' own personal reckoning was not going well. His father was shot long ago on the streets of lower Manhattan for wearing a prayer shawl in public. After that, he and his elder brother, Abraham Jackson, had watched their immigrant mother scratch out a meager existence, taking in laundry. At their unplumbed tenement, she was forced to pound sheets clean in a rain barrel after shattering the ice on top with a rock. After she died, the boys had fled the New York City orphanage, and just kept heading west until they ran out of continent. Jackson got himself a nice shop, and then a wife, and now had two girls, one with brown curls and a scholar's curiosity, the other a little pixie with a merry smile that showed where her teeth had been. What did he have to show for thirty-two years of being Ben Moses? Not much. He'd been sheriff for a while, and too busy to marry. He rented a room that could be anybody's. Sure, he had plans. When he hit thirty-five, he'd look for a wife. Together, he and Jackson would save up the money for a rabbi, and build the Territory's first synagogue. Then he wanted a son to introduce to the pleasures of *Shabbat*, the deep mysteries of *Torah*.

Yes, Ben Moses had it all planned. But he hadn't planned on this. As they sped from the swamp, the burning cold in his lung told him that no matter how hard he gripped the reins, he'd never live to see that synagogue. Or that son.

A mile on, Ben's horse pulled up and Ben slumped down. The others were all ahead; only Tony came up from the rear. *God-damn Jew boy*, Tony thought, as Ben's horse began to circle back. Then Ben lifted himself with difficulty and Tony saw it, the bright red stain on the front of Ben's jacket. Tony reached out to hold a wobbly Ben by the shoulder; winced at what else he saw. A matching stain on the back of Ben's jacket. The ball had passed right through him.

Ben's eyes flickered open. He saw it was Tony; he smiled sheepishly. "Hey Tony, it's all right," he said. Tony said nothing. "Go," said Ben. "Save yourself."

Tony was sorely tempted. But no, he couldn't do it. Not twice in one day, anyway, thinking of poor Miles with his outstretched hand, left behind in the swamp, grasping at nothing. Tony led Ben's mount well off to the side of the road, got Ben down and settled in a dry spot, and covered him with his own coat. He gave him a skin of water to drink. "Hang in there, you ole varmit," he said. Then added, more tenderly, "I'm comin' back, so you better be alive when I get here." Ben's eyes said thanks.

Tony mounted and galloped away down the Military Road, eager to close the gap between himself and the rest of the express riders. About a mile ahead, six Nisqually sentries stood guarding the western approach to *Tenalquot* prairie. They'd heard the shots, but concluded that their tribesmen were hunting game. Sentry duty was long and boring. It dulled the senses. With luck, there would be fresh venison when they returned. With a full belly, a young brave could find the energy to stay up late, then creep up on a pretty young maiden, to give her a gift of a kind face, whittled in alder or pine.

Without warning, the sentries were overwhelmed from behind by an avalanche of hoofbeats and sudden gunfire. A young brave fell, his hands trying desperately to hold together what *Sah-hah-lee Tyee* had made perfect. Boston and Nisqually tangled in the brush, hand to hand, until a knife flashed and the kind face dropped with the woodcarver. A musket shot, another warrior down, his ear running red, the shot followed by a shaggy harelipped madman flying off his mount with a deranged wail. The surviving sentries turned and ran. Dr. Burns never faltered; ignoring the calls of his comrades, he disappeared after the three survivors, into the bush and certain death.

It was then that Tony Rabbeson arrived, bearing sad tidings of Miles and Moses. Against Tidd's better judgment, Tony persuaded them to return for Moses. Riding back east as darkness fell was the last thing common sense would dictate, but they had by now entered into a state of such brittle intensity that no sense was common. When they arrived at the spot where Tony had hidden Ben, he was still alive, though very weak.

"Tony," said Ben, "you've proved yourself a true *khaver.* Please," he struggled for breath, "give this to my brother." Ben extracted a battered oval locket, engraved with a six-pointed star.

Tony opened it. There was a grimy lock of grey hair inside. He snapped it shut. "I will, Ben," he promised.

"Tell Charlie not to take it out on that girl of his."

Tony was silent.

Ben's teeth clenched as he convulsed. Tidd felt in his pockets, produced a flask, from which Ben took a slug. He wouldn't keep it; said "you need it more than me."

"We could work somethin' up to ride you in," offered Tony. Ben just shook his head curtly. "Get goin'," he said. After they mounted, he added, "Boys, if you get out of this alive, remember me!" As Tony pulled the reins to ride off into the gloom, he was surprised to feel his pock-marked cheeks hot and wet.

Although that was the last time any man saw Abram Benton Moses alive, he did not die right away. As he lay waiting for death, he watched night fall, listened to the owl and the wolf, felt the chill of fresh rain over his still-warm flesh, and was grateful for it all. Then he said *Kaddish* out loud to the trees, celebrating the greatness of G-d, praying for peace of mind, peace between people, peace between nations.

Chapter Fourteen
Slaughter

1

Colonel Silas Casey and his adjutant, Lieutenant Augustus V. Kautz, made an odd couple. Casey, unchanged from his West Point days, was a big Irishman with muscles in his head and horseshit on his boots. Kautz was a prim and polished Austrian-American; with his pointy beard, tight buttoned jacket, gleaming saber, and spit-shined boots, he was a monocle short of a young Kaiser.

"Governor!" boomed Casey, as he and Kautz strode into the Governor's corner office overlooking Puget Sound and the Olympics, "top o' the mornin' to you!" Casey reeled in Stevens by his outstretched hand, enveloping him in a bear hug, and thumping him on the back.

"Colonel," replied Stevens stiffly, as soon as he'd disentangled himself from the big man's paws. "It's a pleasure to see you again. I think you know Secretary Mason, and I've taken the liberty of inviting our Territorial commander, Colonel Blunt." Mason flicked his locks back and gingerly stepped within range of a bear hug, while looking down his nose to appear as un-huggable as possible. At Casey's touch Mason jumped back to make room for Blunt, who slapped his paw into Casey's and tried to crush it. He found that Casey crushed harder, even as his bright green eyes professed innocence.

Casey introduced Lieutenant Kautz, who clicked his heels and gave a quick bow from the neck up. "Don't mind Kautz," said Casey, "he's like the stiff Colonel in the old story."

"What's that?" asked Blunt, who had taken an interest in everything involving Colonels.

"The stiff Colonel is at a dinner, ya see, and a pretty young lady seated by his side can't get more than, 'Yes, M'am' or 'no, M'am' out of him for an hour. A young civilian who has been watching the whole thing finally draws him aside and whispers, 'Colonel, can't you see that the young lady is yours for the taking, if you would only loosen up? When was the last time you were with a woman?' '1830' snaps the Colonel. 'Well, Sir, no wonder!' said the young gentleman, feeling quite smug, 'so long ago.' 'not so long,' says the Colonel, taking out his pocket watch, 'it's only 1930 now'!"

Har! Har! Har! bellowed the appreciative Colonel Blunt. Kautz's mustache twitched over a slight smile. Stevens chuckled indulgently, and then proffered a box of cigars, which were accepted all about. Within minutes the room was thick with a satisfying blue haze.

"The Colonel and I fought together down in Mexico," Stevens informed the others. "Battle of Churubusco it was, and we were two green Lieutenants fresh out of West Point –"

"I was green," interrupted Casey. "The Governor here was red-hot. He single-handedly turned back General Anaya's charge, that he did."

"I rose to the occasion," allowed Stevens, modestly.

"Indeed you did, Sir," flattered Casey. "I believe you left the service a Brevet Major?" Stevens nodded. "But you did leave the service, Governor –" and suddenly Stevens wasn't so sure that he liked the turn of the conversation. Casey sat back and puffed at his cigar with a meaningful smile.

The Governor had been expecting something like this. He knew that General Wool resented his direct command over the Territorial Volunteers. Well, Casey was a brute, but he should have learned long ago that he was no match for Isaac I. Stevens. "The Colonel here is himself no slouch when it comes to the manly art of warfare," said the Governor. "He and I trained at West Point, and learned to respect one another." Stevens crossed to a well-stocked liquor cabinet located just behind Casey. "Whiskey, Colonel?" He hefted the bottle over the Colonel's head and cocked an eyebrow.

"That's another thing we share, ain't it Isaac," said Casey, twisting in his seat, then standing to tower over Stevens, "a real nose for the sour mash. Why sure, it's after five – in the mornin' – don't mind if I do." Stevens poured shots all around, though Mason and Kautz evinced no intention of imbibing. "Reminds me of the old joke," continued Casey, "Irishman walks out of a saloon." He stopped, waiting for Blunt to catch up. *Har! Har! Har!*

The Governor merely smiled. "Colonel," he said, "I'm sure you left that comfortable fort of yours for reasons other than to regale us with your witticisms."

"I did. We're sendin' Lieutenant Slaughter to take care of them Nisquallies up by Connell's Prairie. I'd appreciate it, Isaac, if you'd keep your Volunteers out of the way. They've already stirred up a hornet's nest of trouble."

"Pull in yer reins, Colonel!" It was Blunt. "Our boys finished what them *siwash* started, and took down more of them than they got of us."

"They didn't finish a doggone thing, *Colonel*," snapped Casey, with cruel emphasis on Blunt's rank. "Your untrained men burned down the Chief's village, and provoked a fight when no fight was necessary. Now we got dead

Volunteers, dead express riders, dead civilians, and the whole territory in a panic. I'd say it's just starting, wouldn't you?"

"Now, now," said the Governor, "let's not get our dander up. We're all on the same side here. So, tell me Casey," he continued, skipping the "Colonel" part altogether, "what do you suggest?"

"General Wool has ordered me to send troops out to respond to the uprising. What I suggest, if you want to use that word, is that the civilian authority stand back and let the military do its job. There's no precedent for civilian control over the military in the Territories, even with volunteers."

Stevens' eyes narrowed. "I'm not looking for precedents, Colonel, I'm making them." The two men glared at one another. "This is an emergency," continued the Governor. "All measures necessary to preserve the existence of the Territory are legal. Legality follows necessity in time of war, isn't that what Professor Thayer used to say?"

"Yessir," parried Casey, "and the President fired him."

"The same President who wiped out the Seminoles, and ran the Cherokees out of Georgia," shot back Stevens. "It's a law right out of the Old Testament – self defense."

Casey leaned across the Governor's big rough-hewn desk, mussing the neatly arranged territorial seal and ink set. "Listen, Isaac, as long as you're playing military man, I'll feel free to give you a little political advice, which is so plain that everyone in the Territory can see it except you. If you weren't so pig-headed about sticking the Nisquallies up on a worthless bluff for no damn reason at all, we wouldn't be in this fix in the first place." At 'pig-headed' the veins pulsed in Stevens' neck, but he held his tongue. "'Military necessity,' as you call it, might require General Wool and me to tell the boys back in the real Washington who's stirring up trouble out here. Then they can order you to give the Indians a suitable reservation, and take away their reason to fight." Casey leaned back. "Now, you don't want that, do you? It's not too late to bend a little and come out looking like a statesman. Why don't you let our boy Slaughter take Leschi a message – he lays down his arms; you give him a little piece of the river. Heck, its a big river, we don't need every gawld-darned fish, do we?"

Now it was Stevens' turn to lean across his desk. "You trust these savages, Colonel? Or is this meddlesome advice coming from your commander? This isn't about a piece of the river. This is about which race is to be dominant. Your General's always had a soft spot for Injuns, ever since the Cherokee. Well, I don't share that foolish weakness, and I don't think the American people do either." Stevens paused, and silence hung heavy in the room. He intoned the next words one by one, pounding them out on his desk. "*This – is – war.*" Colonel Casey squinted and studied Stevens' face as if he'd never seen him before. "It's a sure bet those poor folks up on the White River don't have any fancy ideas about the Noble Savage." Stevens' voice dripped with ridicule.

"Governor –"

"NO!" Stevens was now in a rage. "You come sniveling in here, asking me to reward Leschi after that massacre?" cried Stevens. "I intend to wipe every hostile Indian in Washington Territory from the face of the map. And I'll use my own troops to do it, if necessary."

Casey rose slowly, shaking his head in disgust. "The President will hear about this."

"My old friend Franklin certainly will. Wait 'til he hears about all the interference I've had to put up with from you and your gutless General."

"Look, Isaac," said Casey, playing his final trump card, "you owe me. You know it, and I know it."

Blunt and Mason were surprised to see their commander falter. What was this secret bond between the two men? "Oh, it's that, is it Silas?" the Governor stammered. "I'd a done the same for you."

"I know," said Casey, but he didn't.

Stevens poured another shot and downed it in a single motion. "All right," he said, "here's what we're gonna do. My volunteers will go out with your Lieutenant Slaughter, under his command, for this one campaign. But I'm warning you, if Slaughter doesn't live up to his name and finish this damn thing, I will not answer to you, or General Wool, or anybody else!"

"Except God," replied Casey, and with a diffident salute he marched out, wondering if he hadn't made a mistake that day on the field of Churubusco.

2

Twenty-eight year old Lieutenant Will Slaughter and his men returned November 1st from their fruitless campaign against the Yakamas. They had endured an arduous autumn crossing of the Cascades, only to beat a hasty retreat back after learning that the troops from Fort Dalles had been defeated by Chief Kamiakan. This vital intelligence was gained by their scout, former Hudson's Bay Company trader John Edgar, the same man who had once fought by Leschi's side in defense of Fort Nisqually. The troops arrived back at Fort Steilacoom exhausted, to find their barracks full of ladies, mewling infants, hissing geese, and squealing piglets. This inconvenienced the men more than their mutton-chopped commanding officer; Lieutenant Slaughter relished the thought of a few nights alone in his Steilacoom home with his dark-eyed wife, Mary.

Gentle Mary Slaughter had sat up half the previous night, consoling Joseph Miles's widow. Dark circles above pale cheeks betrayed the worry she sought to conceal behind a warm smile for her husband. Ever since that day three years before, when seventeen-year-old Mary Wells was prompted by love for a young Lieutenant to leave her merchant father's snug home overlooking Lake Huron, cares and woe had never been far off. She did not complain, though his postings had taken them on the churning seven-month voyage around Cape Horn to San Francisco by mistake, then back through the malarial Isthmus of Panama at the stroke of an Army Quartermaster's gum eraser, and out West yet again by the same yellow-feverish route when the Army finally made up its mind. Each voyage was a nightmare of seasickness for them both, but they held their chins up, except when plastered to the gunnels.

Now they were alone in their room under the covers. This was her favorite time, the time after desire was slaked, when he held her in his arms, and his breathing softened into sleep. Her fingers idly wandered the hairs over his heart as she inhaled his scent, pinning it to memory. Deep inside, she imagined the stirrings of their shared tomorrow, always now at the forefront of her thoughts. Should she tell him? She didn't want him to worry; she could worry for them both. No, not both – *all*. They were a family now, really a family, though for the time being she was the only one who knew it.

The headlines blaring from the Olympia *Pioneer & Democrat* warned that their time together would be short. Already they had seen the shocking story of INDIAN SNEAK AMBUSH ON CONNELL'S PRAIRIE! Only a day later, there was a special edition. MASSACRE OF INNOCENTS!!! cried the masthead – *Chief Leschi Leads Horrible Massacre of White River Settlers – Unarmed Men Women and Children Cruelly Murdered.* The text editorialized in words suggested to Mr. Wiley by the Governor himself: "We trust they will be WIPED OUT – blotted from existence as a tribe."

The next morning, the ruins of breakfast scattered in the kitchen, Will received his orders and was gone so quickly that Mary never had the chance to share their news. She just stood at the door in a daze, a dewdrop of early morning passion moist against her thigh. It was only as she watched his back disappearing at a brisk trot that she cried out, but he didn't hear. She'd meant to tell him. Maybe if he knew, he would be extra careful.

Lieutenant Slaughter went back up the Military Road, leading a company of one hundred men, half Regulars and half Volunteers. For incentive they marched past the scene of the White River massacre, stopping to bury the bodies. They found Mrs. Jones where her children had kissed her, Mr. Jones roasted in the ruined bed, and Enos Cooper by some trampled fruit saplings he'd blistered his hands to plant, shot through the heart. They found Georgie-Porgie's parents, Mr. and Mrs. King, half-eaten by wolves, near the ashes of their cabin. They found Mr. Brannon in a pool of caked blood, tufts of hair, and torn clothing. Some fingers were missing, and his palms were shredded in ribbons from a futile effort to ward off repeated thrusts of the sharp sawmill file left imbedded in his throat. There was no sign of Mrs. Brannon, or her infant son – until Corporal William Northcraft got thirsty, and went to draw water from the well. There, at the bottom of the ten foot shaft, her head square in the bucket and her feet sticking up – a lady. Nestled between her legs, as if it had crawled there for comfort, lay the dead infant.

Slaughter's men sent the bodies of McAllister, Moses, and Miles, west for proper burial. On a bleak November day just perfect for funerals, the Fort Steilacoom bugler sounded Tattoo. Young widows choked out farewells. Martha clutched tight to the bloody hankie she'd so recently tucked, fresh and clean, into Jim's breast pocket.

Back at Connell's Prairie, Slaughter's troops planted Michael Connell beneath the tallest cedar on his claim, and wrote to his father back in County Sligo that he'd died bravely defending his home. "How kin it be home," lamented the old man, "wi' no Lough Gill to fish nor Ben Bulben thar to be traipsed?"

The farewells were no less painful on the Native side. Charlie's sharpshooting ensured that two young children, a boy and a girl, who waited eagerly for their father to return to the longhouse at Mashel Village, would wait in vain. The woodcarving sentry left not only a beloved who rent her garments and swore never to love again, but a crippled mother who relied upon her son for sustenance and daily care. The tribe had always stepped in at such moments, but now the tribe itself was crumbling, as old ways died alongside young men. There was no one willing to drag or carry the bereaved old woman upriver to the Kanasket stronghold, so she kissed her friends goodbye, then drank a tincture of foxglove to usher in eternal sleep.

No sooner had Slaughter's men patted the last shovelful of dirt upon Connell's unremembering head, than they heard muffled shouts and kicks from behind the ruins of Connell's barn. Rifles at the ready, pistols drawn, the Lieutenant took a few men to investigate. The ruckus came from a barrel that stood on one end, with the top wedged firmly shut. They pried it off, and out popped none other than the blustery harelip himself, Dr. Matthew P. Burns, waving a piece of salmon skin and claiming it as a scalp.

"I thent no fewer than eight o' them devilth to their maker," he swore, "afore I was forced to hide in this-here barrel, which sthwelled shut in the night. Me loyal mount, King William, may he rest in peace, took one through the kidneys, and now feeds the crocodiles in these infernal sthwamps." After this amazing account, there never was a crocodile seen again in Washington Territory. Resilient Appaloosa that he was, King William refused to rest in peace, instead trotting unscathed into the camp of some downriver Volunteers three days later.

It was gleaned from Dr. Burns' report that the Indians had beat a hasty retreat up-river when their sentries spotted Slaughter's force. The next morning, a dull grey chilly November 4, 1855, Slaughter gave chase, eastward past the spot where the first shot of the war had felled Jim McAllister, tracking the Indians to a place where the White River's angry torrent funnels through a narrow defile. A man was sent to the water's edge with an axe, instructed to chop some pines for a crude bridge. The troops settled in their saddles, lulled by the rushing water and the *thit! thit! thit!* of the woodcutter's blows, munching on biscuits and jerky. Their horses drank from the river, and foraged for grass and ferns. Suddenly the air split with a retort sharper than any woodsman's blow, and the axe flew unrestrained as the young soldier fell, mortally wounded.

On command Lieutenant Slaughter's forces fanned out along the river bank, taking cover behind scattered driftwood and brush. The Bostons peered across to the opposite bank and steep hillside, but could see nothing other than the impenetrable fir, cedar, and hemlock, that blanketed the area. Still, a man had been lost, and they had plenty of ammunition, so the firing became heavy and smoke choked the western slope.

From the opposite bank, Natives fired more sparingly, conscious of their need to conserve shot. Their inaccurate muskets were no match for the Regulars' muzzle-loading rifles, with grooved bores to impart a spin to the projectile. Kill after kill was reported to Lieutenant Slaughter, as his spotters watched conical hats and cedar tunics fall to the hail of spinning bullets. By nightfall, Lieutenant Slaughter's report estimated the enemy dead at thirty.

On the Boston side, the woodsman was the only death. Two privates were seriously wounded and Corporal Northcraft's boot was blasted to smithereens. "I always was a lucky fellow," he said with a grin, holding up the smoldering remains of his sole.

3

Kwahnesum climbed up with ax in hand and chopped a hole in the roof of her white woman's cabin. At last, she could build a fire on top of the cast iron stove without suffering from smoke. Then she settled in to wait for Charlie's return. She assumed that he would be right back after finding Yokwa village deserted, but as the days stretched into the white man's week, Kwahnesum grew increasingly concerned. She imagined all sorts of different scenarios: her father on the ground, his blood leaking into the earth, with Charlie's rifle muzzle smoking; her father standing at her door, holding by its honey hair the lifeless head of her husband. She was unsure which vision was worse. The isolation nearly drove her insane, but she dared not venture down to the tiny hamlet of Puyallup, for fear of how she would be received. She was unaware of the White River massacre, but she knew that people were expecting trouble. In Kwahnesum's mind she was an unsung hero, the woman who'd averted war by warning her old tribe about her new tribe. She was truly a Sky Woman, watching over the world.

Soon Kwahnesum's idle hands reverted with a will of their own to the traditional tasks in which they had been nurtured. Kwahnesum decided that she would pass the time by making the most beautiful basket in which to store away her husband's uniform forever. Like all Nisqually women, she knew the seasons for gathering the natural materials used in basketry, and had already washed, peeled, split, and dried the cedar root and bark that was the foundation of the basket. She had brought her gathered materials back with her from Yokwa village, and now she carefully unpacked the cedar, and the dried cherry bark, bear grass, maidenhair fern, and horsetail root. She soaked the cedar root in water to make it pliable, and then began the laborious process of wrapping the shiny outer surfaces from just below the bark around the rough and fibrous inner root, to make the coils. Other pieces of root she split and split and split again, until she had dozens of fine tough threads for sewing. She coiled and sewed tightly the thickest root for the foundation. Soon, without thinking, she began to sing the old songs, as she wrapped and sewed coil upon coil. Days passed, and the basket grew under her flying fingers into a softly flaring barrel rising to knee height, wide as a forearm at its rim. With each new coil, Kwahnesum deftly wove in vertical and horizontal bands of beargrass, cherry and cedar bark, maidenhair fern and horsetail root, imbricated in a complex zigzag that captured the ebb and flow of delta grasses in the wind, geese on the wing, river currents swirling over deep, smooth stones. She boiled wild cranberries and rose hips to make red dye in which she soaked the final coil, and boiled lichens for gold dye in which she soaked bear grass. Finally, she stitched the red coil down with the golden grass to make a decorative rim. At last, tired and satisfied, she brought the finished basket to bed with her, and slept peacefully for the first time since Charlie had been pulled from her breast.

In her dreams she danced with Charlie in a big hall filled with white folks and Indians, and everyone was laughing and feasting. Her father was there, and First Mother, too. They were dancing down to the river, into the canoes and down the rapids to *Whulge*, where salmon jumped straight into the canoe. Charlie was dancing with a salmon, her father was singing, and she and First Mother were laughing so hard that the tears streamed down their faces and they could hardly breathe. Now suddenly they were inside the basket she'd made, and water welled up through the woven coils to fill the basket. They were going down under *Whulge* and she was afraid and startled awake to a strong hand over her mouth. She struggled for First Mother's knife, but it was far off in the kitchen. She could feel the blankets torn away and the smothering press of a fat man between her legs which she kicked and kicked until other men grabbed her and held her down, and still she fought and twisted and gasped for breath, but they were too powerful and she could do nothing but inhale the acrid stench of sweat and whiskey. They took turns violating her, three strange scratchy white men, pushing, biting, shoving things roughly inside her, slapping her face, kneeing her in the belly, tearing at her hair, turning her over, ravishing her from the front and behind again and again like mountain goats in heat.

When at last it seemed that they had finished, Kwahnesum coiled herself like a shed snakeskin. "*Siwash* bitch," spat the fat man, as he pulled out a pistol and prodded it towards her privates. She scuttled back until there was no more room for retreat. "You want it?" he asked in English, and Kwahnesum's fear was so intense that she shut her eyes and never saw the lightning stroke of the barrel whipped behind her ear; all she knew was white hot pain, then nothing.

How long she was away, she did not know. She awakened in bed, her head splitting, two Charlies by her side. She blinked. Everything came in twos. "Oh Charlie." She tried to move to him, could not. The room spun and her head split and instead she lay helpless, tears of horror and shame flowing like a hard rain, until gradually she became aware of him. Of his rigidity. He sat like stone.

"Charlie?" she whispered, ten tens of questions fretting about the name.

"Somebody warned your father," said Charlie. "He ran."

So devastated was she that she lacked all guile. "I saved you both."

"So you confess." She said nothing. "I suspected as much. Because of you, lots of good folks died."

"No, Charlie ..." She resumed her weeping, this time quietly, curled inward. "Can we talk later?"

"No, there's more."

"Charlie, something happened ..."

"Because of you my friend Ben ..." Charlie heaved one clipped sob, swallowed like the bitter herb he'd shared with Ben on Passover.

"I'm sorry," she said. "I didn't know –"

"Because of you good honest white folks have been massacred –"

"No, Charlie, no –"

"Because of you the whole Territory is at war –"

"No, Charlie. Please –"

"And here you are, livin' like a savage, tearin' up the house, lyin' around fornicating with every man who comes your way." She froze; no words would come. She managed one sharp shake *no*, though it cost her like a hot poker through the skull.

"I WANT YOU OUT OF HERE!" the two Charlies screamed, yanking the covers away as he stood. She pulled up her legs, trying to hide her bruises.

"Husband –" She reached out an unsteady hand, letting it sway from Charlie to Charlie. Not the hand on her mouth, not the rough unwelcome men inside her, not the blow to the head, none of these was strong enough to kill her spirit. It was Charlie's words, *oh, who would think it could be words that hurt the most?* "Charlie, they raped me."

"Whatever it was, you deserved it."

Unspeakable horror. "Husband?"

"DON'T EVER CALL ME HUSBAND AGAIN!" he commanded, smashing the basket with a hard stroke of his arm. "I would never have married you if the Governor had not ordered it."

Suddenly she saw it all, and her *tamanous* sunk like a stone.

4

Leschi and his people retreated up the steep bank and across the Green River, melting into the woods they knew so well. They had faced the Boston guns and lost only one man, thanks to Leschi's strategy of propping their hats and shirts on sticks to entice the Bostons' wasteful gunfire. The Bostons' rifles were so accurate that they killed many scarecrows.

It made little military sense to pursue the Natives deeper into the wet winter forest, but Will Slaughter was determined to satisfy Colonel Casey's urgent plea for a decisive blow. Nor would he be averse to the accolades due the hero of this little war – or the promotion that would follow. So once he was sure that Leschi had retreated, he ordered a man to finish construction of the bridge. Never were trees felled so fast. The men lashed the fallen timbers together to make a rickety bridge, then hunched low and rushed forward, counting on momentum to save them from a frigid swim. Only Slaughter himself slipped and tumbled into the rushing torrent. Laughing soldiers fished him out from the far bank, his life spared, his powder damp, his dignity impaired.

After that, the young Lieutenant seemed determined to prove himself tougher than anyone else, as he led his men ever deeper into the labyrinthine wilderness. Each day they marched with their fingers on the trigger and their sphincters clamped tight. The light under the giant trees was tinted mold green. They could see thirty feet around them, but not what was three feet away, forcing them to hack constantly at the rotting nothingness enveloping them. The odor of the deep forest was alien, a smell of decay, birth and death measured in eons. Each step was off a precipice into a rotting carpet of leaves, logs, dead things without name, that squished and receded and gave support, or not, at indeterminate depths of the devil's own murky choosing. Lieutenant Slaughter, compass in hand, could see the line he wanted to follow, but could not follow it. Like a serpent from ancient mythology, the forest was alive and watching. It led them where it wanted them to go, on a winding path around fallen trees, through a dozen kinds of thorny branches that clung to their heavy wet uniforms. When at last they tore free, their garments were shredded and impregnated with prickly reminders of each brush with a thorn bush.

And then came night. Relentless waves of drenching mist, the impossibility of a fire even if military protocol had permitted one. The eyes in the darkness. The *hooo, hoo-hoo, hooo, hooo,* of the owl, which could as easily be an Indian with a poison arrow or a musket. The cacophony of wolves, the silent slither of snakes, the crawling of spiders and millipedes, the heavy crackling of the lumbering bear. The rain, the rain, the rain.

They marched and got nowhere, as Leschi's men picked them off, one by one. They camped, and the Natives snuck up and stole their horses. Some said it was the notorious giant Kanasket himself, who suddenly materialized in their midst out of a hollow cedar stump with a shriek, shot a private in the knee, and got clean away. Their wild return fire shot the hat off one of their own.

Their British scout, John Edgar, tried to cheer his comrades with the inexhaustible supply of stories he'd picked up in his many years as a trapper and trader. "A Hertfordshire farmer went out on a snowy day to milk his cows," he began, as they slipped and grunted through lichen-covered-moss-covered lichen. Though most of the men didn't know Hertfordshire from Worcestershire, they'd come to rely on Mr. Edgar for entertainment and sound advice. "He saw a little bird lying half-frozen in the snow," continued Edgar, "so cold that it was silent. 'Poor wee thing,' he said, and he picked it up. He wanted to find some way to save the little bird, to warm it, but he had to get on with his chores; he couldn't go back to the house. Well then, he looked about and saw a nice big cow patty, steaming in the snow. That's it, he thought, and plunked the wee birdie into the cow patty."

"Sounds good after my bed last night," groused one of the company wags.

"Indeed it was," continued Edgar, "soon enough the warmth of that patty did the trick, and the little birdie was singing at the top o' his lungs. Just then, a fox come through the forest, and he heard the little bird singing. That fox -" was as far as he got when a shot rang out, a ball pierced Edgar's windpipe, and he dropped into the mossy stew and died, a froth of blood at his lips.

Edgar's comrades fired back at shadows, hitting nothing. Silence closed over the forest, as though nothing had happened. The survivors' first thought was always, *glad it wasn't me*. The second was sorrow for the poor Limey; this wasn't his fight anyway. The third, fourth, fifth, and every sucking next step's thought was, *any second now, it could be me.*

As Slaughter struggled to find ground for a decisive strike, more and more of his men died, shot down while fording a creek, plodding nowhere on numbed feet, climbing a tree to try to get their bearings, relieving themselves in the brush. They thrashed, more than marched, along the slippery twisting route that the forest pressed upon them, a deeper and more unrelenting gloom settling over them all. The only thing preventing desertion was that there was nowhere to go.

5

Though Slaughter's men suffered, it was not one-sided. The white man's sharpshooting rifles made their mark: a spy who sneezed, a brave tending his horse, a sister feeding broth to an ailing brother, a father sleeping fitfully in a cold cedar bark bed, a hunter thanking the deer spirit for surrendering its life to nourish the tribe. All fed the growing fury.

On the east side of the Cascades, the force mustered to avenge Kamiakan's victory moved swiftly along the Columbia, to the mouth of the Yakama River, then northwest into the heart of Yakama country. Three hundred seventy regular Army joined by a hundred fifty Washington and Oregon Volunteers, under the command of a square-jawed Vermonter, Colonel George Wright, made this the most powerful force ever assembled in the Pacific Northwest. Wright's troops were equipped with eight mountain howitzers, and the latest breech-loading rifles.

Chief Kamiakan's outnumbered braves attempted to make a stand in a cold November wind on rocky Twin Buttes, but the howitzer bombardment followed by a charge of well-armed soldiers and determined Volunteers quickly broke their defenses, and they were forced to fall back. Wright's troops pursued them as far east as the Columbia, then watched as elders and children joined young men, women, horses and cattle, in the icy waters of the Columbia. Some swam for their lives, others to their deaths. From the opposite bank, teeth-chattering survivors quickly dispersed to winter camps. The momentary blaze of Yakama glory was ended, almost before it began.

Natives small and grand suffered throughout the Territory. A Puyallup in the employ of the Hudson's Bay Company was shot down in cold blood, while chopping wood just outside the gates of Fort Nisqually. Charlie Salitat, the Duwamish Paul Revere, was awakened in his Seattle bed from a dreamless sleep, by the sting of his own throat being cut; revenge for aiding the white man. Peopeomoxmox, Chief of the peaceful Walla Wallas, surrendered himself to a company of Territorial Volunteers, under a pledge that his people would be left unharmed. The Volunteers made him watch, as they attacked and razed his village in violation of their oath. Then they scalped and butchered the old Chief; a man who, as a child, had feasted with Lewis and Clark, honored guests of the Walla Wallas. The Volunteers pickled choice parts of the Chief, for souvenirs to be traded and displayed in taverns from Portland to Bellingham.

6

Kwahnesum left Charlie with only the clothes on her back, and First Mother's obsidian knife tucked in her belt. Head spinning, insides like soured milk, she rode to Muck Creek. There, she slumped from her mount and vomited at the doorstep of her mother's childhood friend from Puyallup days, John Edgar's wife, Betsy. Betsy undressed her, cleaned her, and put the girl to bed.

Though Kwahnesum never spoke of her ordeal, the nature of her bruises and the way she moaned in her sleep, fighting off invisible attackers, told Betsy all she needed to know. Laying her big warm hands and cool herbal compresses upon Kwahnesum's belly and brow, Betsy did her best to sooth the battered girl. Kwahnesum's eyes opened but did not see. She cried out and reached for her mother, for Charlie, for a knife just beyond reach.

Betsy sat many long days and nights with Kwahnesum. When Betsy had other chores, her place was taken by Alala, a young Cowlitz beauty from the next homestead. Alala was named for the common nettle plant, which, as her husband Sandy Smith was fond of pointing out, could be both irritating and soothing. Gradually, Kwahnesum's outward wounds healed, but she was withdrawn and sullen. When one day Sandy Smith came in to feed her his special stew, she pulled away and would not look at him. Sandy, a gentleman and a gentle man, handed Betsy the dish over which he'd labored, mumbled his apologies, and retreated.

Kwahnesum always took the stew from Betsy's hand. As she fed the girl nourishing chunks of carrot, parsnip, potato and venison, Betsy hummed an old song that Sara used to sing. Kwahnesum could hear the words in her head:

> *The sun shines in your eyes, my dear,*
> *The moon glows in your breast,*
> *Sun and moon will still be here*
> *When we've gone to our rest, dear,*
> *When we've gone to our rest.*

Oh, if only First Mother were here!

"Sssssshhhhh," said Betsy, reading Kwahnesum's mind. "Remember, child: the dead have their own tasks; we cannot know them." Kwahnesum was still.

"Your mother often spoke of you to me. She was amazed by your strength, though concerned about your restless spirit." Kwahnesum fretted at even the gentlest chiding, so Betsy quickly added, "She worried about you, dear Kwahnesum, because of her love for you. She used to say, 'Betsy, we are like *Ta-co-bet*, we make our own weather. What weather will you make today?'"

Kwahnesum turned away, her face cloudy. Betsy pretended to take no notice. "Like you, I married a white man. Like you, I sit here, alone, as he fights my own people. It is painful. I do not know whether he is alive or dead. I want him to live, but I do not want the white man to win this war." Kwahnesum turned back to search Betsy's face. "Yes," said Betsy, "we share much. Like you, I left our way of life for the white man's way, but our way has not left me."

Kwahnesum looked away. The elder woman took the girl's chin, and brought her wide, dark eyes back up to meet her own. "Kwahnesum, your mother is watching from *Otlas-Skio*. She was the daughter of a Chief. So are you. We cannot escape our blood." Kwahnesum pulled her chin free, then turned back to gaze at Betsy of her own volition.

The next day, Kwahnesum was up and testing out her shaky legs, as the color returned to her cheeks. She found First Mother's knife, tucked it again by her belt. It made her feel, not good, but more focused, to know it was there. Still, there was no smile.

The next grey and sodden day, as Kwahnesum sat around a rough pine table with Betsy and Alala quietly weaving cedar mats, a lone rider galloped up. Sandy exchanged a few words with him as he watered his horse, re-mounted, and rode on. The women watched as Sandy trudged back to the cabin, face ashen. He entered, placed a hand on Betsy's shoulder. "John's gone," was all he said. Kwahnesum just sat, stone cold, watching as Betsy's hands crumpled cedar bark into shavings, which fluttered like dry tears, slick to the floor.

Alala led Betsy to bed. Kwahnesum stumbled out without any farewell. She was poison, she was bad luck, she was dirty. She had caused this war like Charlie said, so she had killed dear Betsy's husband. She needed to go far away; to lose herself, to bury her own stinking evil carcass deep in the belly of the Bostons, where it would fester and kill them all. She headed northwest, towards Seattle.

The stench of raw sewage mixed with rotting garbage, milled logs, and composting sawdust, struck her nostrils well before she could see the town. It was an apt welcome to the most dismal collection of dwellings ever dropped askew into the muck of a tide flat, and stuck willy-nilly onto steep, forested hills. Recently swelled by war refugees and the marines of the Sloop-of-War *Decatur*, Seattle boasted tens of frame buildings, with planks milled at Yesler's steam mill, and brick hearths and chimneys from two working kilns. Steam belched morning, noon, and night, from Yesler's mill. The huge cookhouse and mess hall in back, that served as the social and political center of town, was the size of two longhouses. Around the mill were four man-made mountains of sawdust, and then just south, a row of gambling dens and saloons, where the "sawdust women" hung out – Indian prostitutes who worked the dangerous, muddy streets of Doc Maynard's plat.

At the southern tip of Maynard's plat rose the large, three-story boarding house known as Mother Damnable's, where Mrs. Conklin and her girls welcomed all comers who carried gold or coin. Between Mother Damnable's and Yesler's mill, stood the first of two new blockhouses, monuments to prudence or fear. Just north of the mill stood the genteel white-picket-fenced houses of Arthur Denny, C.D. Boren, Charles Terry, and their families, the North Blockhouse, and the Methodist Church established by Denny, with its squat belfry.

Slicing it all neatly in half, a long greased wood-plank road plummeted down from the hills towards Yesler's mill – Skid Road it was called, where logs twice the length of grey whales careened from forest to ocean at unimaginable speeds. The skidding of timber was an unending source of entertainment for the drunks who could not afford, or were between, visits to the sawdust women. They arrayed their wobbly selves along the path, occasionally contributing to the merriment by slipping into the greased path of an oncoming Douglas fir.

Seattle was modern, Seattle was a coming place, a town of gumption. It boasted elevated plumbing. Great hollow-log sluiceways of excrement, built up on pilings, descended from the hills to the Sound at regular intervals, fed by tributaries from each building by which they passed. Seattle had embraced Thomas Crapper's plunger watercloset with all the entrepreneurial zeal of its bottom-line heart. As long as you didn't flush at highest tide, waste flowed to the sea, freeing man of his stink. The newfangled Crapper Throne fit the mood of Seattle – a town in too much of a hurry to go outside, even to answer the call of nature.

All of this was so far beyond Kwahnesum's experience that she hardly knew what she was looking at. It mattered little; if she absorbed the town's stench it only added to her allure for certain men. Already they were circling like jackals. She saw their yellow eyes, the eager way they licked their lips. The men closed in around her pony, but that was what she wanted. She was comforted by the cool weight of the sharp stone blade, tucked in her belt against the small of her back. What little plan she had, was to take one or two with her before she died. Now they were closing in, feeling her leg, shying the pony to a stop.

"Hey, pretty Miss, wanna come play with me?"

"Where you off to in such a hurry, sawdust lady?"

"C'mon, darlin', I'm the *tillicum* with the greased timber just for you!"

Kwahnesum dismounted in a quick athletic twist of her body. She planted herself on the boardwalk, hands on her hips, legs spread, smiling a wicked smile that gave even the meanest wrangler a momentary pause. "You want me?" she said in Chinook. "*Chahko pee iskum nika*" – come and get me. They moved forward as a unit as one of her hands slipped around behind. Just as she gripped the mother-of-pearl handle, a dandy of a man with a salt-and-pepper pompadour stepped between Kwahnesum and the pack, and raised his silver-tipped walking stick.

"Any man among you who molests this young lady shall find his head split open," announced Doc Maynard, who was well known for splitting heads, then sewing them back up at no charge. The men encircling Kwahnesum all knew Doc, and liked him well enough, except for his strange partiality towards the *siwash*. There was plenty of other Injun *poontang* on the street, so it didn't seem worth the trouble. The crowd dispersed.

Kwahnesum scowled at Doc's misplaced gallantry. "I didn't ask for your help," she said in *Whulshootseed,* and Doc answered right back in *Whulshootseed,* "No, but you needed it, Mrs. Eden." He held out a crooked arm. Kwahnesum hesitated a long time before taking it.

At Maynards' house, Doc's wife Catherine bathed the girl, and put her to bed. Lying in the big, soft bed, Kwahnesum realized she was crying. Once the tears started, they were inexhaustible as the Seattle rain. Finally, her stomach sore from sobbing, she crawled from the Boston bed to a mat on the floor, and fell into a deep sleep.

7

By December 4th, exhausted, sick, and on the verge of mutiny, Slaughter's company at last returned to Brannon's Prairie, near the scene of the White River massacre. They'd begun to make camp when Captain Erasmus Darwin Keyes arrived to greet them. The bearded Captain had just disembarked, bringing reinforcements by order of General Wool. Captain Keyes had a kind word, an open ear, or an encouraging pat on the shoulder for each man he passed. He spoke with a New England accent – was it Massachusetts or Maine? – but he immediately made Kentucky boy Will Slaughter feel like an equal, despite the gap in years and rank.

They conferred in a little abandoned root cabin that the Lieutenant had chosen as his quarters for the night. Captain Keyes suggested that they could press on to Fort Steilacoom that very night, but though Will valued the elder man's opinion, he declined. "My men are exhausted; they must have their rest," said Will. Captain Keyes was too respectful of the hardships endured by Slaughter over the past month, to make his suggestion an order. "Besides," added Will, "we haven't seen any sign of the enemy in over a week."

A merry blaze was set for the Captain and Lieutenant on the dirt floor of the vented cabin. The men were too tired to cheer, but the warm glow of camp fires and hot food in their bellies, was more than welcome.

Though near collapse himself, Lieutenant Slaughter huddled with Captain Keyes to go over maps, and try to organize his report. "They won't stand and fight," complained Slaughter. "It is like shadowboxing, 'cept the shadows shoot back." He looked grim. "We have superior weapons, and they gotta be short on shot. But they know how to live out there; we don't. I cain't see that a winter campaign in those thick forests is going to do a lick of good."

"What do you recommend, Lieutenant?" asked the Captain.

"I think we should hold our defensive positions around the populated areas until spring. If the Indians are fool enough to attack, or even come downriver, then we can get 'em. If not, we go after 'em when the weather is more hospitable. Meanwhile, I 'spect they're short on food, which oughta soften 'em up."

"A good plan," said Captain Keyes, laying his hand on Will's shoulder. "You can count on my support with the Colonel. Oh, and by the way," he added, his thick lower lip hinting at a smile, "I had the pleasure of Sunday dinner with the Governor and his wife. A lovely lady from Michigan was there; she bids you a fond hello."

The Lieutenant's face lit up. "Mary!"

"Yes, she is very well, spending the week with her friend, Mrs. Stevens, in Olympia. She'll be real pleased to see you, I can assure you of that! She'll fly to Steilacoom the moment you arrive; she has some news for you." Morning sickness had led to gossip, and pretty soon everyone knew – except the father-to-be, lost in the woods fighting Indians.

"What news?"

"Oh, it's not for this old bachelor to spill the beans," chuckled Keyes.

Could it be? thought Will. He rose and crossed to the doorway to draw an exhilarated breath under the waning crescent moon, where he made a smart silhouette against the fire-lit doorway. A shot rang out and Will Slaughter fell, a bullet in his heart, the beginnings of a smile frozen on his lips. Leschi and his warriors charged forward, the breech-loading rifle he'd commandeered from a dead soldier still hot in his hands. Shot followed shot, battle cries rang across the prairie, and once again all was confusion and death.

8

Sunday, December 9, 1855, broke gusty and cold. Though the funeral was set for two o'clock, the little burial ground at Fort Steilacoom was crowded by noon. The many settlers already billeted at the fort all turned out. The Territorial Legislature was adjourned, and many representatives were present. Mourners arrived by horseback and buggy from Olympia, Tacoma and Seattle. A company of Volunteers came from Olympia's Camp Montgomery, along with the McAllisters and other displaced settlers. People walked up from the village of Steilacoom, where Will and Mary Slaughter had so quickly woven themselves into the fabric of daily life.

By the time of the service, a pelting sleet stung the mourner's cheeks, blown in horizontally from a slate sky over the Sound. Mason spoke, and Captain Keyes. Mary Slaughter held her sides and could not lift her stricken gaze from the muck underfoot. Meg Stevens and Martha McAllister had to hold her up, and then Mr. Mason had to hold up Martha. As the casket containing Will Slaughter's remains was lowered into the earth, a thin bugle cry flew east, towards Kentucky.

After it was over, everyone was subdued, even the Governor, who stepped gingerly around the soft earth of fresh graves. The Governor had uncharacteristically declined to speak; he was only present because Meg said if he wouldn't go, Mr. Mason would escort her, and he hadn't liked the way she said it. He fidgeted all through the service. He just didn't see how this kind of wallowing could help win the war. He was grateful when it was over, and he could join the men back at the fort for whiskey.

Stevens was also fretting over the sharp criticism in the new opposition paper. The *Puget Sound Courier*, published right here in Steilacoom, had the temerity to blame the war on his treaties. The *Courier* charged that he "stole the Indians' land and gave them almost nothing in return." It impertinently dubbed him, "King Stevens." Lies, all of it! The Indians started it by shooting McAllister and massacring innocent settlers. The massacre proved that no amount of generosity – and he had been very generous, going to the very limit of what Congress would ratify – would ever slake the savage thirst for blood. Why couldn't these Republicans see what was obvious to most folks in the Territory? Did he detect the hand of Wool and Casey behind all this? Or were there others? A free press was a good thing, of course, but this went too far. Publishing a newspaper carries a duty of responsibility to the community. *Don't these fools realize that this is war?*

The Governor was comforted somewhat by the advance proof of the *Pioneer & Democrat* in his pocket. Scheduled to come out tomorrow, in a front-page editorial his friend, Mr. Wiley, decried the attacks on the Governor as, "libelous and scurrilous." Stevens licked the nib of his pencil, and wrote, "Exactly!" in the margin, then penciled in a few minor additions of his own. After "libelous and scurrilous," he added, "amounting to treason." Not quite satisfied, he added, "The reckless expression of such sentiments gives comfort to our enemies, while undermining our brave soldiers in the field." He was gratified the next day, to find that Mr. Wiley had incorporated his suggestions verbatim. Mr. Wiley was just the kind of responsible journalist needed at a time like this.

Chapter Fifteen
Balls

1

It was the New Year, 1856, anything but happy. The Boston and Puget Sound tribes had battled one another to stalemate. Crops rotted in the fields, as white bellies went hungry. Salmon carcasses rotted in the streams, as red bellies went hungry. Domesticated animals roamed free, hogs rooted in abandoned pantries, cows heavy with milk lowed in the forests until the wolves got them. Winter longhouses were cold and silent, crumbling in disrepair. Thousands of Natives, too sick or wise or scared to fight, were held in temporary reservations on Fox Island, Point Monroe, Whidbey and Squaxon Islands. These reservations were little better than cattle pens, muddy fields ringed by high picket fences and guard stations. Tribes were thrown together willy-nilly, fed government rations, and prohibited from singing the ancient songs. Listless Natives found comfort in adultery, black market booze, gambling, and homicide; their eyes sank to a uniform slate; they cringed at the approach of a white man.

The mercury fell to nine degrees, and half a foot of snow fell in Olympia and Steilacoom. Displaced families suffered deprivations all through the bitter cold winter, drawing stinking shirts and tattered shawls to their shivering bones, terrified by every hoot in the night. They watched helpless as their idle, hungry children learned the pleasures of cruelty, while the back-breaking labor of their best years disappeared. Pioneers by the hundreds boarded ships to San Francisco, businesses failed, shop fronts were boarded up, entire fledgling settlements vanished under a fecund Pacific Northwest stew of evergreens, liverworts, lichens, moss and shrubs. People paid a buck a pound for rancid butter. A sawbuck musket now sold for two double sawbucks – to the very few who had the cash. Hard cash was scarce; the scrip paid to Volunteers in lieu of wages was passed in discounted bucket loads, like the hot potato game in which the one left holding it when the hurdy-gurdy stopped got burnt.

Even the Governor felt the pinch. Volunteer companies were disbanding, having reached the end of their initial three-month enlistment, disgusted with the hard, dangerous, futile work of soldiering. The regular Army adopted a defensive posture around the coastal towns, to wait out the winter. The first bills for the extravagance of raising up companies of Volunteers had made their way to the other Washington, and neither the President nor Congress was amused. The letter from William L. Marcy, Secretary of State, was terse:

The purpose of strictly limiting you in expenditures for the purchase of Indian lands was to maintain a fiscal prudence exigent upon the sound discharge of the public business. Many Representatives (who, I remind you, hold the purse strings) recall funding the Army of the Pacific to fight our wars, and they question the necessity of a costly and duplicative volunteer effort. In this, the President concurs. We will endeavor to obtain payment of a portion of the seriously over-budget requests presented to date, but the President instructs that you should most earnestly seek a less costly means of extricating yourself and the Territory from its present difficulties.

I am, Sir, your obedient Servant,

Wm. L. Marcy

Stevens crumbled the letter in his hand with a snarl. "MASON!" he shouted, and Charles appeared. "Haven't we got some money somewhere?"

"Yes, Sir," replied Mason. "We received a treasury draft for $3,875, that was too large for any bank in the Territory to negotiate, so I placed it in the safe for a rainy day."

"It's raining right now. We need hard cash to muster troops for the decisive blow. Wool and Casey want to sit on their hands 'til summer. Now, it looks like they've turned Mr. Pierce against us." Stevens shared the crumpled letter with Mason, before wadding it back up and chucking it onto the fire. Mason watched in dismay as the official Territorial document turned to ash. "Mason, here's what I want you to do. Have my pal Henry Cotter, of Parker & Cotter Express, run the damn draft down to Portland and get it cashed. We'll pay him 1% for his trouble."

"In wartime, Sir? I think we may have to go higher."

"Well, then, get the best deal you can, but not a nickel over 3%."

"Yes, Sir, I understand." Mason pushed his glasses up. He noticed that Stevens looked uncharacteristically weary. His eyes were bloodshot and sunken. He was a man of action. When he couldn't act he could barely function. All he could do was drink, something he'd been doing round the clock since Lieutenant Slaughter's funeral.

"If it wasn't for you, Charles," confided the Governor, sidling so close that Mason cringed in anticipation of feeling the Governor's drunken arm around his shoulder, "and Meg of course – well, I don't know."

"Yes, Sir, thank-you, Sir." Mason heard footfalls in the hallway, and scampered out of the room. The Governor barely noticed.

"The key is to get Leschi," he muttered. "Get him; make an example of him." Stevens dropped into an overstuffed armchair by the fire, put his feet up on the ottoman, his head lolling to one side. "Make him pay, God damn it; then the savages will lay down their arms. They'll beg me to put 'em on the reservation."

Meg, who'd been eavesdropping from the doorway, padded in, in stocking feet. "What's that, Ingy?"

"Oh, nothing. I was just thinking up how to win this war." She knelt before him, removed his boots, and began massaging his feet. "They always pay the bills for a winner, Meg. Doesn't matter what the cost – if you're victorious, every God damn politician from ward boss, on up to President, wants to get on the bandwagon. You just wait. Next week I address the Legislature, then on to Seattle. They'll get an earful."

"Yes, Ingy, I know." She felt his tension and kneaded deeper, paying special attention to his war wound. "Everything's going to be fine."

Isaac leaned back. "What I've done, I've done for the children, you know." She believed him, knowing how loving he had always been with their own. "They can't live in fear all their lives." He sat quietly, watching the fire, as Meg worked at his toes, his scarred instep, his ankles and calves. "Everything will work out," he said at last, echoing his wife. "We're on our way, Meg. Into the history books! Who knows, maybe even the President's Mansion." She must have let slip a glint of skepticism, because he pressed forward, practically pleading with her. "No, Meg, why not? Why not? Now, fix me a drink, there's a good girl."

"Isaac, no –"

Did he only mean to pull his leg away or was it well aimed? She was on the floor, her nose bloody from a swift kick. Mason materialized too quickly, dabbing the blood with his own clean starched handkerchief, whispering reassurances. "GET OUT OF HERE! BOTH OF YOU!" bellowed their Lord and Master.

Stevens got his own drink; took a big pull straight from the bottle. Perhaps Mr. Mason would be of more use pleading their case in person back in Washington City. Stevens smiled. That would probably be more politic than killing him here and now with his bare hands, though not nearly as satisfying.

2

By light of a full moon framed by ghostly clouds, Olympia's brand-new whitewashed Hall of Representatives impressed the men gathered to hear the Governor's State of the Territory Address. It was January 19, 1856, a cold Saturday night. At precisely 7:30 p.m., Governor Stevens stepped into the packed hall, where he was met with polite but hesitant applause. He shook hands right and left up the central aisle, bounded to the podium, shook hands with droopy-eyed William Wallace, leader of the opposition Republicans, and Elwood Evans, his hand-picked Secretary to the Legislature.

Stevens grasped the lectern firmly and began to speak without notes. "Washington Territory, our home, our land, our blessing, our future, is under attack. This is not a war with a civilized foe. It is a determined effort to wipe us out, men, women, and children. It is a war of extermination, carried forward by a savage race that knows nothing of Christian charity, nothing of the rule of law, nothing of democracy, nothing of freedom, nothing of property, nothing of justice, nothing of mercy." *Here-here!* came a few cries.

"I see among you some who are skeptical. What I say was fully demonstrated by the Indians' immediate breaking of their solemn contract, contained in a treaty signed by no fewer than sixty-two of their Chiefs, head men, and braves, including their war leader, Leschi." *That's right!* "It was demonstrated by the unmanly way Leschi ambushed his old friend and protector, Jim McAllister." *Yes!* "And it was horribly and incontestably demonstrated by the renegade Leschi's massacre of defenseless men, women, and even innocent children, at White River." *Cruel murder!* cried a voice, and now the Legislators were beginning to unite. "Since then, it has been demonstrated time and again by their cowardly method of warfare, hiding behind trees, killing without formation or flag, sending even our brave and beloved Lieutenant Slaughter to an early grave, never to see his first and only child." Grim vengeance filled the hall.

"I know, there are a few who would argue that we should make a new treaty with these treaty-breakers." *Never!* "A few who say we should reward the massacre of innocents, by giving in to new and unjust demands that go well beyond the broken bargain the Indians themselves made." *Fools! Cowards!* Stevens leaned back and let the hall speak for him. The audience was his keyboard; with expert fingers he struck the chords, and it responded.

"I have come here tonight, before this great and august symbol of civilization in Washington Territory, to tell you where your Governor stands on this vital issue." Here he began thumping the lectern with each phrase, softly at first, but then building to a crescendo. "I am opposed to any new treaties." Loud cheers. "I will protest against any and all new treaties to my last breath." Louder cheers. "Nothing but death is mete punishment for their perfidy; their lives should pay the forfeit." The hall erupted, giving voice to all the fear and anger that had been building since October. Stevens let it go, and go, and go, until finally he held up his hand.

"To those misguided white men among us, who criticize our efforts, and offer support for the savage cause, I say this: in time of war, aid and comfort to the enemy has a name, and that name is treason. This administration shall not hesitate to prosecute traitors." Some cheered harder than ever; others joined the cheering nervously; a handful stood mute, and their silence was noted. One or two of these even added a dilatory, *here-here!* in self-defense.

"Leschi does not represent his people," continued the Governor. "He leads a small, but dangerous, conspiracy of criminal elements. Their object is to hold civilization itself hostage. They are armed and crazed with hatred for our way of life. They hate our machines, our material progress, our faith in the one true Lord Jesus, and our American liberty. They hide in the forests and strike without warning. They could strike at any time, at any place. Where is your wife tonight? Where are your children?" A fearful silence. "Yet at this time of peril, the Army, led by General Wool and Colonel Casey, two well-known Indian sympathizers, stands by idly, waiting for the next attack."

Stevens paused. The fear was palpable; the people wanted someone to show them what to do; someone strong to rely upon for protection against the terror of the dark forests. "As a West Point soldier, Isaac Stevens does not wait to be attacked. We must wipe these savages from the map, before they attack again!" Thunderous cheers.

"To Leschi and his band of renegades," concluded the Governor, "I have only one message. It is not a message of conciliation. It is not simpering cowardice. I say this: *the war shall be prosecuted until the last hostile Indian is exterminated.*" This time the cheers rocked the chandeliers. Stevens supporters demonstrated in the aisles. Secretary Evans repeatedly pounded his gavel for order, while at the same time joining the raucous cheers. Stevens' little frame was hoisted up onto the shoulders of several of the biggest men, and swept from the hall in triumph.

3

Colonel Blunt told Charlie that it was a vital job, and that it would only be temporary, but Charlie knew a demotion when he saw one. The Eden's

Rangers banner was balled up on the floor in a corner of the shack that passed for his headquarters. No more was Charlie at the vanguard of a proud column of soldiers. Now he was Captain of a rag-tag collection of broken down ex-warriors and toothless *klootchmen*, squealing infants and sullen boozers. He was Indian Agent in charge of the Fox Island Reservation, where eight hundred sixty-eight – he'd personally counted them – Indians, mostly Nisquallies and Puyallups, harmlessly waited out the war.

As Charlie nursed a mug of hot java out in front of his headquarters, chair tipped back, feet resting on a stump, he couldn't help thinking about Kwahnesum. The more he thought about her, the worse he felt. After all, he'd been the one who had leaked military secrets – he'd told Kwahnesum that they were out to get her father. How could he blame her for having warned him? Isn't that what any daughter would do?

Charlie didn't figure anyone flat out knew that he'd spilled the beans, but he couldn't help feeling that they suspected it. Tony didn't seem to have much use for him, and he never saw the Governor anymore. Well, that was just fine with him. He could get along. Stuck here in this backwater, he wasn't likely to see any more action, which sure beat tromping through the woods waiting to get shot at. He could still see that man – barely more than a boy – go down with his own bullet in his back. He'd been watching that over and over at night, then waking with a cry on his lips. Alone.

Charlie's feet on the stump framed a blue slice of Sound called Hale Passage, that cut between Fox Island and the Kitsap Peninsula. To the northwest loomed snowcapped peaks so close he could practically tap them with his toes – Mt. Skokomish, the craggy and sharp Brothers, Mt. Constance, the Warrior Peaks. The Territory supplied him with a roof over his head that didn't have a damn-fool hole cut in it, and three squares a day. When they won this thing, he figured the Governor'd find some way to get the boys back in Washington City to pay off the Volunteers' scrip. Charlie was quietly using his gold to buy up other men's scrip for a fraction of its face value. He didn't need any more excitement; he'd had plenty. He was ready to sit out the war right here, getting rich. Charlie Eden would land on his feet, yes siree. So why did he feel empty inside?

Charlie was jolted from his reverie by something so startling, it knocked him over backwards in his chair. His spilled coffee scalded his lap as he leaped back up, but it was too late to fetch his rifle. Besides, that would have been mighty stupid, considering that the prows of six war canoes were already landing Leschi and Kanasket on his doorstep, with over thirty heavily armed and painted warriors. So Charlie just stood his ground, trying to look dignified, despite the large soggy patch across his belly and down to his crotch.

Leschi kept a straight face, but his eyes smiled as he held Charlie by the shoulders. "*Klahowya, Challie* Eden, we come in peace," he said in Chinook, as Charlie tried not to tremble. So many canoes for so few warriors – the meaning did not escape him. Leschi's men quickly fanned out, and took Charlie's tiny command without firing a single shot.

"I am glad it is you, *Challie*," said Leschi, inviting him to sit, and offering him a pipe. As they smoked together, Leschi explained why he had risked the passage down the Puyallup River, through Commencement Bay, down the treacherous Tacoma Narrows, past Wollochet Bay, where his kinsmen had died from the pox.

"On the way here, we met some men in a canoe filled with potatoes. Two white white men, and one black white man. Some said we should kill them, *Challie*, but I said no. They gave us their potatoes; we gave them their lives. So it is; we all have something to trade. How is my daughter?"

Charlie wasn't sure if the last remark was connected to the first or not, so he lied, "She is well, Chief Leschi; you need not worry about her."

"I do not worry about her, *Challie*. When she left me, she became your worry." Charlie concentrated on his poker face, and said nothing. "But if you will remember," Leschi continued, "it is the prerogative of the father to set a test for the groom. You never passed my first test, so now I will set you another." He scrutinized Charlie as if he were a stallion at the market. Charlie wondered whether he measured up.

"We could have attacked Steilacoom – we passed within a few of your *miles* – but instead we came here to parley. I want you to send word to Colonel Casey at Fort Steilacoom. Tell him we are ready to make peace. Tell him I was forced into this war by *Govenol* Stevens, and tricked into it by Mike Simmons and Jim McAllister, who placed my mark on a treaty I never signed. But now my heart is sick, and I, and all my people, wish to live in peace. Tell him we need only a little land by our sacred river, and we will lay down our arms." Leschi took both of Charlie's hands. "Tell him this, make him believe, and you will truly be my son."

Leschi's words touched a long-abandoned place in Charlie's heart. Could it be that he had roamed all these thousands of miles from home, to find in this alien man the father he never had? He knew he wasn't worthy, especially after the way he'd treated Kwahnesum, but perhaps, just perhaps ... What was it that Leschi had said to him, that awful day of the failed wedding? *There are no small men. There are only men who lack the courage to become big.* He didn't know if that was so, but suddenly nothing on earth mattered so much as showing this man that he had the courage to become big.

Charlie wrote out Leschi's words exactly. He added his own assessment that the Chief appeared sincere, and had not harmed him, or any of his other prisoners. Then Leschi permitted him to dispatch a small canoe with two men, to carry the message to Steilacoom.

The news was a thunderbolt to the town. The dreaded foe was only three miles across the water! Men grabbed their muskets, women grabbed their children, and dogs ran alongside, barking excitedly, as everyone rushed to board themselves up in blockhouses. A messenger galloped to the fort, bearing Charlie's note. "Ride on to Fort Nisqually," ordered Colonel Casey. "Ask Dr. Tolmie to lend us the Hudson's Bay steamer *Beaver*, then bring word to Olympia!" Casey, Captain Keyes, Lieutenant Kautz, and a company of Regulars rode out to Steilacoom, where they impatiently awaited the arrival of the steamer. The squat little vessel puffed merrily into view within the hour, carrying Chief Judge Lander, now a Lieutenant Colonel in the Volunteers, and – Casey was sorry to see – that pesky newspaperman, Mr. Wiley.

The Regulars boarded hastily with a howitzer in tow. Because there were no gunports on the little steamer, they had to take a moment to cut into the *Beaver's* gunnel to accommodate the barrel. They strapped it in place with hemp rigging. Throughout this hasty modification, Kautz paced up and down the deck yelling, "*Schnell, schnell,* faster, faster!" As soon as the howitzer was secured, they embarked for the short crossing to Fox Island, arriving in the little harbor outside the reservation just as the late afternoon shadows of the Olympics began to settle over the island.

Leschi's warriors were arrayed the length of the beach. In addition to the original landing party, hundreds of other Indians, newly released from their holding pens, stood watching. The adversaries studied one another in tense concentration. Charlie and a half-dozen other disarmed soldier-hostages, were dotted among the native forces, as a kind of human shield against bombardment. "For friendly Indians," remarked Judge Lander, "they don't look too friendly."

"We can't land our forces without grounding our steamer," reported Captain Keyes to Colonel Casey. "The dinghy only holds ten or twelve men at most. Even if we managed to land, we couldn't get enough men to shore to engage the enemy. We can't blast them without killing the hostages. Frankly, Sir, I'd say we've got no choice but to talk."

Colonel Casey stared longingly at the enemy, so close, yet beyond his grasp. He was surprised when Captain Eden stepped free from Leschi's side, and casually crossed to a small canoe. Charlie proceeded to launch himself and paddle the forty or so yards over still water, out to the spot where the *Beaver* had weighed anchor.

"Well, Captain," said the Colonel, "as the preacher said to the prostitute, 'You may be damned, but you sure look like you're havin' a good time!'"

Charlie chuckled. "Fact is, Sir, we're being treated real good."

"So why don't you tell me what's going on here, Captain."

"I put it all in that note, Sir. Like I said, Leschi wants to make peace."

"Peace is all anybody's talked about since the time of Jesus, Captain, but it hasn't worked out that way. Last I heard the Governor wants me to bring him back dead or alive." The Colonel smiled. "Half-dead would probably suit him just perfect."

"And if I may interject –" It was Lieutenant-Colonel Lander.

"Yes, Judge?" encouraged Casey.

"In light of the Governor's recent words to the Legislature, every member of Leschi's band there would have to surrender themselves to trial."

"Colonel," said Charlie, straining to think like a big man, "before I deliver a bitter pill like that, you gotta give me something to sweeten it." He looked Casey in the eye. "I don't know about these other Injuns, but Leschi might just give himself up if you pledge that his people can have a couple miles along the Nisqually River."

Casey was sorely tempted, but he knew he didn't have the authority. He saw Wiley watching him, pen poised to take down his response. "You tell Leschi that if he gives himself up, I'll work day and night for that. But I can't make him any such promise. That would be up to the President of the United States." He paused, gauging his words. "Now, if the Governor recommended it, I'm sure the President would do it. And you tell him for me, that my *Tyee*, General Wool, will recommend it to the President. But if the Governor is against it, well, I'm just not sure."

So Charlie carried this message back. "Tell the Colonel," said Leschi, "that I can see he is a good man, and if I face him in battle I will be sorry to kill him. Tell him he has fifteen of your minutes to get his ship out of here, or we will board it and take him. And you, *Challie* – promise me – after delivering this message, you will come back."

"I will, Chief." Charlie paddled back out, each stroke heavier than the one before. When he had delivered each word of Leschi's message, the Colonel just smiled. "Captain," he said, "Leschi might kill you outright, or take you hostage. You're safe now. Don't go back."

"Thank-you, Colonel," said Charlie, "but I gave my word." Charlie hastened overboard to his canoe. He paddled back with light strokes, through settling evening mist, to whatever his destiny might be.

When he got to shore, Charlie turned to see the *Beaver's* plume melting into the shadows. It steamed around the bend, heading southeast, back towards Steilacoom. Leschi loaded the war canoes with sixty new recruits from among the strongest young men, and with Charlie's ten rifles, and stores of ammunition. Then he turned to face Charlie, eye to eye. Once again, Charlie was impressed by how powerfully Leschi was built. But this time, he was not afraid.

"Tell your *Govenol* that I will send for you again in one moon, and once again we will talk peace. Until then, we will make war, and many will die. From this day forward, each new death is on his conscience. If he does nothing to stop this, then he is not a man."

Leschi embraced Charlie before rejoining his men. The canoes leapt out into the small bay. At the last minute, Leschi turned and shouted back over the water, "Tell our Kwahnesum that her father misses her!" Charlie fought to hold back unmanly tears, as the war canoes faded into the mist. If only he could!

Leschi ordered his men to cross Hale Passage, and hug the northern shore. Sure enough, as he suspected, the *Beaver* was lying in ambush just around the eastern tip of Fox Island. "Ready the howitzer!" ordered Colonel Casey.

"Sorry Sir!" reported the flummoxed gunner's mate. "Looks like in our hurry, we forgot to load the bloody balls."

Casey scowled, but his scowl soon turned to a great big belly laugh, as he watched Leschi's forces disappear northward, up the swift-running Narrows. "You want balls?" he cried. "That man up there's got 'em!"

Chapter Sixteen
The Battle of Seattle

1

O n January 25, 1856, the steamer *Active* rounded Alki point, carrying Governor Stevens, Mike Simmons, and Tony Rabbeson, past the place where the original two dozen settlers of what would become Seattle had first touched ground. Those settlers had ostentatiously named their improvised hovel of muslin stretched over blackberry bushes, "New York." When it did not immediately sprout tenements, the addition of the Chinook word for "by and by" made it "New York *Alki*," and eventually just *Alki*.

From the deck of the steamer, the Governor could just make out the shapes of the North Blockhouse, the Methodist Church, Yesler's mill and cookhouse, the South Blockhouse, and Mother Damnable's, the five major Seattle landmarks from north to south. There were half a dozen ships at anchor in the deepwater harbor of Elliott Bay, most impressive of which was the war sloop *Decatur*, commanded by the large New Yorker, Captain Geurt Gansevoort. Sounding their approach, the Governor's party awaited permission to board, then pulled alongside and grappled the ratline of the great triple-masted ship.

Once on board, the Governor and his party strutted about the bridge deck, doing their best to admire Captain Gansevoort's battered command. Once a 566-ton vision of polished New England maple and brass, the *Decatur* was reduced to a patchwork of maple, cedar, and dry rot. Her former Captain, Mr. Sterrit, had managed to ground her on a reef by Bainbridge Island, and she'd nearly sunk during the humiliating tow in to Yesler's wharf. It was only the past week, after three months of repairs, that she was again seaworthy.

The Governor had little interest in her past. She was well armed, with seven 32-pound carronades along each side of her hull, a 12-pounder at bow and stern, and an effective range of 150 yards. To Stevens, as to most of the pioneers, the *Decatur* represented two essentials: the protection of its mighty guns, and a boost to the economy.

A young boy tagged along on their tour of the top deck. "Hey, young feller," said Mike Simmons, squatting down beside him, "what's yer name?"

"Johnny King, Sir," said the boy.

"That's right," said the Captain, in response to Mike's inquiring glance. "This here boy is the one that led them *kinder* away to safety from the massacre. He's staying right now with Arthur and Louisa Denny."

"Governor," said Mike, "we got us a young hero right here."

The Governor's mind was elsewhere. That swine Henry Cotter they'd sent down to Portland to cash the Federal warrant had kept right on going, disappearing with the people's money. That's why Stevens had to come to Seattle, hat in hand, begging. It was the side of politics he could least abide. "Governor?" prodded Simmons.

"Yes, Mike, sorry."

"This here is Johnny King, the young feller who rescued his brother and sister from the Injuns at White River."

It warn't my brother an' sister, thought Johnny. *My real brother's dead.*

"Congratulations, son," said the little man with the big head, and he stuck out his hand. Johnny shook it; what was he s'posed ta do?

"Smile, young feller," prompted Mike, "this here's the Governor! Yer shakin' hands with the Governor himself."

"Really?" asked Johnny, getting excited. "Kin you git my friend, Georgie King, back? The Injuns took him."

"Well, son, I'll sure try."

Johnny's face fell. Seems the Gov'nor was just another do-nothin' grown-up.

"Captain, you got any reporters on board?" asked the Governor.

"No, Sir."

"Well," said Stevens, losing interest, "nice meeting you, Jimmy."

"Johnny," said Johnny, but the Governor had already moved on. The money he needed sure wasn't going to come from some orphan kid.

"Governor," said the Captain, "the Seattle delegation is waiting in my private dining room." *Down to business*, thought Stevens, as he followed the Captain below to the berth deck. All the big money in Seattle was there – Yesler, Denny, Boren, Terry, Bell. Doc Maynard was there too. Though personally he wasn't worth a fly's fart, he represented Mrs. Conklin, who had access to an inexhaustible supply of hard currency. Stevens was suddenly a different man, attentive and charming, as he pressed the flesh in the Captain's mess.

They wedged the Governor in at the head of the table, between the Captain and an irascible coot with sawdust in his ears, snot in his beard, and hair standing straight up, as though trying to abandon ship. The coot wore a tight-lipped scowl, which deepened as the man to his left, Arthur Denny, stood to raise his glass of milk in a toast. "Governor, on behalf of the Seattle business community, we welcome you to our humble but growing settlement.

I believe you are acquainted with most everyone here. That fellow to your left is our friend, Henry Yesler, whose mill employs half the town."

The Governor raised his glass – not of milk. "Mr. Yesler, a pleasure, Sir."

"Yeah, well, the pleasure's all yers, Gov'nor," growled the great engine of commerce. "I'm tryin' to figure out how we're gonna pay fer this war of yers, which ain't so hot fer business, I'm tellin' ya!"

Stevens maintained a steady tone. "Well, Mr. Yesler, I was thinking of asking for a tax on milled lumber." The room fell completely silent. Then Yesler did something he only did once a year: he laughed, and Stevens laughed with him. The two most powerful white men in the Territory clinked shot glasses and drank their whisky down. The rest of the room heaved a collective sigh of relief, and joined them in a belly laugh over the Governor's joke. Stevens might be a little wild, but he was their kind of man. Soon everyone in the room had shared a word and a drink with the Governor, and Mike had noted down quite a few special requests, to carry back to Olympia.

"But seriously, Gov'nor," said Yesler, at last, "this damn war is killing us at the mill. What have you got in mind?"

Stevens rose to his feet. "Gentlemen, first off, you've got nothin' to worry 'bout up here in Seattle," he assured them. "There aren't but fifty or so hostiles on this side of the mountains, and they're all high-tailin' it back into the forest as we speak."

"I don't know, Sir," piped up Doc Maynard. "With all due respect, there's a lot of chatter among the friendly Indians about an attack on Seattle."

"Attack on Seattle!" mocked Stevens. "There's as much chance of an Indian attack on New York. Captain, you ought to remove your ship to the harbor by Steilacoom, where it's more likely to see action."

Captain Gansevoort squinted and showed his teeth. Mr. Denny checked his pocket watch. The rest of the men looked solemnly at their hands. "Well," whispered Denny to Yesler, "he is the Governor. Perhaps he knows something we don't."

"If I may, Governor –" It was Doc again, and Stevens was beginning to get vexed. Hadn't he given him some kind of an appointment? Didn't he know that meant keep yer mouth shut! Still, Doc jabbered on. "I've talked to the Indians about your policy of extermination, and I'm worried it's turning the friendly ones against us. Not only that, but it's likely to prolong the war. They asked me, how's a fellow supposed to surrender, if he knows it means death?"

"Our policy is clear, Doctor," replied the Governor with cool precision. "Any hostile who turns himself in can rely upon the justice and mercy of the

Government. There can be no other terms with criminals who have terrorized our people. As for the so-called 'friendly' savages, let's not deceive ourselves. They'd all slit our throats if they thought they could get away with it. Keep 'em in fear and you keep 'em down, that's what I say."

Stevens barreled on, rather than give Doc a chance to reply. "Now, about this war. Gentlemen, this war is not my war. It's your war. That's right," he added quickly, holding up his hand as if someone were about to contradict him, "your war, Gentlemen, and the war of every man who wants to make a little something for himself out here in God's country. Now, with all due respect to our friend Mr. Yesler, if you think a little war is bad for business, you're thinkin' short term. Where would you rather live and work, a savage land, or a land where the savages have been put in their place? Where would you rather raise a family, a Territory where you'd have to wonder whether your kin were about to be massacred, or one where the Indians have been beaten? Where would you rather invest in a mill or a factory, a store or a hotel? A Territory that's half *siwash*, or a nice white Territory where Christian folks own all the good land, and the few remaining red men are safely out of the way?

"So remember, Gentlemen, whether you're a good Democrat or one of those other kind," and here he looked Arthur Denny in the eye, "we're all white men, and all on the same side. Who am I? Am I the Democratic Governor? Hell, no! I'm the white man's Governor; I'm the fellow protecting your investment."

Mr. Yesler started the applause, and it spread around the room. Soon they were all standing, and Stevens basked in the glow of their approbation.

"Thank-you, thank-you, Gentlemen. Coming from you, this means a lot. But I have to ask more from you than just your applause. Mr. Yesler, Mr. Denny, the rest of you Gentlemen – as a little favor to me – I would like you to put together a special fund. Tony or Mike here will be by next week to collect, and then once a month until these troubles are over and prosperity is back. Let's call it the Governor's War fund. Consider it an investment, same as patching up your store or your mill. I'm going use it to keep you all in business, and to raise your land values. It's an investment, Gentlemen, pure and simple."

"Now wait just a minute," said Mr. Denny. "This is highly irregular –"

"So's war," spat Yesler. Denny nodded gravely, and consulted his pocket watch again. "What you gonna do with our money?" Yesler asked the Governor. "Specifics."

"Well, Sir, the first thing I'm gonna do is offer a reward for the heads of every hostile Indian, including extra for the leaders. That's how we're going to end this war, Gentlemen. We're going to decapitate the enemy!"

"Governor!" protested Doc Maynard. "Cash is scarce these days. People are desperate. We'll have bounty hunters bringing you the heads of friendly Indians."

Stevens paused just long enough to watch Doc sweat. "Doc," he replied, "as Mr. Yesler here has just pointed out, this is war. Whose side are you on?"

"I'm in," announced Henry Yesler. Doc suddenly recalled who had appointed him Justice of the Peace. They were all in.

2

Leschi was not high-tailing it back into the forest. After his parley at Fox Island, his reinforced army took the Black River up to the eastern shore of huge Lake Duwamish, near the place he had camped so long ago with Dr. Tolmie, when they first went to confront Patkanim over the murder at Fort Nisqually. There, he joined the rest of his forces, led down from the upper Green River by Quiemuth. Then they waited for reinforcements.

Nelson brought bitter disappointment. The thousand warriors promised by the Chiefs of *Whulge*, turned out to be a paltry column of twenty stragglers, left behind when the tribes were ferried to reservations across the Sound. Leschi and his men were on their own. The promised general uprising of all the tribes on *Whulge* would not come.

Their only other hope lay to the east. They expected Owhi within a few suns; instead, he took ten, delayed by the deep snows of Snoqualmie Pass, that forced his men to dismount and cross on snowshoe. Each day, Leschi paced and watched nervously, afraid that his camp would be discovered and attacked by the Boston soldiers. His people were nervous too, camped so close to Lake Duwamish. How often had they been warned as children about the *Zugwa*, the demon beneath the lake, whose great black hand could snatch a man and pull him to a cold and airless death?

True to his word, Owhi did come, leading ten tens of warriors. When his right fist pounded his chest in greeting, Leschi was overjoyed. With the addition of Owhi, Leschi now commanded the largest Indian army ever assembled west of the Cascades – well over two hundred men. A problem remained, however. They were mostly armed with muskets, spears and clubs. They had only a dozen of the accurate, breech-loading rifles, and precious few bullets.

"We must have better guns," Leschi insisted that night, as the leaders huddled in the cold and dark of a fire-less camp. "Our spies tell us that Volunteers have been mustering out. They have breech-loading rifles, and plenty of ammunition. When we learn where the arms are hidden, we will seize them."

Owhi exulted to hear such manly talk. Ever since Chief Kamiakan had been defeated, he had thirsted for revenge. He scoured the Umtanum and Manastash, even into the land of the Kittitas, to assemble this new army. Uncertain where to strike the many-headed Boston hydra, he was pleased when Winyea reached him with Leschi's call. "I will be proud to help you lead such a raid," he said. "Many white men will die. They will learn the folly of stealing our land."

In the wee hours of the next morning, under cover of darkness, Leschi's army broke camp and crossed the big lake to within a few miles of Seattle. There they camped for one more night, on the western shore, gathering intelligence, resting Owhi's travel-weary warriors, and preparing their weapons for battle.

In the winter dark of early evening, a large, middle-aged Nisqually with a three-fingered hand, crept into camp. "Here is what I know," whispered John Hiton, who'd been rewarded for helping the King and Jones children, with a job in Yesler's kitchen. "The rifles are in the cookhouse under the floor by the big oven. I will try to be there to show you exactly. There are maybe seven tens, with plenty of bullets. I have heard tell that there are also rifles hidden in a shed behind Plummer's house, by the swamp near the water, but I have not seen them."

"I know Plummer's house," said Wyamooch.

"Good," said Leschi. "You will lead a raiding party to it."

"But there is a problem," warned John Hiton. "The marines from the *Decatur* sleep in the cookhouse every night, and guard the town."

"How many?"

"Maybe four tens, well armed."

"We can take them!" cried Kitsap, and Owhi and Sluggia joined in approval.

"Maybe," said John, "until the ship opens fire. To those big guns, a man is like a mosquito."

"What do you suggest?" sneered Kitsap, his scar dark in the thin light of a cloudy day. "Should we go to the reservation? I would sooner die now!"

"There is a better way."

"Go on, John Hiton," urged Leschi.

"The marines go back to their ship every morning at dawn. Time your raiding parties to arrive when they are out in their boats. Creep down in silence under cover of darkness, just before the dawn. With luck you can grab the guns and get back to the cover of the trees, before the ship knows anything has happened."

"This is a cowardly way to do battle," cried Kitsap. "Why should we sneak around? At last we have many warriors. Now is the time to wipe out the white man, once and for all. I say we attack in one great mass before dawn. We will drive them into *Whulge*. She is thirsty for their blood!"

"Yes!" cried Stahi, who'd been sober ever since he'd led McAllister into the ambush. Sluggia quickly agreed with his father. After the years of Stahi's drunkenness, at last they were united.

Leschi did not agree. "I know John Hiton. He speaks with wisdom. I say we follow his plan." Quiemuth, Kanasket and Nelson nodded in agreement.

"I have seen their big guns," said Owhi. "I am with Leschi."

They all looked to Wyamooch who, for once, had not spoken. Kitsap confidently puffed out his chiseled chest, knowing that Wyamooch had always followed his lead. Wyamooch surprised everyone. "I too am with Leschi."

3

Many cheerful libations after his successful fund-raising dinner, the Governor staggered out of the Captain's mess and up the companionway to the bridge deck, arm in arm with Tony and Mike. From there, he was lowered in a net to the waiting *Active*. "Tony," he said, when they'd gotten him vertical, "wasn't there a friend of yours in this town, a Mrs. Conklin, who you like to visit?"

Tony allowed a rare grin to plump his sunken cheeks. Mike Simmons slapped Tony on the back – something he didn't ever dare to do with the Governor. "That lady's got more pussies than a momma cat!" he cried with delight. "I'm game, Gov'nor."

"Then what are we waitin' for, boys?" The Captain of the *Active* was informed that the Governor had an important engagement shoreside, and they set course for Yesler's wharf under a full head of steam.

"Tony," said Stevens, "there is a kind of delicate problem here, me being the Governor and all. You've got to go ahead and arrange things for me with the lady, so I can use a private entrance, and, well, she'll understand; I've got to be a little bit discreet. I'll meet you boys back here, tomorrow morning." So Stevens waited eagerly, his manhood already straining at the buttons of his trousers, while Tony made the arrangements. Soon, he saw the red-haired lady herself appear at a side door, carrying a candle. Isaac hurried to join her.

"Dear Sir, such an honor!" gushed the buxom Mrs. Conklin, as she ushered the Governor inside and up a private stairway. The landing opened onto a richly furnished apartment with oriental carpets over burnished floors, tapestries covering the walls, potted ferns and palms tastefully dotted among velvet loveseats, and ornate Persian brocade divans. "I attended that marvelous welcoming dinner, Sir, and was entranced with your very dominating presence. You are a fighter, Sir, a true military man, and I'm proud to have you as my," here the lady dropped into *sotto voce*, as she leaned her swollen bosom towards his chin, "Governor." *Cackle-cackle.*

Stevens blanched inwardly, but smiled gamely. "No need to worry, Sir, this is a completely private apartment, reserved only for the most respectable Gentlemen. All my ladies are thoroughly instructed in the courtesan's creed of confidentiality." She fluttered her eyelashes and jiggled her breasts ever so slightly, as she nestled him onto the softest plump sofa, and fixed him a whisky and soda.

Drink delivered, the High Priestess of Pleasure positioned herself behind the Governor, dipped her fingers in warm scented oil, and gently massaged his temples and neck. "I am sure that current events are creating great strain, even for one so powerful as yourself, Sir. I am honored that my humble services might play a part, however small, in easing your cares, thus bringing us ever closer to that certain victory which God intends. This house is a place of perfect freedom and relaxation. You may trust us totally. Your pleasure is our only aim. All you need do is relax, let yourself feel the tonifying comfort only the weaker sex can bestow. Would you care to inspect the young ladies in person, which has the advantage of touch as well as view? Or perhaps you would prefer a special service offered to a Gentleman of your stature, the perfect privacy of having the ladies pass by our special viewing portal, where you can see them, but they cannot see you?"

Excellent, thought Stevens, his stature growing even as he melted under Mother Mary's well-practiced fingers. "The latter, Madam."

Mrs. Conklin sauntered over to a large tapestry, depicting an oriental scene of highly stylized copulation, in which a little Kama Sutra figure no bigger than the Governor, held an engorged lady entranced upon a horse-sized erection. She pulled a cord that rolled up the tapestry to reveal a darkend window. "On the opposite side, it appears as a mirror," assured dear Mother

Mary, as she pressed a special call button. She returned to her place behind the Governor, and resumed the massage as a warm yellow glow brightened the mysterious window, the gaslight in their chamber faded, and the ethereal tones of the wood flute wafted over them.

"Governor," whispered the notorious Madam in his ear, "I give you the world-famous Mother Mary's Portal of Pleasure."

The first girl appeared, a vision of golden-haired feline grace. Her breasts, barely concealed beneath a gauzy wrap, were firm and inviting. She moved with the fierce, balanced purpose of a tiger. "This is Chloe," whispered Mrs. Conklin in the Governor's ear, "a direct descendant of the Greek Goddess of Love, Aphrodite." But the Governor had no interest in a woman so much taller than himself, and shook his head.

The next temptress had long, flowing red hair, a skirt and brassiere of iron mail, and a sword at her belt. She strode to the glass and licked it, then turned contemptuously, bent at the waist to slap the ground with her flaming mane while displaying her taut haunches, then turned again and snarled. "Diana, the huntress," whispered Mrs. Conklin. "No," replied the Governor firmly, as he crossed his legs. Stevens would be the only swordsman at this tryst.

Next was a Negro with shining bronze skin. "No Africans," said the Governor. "Naomi is from the Island of Fiji, Your Excellency." "No Fijians, then," said the Governor, and he dismissed her with a wave of his hand.

Next was a light-skinned Indian girl, with flowing black tresses, an elegant aquiline nose, dark curled lashes under plucked brows, eyes pellucid and quick. Her toned body shimmered in the soft light, as she swayed to the wood flute, like a cobra entranced by its charmer. "A fresh arrival," cooed Mrs. Conklin. "A real Indian Princess." The Governor admired her smooth fine thighs and the way her back dipped and swelled into rounded buttocks, radiant as any ocean wave under moonlight. "I can see that you have an eye for the best," encouraged the Madam. "You would be the first client to sample this delight, Sir." He was rock hard, he'd waited long enough. "Yes," said the Governor, aroused by the thought of ravishing the enemy. "Yes, she'll do nicely."

Mrs. Conklin clapped her hands three times. Bowing low, she withdrew in a swish of crinoline. The light faded from the magic portal, leaving the Governor in the agreeable dim glow of the gas lamps, every sense aroused. A shadow shifted by a small door to his left, then formed before him into the winsome Native, clad only in a translucent silvery nightgown, wrapped with a boa of eagle feathers. Though the light was low, the Governor was aroused by the lingering shadow where the girl's erect nipples tented the silk of the gown, and the deeper mystery where her legs converged.

Kwahnesum could not believe what her eyes beheld. It was that dreaded little tin-pot tyrant from Medicine Creek! Doc and Catherine Maynard had been too kind to her. When they'd sent for Charlie, she knew she had to go. She'd run to the house of Doc's good friend, Mrs. Conklin, who was more than happy to take her in. Kwahnesum was no fool; she knew what kind of house this was. She went willingly. She deserved no better.

Oh, for First Mother's obsidian knife! She'd plunge it right into his chest. But there was no place to conceal it in this sheer costume, so it was stashed with her clothes at the other end of the house. Kwahnesum struggled to master her emotions. She saw immediately that there was no danger of being recognized. If Stevens had seen her at all, it had been amongst crowds of her people. Besides, he was too besotted with lust and whiskey to recognize a face, and his eyes were busy elsewhere.

He was handsome, she had to give him that: dark-eyed and intense, a proud, high-for-a-Boston forehead over delicate features. Let him look, she decided, and she began to sway, slipping first one shoulder and then the other from the nightgown, letting it slide down in front until her breasts strained upward at the hem of the bodice, held up only by her nipples. With a surprisingly smooth and gentle touch, he caressed first one, and then the other breast, out from where they nested, causing the nightgown to drop to the carpet. He drew her forward, and began to suckle, careful and methodical in his lovemaking, giving each breast its due. As he took his pleasure, she looked down upon his curly locks, then took his head in her hands because she was curious. Under guise of passion, she tested the powerful muscles of a neck she lacked the strength to snap.

He ordered her to lie down on the divan, which she did. He removed and carefully folded his strangely formal clothes, the frock coat and chemise with separate stiff collar and cuffs, the woolen trousers with the sharp crease, the one piece union suit underneath, slowly revealing a strange, composite man. The Governor, naked, appeared to be two entirely different men, fused at the waist. The top man was lusty and powerful, the bottom man, scrawny and shriveled. Because the weakling dwelled below, the Governor's comic little erection poked from his crotch like a field mouse alert for a hawk.

Then he was on her and inside her. She closed her eyes, pretending she was far away, running through *Tenalquot* Prairie, a little girl out with momma in the time before Bostons. She was a bit too dry and he felt rough, like the horsetail her mother taught her to cut and use for scrubbing things clean. Oh, she remembered, how she loved to scrub and burnish and polish to get the bowls and baskets and men's spears to shine in the sun. And then with a cry, he came inside her, and she knew she could never get clean again.

He didn't just roll over and go to sleep; no, he wanted to talk. "What's your name?" he asked in surprisingly good Chinook, and she told him, "Tenalquot."

"After the prairie? I'll bet you hate my people, don't you?" he mused. Kwahnesum only smiled a bit, surprised that he would be so blunt. But of course – Mother Mary had already told her. *The courtesan is so powerless that she hears everything, and becomes powerful.*

"Tenalquot," he said, turning back towards her, running his soft hands gently over her breasts and down across her stomach, "you are so beautiful." How little you know, she thought. "I don't want you to hate me, dear Tenalquot," he murmured, kissing her breasts again. "I'll tell you what – ask me anything, and I will tell you the truth."

She looked at him doubtfully, but ventured, "Why make war on my people?"

Stevens scowled, but a pledge was a pledge. "Self-defense. My informants tell me that Leschi went to a great war council east of the mountains last summer, where he made a solemn pact to join the Yakamas in exterminating my people."

His informants! She would have to find a way to warn Leschi. "Who says such a thing?"

Stevens, drunk with liquor and pleasure though he was, still had a modicum of guile left. "That goes too far. But I will tell you something more. Even if it were true that Leschi wanted to make peace, I would still press this war to its end. Chief Se-alth said it best at Medicine Creek, 'Day and night cannot dwell together.' Were you there?"

Kwahnesum shook her head, "No." Why should he know?

"That is when Leschi made himself known as my enemy. It is strange, my dear. In some ways he and I are alike. Like me, he realizes what the weaklings refuse to accept – that two such different races cannot live side by side in peace. One race must govern, the other must submit or perish. It is no different with the salmon that you catch. You govern the salmon; the salmon submits. Many salmon perish to feed your people."

Kwahnesum worked up her courage. "Sir," she said, "we do not try to move the salmon from their river home. Couldn't you –"

"What has the salmon ever made besides more salmon!" interrupted Stevens. "There's the rub, my savage beauty. Your people say that they have lived here a thousand generations, yet you have nothing to show for it. The white man's turn has come. In just a few generations, we will build railroads, huge ships, cities that will dwarf even the Douglas firs. We will have riches and comforts beyond your imagining. It is selfish for your Chief Leschi to stand in the way. Your people do not use the land. We can make much more of it."

"Yes, Sir, I believe that what you say is true. My people have loved the land, and loving and using are not the same thing." Stevens looked into her eyes for the first time. For a moment he thought that he had seen such eyes before. No, of course not; he shook it off.

"Sir, I have lived in your houses. You are right, they are better than ours. Except they are empty and lonely. Our longhouses were always full of life and joy."

"Tenalquot, little child, do not lie to me." His hand slipped down between her legs, and he pressed a little too hard until she gave a cry. "Your people raided and murdered one another; took slaves; suffered like any other people. Isn't this so?"

She knew there was some truth to what the Governor said. For his part, he was content with her silence; his tone became kinder. Once again he was the Great White Father, instructing the heathen. "Our Lord, Jesus Christ, put us on this earth to be fruitful. We must love one other, but there is no reason to love the wild animals who threaten our stock, or the untamed forest, or the stone mountains. Those are the raw materials He gave us to build his Kingdom on earth. If we do not use his bounty to the fullest, we are not good Christians."

"Yes, Sir," she ventured, making her voice as gentle as possible. "But there is plenty for all. Couldn't you spare just a little land by the river for my people?"

He drew his hand away and sat up. "You are Nisqually?"

"Yes."

"Leschi's murderous ways have sealed the fate of your tribe."

"But he did not order the massacre at White River!"

"How do you know that?" The Governor looked at Kwahnesum quizzically.

"I – I just know it."

"No matter," said the Governor, relaxing again as he traced the outline of her thigh. "It happened, and people think Leschi was responsible."

"Do you?"

"For a whore, you ask too many questions," he replied, tangling his fingers into the hair of her pubis. She pushed his hand away and sat up. "Don't go, Tenalquot," he said, reaching for her. "I'm not a bad fellow. I feel sorry for what's become of your people, but you must understand – no great thing can be accomplished without some sacrifice. I am trying to build something new here in Washington Territory. Some day, all this unpleasantness will be forgotten, and people will simply say, 'What a wonderful place to raise a family!'"

"Sir, who will say that? The white man, or the red man?"

"Both. But even if it is only the white man, that is enough." He laid her back down, and returned his hand to her pubis. "It is like this house, Mother Mary's; think of all the joy it brings! If, in the process, the innocence of a few girls gets sacrificed, so what? It is sad, perhaps, but it doesn't really matter, because whores don't write history." Kwahnesum tensed as his finger slipped inside, but Stevens held her down with his strong arms, as he took a second helping of God's bounty.

4

Su-quardle, known to jocular Bostons as Chief Curly due to his bald pate, was always up before dawn, and the morning of Saturday, January 26, 1856, was no exception. Like his father and grandfather before him, Curly was a Chief of the Duwamish, but he had made his peace with the white man. Henry Yesler was now his son in law, and he worked at Yesler's mill doing a little bit of nothing too strenuous. His light-skinned granddaughter was already being raised as a Yesler. As he liked to say when the young braves challenged him, "You can't get far swimming upstream." "Tell that to the salmon," they'd say. "Look what happens to the old salmon when he gets there," Curly would reply.

As Curly left his little shack on the southeastern edge of town to fetch some water that cold and misty morning, he heard a familiar voice call to him from the brush. There, by the side of an old fishing camp, he found his friend Wyamooch. "Listen carefully, Su-quardle," said Wyamooch. "You and I will be big men today." Curly liked the sound of that. "Tell your boss-man Yesler that Leschi attacks at dawn. Leschi's aiming for the cookhouse, while I lead a raid on Plummer's for what they're hiding there. Tell him Wyamooch says so. Tell Yesler to tell Stevens who it was that gave the warning. They will pay many blankets. Now I have to go; I'm supposed to be scouting." Curly dropped his bucket and ran off to find Henry Yesler.

In the dim light, Kwahnesum could barely make out the sleeping form of the Governor beside her. Ever so silently, she slipped from under the sheets. Careful not to bump anything, she felt about for a suitable weapon. She picked up her feather boa, but decided it would snap if she tried to strangle him with it. Besides, he was so strong, she feared he'd fight her off and kill her. She felt about at a side table, and had to catch a statuette before it fell over. That was it! A stone carving of a nude woman carrying a basket on her head. She picked it up – it was heavy. One well-aimed blow, and he'd be finished. She just needed a few more minutes for the sun to top *Ta-co-bet*, so she could be sure her aim was true. She knew she would have only one chance. She drew the Governor's frock coat around her shoulders for warmth, and waited.

Leschi's men had the town completely encircled, the line along the woods stretching from the Methodist Church in the north, to Mother Damnable's in the south. Leschi, Quiemuth and Kanasket commanded the center; Owhi and Stahi commanded the northern flank; Kitsap and Wyamooch commanded the southern flank. Just before sunrise, the marines filed out of the cookhouse and down to waiting rowboats. As the boats were launched, Leschi led a small raiding party out from the cover of the wooded hills, gingerly stepping and sliding down the steep bank beside the greased planks of Skid Road, towards the cookhouse. Simultaneously, Wyamooch led a small party out of the woods on the southeast, along the beach towards Plummer's cache.

Chief Curly reached the mill just after the marines embarked for the *Decatur*. The foreman thought he was drunk, and refused to awaken Mr. Yesler. Curly sought out his daughter, who listened with ever-widening eyes, then immediately awakened her husband. "Leschi's going to attack right after dawn!" she cried.

"Says who?" asked Yesler, shaking the sleep from his head.

"Wyamooch," said Curly, and he quickly filled in Yesler on his morning rendezvous in the brush.

Made sense, thought Yesler. Wyamooch had been on the Governor's payroll since Medicine Creek. Yesler dressed hurriedly. "Did he say anything else?"

Foggy old brain, thought Curly, rubbing his bald dome. "Leschi's hiding in Plummer's coop," he spat out quick, before he appeared as befuddled as he felt. He was sure Wyamooch had said something about Plummer's, and that man had the fattest chickens in town. Yesler took Curly into his rowboat, and together they chased the marines out to the *Decatur* to sound the alarm.

As soon as he heard the news, Captain Gansevoort had the men load a howitzer with a few balls on board the row-boat, leaving it dangerously low in the water. He sent the squad of marines right back to town, with instructions to demolish Plummer's coop. The marines rowed like their lives depended on it, which, for the non-swimmers, seemed likely. By some miracle they made shore. Meanwhile, the *Decatur* herself quietly weighed anchor, and moved in on the rising tide, to just off the end of Yesler's wharf. She came about, and trained her starboard guns on the hills looming from nighttime mists, over the awakening town.

Back shoreside, Johnny King watched as Mrs. Denny took a tray of biscuits out of the oven. The Denny's little girl, two-year old Emily, reached out her hand and said, "Eat!"

"Too hot, Emily," said her mother. "Just wait."

"EAT!" demanded Emily. With a two-year old's fury, she began to wail. Johnny winced. Emily's tantrums could shake the house and rattle the windows.

Kwahnesum strained her eyes, barely perceiving the outline of the Governor's broad white forehead. Taking a deep breath, she lifted the stone statue high.

The explosion of the howitzer was much, much louder than Emily's tantrums, shattering the kitchen window, and silencing even Emily in mid-howl.

Stevens bolted upright just as the statue smashed his pillow, sending feathers flying everywhere. For a moment he thought he'd been shot. Kwahnesum leaped up and fled, naked but for the Governor's frock coat.

More feathers flew as Plummer's chicken coop exploded in a direct hit. None but chickens were the worse for the marine gunner's excellent marksmanship; the raiding party fled the adjacent shed in terror, through shot-roasted chicken, dazed birds, and flying debris. Their search for weapons had been in vain, their intelligence faulty, and all they had to show for their trouble was a few dozen sprouting potatoes, and a jug of corn mash whiskey.

Leschi's raiding party, empty-handed and only half-way to its destination, did an about face, and fled back to the sheltering forest, cursing the loss of the element of surprise. The moment Leschi's men made cover, the forest erupted in a huge volley of musket fire.

Throughout the town, wood splintered and glass shattered. Mrs. Denny screamed, then shook the muffins out into her apron, grabbed Emily by the arm, and ran out with Johnny on her tail. Everywhere Johnny looked, people in their underwear and even Mr. Butler in his wife's red flannel petticoat were running and flailing and falling and getting up, grabbing at children and scrambling over one another, to reach the South Blockhouse. A huge line of smoke rose from the woods all around, marking for the terrified inhabitants the longest skirmish line they'd ever seen.

To get to the safety of the blockhouse, they had to run straight into the guns of the enemy, then around to the side facing the wooded hills to get in the door. Johnny ran without any regard for Mrs. Denny, who fell behind. What the heck; she wasn't his maw. As a second volley of balls flew all about him, it seemed like he heard Maw's voice, guiding him towards the blockhouse at the top of the hill. "Don't you ever be scairt," it said, and he wasn't, he was just mad. He saw a young man he recognized run out of his house and then, stupidly, go back to close the door. Johnny flew past Mrs. Blaine, the minister's wife, sitting in a rocking chair, with her infant daughter in her lap, carried by her two sons. Then he was up to the blockhouse, around it and in, just as a sound like thunder rose from the *Decatur*, and he knew the Indians were getting shelled by those big 32-pounders he'd seen just the night before. Johnny was yelling again and again, "Blast them heathens, c'mon, blast 'em, blast 'em to smithereens," but in all the noise and confusion he couldn't hear himself. Soon he quieted down, and didn't even bother to cry.

The Governor, disoriented, scrambled for his clothes. In the rush, he ended up in his trousers and Kwahnesum's silk nightgown, a few feathers from the exploded pillow still decorating his hair. Searching frantically for a way out of the hell-house of pleasure, he ran into a hallway. Down the hall was a broad porch, where several other half-dressed customers and girls were floundering about.

That was the moment the *Decatur* fired the first round of shells that Johnny cheered from within the blockhouse. They fell short, plowing up the ground behind Third Street, destroying a livery stable. All was quiet for a moment. Then the delayed-fuse shells exploded, spattering hot metal and wooden splinters, mixed with mud and horsemeat, in all directions. Exploding shells, thought the Governor. Good enough if they can get them up to the enemy's position.

"What in heaven's name was that?" cried a man in a frock coat and bloomers. "I'm just a bible salesman; I didn't reckon on stumblin' into a war," he confided to the Governor, then stuck out a trembling hand. "Robert Wilson," he said as if he were making a sales call. It was his last. A bullet blew off the top of the bible salesman's head, and he fell heavily, spattering Kwahnesum's nightgown in bloody grey matter. Disgusted, Stevens yanked it off, just as a strong arm pulled him back.

"C'mon, Governor," cried Simmons, throwing his coat around the soiled leader. Simmons, in chain mail that hung to mid-thigh, looked like a great Irish knight whose squire had forgotten his trousers. Tony was right behind him, wearing a red flannel union suit. Their dash to the waiting Active made up in alacrity what it lacked in dignity.

Johnny surveyed the folks huddled in the blockhouse. In their haste, most had forgotten their guns. "Keep clear of the rifle slots," said an old man with a long droopy face, shooing some children back. Right next to Johnny sat Milton Holgate. Everybody in town knew Milton. Though barely fifteen, he'd killed a drunken marine who'd tried to rape his sister. Milton had his shotgun in hand; yes sir, he didn't forget to grab it.

"I ain't keepin' clear of nothin'," Milton confided to Johnny, as he breech loaded a shotshell.

"Yeah, Milton, you get us some Injuns!" said Johnny, delighted with the opportunity to fight back. "How 'bout we take turns?"

"I ain't takin' turns with no little kid," said Milton, hopping down from the bench. He stuck the barrel down the angled chink in the wall, and sighted a shot. "Dang, I can't see nothin'!" he cried. Then, cool as a dipper of spring water, he popped open the door.

"What in tarnation you doing boy?" yelled the droopy-faced man, but Milton had already slipped out and sighted like he was shooting ducks on a pond. There was a loud report and an almost simultaneous thud, as Milton fired and was hit square between the eyes with return fire, knocking him straight back through the door to land at Johnny's feet. Women screamed and the old man slammed the door shut. Johnny stared at Milton, who stared right back without seeing a thing.

The *Decatur* came about and fired its portside guns, while starboard cooled and reloaded. Quiemuth, who had just fired Leschi's rifle at the man in the doorway of the blockhouse, couldn't hear the volley coming in. Leschi heard it; a great humming like a pack of giant bees. The trees above shattered. A minute later, angry demons in the ground exploded, flinging stones and hot metal everywhere. "This is an evil magic," yelled Leschi to his brother.

"We must fall back," cried Quiemuth, "out of range of shells that *mox-poo!*"

"If we retreat," shouted Leschi over the din, "we cannot reach the town with our muskets. We must hold our ground, and launch a raid to get in closer." But few of his warriors were waiting for Leschi's opinion. When the huge shells exploded a second time, nearly all the Natives fell back in panic, and neither encouragement nor threats from their commanders could induce them to step within range of the *Decatur's* cannons.

"Send word to Owhi," hollered Leschi to Quiemuth. "I want him to attack from the north. Have Kitsap and Wyamooch attack from the south. I will attack from the center. Go!" Leschi felt as if one of the Boston's cannonballs was in the pit of his stomach. He had heard of the power of the white man's guns, but he had never felt it before. How could they defeat such a foe, armed only with a few rifles, muskets, spears and clubs?

Lieutenant Colonel Lander of the Volunteers, who happened to be a guest at the Boren residence while in town to preside as Chief United States Judge, had sprung from bed at the first sound of the howitzer. Without bothering to change out of his nightgown, Lander grabbed his rifle and a few men to aid in the defense of the town. Now they were arrayed at the second-story windows of the Boren home, training their rifles on the northern hills.

Owhi's men, who had heard the howitzer before, were steeled to face it. Owhi and Stahi, with two tens of men apiece, boldly swept down out of the northern hills, but just as they passed the Methodist Church, Lander's impromptu force opened fire. The attackers fell back to the church for only a moment. Realizing that they outnumbered the defenders, Stahi let loose a banshee cry and charged the house with his half of the force. Lander and his men fled for their lives, the Judge's nightgown billowing out behind him like bleached judicial robes. Just as Stahi's force reached Boren's picket fence, a round of carronade shells landed in their midst, tearing up the ground beneath their feet, tossing warriors into the air like sparks from a campfire. Owhi led a second wave behind Stahi, but delayed explosions stopped them in their tracks. Dazed survivors stumbled about, half-blind and deafened, easy prey to be cut down by crossfire from Lander's regrouped force, and a company of marines coming up from the shore.

A delayed shell exploded, and Owhi fell with a cry. Stahi lifted Owhi over his shoulder, and ordered a retreat. As he neared the sheltering edge of the forest, Judge Lander leveled his compression rifle, sighted, exhaled, and gently squeezed the trigger. Stahi fell, a bullet between his shoulder blades. Owhi, half-conscious, clung to his dying rescuer as many hands tried to pull him to safety.

"Go, Owhi," said Stahi. "Tell Sluggia I am sorry. Tell him," he whispered, choking back blood, "to obey his uncles."

In the south, Kitsap lay dazed, bleeding from both ears, after leading a charge across a beach that was torn in half by one shot from the marines' howitzer. Sluggia, himself bleeding from shrapnel wounds, helped his friend to his feet. Together they staggered back into the forest. Kitsap's injuries left Wyamooch in command, and he chose to lay low, rather than attempt an advance. The marines fired their howitzer parsimoniously, trying to give the impression that they had plenty of shells, when in fact they were almost out. Without the howitzer, they would have to retreat or be overrun. Wyamooch had no desire to test the defenders' resources; his loyalties lay elsewhere. Both sides kept their heads down, and refrained from further heroics. It seemed a satisfactory arrangement, during which the Bostons even managed to partake of some of Plummer's roast chicken.

As Kitsap and Owhi fell, Leschi charged with the few men brave enough to run straight into the shells that *mox-poo*. "We must get so close that those big guns are useless," cried Leschi. Only a few handfuls of men followed him. Quiemuth volunteered, of course, but Leschi would not have him. "Someone must lead our people if I am killed."

Leschi and Kanasket mounted a desperate charge down the steep incline of Skid Road, around the north end of the swamp, and through the sawdust mounds towards Yesler's wharf. As his warriors came roaring down out of the hills, the *Decatur* turned its carronade from Owhi's forces to Leschi's. A round of shells flew high and wide, splintering the log chute. Ears ringing from the earth-rattling explosions, the Natives ran through the deserted town, giddy to have made it below the firing perimeter of the cannons. Muskets primed, they launched themselves into the great mounds of soggy sawdust piled east of the wharf, intent on reaching Yesler's mill.

It was not to be. When they topped the first rise, they found themselves staring into the sights of the breech-loading rifles of Lieutenant Phelps, and thirty marines. As the first volley rang out and most of the Natives dived back for cover, the mound gave way under Leschi, burying him in heavy sawdust in no man's land.

"Leschi is lost!" cried Winyea, firing wildly through his tears.

"Not if Kanasket has anything to say about it," boomed the big man, and with a howl he was over the edge, slopping down over wet sawdust, through whistling bullets and clouds of smoke. Kanasket half ran, half tumbled, to the spot where Leschi's hand waved up out of the ground. He began to dig frantically as bullets kicked up the sawdust all around him. Nelson, Winyea, Wahoolit, and the others, concentrated their fire as best they could to try to cover him. There! Kanasket felt a head and cleared it quickly, then pulled with all his strength, just as Wahoolit and Nelson led a small band of Leschi's men over the lip of the dune to draw some of the marines' fire. A bullet tore open Wahoolit's hand and he fell back. Nelson charged on, giving Kanasket the extra moments needed to pull a sputtering Leschi free. The two of them sprinted, zig-zagging and tumbling through flying sawdust and worse, back over the mound to cover.

Old Nelson, he of the scraggly salt and pepper hair, rescuer of the King and Jones children, never made it back. He fell in the sawdust, shot through the head.

It soon became apparent that Leschi's desperate frontal assault was stopped. To linger before the marines' rifles would have meant certain death. Musket fire from above, organized by Quiemuth, helped cover their retreat, as they scrambled back through the town and up the hill. The smoke of battle was so thick that they escaped the spotters on board the *Decatur*.

A Yakama brave from Owhi's force reported back to Leschi. Stahi was dead. Fortunately, Owhi's wounds did not appear to be life-threatening. His men held a few buildings along the northeastern outskirts of the town, beyond the range of the *Decatur's* guns, and were plundering beef and pork, and a few arms. The town was terrorized, but nothing of strategic value had been accomplished.

Wyamooch came on the run, breathing heavily. "Leschi," he said, "I have just come from our southern flank. Our men have fought bravely. Kitsap and Sluggia are both wounded. It is no use to attack that way. A powerful force of defenders has it secured with big guns that toss men into the air."

It was mid-day; the battle had raged for four of the white man's hours. The arms Leschi had wanted to capture were by now hopelessly beyond reach. Leschi signaled retreat. They fell back, to feast on captured cattle.

A group of Native women found an unexploded shell. They sang a song to exorcize its evil medicine, then killed it with a spear. The explosion killed them right back.

As Leschi's people feasted and died, the Bostons evacuated women and children to the *Decatur*, and to the lumber bark *Brontes*. Leschi didn't mind; he had no stomach for killing women and children. Nor did he have any stomach for the fresh roast meat that Ann and Moonya set before him and his brother. Against his wishes, some of his men insisted on going back to the skirmish lines – at points beyond the range of the *Decatur*. They believed that because the women and children were evacuating, the Indians had won the war. "It is a waste of ammunition," said Leschi, but he was too discouraged to prevent it. As the battle sputtered uselessly into evening, already Leschi was mourning their losses.

"Winyea told me of Kanasket's valor today, and also that of Wahoolit," said Quiemuth, between great rips at a meaty rib. "I have thanked them both. Will you?"

"Yes, my brother," said Leschi. "There are men I will have to wait to thank in the next world. Old Nelson, my dear brother Stahi ..." His voice trailed off.

"I pity Sluggia, who just got his father back, only to lose him again. It would have been better to let me die."

"You must have some purpose left," said Quiemuth, grabbing Leschi by the shoulders. "You think *Sah-hah-lee Tyee* doesn't know how to get rid of a fool like you?" The brothers embraced.

As night fell, the Natives retreated, leaving hundreds of precious slugs in the walls of Seattle's dwellings. It was a mighty cry of futility. Too many of their people were dead, and many more wounded. Of those that survived, most were too terrified of the white man's deadly sorcery ever to fight again. Only two whites were killed, none of them soldiers. No rifles were captured. It was a terrible defeat. The greatest might the Indians had ever assembled west of the Cascades, was useless against one battered old Boston war ship.

Chapter Seventeen
Heads

1

The steamer *Active*, bearing the august presence of a newly bathed and appropriately attired Governor Stevens, lived up to its name during the Battle of Seattle. The Governor issued a series of conflicting orders, sending the little ship to Bainbridge Island for "a strategic view," then up to Port Madison, ostensibly to "check on the Suquamish." Most of the Suquamish were safely penned up in reservations, and the rest were more likely to be found firing upon Seattle than lolling about the beach by their ancestral village. The Governor, by this time under the influence of a bumper of the Captain's best champagne, proved impervious to such reasoning. Instead of returning to Seattle, he had the *Active* investigate Shilshole Bay, located safely around the tip of Magnolia Point, well north of the action. From there, the *boom-boom-boom* of the *Decatur's* guns lulled him to sleep.

The next morning, the Governor directed the *Active* to head north to Whidbey's Island, under a sky as grey and heavy as his hangover. They steamed up the east side of the island and around Sandy Point, into the mouth of Saratoga Passage. Patkanim's summer lodgings were there, to which the Snoqualmie Chief had retreated, in an effort to stay clear of the war.

The handsome Chief, with Leschi's sister, Skai-kai, two other *klootchmen*, and his personal bodyguards, hurried down to the shore to greet the steamship in person. Patkanim and the Governor seemed a funhouse mirror image of one another, both short and powerful, both decked out in frock coats over flannel shirts, each with their politician's wariness under false smiles.

"Governor Stevens," said Patkanim, in perfect English, extending his hand in the white man's fashion. "It is good to see you again, my friend. I am honored by your visit."

"Chief Patkanim," replied the Governor, "it is good to see you as well. If the other Chiefs were like you, we'd all get along a lot better."

The Chief inclined his head in a proud display of modesty.

"You know my assistants, Mike Simmons and Tony Rabbeson?"

"Yes, Governor, of course. Mr. Rabbeson and I took a most interesting voyage down to San Francisco together." Patkanim smiled some more. Mike smiled. Tony nodded.

Patkanim invited the Governor and his party to accept his hospitality. His huge cedar longhouse was cluttered with comfortable chairs, tables, mirrored dressers, full length mirrors, and bed-stands with feather mattresses, haphazardly strewn everywhere. No room seemed to have any particular function.

The Chief's *klootchmen* served a feast. They began with fresh geoduck steamed on a bed of seaweed, followed by thick roasted shanks, honey-glazed to perfection, spiced with cinnamon sticks from the orient. The meat was delectable; it fell from the bone, and the men ate greedily.

"Now that's finger-lickin' good," complimented Mike as they finished the last morsels. "What was that, Chief? Maybe wolf or bear?"

"Haida," said Patkanim, naming the enemy tribe from the North. The Boston stomachs churned. "No!" said Patkanim. "You don't really believe that I would serve you such scum!" He roared with laughter, and the Governor joined in. Mike wasn't too sure, but he chuckled in the interest of diplomacy.

"A memorable feast," Stevens complimented, as the *klootchmen* passed pipes loaded with Virginia tobacco. "After a dinner like that, a man knows he is dealing with a man of substance." Patkanim glowed. "Knowing you for a great *Tyee*, Patkanim, I wanted to come to you in person to make a special request." He paused to further pique Patkanim's interest.

"Women, go!" commanded Patkanim, snapping his fingers. His *klootchmen* scattered – but not so far that they could not eavesdrop. "Please, Governor, do go on."

"On open ground," said Stevens, careful not to give the impression of weakness, "the Boston soldiers are the best in the world."

"I have heard tell," allowed Patkanim, magnanimously.

"The difficulty is that they do not know this land like the red man, like a man such as yourself knows it."

"It is true."

"And so, whenever Leschi shows his face he is defeated, but then he runs back to his hiding places deep in the forest, and we cannot finish him off."

"Ah," was all Patkanim said. He saw where this was headed, but tipping his hand was not in his nature.

"So I have come to ask you to lead an expedition into the forest. I want you to find Leschi's hiding place, to kill him, and bring me his head."

Patkanim was delighted. He would have revenge at last for all of Leschi's meddling! Still, he did not tip his hand. "This I would like to do out of respect for you, Sir, as Governor. But it sounds dangerous, and I would not expose my people to danger without any hope of reward."

"You shall have reward a-plenty: twenty dollars per head for every hostile warrior; fifty dollars per head for the –" Stevens hesitated "– head men –"

"The head men, that is very good!" said Patkanim, laughing. He repeated the joke to his bodyguards in their native *Luhshootseed*, and they all laughed with him. "For which 'head men' do you pay extra?"

"Kanasket, Stahi, Kitsap, Nelson, Winyea, and Quiemuth," answered Stevens.

"What about Leschi?" asked Patkanim, his black eyes shining.

"For Leschi," said the Governor, his jaw tensing, "one hundred dollars. But on one condition."

"What is that?"

"I don't want his body attached." Skai-kai ducked her head to hide her revulsion from the other *klootchmen*. "Make a stew out of it!" added the Governor. As the men laughed, Mike felt the first bubble of indigestion pushing at his heart.

2

Following the Battle of Seattle, Leschi and six tens of surviving warriors had fled to Kanasket's hiding place on the upper reaches of the Green River, to regroup and lick their wounds. Owhi and his surviving force fled back across the mountains to the land once held by the Yakama.

Ten suns later, Leschi galloped with a small band of thirty warriors out of Kanasket's stronghold, following the Green River Valley west to Muckleshoot Prairie, then across to the home of Sandy Smith on Muck Creek. Their mission was to renew peace talks. Around each bend lurked war and death, as Regulars and Volunteers scoured the countryside for them.

Sluggia's words echoed in Leschi's skull. "Why," he pleaded from the pallet, where fever wracked his shrapnel-studded chest, "why is it always peace with you? Did my father die for nothing?"

It hurt Leschi to hear such questions. Had he not been bold in strategy and in battle? Had he not twice led the most dangerous charge into the center of the town? Yet it was true, when it came to death he was never reconciled. He still saw the surprise on the face of that young brave Patkanim had left to watch the canoes, that moment of understanding just before darkness. What was this weakness? Did it endanger his people? As Leschi's horse followed the familiar paths to Muck Creek, such a longing for the days of peace gnawed at Leschi's heart that he almost cried.

"I seek peace," he'd told Sluggia, "for the same reason I once agreed to go to war. It is because I think it is the most likely way to get our land."

"So, Uncle," Sluggia had replied, "you are still waiting for crumbs from the white man's table." The words stung, but what could he do? They had all felt the power of the Boston guns. His people were starving, sick, full of despair. They would not survive another attack by shells that *mox-poo*. Indeed, they would barely survive the winter, for there had been little time for the men to fish, and the *klootchmen* had not dried enough berries or smoked enough salmon and clams. When spring came, they could no longer return to the warm lowlands where food was plentiful. Despite Sluggia's bravado, most of his people now clamored for peace at any price.

Leschi had replied, "What is rightfully ours is no man's crumbs. We must learn to live in a world in which the Bostons rule. We have fought well; we have nothing to be ashamed of. I will take what I can get, and you should too."

Oh, the look in his sister's eyes, staring out from Sluggia's face. If only he could shake that memory.

That night, Mary had refused to come to his bed. Ann stood by quietly, but he would not invite her, and she slept alone. She was accustomed to it. There was no point in stirring hopes he could not fulfill.

Suddenly a projectile flew from the brush by the side of the road. It smacked Winyea square in the chest. "Dismount!" ordered Leschi. His men pulled up short in a shower of stones and rearing ponies, as they slid off to the side away from the brush, using their mounts as cover. They raised their weapons, but Leschi signaled "hold fire." Was it the need to conserve precious ammunition, or his wretched weakness?

They heard a snap in the brush, a loud "*sssssshhhhhhhhh,*" followed by a nervous giggle and a frightened, "shut yer trap!" Leschi's men tensed their trigger fingers, even as Leschi relaxed.

"Come on out, *tenas men*" – boys – he hollered in Chinook. More crackling, then out stumbled four white boys, maybe eight or nine years old.

"Show me," commanded Leschi, holding open his palms.

The tall boy in front held up his own hand. In it was a seedpod, about the size of a crabapple. Leschi took the pod, displayed it to his men, then crushed it in his hand and tossed the pieces in the air, laughing as seeds floated about the terrified youngsters. "Let's go!" he ordered, leaving the boys with the tale of how they attacked the savage Chief Leschi, and escaped with their lives.

206

Leschi's men pulled up in front of the Smith cabin. Sandy and his neighbor, John McLeod, were riving shingles for repair of the rain-battered roof. John, himself half Algonquin and half Scottish, had lost his Nisqually bride to the pox. Now he struggled to raise two daughters on his own. As soon as they recognized Leschi, the greetings were cool and cautious. Not being Bostons, the men were not afraid, but still, they did not want to get caught in the crossfire.

Sandy's wife, Alala, held no such reservations. Running from the kitchen, she warmly greeted the new arrivals. "Mr. Smith," said Alala to her husband, "don't you think having a Chief to dinner is reason enough to butcher that pig you're so fond of?" In an aside to burly Kanasket in *Whulshootseed*, Alala added, "He calls her Miss Buttercup. Butter-arse is more like it. She's raised two litters and I say she's had a better life than most. I swear, he'll have me making that sow a dress if we don't kill her off soon."

Reluctantly, Sandy went off to the pen to bring back the bacon. He slaughtered another pig, instead of Miss Buttercup. Roasted on the spit, it was just as good. Betsy Edgar smelled the roast, and wandered down to see what the occasion might be.

"Betsy," called Leschi when he saw her. "I am very sorry about your husband."

Leschi moved to slick her down, but Betsy stepped away. "Your first wife and I used to marvel at the stupidity of husbands," she said. "When women rule the world, do you think we will spend our days looking for new ways to kill each other?"

"You may have the world today, as far as I am concerned," replied Leschi. "I miss her," he confided quietly. Almost involuntarily, his hand went to the tortoiseshell and bear tooth necklace at his throat.

"So do I," breathed a voice so deep in his soul that he thought at first it was his own mind playing tricks. It was the voice of songs cast upon the waves of *Whulge* in peaceful times. He spun with amazement to find his daughter, and there was no hesitation as he enfolded Kwahnesum's near-starved frame in his strong arms. "I want to come home now," was all she said, and though he knew there was no longer a home to which he could bring her, he managed to say, "Yes, Daughter," before he was too overcome to say anything more.

3

Much later, after the men had licked the grease from their fingers, smoked their pipes, and drunk their kalse root liquor in Hudson's Bay coffee, Leschi spoke. "The Governor is an evil man. He sets cruel terms for his bargain, and never wavers. He is not moved by the suffering of any people, not ours, or even his own. He does not learn from the world. His listens to no voices, aside from the voices in his own head.

"Still, I am afraid that the terrible power at his command may be too great for us. We must find a way to make peace with the Bostons. I have been thinking; if we could go around Stevens, and be heard by the *Tyee* of *Tyees* in Washington City, perhaps there would be hope."

"I don't know," said John McLeod. "You might find the two Washingtons to be the proverbial horse with two asses!" The men chuckled.

"Leschi," said Sandy, "I for one was not happy to see you, when you rode up this afternoon. Your presence puts my family and friends at risk. But maybe I was a bit hasty. It is good that you want peace. We want peace, and many Bostons want peace, too. There are many who dislike Stevens, and who are sympathetic to your cause."

"What can I do to reach such people?" asked Leschi.

Sandy thought a moment. "I'm just a Limey bastard to them. You need a Boston to reach the other Bostons."

"Good," said Leschi. "I know just the right Boston. Sandy, would you please go find *Challie* Eden. Tell him the time has come again. Bring him here. I will leave a man nearby, who will lead him to our camp."

"I will do as you ask," promised Sandy. "I ask only that you move your men away from our cabins. It is too dangerous for us to be seen with you."

"So be it. We will make our camp in the forest to the east. No one will know of this visit."

Leschi picked a campsite not far from the burned-out remains of Yokwa village. Once camp was set, his feet of their own will carried him over a carpet of decaying boughs, to the deodar where Sara once rested. Under the enigmatic smile of a crescent moon, Leschi asked, "First Wife, what shall I do?" He sat cross legged on the spot where he'd picked up the desecrated remains of her earthly bones, feeling the slow drip of night rain, listening long for the spirit's answer. Near dawn a bear passed by, leading her cubs straight for the river.

Leschi nodded and rose, returning to camp exhausted, but more confident. To his surprise, he was just in time to see Alala slipping from Kanasket's blanket. She met Leschi's gaze and refused to look down. "I won't lie," she said. "But I am not just here for my own pleasure. I have also brought something for the tribe." She took Leschi's hands. "Please, don't tell Mr. Smith." She hurried back to her husband.

Kanasket looked sheepishly at Leschi. "She is a spirited girl," said Leschi, smiling. Kanasket nodded. "I know what she gave you," teased Leschi, "but what did she bring for us all?"

Kanasket pointed to a small chest. Leschi opened it, and found that it was brimming with powder and shot. "A spirited girl!" crowed Leschi.

"She said that if anyone finds out where we got this, it will be her death," said Kanasket, his open face darkening with uncharacteristic worry.

"My friend," said Leschi, patting Kanasket on his broad shoulders as dawn pricked the treetops. "My dear, dear friend, no one will ever know."

4

War canoes launched eastward, in search of heads. Patkanim, in derby hat and frock coat, stood in the prow of the first of six long cedar canoes carrying fifty-five warriors. Up the Snohomish they surged, to the point where it intersects with the Skykomish and Snoqualmie Rivers. There, a small settlement of Skykomish huddled beyond the tree line, trying to avoid Stevens' Indian Agents. When Patkanim disembarked, their head men came running to hear his command. The head men flinched when they saw the Indian Agent Mike Simmons, then marveled to see that Simmons was no threat to them this day, thanks to the great power of Patkanim. The price for Patkanim's favor for another few months was manageable: one wild boar, a night's lodging, ten warriors, a few women.

After a breakfast of venison and *charlaque* roots, the reinforced war party took off into the stiff current of the rain-swollen Snoqualmie. Patkanim's powerful braves stroked and chanted in unison, as the dappled meadows and rich woodlands of the Tualco Valley hypnotically slipped by. They passed Tolt Lodge and other lands once teeming with peaceful Natives, now deserted. Soft swells of soil along the river grew into steep hills, and in the distance snow-covered peaks loomed. Finally, growing bored with the scenery, Mike Simmons decided to try to learn something of this enigmatic Chief with the perfect English.

"Chief Patkanim," he called, addressing the Chief's back, as Patkanim knelt watching the river ahead. "Do y'all know where Leschi is hiding himself?"

"Not yet."

"Then how will you find him?"

"I will find him."

"But how?" Mike pressed.

Patkanim didn't answer for so long that Mike thought he'd insulted him. He was figuring how to make amends, when Patkanim turned his head and said, "Do you know who we are?"

"The Snoqualmies. Named after this river, I expect."

Patkanim turned his back again. "We are the Snoqualmies," he announced, "and this is our river, but you are an ignorant fool if that is all you know of it."

Mike checked his temper. This man was too important to antagonize. "I'm sorry, Chief, I'm just a feller from Kentucky, so I guess you're right. I don't know beans about your people, but I'd like to learn."

This seemed to placate Patkanim, who turned around and squatted in front of Simmons. "Snoqualmie means, 'People of the Moon.' Many generations ago, the first Snoqualmies climbed down a frozen moonbeam to find our river." Mike's skepticism changed to wonder as the river opened on a huge vertical cataract dropping some three hundred feet from a distant chasm in the rock, into a great thirsty bowl. Mist rose like steam from the bowl. The roar of the water was deafening.

"You see, white man," hollered Patkanim, pointing back at the glistening waterfall, "this is all that remains of that beam of light. It broke off from the moon when my people first arrived in this land."

"That's a beaut of a waterfall," cried Simmons. "But I still don't know how you're gonna find Leschi."

"You will see," replied Patkanim, "if you open your eyes." Mike blinked. "You say, 'That's a beaut of a waterfall,'" Patkanim said, mimicking Mike's drawl, "but to me, it is no waterfall. To me, this is a sacred place, where the power of the moon falls to earth. This power guides my people to victory over our enemies. For example, those fools camped over there," and he pointed to a small encampment where a few Natives were admiring the falls so intently, that they were oblivious to six war canoes closing fast.

"What about them?" asked Mike, but Patkanim had already turned to face his quarry. Before they had even touched the shoreline, Patkanim's warriors leaped out. Effortlessly, they subdued the small family, two men, a woman, and three children. Even the children were quickly trussed, hands and feet tied behind and together, then dragged twisting and crying before Patkanim, who brandished a gleaming steel army sword. Quallawort, Patkanim's loyal brother, interpreted the proceedings for Mike Simmons.

"Silence! I am Patkanim, Chief of the Snoqualmies. You are trespassing on our sacred lands!"

"Great Chief," said the eldest, a man with white hair, "we beg your forgiveness. In these troubled times, it is difficult to find a safe place. We meant no harm."

Patkanim held the tip of the sword to the man's throat. "Insolent slave! I said, be silent. You did not wander here by chance. You were pulled by the moon to lead us to our enemy." Simmons felt he was somehow responsible, but he dared not interfere. The waterfall roared, drowning choked sobs of the woman and children.

"You are Klickitat, like Kanasket, Leschi's cousin," announced Patkanim. "You must know where Leschi is. Speak!" The men looked down in silence.

"Did you hostiles know that your heads are worth many *hiqua* to this Boston man?" Patkanim indicated Mike Simmons, who flushed, but held his tongue. The prisoners kept their gaze averted downward.

Patkanim flashed the sword just inches above the heads of the two men, who flinched despite themselves. "I've heard that a cleanly decapitated head knows its fate for a few seconds after it leaves the body," he mused. "Which one of you is going to lead me to Leschi?"

"I am," said the younger man. With two-handed fury, Patkanim flung the steel blade through the older man's neck so cleanly, that his head jerked to the side only slightly as it popped up. It was as surprised as anyone to find itself tumbling down onto the beach, rolling to a stop in the sand. Its open eyes blinked twice, fixed on liquid moonbeam.

"A wise choice," said Patkanim to their new guide. His voice was devoid of inflection. "Mr. Simmons, have you any more questions?"

5

"*Challie* Eden, it seems that you cannot be rid of me," said Leschi with a weary smile, as he stood to welcome the young Captain. Charlie had been brought blindfolded on horseback from Sandy and Alala's cabin, to Kanasket's hideaway on the upper reaches of the Green River. A hastily constructed log-frame longhouse and a few cabins were tucked against the base of the ridge, camouflaged behind spruce trees, and a lichen-encrusted wall of fallen timbers. Even after the blindfold was removed, Charlie would have walked straight past the well-hidden camp, had Kanasket not grabbed him by the arm and led him towards it.

Charlie was shocked to see how the work of only a month had chewed so much flesh off of Leschi. He surveyed the cramped longhouse, packed with sixty warriors and an equal number of women and children. Many were wounded or sick. Charlie heard the anxiety in their voices, saw the fear in their eyes, the hunger hollowing their cheeks, and knew their desperation.

"I am here to serve you," said Charlie, almost adding "Father," then biting his tongue.

"To serve us all, I hope," answered Leschi. They sat by a small fire off to the side, where Leschi's inner circle could hear the conversation. "I want you to help me write a talking paper that lists the wrongs of the white man, and the wrongs of my people," announced Leschi. "Bring this paper to my friends among the Bostons. Ask them to send it to the Great *Tyee* in the East. If he thinks we should get our land by the river, he should say so, and he will have the blessings of our people forever. If, after reading it, he does not think we should get our land, I will abide by his decision. Either way, we will lay down our arms."

"But the Governor has promised to wipe out every hostile Indian," replied Charlie. "You must surrender without terms, to what he calls the 'justice and mercy' of the government."

"I have seen this 'justice and mercy' before, with poor Kassas, Patkanim's brother. He was hanged for a murder he did not commit. When the white man says 'justice,' he means he wants to kill while feeling righteous."

Charlie nodded. "I have more grim news. The Governor has posted a reward for your heads. As we speak, hundreds of men are out hunting Indians – and the Governor isn't particular about the heads he gets. Except –"

"Except what?"

"Except, that he is very particular about you and your fellow Chiefs." Charlie looked around the circle. "Your heads, to a bounty hunter, are worth fifty dollars each."

A few looked startled, but Kanasket stood. "It will cost them many of their own to get it!" he announced.

Wahoolit held up the raw stump of his left hand, shot during the Battle of Seattle. It was curled into a tight, useless claw. "Tell the Governor I'll take one fresh salmon for each finger I got left – and I'll cut them off myself!" The men laughed.

"Wyamooch!" demanded Leschi, with sudden vehemence. "How much is your head worth?"

"Not for sale," replied Wyamooch, uncomfortable with the taunt lingering in the question. He had been nervous ever since Kwahnesum's return, and even more now that John Hiton had arrived that morning from Seattle, bearing food and fresh intelligence.

"Chief Leschi," said Charlie, "your head is now worth one hundred dollars!"

"Such a valuable head ought to be worth even more while still on its shoulders," replied Leschi. "Let's see if it can't write up a talking paper."

Charlie and Leschi conferred late into the night, drafting papers for Charlie to carry to sympathetic Bostons. Ann quietly padded about, tending the fire, and making sure they had food and drink all the long hours of their labor. When at last their work was done, Ann brought out Leschi's most ornate clay pipe, the one with the dangling eagle feathers. Leschi lit the intoxicating *kinnikineck* leaf, took a long draught, and passed it to Charlie.

"To peace and friendship," said Leschi. Charlie smiled as he took the pipe. He inhaled the sweet smoke.

"To peace and friendship, my – Chief," Charlie replied, again suppressing the urge to say, "Father."

"We both have unfinished business this night," said Leschi, his face still careworn. "Yours is more pleasant than mine." Charlie looked puzzled. Leschi led him outside, around to a small cabin behind the longhouse. "Goodnight, my son," smiled Leschi, and there it was – the word, and with it, that feeling of belonging.

"Goodnight, Father."

Charlie's heart soared as he pushed back the cabin door to find Kwahnesum waiting. She was dressed all in soft deerskin, seated straight on a blanket, her dark braid snaking over her shoulder and down her breast, shining by the light of pine-pitch torches. Had Charlie been less enamored, he could have seen in the way she held her body that this was a different Kwahnesum, one with stress fractures ready to separate at the slightest touch. But he was overcome. He fell before her, begging forgiveness.

"Tomorrow, Kwahnesum, I will take you home with me, and we will never speak again of that time I was away, or of the time I came back. I will do our father's bidding, and I will never leave you. I will resign my commission with the Volunteers. Soon there will be peace, and we will live quietly, and raise a family."

She had yet to speak; she only ran her hands through that cursed honey hair. Ghost hair, Sluggia had called it. Hair like rays of the sun. "Day and night cannot dwell together," she whispered. "I will stay with my people; you must go with yours." Although he protested long after their limbs entwined and she opened to let him enter, she sent him away firmly by the cold light of dawn.

Stumbling from the cabin, Charlie found Leschi already up and waiting with a small boy at his side. "As a token of my good faith," said Leschi. He nudged the frightened child towards Charlie. It was only then that Charlie saw that the boy was white. "George King," said Charlie, more a statement than a question.

The boy nodded. Charlie knelt down before him. "My name's Charlie. You wanna go home?" No sooner had the words slipped out, than he realized the boy had no home.

"I din' cry," Georgie said. "You tell Johnny, I din' cry." Then he began to cry.

6

Patkanim and his warriors pressed on, portaging around the liquid moonbeam to the South Fork of the Snoqualmie River, then down the Cedar River to the mouth of Green Valley. There they abandoned their canoes and marched overland due south, to the Green River. Their guide led them up the Green River, straight to Kanasket's hideaway, which they reached on the very day Charlie and George King departed.

Patkanim's plan was to launch a surprise attack that night, by the light of a full moon, just after midnight. But as the men settled in for their rest, Skai-kai slapped a pony's rump, sending it whinnying and clattering into plain view. Leschi's alerted sentries soon returned reports that Patkanim was at their doorstep, armed and painted for war, in the company of a big white man with a red-grey beard.

In the early twilight of a winter mountain pass day, Leschi emerged from behind the timbered barricade protecting the camp. "Patkanim," he shouted, "will you step forward like a man, to speak with your brother?"

"You are no kin to me," cried the Chief who stepped from the swampy stew of alders, ferns, and elderberry, beneath the camp.

"What of your first wife, my sister?" asked Leschi.

Skai-kai was pushed forward, her face pinched with fear. "Tell him," ordered Patkanim.

"Brother, I am Snoqualmie," she said. "I spit on your name." She was roughly yanked back.

Leschi was shaken, though he knew better than to believe Skai-kai was speaking freely. "So now you speak through women, Patkanim?" he taunted.

"I do not speak," said Patkanim. "I fight."

"What are you fighting for?" probed Leschi. "A nice warm spot in the reservation, where you can be Chief of Government hand-outs?"

"I am fighting for your head," replied Patkanim.

"I think perhaps by high sun tomorrow," answered Leschi coolly, "I will have your head."

"No," countered Patkanim. "By that time I will have yours."

"Well," said Leschi, "at least mine is worth something." He laughed contemptuously. "One more thing," he called, as Patkanim turned to go. "I hear my old friend Mike Simmons is here." Mike stepped out from the cover of the swamp bushes.

"*Klahowya*, Chief Leschi."

"Are you here to pay for heads?" asked Leschi, through a young interpreter.

Mike licked his lips nervously, glancing from side to side. "Leschi, old friend, if you was to just surrender peaceable right now, I'd be pleased as a hog in shit. I'd work with the Gov'nor to be sure you got a real fair trial."

"Fair, like that treaty you signed for me?"

Mike grinned but he didn't look happy. He shook his head. "You know well as me, you made yer own mark on that paper."

"Mike Simmons, you're a liar." Leschi reached back behind the barricade and grabbed something big and round which he heaved downhill. Both Simmons and Patkanim jumped back into the brush. When nothing exploded, they peeked out to see Wyamooch's head roll to a stop, not five feet from where they'd been standing. "See what the Governor will give for that," spat Leschi.

A hard, cold rain established itself soon after dark, then let up around midnight. Both armies were shivering. Even after it passed, the clouds hung low, cloaking the opposing forces. All the long, nervous night, sentries peered into darkness, but no attack came. Leschi's men slept in shifts along the barricades, and behind them women and children huddled in the cold longhouse without telltale fires, too frightened to sleep.

The crack of the first volley echoed up the mountain passes at dawn. Leschi's people felt a strange sense of relief, after the long tense hours of waiting. Leschi was pleased to observe that, aside from Patkanim, no one carried anything more deadly than a musket. Volley after volley smacked against the barricades and longhouse walls, with little effect. Patkanim's forces were stranded in the swamp, with too much open ground between themselves and the camp to risk a charge.

As morning wore on towards mid-day, the reality became apparent. No matter how they husbanded their shot, Leschi's men were dangerously low on ammunition, even with Alala's treasure chest at their disposal. Then a mother's scream came from the longhouse as a child was struck by a shot that penetrated a chink in the logs. Fear was mounting.

Without warning, a terrible rain of flaming arrows descended on the longhouse from up the ridge. "Patkanim has outflanked us!" cursed Leschi, but it was too late to do anything about it, as panicked women and children poured from the burning building. Leschi had no choice but to lead a wild charge across the sand spit in front of Patkanim's guns, into the swirling waters of the Green River. A handful of warriors and twice as many women and children never reached the water. The icy river claimed another ten, mostly children and elders.

Just as Leschi reached the edge of the river, one of Patkanim's warriors stepped from the brush and drew a bead on the Chief. "Uncle!" cried Sluggia. He pushed Leschi into the water just as the shot rang out. The ball harmlessly tore at the trailing flap of Leschi's coat. Sluggia returned fire, and Patkanim's warrior fell wounded. Then Sluggia dived in behind Leschi, and they both swam for their lives.

From the opposite bank, Leschi and his men reloaded with powder kept dry in pouches made of tightly sewn otter pelts. They fired a retreating volley at Patkanim's men, who had emerged from cover a moment too soon, and one man fell. The withering return volley sent them scampering into the woods for cover.

Patkanim stepped out to celebrate his glorious victory. Though outnumbered, he had dislodged Leschi from his hiding place, and decimated the Nisqually force. Calling Mike Simmons as his witness, Patkanim boldly marched across the sand spit, tallying the value of heads, some of which still moaned in the dirt. At the riverbank he lifted the body of a young Nisqually warrior by the hair, drew his army sword, and lopped off another gruesome prize. He lifted the trophy and whooped in triumph just as Leschi raised his Kentucky rifle from the cover of the tree line, sighted first one head and then, out of respect for Skai-kai, the other. Leschi fired a precious bullet. The decapitated Nisqually's brains spattered Patkanim. Twenty dollars worth of gristle and bone flew from his hand into the river where, with a parting sneer, it tumbled and sank.

Chapter Eighteen
Diplomacy and Anger

1

The children sobbed under clouds that blotted the sun. The way was long and dangerous to Leschi's only other known safe harbor west of the mountains – his ancestral village at Mashel Falls. To get there, they had to sneak undetected across the White River east of Connell's Prairie, then cross South Prairie, the Puyallup, skirt the western edge of Elk Plain, and cross the upper reaches of Muck Creek. It was a three-day march with women and children in tow. As they marched, they were exposed to ambush from the west. Leschi feared that the Boston troops could easily guess which way they were headed, if they weren't already waiting for them.

With so much daylight lost to battle, and such exhaustion and sadness weighing them down, Leschi's people got only as far as the White River that first night. There, they made camp, huddled together wet and shivering. They covered themselves with fir boughs, for they had been unable to salvage any blankets or skins during the desperate escape across the Green River. People chewed pemmican they carried in waist pouches. It was too early in the season for fruit, so food was scarce. A few squirrels, rabbits, edible mushrooms and roots, supplemented their thin repast. They would have roasted the loyal dogs that had followed their masters through the hail of shot across the frigid river, but they didn't dare build fires.

Leschi settled himself heavily between Kanasket and Quiemuth, who sat with Moonya, their son George, and their little bright-eyed daughter, Kiya. Across from them, Sluggia sat with Ann, Mary, and Kwahnesum, who was pale and trembling with fever. Ann located pemmican in her pouch, which she fed lovingly to Kwahnesum. Mary moved behind Leschi, and began massaging his back and neck. As her soft hands moved over his tired muscles, her eyes were locked on Sluggia.

"You fought well today, Sluggia," said Leschi. Sluggia said nothing. "Thank-you, nephew," added Leschi. "I believe I owe you my life."

Sluggia nodded curtly. "Use it well," he said. "No more running."

"The wolf runs, but he is no coward," said Quiemuth. "It is called survival."

"Survival," echoed Kanasket. "We cannot survive like this. We must have food and ammunition. My Chief, allow me to lead warriors downriver to find supplies. I will bring them back to Mashel."

"Where do you think you might find supplies?" asked Leschi.

"We have friends at Muck Creek," said Kanasket simply.

Leschi smiled, despite himself. He and Quiemuth had their women for comfort; why should his friend be denied? "Very well," said Leschi. "But be careful. Always use advance scouts, and set a rear guard as well. I can spare you ten men, no more."

"Thank-you," said Kanasket.

Leschi looked with fondness at this calm giant. Was he slightly simple of mind, or merely wise enough to keep his life simple? Leschi handed his precious rifle to Kanasket. "My friend, take this."

"Oh no, I cannot."

"Please." Their eyes locked. "As a favor to me."

"Very well." Kanasket took the rifle, and gave Leschi his old musket in return. "I will oil it tonight."

2

Frank Clark was just about cross-eyed with boredom as he sat in the three-room log cabin that served as the United States Court for the Third Judicial District of Washington Territory. Hugh Goldsborough, an Olympia attorney who had once counted the Governor himself among his clients, droned legal *arcana*: defeasible remainder estates, the rule against perpetuities, how many contingent beneficiaries could dance on the head of a pin. *There oughta be a law*, thought Frank, as he idly watched Judge Chenoweth's silver eyebrows droop beneath his shiny bald dome, *against the prosecution of actions to quiet title during wartime*. Frank knew the rule was just the opposite; so long as the courts were able to function in what might nominally be called a theater of war, civil law prevailed over military. By this point, Steilacoom was as nominal a theater of war as any – the closest it had come to seeing action was when Leschi and his men paddled through the Tacoma Narrows out to the Fox Island Reservation. Now that the Indians had suffered the power of the white man's cannons, and with nearly two hundred fifty Regulars, over a hundred Volunteers, and God knows how many mercenaries, all out beating the bushes for any sign of the rag-tag remains of Leschi's forces, there was little chance that this insignificant log cabin snug in the heart of Steilacoom would come under attack.

So Clark dithered, waiting his turn to point out the undeniable flaw in Goldsborough's convoluted argument. Clark's client's interest in the disputed property must vest within twenty-one years of a life in being at the time of the making of the grant, because no one except the savages had even been around these parts for that long. While he waited, his active mind was a thousand other places at once, flitting from keeping the Sheriff bought, to decanting his next batch of homebrew, to getting into the bloomers of the Sheriff's pretty daughter, to finding new sources of cash to pay off his old creditors, to his next visit to Mother Damnable's. Then – *Glory Hallelujah!* – Clark's law partner, William H. Wallace, burst in to beg the Court's indulgence for an early lunch recess. Wallace had to consult his partner in a matter of great urgency.

Back at the office, Clark was introduced to a mud-spattered, honey-haired fellow, named Captain Charles Eden. "Dr. Tolmie suggested that I come see you, on behalf of a certain party," began Charlie, cautiously. "That party is a very important person, who needs to communicate certain information to persons in high authority. Owing to certain, uh, circumstances, he needs to work through intermediaries. Knowing that Captain Wallace here is head of the Republicans in the Territorial Legislature, it was natural to think that perhaps you would help us."

"It's Mr. Wallace, now, Captain," said Will. "I've finished my tour of duty." He had buried the memory of slogging about the dark sodden forest with Lieutenant Slaughter as deep as a festering wound could go. "What is the nature of your principal's instructions?" Oh, how he loved the intrigue of politics.

"My principal is in a position to broker a peace settlement between Chief Leschi and responsible Federal officials."

"Time to muck out the stable, Captain," said Clark. "I happen to recall that your father-in-law is Chief Leschi. I say your principal is one and the same."

Charlie wasn't much good at this sort of thing. His face gave him away. He feared they'd send him packing and he'd be court-martialed for aiding the enemy, but Frank Clark just grinned, and slapped him on the shoulder. "Why didn't you say so? I love impossible cases, and his is the worst."

Will Wallace wasn't so eager. "I don't know, Frank," he said. "I mean, that son of a bitch –" and his eyes teared up as he turned abruptly away, once again sucked back to the carnage at White River.

"Will," said Frank, putting on his most sympathetic look, "our professional calling does not require that we approve of the criminal's ways."

"Leschi's no criminal," objected Charlie.

"Of course not," said Frank, who didn't seem to care one way or the other. He turned back to his partner. "Besides, it's a great opportunity to stick it to the Governor."

At this, Mr. Wallace's eyes refocused. He nodded sharply. "All right," he said, turning towards Charlie. "What kind of deal does Leschi have in mind?"

"He is ready to surrender," said Charlie. "He wants the Indians who stood with him to be free to go to the reservation. He alone will submit to trial."

"And their land claim?" asked Wallace. "What about that?"

Charlie produced a document. "This is a list of the wrongs of both the white man and red man since we Americans first settled in Puget Sound. Leschi wants this sent to the President, with a request that his people be given land by the river. He will abide the President's decision – either way."

The two lawyers studied the document. It was a grim but accurate summary of man's inhumanity to man. No one's hands were clean. It did not try to soft-peddle the White River massacre. Even so, tracing it through, they could see the despair of an independent people who had lived the life given to them by their Great Spirit for generations, suddenly ordered to give up their way of life or perish. "We can make this into a memorial, gather signatures –" Frank Clark began, but Will cut him off.

"Now you're going soft on me, Frank," said Wallace, ever the shrewd politician. "This is politics, not a popularity contest. Do you think we'd get even fifty signatures at a time like this? Private influence, secret channels, that's the ticket! Write a brief, you know, the Governor's arrogant policy, no, make that 'arrogant and inflexible policy,' he led us into this war, no, make that 'this costly war,' *etcetera, etcetera*, that kind of thing. I'll sign it, by gum. This will go to Washington on the next steamer."

"There's more," said Charlie. He stepped outside, returning a few minutes later with a small boy in hand. "Gentlemen, this here is Leschi's olive branch. Meet George King, a very brave young fellow who spent four months living with the Indians. He reports that he was well treated. Is that right, Georgie?"

"It was kinda fun," said George. "I'll bet I know a lot more Injun stuff than Johnny."

Will Wallace, who knew political manna from heaven when he saw it, looked like a kid on Christmas morning. "Georgie," he said, "you like candy? You and me, we'll go get some candy, and then we'll pay a little call on the office of the *Puget Sound Courier*, OK? That's a newspaper. You won't be scared, will you?"

"I don't cry for nothin'."

"All rightee, then, me neither. Let's go!"

3

The next issue of the *Puget Sound Courier* reported: *LESCHI RELEASES CAPTIVE CHILD IN BID FOR PEACE* – *Representative William Wallace Vows to find Good Home for Orphaned Boy* – *Says Showing of Good Faith Should be Reciprocated* – *End of War in King Stevens' Hands* – *News of an amazing meeting at Muck Creek, followed by a daring visit to the enemy stronghold by Captain Eden to rescue the boy.*

"Muck Creek, eh?" said the Governor, crumpling the paper and throwing it to the floor. "Haven't we heard suspicious reports about goings on in that neck of the woods?"

"Reports?" asked Blunt blankly.

"Yessir," interjected Tony Rabbeson quickly. Blunt was fine for carrying out orders, but creativity was beyond him. "Seems them half-breeds have been livin' up there untouched by any hostile through the whole dang shootin' match. Now, way we figure it, them and their squaws must be up to no good or they'd be pushin' up daisies, just like the good folks of White River."

"Tony," said the Governor, "I want you to notify Colonel Casey about the threat posed by the Muck Creek settlers. Ask him to send a patrol up there to look around."

"Yessir." Tony headed out the door.

"What about Leschi?" asked Blunt, genuinely befuddled.

The Governor gave his big Commander a look of pity. "Leschi? Do you figure on capturing him in time for the next edition of the *Pioneer & Democrat*?"

"No." A long pause. "Oh."

Har! har! har!

4

On a Friday morning in late February, 1856, Colonel Casey broke camp and headed south on the White River, towards the Puyallup. By mid-afternoon his troops had reached a point about a mile east of the town of Puyallup, where they pitched their tents at the base of Elhi Hill, the steep ridge that led to Connell's Prairie. Captain Keyes, officer of the day, remembered well the lessons he had learned that fateful night in Lieutenant Slaughter's camp. He posted double sentries in three groups at key points along the hillside. "That oughta get 'um, Bustah," he advised his chestnut Morgan, who was adept at keeping military secrets.

All the long night the sentries peered into the gloom at nothing. At five in the morning, nearly two hours before sunrise, Casey – over Keyes' dissent – allowed the men to build cooking fires. The light from one fire shot up Elhi hill and glinted on something shiny. Private Kehl, the sentry who spotted it, froze. Were his eyes playing tricks on him after the long hours of strain, or was that ephemeral glint real? He squinted into the gloom. Now that his eyes knew where to focus, he could make out a lone shadowy figure in the dim light cast by the fires, creeping down the hill. The giant seemed an apparition. Kehl raised his percussion rifle, exhaled slowly, and squeezed the trigger. The giant fell.

It took Kehl and three others to drag the huge wounded Indian into camp. Though the bullet had paralyzed the Indian from the waist down, he was still very dangerous. He cursed and swung his powerful arms. The soldiers' barrage of swift kicks dislodged the long bone-tipped spear to which Kanasket clung with the strength of two men. Lying just beyond his reach was the freshly oiled Kentucky rifle that had betrayed him.

Captain Keyes and Colonel Casey both came out to see the wounded giant. "Congratulations, Private," said the Colonel, bending down for a closer look. "You've bagged Kanasket himself. He's a vicious bugger." As if in answer, Kanasket pulled an iron butcher's knife from his belt with murderous intent, slashing at the Colonel's neck. Casey tumbled back just in time, as quick-thinking Private Kehl smashed Kanasket's arm with his own bone spear, jarring the knife loose before Kanasket had a chance to throw it. Blood now spurted from fresh wounds where the spear had removed a chunk of flesh and muscle.

Kanasket stopped flailing as more and more of his blood puddled in the dirt. "My heart is wicked toward the whites and always will be," he hissed in Chinook. "Kill me now, or I will find a way to kill you."

Colonel Casey had regained his feet. "You heard the man. Hang 'im."

From their hiding place on the hill above the camp, the small band of warriors Leschi had detailed to accompany Kanasket looked on with dismay. "He should not have scouted alone," said Wahoolit.

"We must save him!" whispered the Sluggia. The rest ignored him, as the soldiers below extinguished the cooking fires, and all was shrouded again in darkness. Sluggia yanked on Wahoolit's arm. "How can you just stand by and let him die?"

"There are many soldiers; we are few. He is already dead," replied Wahoolit.

Down below, a small detail was looking for a strong enough limb to hold the noose, as the rest of the soldiers set up a skirmish line around the perimeter of the camp. Kanasket cried out to his tribesmen. "Remember me! Fight for me! Kill these devils!" Soldiers tried to stuff a cloth into his mouth, but though he was one and mortally wounded, and they were many in prime strength, they could not silence him. Kanasket twisted his lion's neck, spat out their gag and snapped at their fingers with his teeth. "I will watch you from *Otlas-Skio*," he cried to his comrades in arms. "I will cheer when you destroy the white devil! Goodbye my friends. Say goodbye to Leschi for me. I loved him above all others."

As Kanasket called out his farewells, Sluggia crept down the hillside until he was within thirty yards of the execution squad. He could see them stringing a noose over a limb. Kanasket cried, "Say goodbye to Alala for me. Goodbye, fight on, my brothers, never –"

Sluggia's mercy shot silenced Kanasket forever. A return volley scattered stones at Sluggia's feet, forcing him to scamper back up the hill.

"Hold your position, men," ordered Colonel Casey. He dared not give chase in the dark, for fear of being lured into an ambush.

The soldiers gawked at the remains of great Chief Kanasket. They took turns spitting and urinating on him, then moved out at daylight, leaving Kanasket to the wolves. The small band hiding on Elhi hill easily avoided them. After the soldiers were long gone, Sluggia and the other warriors crept cautiously down the steep hillside to retrieve the remains. They built a bier of hemlock boughs. It took four men to hoist him into the branches.

Seething with anger, Sluggia vowed revenge.

5

Governor Stevens stepped around his new burnished mahogany desk, a masterpiece of the woodcarver's art that was the size of a sloop's quarterdeck, to shake Charlie's hand. "Brave lad," he said, "going into the heart of enemy territory like that. Risking your life for that boy. Brave lad."

"But Sir –" began Charlie.

"No!" barked the Governor, throwing up his hand, "don't be modest. I think there's a commendation in this for you. Don't you think?" Stevens shot the query over to Blunt, who was smirking in a seat by the wall.

Blunt didn't even unfold his three chins to give the answer he'd spent the past hour memorizing. "With respect, Sir, some might see it as an act of treachery."

"Treachery!" cried the Governor in mock horror, and Charlie's mouth went dry.

"Seems the Captain here was in touch with them Muck Creek traitors who do the Injuns' bidding," explained Blunt. "Could be said he was aiding the enemy."

"Charlie? Oh no, I can't believe it!" the Governor exclaimed. "Charlie, your loyalty is being questioned here. What do you say?"

Charlie just stood rooted to the floor, dizzy, not a cogent thought in his head.

"You know, young man, considering your position as a military officer, if I thought there was a grain of truth to what Colonel Blunt is suggesting, I could have you marched right out and shot!"

Charlie nearly wet himself. "But, but –" was all he got out.

The Governor put both hands on Charlie's shoulders, looked him straight in the eye, and said, "Charlie, I want you to take an oath."

"Yes, Sir."

"Loyalty, Charlie. That's all. Loyalty. Have I got your loyalty?"

What could he say? "Yes, Sir," he croaked.

"I don't hear you, Charlie."

"YES, SIR!"

"That's better," said the Governor, still holding Charlie before him like a hooked fish. "I don't happen to agree with the Colonel, but I'll be watching you, understand?"

"Yes, Sir."

"You won't disappoint me?"

"No, Sir."

"As a Captain in the Volunteers, your job isn't to make peace, got it?"

"Yes, Sir."

"Do you know what your job is?"

"To fight, Sir?"

"To kill Indians, Captain."

"Yes, Sir."

"What's that?"

"YES, SIR!"

"Dismissed!"

Charlie didn't get quite out the office door before he ran into the bespectacled Charles Mason, newly returned from the other Washington. "I bring excellent news from our friend President Pierce," blurted out Mason, unable to contain himself. Charlie lingered by the doorway. He should have resigned his commission, that's what he should have done.

"The President says he fully supports the most vigorous efforts against any hostile Indians in the Territory." *Vigahrous effahts.*

Well, of course he does, thought Charlie. Killing Indians never lost any American President an election, and this was an election year.

"And?" prodded Stevens.

Mason beamed like a schoolboy who knows all the answers to the final exam. "And he will be pushing Congress to authorize full payment of all Territorial debts during the next fiscal year."

Suddenly Charlie knew what he must do. He crept from the doorway, pausing only at a clerk's desk to write up a letter resigning his military commission. Treason? Horsefeathers! He was the hero who'd rescued the King boy. Treason was all a big bluff, and he was no longer willing to play the Governor's fool. He was going to book the next passage on a steamer to San Franscisco, from there Panama, then Washington City. He would deliver Wallace's brief and Leschi's memorial to the President in person. Charlie Eden was ready to play with the big boys.

At least, he hoped so.

Chapter Nineteen
The Burial Canoe

1

T he headline in the Olympia *Pioneer & Democrat* blared: ARMY LOOKS INTO TREASON AT MUCK CREEK - *"Nefarious practices" cited in letter to Governor - Governor Stevens vows to take swift action against traitors.* The fine print continued: "In a message to the Territorial Legislature, the Governor explained, 'There is no such thing as neutrality in an Indian war, in my humble judgment. Whoever can remain on their claim unmolested is an ally of the enemy and must be dealt with as such.'"

Alala had curled on her mat and cried until sleep overwhelmed her every night for a week since she received news of Kanasket's death. Her British husband Sandy Smith, courtly and respectful, let her mourn at night. Daytime, however, was for chores; no one had the luxury to weep around the clock.

Alala was hanging out wash when the soldiers came. It was a company of Territorial Volunteers, under the command of twenty-eight year old Major Benjamin Frank Shaw, the red-bearded hat on a stick from Medicine Creek, whose high rank was reward for getting the Indians to sign their own death warrants. The men galloped through the kitchen garden, tearing up the early peas, the potatoes, and the remains of the winter chard. Then they leveled their guns straight at Alala's broken heart.

"Where's you husband, Missee Squaw?" chirped Shaw, none too kindly. *Out the back of the barn and into the forest,* she hoped, but before she could muster a lie to cover his tracks the *pelton* wandered out the front of the barn, using a rag to wipe the pig shit off his hands.

"Gentlemen," he said in the dulcet tones of the Queen's English, "may I be of assistance?"

His answer was a rude blow across the neck with a gun barrel. Two young men wrestled him to the ground and bound his hands behind his back. "Alala! Get Dr. Tolmie -" he was able to cry before they gagged him with the shit-encrusted rag, and rode away. Alala ran to Betsy's cabin. Together they ran to warn John McLeod, but it was too late - they were just in time to find his daughters screaming at the disappearing hooves of his captors.

2

A knock came at the Governor's door. "Mike Simmons is here, Sir, with an Indian," announced a clerk. "It's a Mr. Pat Kanim."

"Very good," said Stevens. "Send them in."

The Governor rubbed his hands together eagerly. Since the day when he had rallied the marines in defense of Seattle – as reported in the *Pioneer & Democrat* – everything had been going well. The Army was having some effect against Leschi, and public opinion was firmly behind his policy of extermination. Of course, there were still some who nattered on about making peace with the poor downtrodden savages and giving them more land, but they were distinctly in the minority. It didn't hurt that the better elements in the Territory were holding fistfuls of scrip, which wouldn't be worth a damn if Congress didn't agree that Stevens was right to prosecute the war in the first place. Most folks could plainly figure on which side their bread was buttered.

Still, there was one thing the Governor didn't have that he wanted above all else: Leschi's head. Well, he'd see about that. He positioned himself, standing behind his polished new desk, the better to strike an imposing executive demeanor. Mike and Patkanim lumbered in, followed by a brave carrying a large, stinking gunny sack.

"Mike! My good friend, Chief Patkanim!" cried Stevens. "Have you brought me good news?"

Patkanim's quick eyes darted over the massive gleaming desk, the red, white and blue flag, the various awards and diplomas arrayed on the walls and shelves, the thick inscrutable books lining one wall. He took in the energetic face of the Governor, as compared to the lethargic bulk of his Commander, Colonel Blunt, seated in the back corner.

"Yes, Governor," said Patkanim. "We have chased Leschi from his Green River hideout, and burned it to the ground. I have brought you trophies," and he signaled to the brave. Before the Governor could stop him, the young man inverted the sack above his new desk. Out thumped head after head, tangled black hair matted with dried blood, caked with mud and swarming with flies, some with tongues blue-black and protruding, others with eyeballs hanging from the thread of an insensate nerve. They thumped and cracked and rolled, and a few overspilled the desk onto the floor. One even bumped up against the astonished Governor's foot.

Stevens knew better than to betray his disgust before the Snoqualmie Chief. He lifted the head at his foot by its hair. The countenance was familiar. It was Wyamooch.

"I already paid for this one," said Stevens.

Patkanim frowned. "Where is it written, 'except Wyamooch?'"

The Governor reached with his free hand to dip the nib of his steel quill. "X" he marked across the stiff forehead. Then, with a flick of his wrist, Stevens sent the head flying back at Patkanim, who caught it.

"Anyway," said Simmons with a nervous laugh, "you didn't kill him, did you, Chief?"

Patkanim dropped Wyamooch back on the Governor's desk. "No, but I killed another that got away in the river, so you pay me for that one."

"I pay by heads," snapped the Governor, "not fish bait. What I want is Leschi's head. Have you got that in your bag?" Patkanim glared back in silence.

"Eight heads, no Chiefs." The Governor pushed aside the gruesome trophies and found some stained writing paper. Dipping his nib in the inkpot again, he wrote: "Pay to Chief Patkanim from Governor's War Fund: $160." He held out the signed requisition until Patkanim reached for it, then snatched it back. "And don't ever bring another head into this office, until it is Leschi's." The Governor placed the warrant on his desk; Patkanim, scowling, picked it up and stalked out.

Meg gave wide berth to the smelly Indian Chief exiting her husband's office. Iggy was so busy these days, but it wouldn't do for him to miss their dinner engagement with the legislative leaders that evening. Meg had so many things to do to get ready for their housewarming party to inaugurate the new Governor's mansion. She'd just had the most wonderful idea; she would place luminaria all the way up the walk and through the gardens. As she worried about whether the landscaping would be ready in time, Meg peeked her head in, to give her husband a quick reminder about dinner. What were those horrible things all around Iggy? The stench of rotting flesh hit her, contorted faces swimming before her eyes, a mocking pageant of agony. Meg shrieked; dropped in a dead faint.

3

Leschi was despondent over the loss of Kanasket, but there was no time to pay him the honor he was due. The situation was desperate. Leschi's people numbered fewer than ten tens, half of whom were women and children. Leschi sent Winyea back across the mountains to deliver an urgent plea for help to Owhi. At least fierce Kitsap still stood by his side. With determination but little hope, Leschi steeled himself for the final battle.

Kwahnesum begged her father to take her to war with him. He denied her. Although she was on the mend, she was still weak from fever, and he could not risk being slowed down by infirmity. About thirty women, children, and elders, remained behind at Mashel Village, including Kwahnesum and Mary.

"You will be safer here, Daughter," said Leschi. "You are now *Tyee* of Mashel." Mary glared at Leschi, then spun and marched away. He ignored her; bent to kiss Kwahnesum on the brow. "I will return soon," he said. Kwahnesum saw that he did not believe it to be so. With sudden clarity, she felt that this would be the last time they would see each other in this world. To honor him, she slicked his arms while smiling, though she would much sooner wail, and then she let him go.

Young George, Quiemuth's son of thirteen summers, also begged to go into battle. "We need all the men we can get," he argued to his father, who knew it was true.

"And we need our boys to live to grow into men," interjected Moonya. She appealed to her husband. "It is too dangerous. He is too young. I could not bear to see him in battle."

"Mother," said George, "how could I live, knowing I did not fight for our people?"

Moonya shook him off. "Look after your sister, Kiya," she replied.

"Kwahnesum can do it," said Quiemuth. "Moonya, George is ready to become a Nisqually warrior. It is not our place to stop him." So young George went with his people to fight the white man, downriver – down their river – in one of six war canoes, then overland back to *Tenalquot* Prairie, where it had all begun.

4

Captain Tony Rabbeson had his orders. They were to march straight up the Military Road across Connell's Prairie, through the forest, and down the steep bank to the White River crossing. There, they were to build a blockhouse and ferry. One hundred forty Volunteers left Fort Steilacoom on a bright Friday in early March, armed with muskets, rifles and bravado. They numbered seasoned veterans like Andrew Laws, who'd shot too soon out of the Indian camp on Connell's Prairie the previous October, and Jackson Moses, Ben's bitter older brother, who'd joined up to avenge Ben's death. Ben's locket, engraved with a six-pointed star, brushed against Jackson's chest with every beat of his Appaloosa's hooves, a constant reminder of loss.

On March 10, 1856, after tramping through the swamp where Ben received his fatal wound, Rabbeson's force safely arrived at the newly-constructed blockhouse on Connell's Prairie. "I saw it clear as you're standin' there," Tony Rabbeson told Jackson, as they slogged through the swamp. "Out steps three Injuns, including ole Chief Leschi, and before you could say 'jackrabbit' he raises up his big musket and *boom!* your poor brother was hit. I pulled up the reins and returned fire, but the cowardly devil'd already disappeared into the brush."

"How'd you know it was Leschi?" asked Jackson.

"Well, I'd just seen him when we first rode in. Scar-faced bugger in a felt hat."

"I'll keep an eye out." Jackson thought he remembered the Chief from the wedding, though he didn't recall any scar.

Tony sent Jackson on ahead as part of an advance scouting party. Slowly, they crept through the woods where McAllister and Connell were ambushed, then down the jumbled hills towards the river.

Two hundred yards further ahead, on the brow of the next furrow in the ridge, Leschi and his people crouched, hidden amongst boulders and a stand of low bushes. Leschi's forces had an excellent vantage on the four Volunteers creeping towards them. The plan was to wait until the soldiers reached the sag between hills, and then fire down upon them. At that point, the range would be about fifty yards – close enough for an accurate shot, even with their clumsy muskets.

The scouts crept cautiously downhill, sniffing the wind, pausing frequently to scan the horizon and listen for telltale hoots or crackles. Nothing. Nothing specific anyway. Jackson just didn't like it. Was it nerves, or something real? Silently, he signaled to press on. They were about fifty yards from the sag at the bottom.

Kitsap watched as the white devils crept closer, almost within range. Then something high up drew his eye. There, cresting the ridge of the hill from which the scouts had come, a line of soldiers. Ten, no two tens, no, more – more than he could count. He turned to signal that they hold their fire against the scouts and wait for the main force. In his hurry, he snapped a twig with a sharp crack. Kitsap cursed himself silently. He must find some way to atone for this unforgivable blunder.

Jackson heard it. The others didn't seem to. Sure, it could be anything, a squirrel's chatter, a bear in the brush, a tired old limb picking this particular moment to fall, out of all the quiet moments in eternity. But the locket pricking his breast said otherwise. Those boulders, right up there, barely fifty yards overhead – they'd make a great place for an ambush. He held up his hand, and his men halted. "Real calm now," he said, "like we're just jawin' 'bout the price of beans, I think them boulders up there are full of Injuns." The scouts tensed, but gave no visible sign. "Make like you're settin' down fer a drink of water, but find some cover."

The men settled, trying to look calm. "Billy," said Jackson to the youngest, "get up nice and slow, and saunter on back to warn the boys comin' down."

It was Billy's move back that tipped Leschi. "Fire!" he ordered. A huge volley rang out, just as the advance scouts dove into the grass and rolled behind logs, rocks, and into any small crevice they could find for cover. Billy went down; two others were wounded immediately. Jackson was lucky. He fired his rifle with intensity and hatred, willing every bullet to find flesh.

Tony had left Lieutenant Urban Hicks back at the blockhouse on Connell's Prairie with half the men, but he still had seventy. The men scrambled and slid down the steep bank into the field of battle, firing their weapons willy-nilly at the smoke rising from the boulders. Soon, the battle settled down into two entrenched lines trading shots with little effect. Each line unsuccessfully tried to outflank the other. *Klootchmen* beat rhythmically on war drums to bolster the courage of the warriors, calling upon *Tobcadad* – the war spirit – to guide the tribe's lead balls into the heart of the enemy. The white men had their own sorcery. Rabbeson's other Lieutenant, a braggart named Van Ogle, had once astounded some Nisquallies working in his field by putting a bullet through a hat on the ricochet. As the drums beat their ominous rhythm, Van Ogle spotted one of those same Nisquallies pop up and then drop down again between two boulders. Van Ogle winged him on the ricochet. "This *s'kookum* Boston," panted the warrior as his *klootchman* pressed herbs into his wound, "he shoots around corners."

Leschi looked up to behold a sickening sight. On the ridge from where the first soldiers had come, an equally large force of reinforcements appeared. Lieutenant Hicks had heard the shots, and ordered his men into battle. He had also sent an express rider back to the Puyallup River, where Lieutenant Kautz's forces were operating.

Outnumbered more than two-to-one, Leschi had no choice but to order a hasty retreat. The Bostons pursued them relentlessly towards the river. If Leschi's people could reach the river and get across to where they had hidden their ponies, they would have a chance of escape. If not, this would be the end.

The Nisquallies retreated, covering their rear as best they could, but Rabbeson's pursuing force was too close, and their fire too intense. The Nisquallies were soon pinned against a swamp bordering the river. Either they could wade in and be slaughtered like the helpless river otter wiped out by the white man, or make a stand and die like men. Leschi's order passed from man to man to take cover at the edge of a swamp. They would make their final stand.

Now the Volunteers pressed upon the desperate Natives, curving the skirmish line until Leschi's people were surrounded on three sides. Women abandoned their drums and came to the front line, taking up muskets from men who fell, loading them with practiced hands, and firing with equal accuracy. Ann was there by Leschi's side, and Leschi saw her as he had not seen her in years. She was beautiful to him, and his heart was full. There, to the other side, Quiemuth loaded and fired, loaded and fired, his face calm despite the hopeless odds. Quiemuth's son George was there too, with Moonya by his side, helping George reload, while chanting a prayer to her *tamanous*. Further down the line, Sluggia sweated and fired, ready to join his uncles in death. Aside from the smoke, the sky was blue and the air warm and sweet. Now, thought Leschi, it is a good time to die. He fired and loaded, fired and loaded, as the incoming bullets and balls snapped limbs, cut leaves, exploded the muck around him, and the soldiers inched ever closer. But for some reason, *Sah-hah-lee Tyee* would not take him.

Suddenly Leschi heard a great battle cry behind them, and he knew at that instant that they had been completely surrounded. He prepared to die. No! It was Winyea, his eyes wide with excitement, and there, by his side, Owhi, thumping his chest and firing – a sleek compression rifle! In an instant their ranks swelled with forty new men, and though they were still outnumbered, now they could spit rifle fire back towards the advancing soldiers, whose lines wavered in confusion as men dropped. The Volunteers' advance was momentarily halted.

"Owhi," said Leschi from his position behind an ancient, rotting fir trunk, "you have saved my people. Thank-you."

"It is I who must thank you, Chief Leschi," replied Owhi. "You give me another chance to kill Bostons."

"Enough talk," scolded Quiemuth. "Look up." Their gaze followed Quiemuth's. Lieutenant Hick's express rider had reached the Puyallup, and the ridge behind the Volunteers darkened with Lieutenant Kautz's blue coats.

In four ranks of twenty-five the professional soldiers' horses pawed the dirt. Each man whispered whatever goodbyes he had to say, or tried to broker a special deal with that old, forgotten friend in the sky. The Volunteers below gave a cheer, then parted to make way. Lieutenant Kautz raised his sword, looked from side to side down the long rows of wide-eyed, sweating bluecoats, then slashed the air and cried, "CHARGE!"

They came like a buffalo stampede across the trembling ground, tearing up great clods of dirt as they went. Leschi's men had never seen such a thing as a cavalry charge; no Native would be so foolish. It brought fear to their hearts. What kind of medicine did the Bostons have, that they could throw their lives into the breach without care? Leschi and Quiemuth had all they could do to hold their men on the line long enough to get off one volley. Most of the men fired too quickly and wild, they were so eager to flee, but a few shots killed. Leschi sighted his musket carefully on the officer leading the charge. He fired and was pleased to see the officer go down.

Lieutenant Kautz fell with a musket ball in his thigh. His last memory before losing consciousness was of the rear of a fast-disappearing cavalry line that did not falter. Other men up and down the line fell too, but there were many more to fill their places, including the Volunteers, who joined in the charge screaming for blood.

Outnumbered beyond reason or hope, the Natives broke for the river in a run for their lives. With all the fury of utter hopelessness, Kitsap hurled his war axe at the advancing line. It flew from his hand straight at Jackson Moses' head. Jackson dodged at the last instant; the axe paused only long enough to take his left ear before imbedding itself four inches deep in the chest of an unfortunate bluecoat. Jackson never missed a step, his charge made all the more fierce by the blood frothing from the side of his head. As the Nisquallies flew through the swamp towards the river, mere steps ahead of their pursuers, many men fell, and women too, suffering death and worse.

Leschi led his family into the densest part of the swamp, expertly navigating the rotting trunks, thick primordial stewpots of sucking mud, and swarming thickets of lichen-encrusted thorns. Soon, the sounds of gunfire and chaos melted away, as they took a circuitous route to a crossing he knew further upriver. After the terror and the long sprint, Ann doubled over with a cramp. "Go," said Leschi. He had to push Quiemuth on to convince him to save the rest of their family. "We will catch up soon."

Together, Leschi and Ann crouched behind a liverwort-smeared stump, from which ferns sprouted and mushrooms glowed with otherworldly light. Gasps from Ann's heaving lungs attracted the attention of Jackson Moses, who crept into a nearby clump of Pacific Willow. As the blood continued to gush from his amputated ear, he raised his government-issue rifle. Breathing heavily, he tried to steady himself. He sighted down the barrel through spots dancing before his eyes, at the tall, strong back of the Indian helping the *klootchman*. My God, *it's Leschi hisself*, thought Jackson. He took a deep, light-headed breath, squeezed the trigger, and watched as blood spilled from the man's mouth as he died. Odd; neither the man nor the gun made any sound, and then the man he'd just killed stood over him laughing. The next thing Jackson knew, he was lying in the silty bear grass with a throbbing head, as another Volunteer pressed a balled up kerchief to his ear. He looked around and realized he had passed out for lack of blood. His rifle was gone, but his life had been spared.

A short time later, Leschi, with Ann and his new rifle, emerged on the bank of the White River. As they were preparing to cross, Leschi looked up to see *Ta-co-bet*, resplendent in royal robes painted by the sunset on its glaciers. He felt betrayed by his *tamanous* – the mountain that had done nothing, that had stood mute and indifferent as the last battle ever to be fought by Indian warriors on its *Whulge* side ended in bitter defeat. *It is Ta-co-bet no longer*, thought Leschi bitterly. Now, it is Mt. Rainier, named for a man who never laid eyes on it. *The mountain whose name means nothing.*

Arm in arm, weary and shivering, Leschi and Ann forded the numbing river. Before slipping under cover of the dark forest, Leschi paused again to study the mountain. He blinked twice. How could he not have noticed it just a moment before? There, over the mountain, hung that strange cloud he'd seen so long ago – the great war canoe, launching from the crater into the sky. But there was a hole in the cloud, through which the magenta sunset poured like blood. *A hole punched in the canoe.* Could it be? What he had taken for a war canoe, was in fact a burial canoe.

IV

Treason & Surrender

(March 11 – November 14, 1856)

Chapter Twenty
Knife to the Gut

1

This is what John McLeod knew: they'd taken a few others along with him, because he'd heard the commanding officer give instructions for handling "the prisoners"; he was in a small frame cabin with a splintery planked floor; the heavy door was locked and barred and there was only one high, narrow window, also barred; he had a slop bucket, a water bucket, and a pallet with blanket; there was a soldier guarding the door, who passed him his biscuits and beans, and took his slops twice a day. This is what he didn't know: where he was; what he was charged with, if anything; how long he'd been here; when he'd get out, if ever; what had become of his daughters; whether anyone knew if he was dead or alive; whether anyone besides his daughters even cared.

At first they'd questioned him, the hatchet-faced officer and his men. Though he figured this had something to do with that visit by Leschi, they seemed just as interested in the details of his Algonquin lineage and intermarriage. They'd tried to get him to sign a confession saying he'd supplied food and arms to the Indians. When he refused, the officer gave a sharp nod and he'd felt the butt of a rifle crack against his rib. That seemed long ago now. He had a dull ache each time he drew a breath, sharp pains when he twisted wrong.

No one came to question him any more. The vastness of time fretted the ragged edge of his composure. At first he had paced and sung and tried to speak to the guard, but he got no answer and tired of the sound of his own voice, so now he just sat huddled on his pallet, and slept. Sleep, blessed sleep; he never knew he could sleep so much, he was like a great cat. At least in sleep the time passed quickly, and he could visit his laughing daughters splashing in the creek, joined by his dear Nisqually wife, Ohanapecosh. John McLeod smiled, eyes shut, remembering their first time together, how he looked down into those nut-brown eyes, soft with warmth and welcome.

"What is the meaning of your name, me love?" he'd asked.

At first she wouldn't answer; it took him days to get it out of her. *Looking down on something wonderful*, she'd finally said; then she bit her lip and smiled in that secret way of hers that quickened his pulse. She was something wonderful, something he'd never known in the lonely hard days trapping mink and muskrat, or the lonely cold nights guarding the company's sheep against the yellow-eyed stealth of the wolf pack. She'd given him children, one copper beauty to whom he'd wanted to give an Indian name, but Ohanapecosh, she of the most beautiful name in creation, sensed the changing winds and said, "No, John, give her a proper white woman's name." They'd settled on Jane, in honor of Dr. Tolmie's wife. Then, two years later, a rosy-cheeked *wean*, and he couldn't resist, so she was christened *Tupso* – Rose.

Yes, those were good years. He'd left the company, they'd built on Muck Creek, and everything they planted flourished. Until one day, he'd looked down upon someone so wonderful, and found her eyes deadened like stagnant pools, the pox upon her cheeks. Poor Ohanapecosh, and their dear lassies, to lose a mother when they were so young. And now, just a few years later, how terrified they must be to have their pappy taken too.

John felt wetness on his cheek, and realized he'd been crying. So what? There was no one to see, nothing to find out, nothing he could do but rage or sleep or cry or laugh, and it made no difference which he did, for nothing changed. The nightmarish succession of emptiness went on, hour by hour, day by day, eternity by terrifying eternity.

Though John didn't know, the nightmare was repeated one hundred feet away for Sandy Smith. And though neither John nor Sandy knew, it was repeated yet again one hundred feet away for their Muck Creek neighbor, Henry Wren. And though Henry didn't know, he was now a widower. After his arrest, his Nisqually wife had gone to find her people, but she was shot on sight as she approached the outskirts of Olympia. It was an act of revenge by James Brannon, brother of the man who'd tried to fight off a sharpened file barehanded on the White River only five moons – but uncountable lifetimes – past. The neighbors looked the other way. Poor man, he'd suffered enough.

Sandy's wife Alala had canoed downriver together with Henry Wren's wife, but Alala hadn't made the fatal error of trying to go on to Olympia. Instead, with money secretly provided by Dr. Tolmie for the aid of the former Hudson's Bay employees held by the military, she consulted with Attorney Frank Clark. Frank hired a canoe and team to take him from Commencement Bay northward, up the Colvos Passage, past Vashon and Bainbridge Islands, around the southern tip of Whidbey's Island, into Useless Bay. It was April 2, 1856, when Frank touched down by the home of Judge Francis Chenoweth. There, Frank presented his affidavits and petition. The next morning he returned with a freshly inked writ of *habeas corpus* – the ancient bulwark of Anglo-American liberty issued by courts of justice, which commands the executive to "produce the body" of any prisoner before the judge in open court, to examine whether there are legal grounds to hold him.

2

Leschi's people, joined by Kitsap and what was left of Owhi's force, rode due east on the Naches Pass Road that Leschi and Quiemuth had helped the pioneers build just three years before. No longer an army, they'd been reduced to a defeated band of refugees. By midnight of the disastrous rout at White River, they reached the base of Mud Mountain, some eight miles further into the wilderness. Leschi dispatched Winyea and ten braves to escort the women and children from Mashel Village over the pass, to join them east of the mountains. Others simply broke off in small groups, dispersing like seedpods to the wind, unwilling to follow Leschi any further. Even Leschi's old friend, Wahoolit, begged off the arduous trek across the mountains.

"I must now go my own way, Chief," Wahoolit said, tears in his eyes.

"You fought well, Wahoolit, despite your wounded hand," said Leschi.

"It is not my hand, but my wounded heart, that tells me I must go," replied the old warrior.

"I am going with Wahoolit, Uncle!" cried Sluggia.

Leschi looked with surprise at his nephew. "You, too, Sluggia?" he said. "You and your father fought bravely when we attacked Seattle. You saved me at Green River. How can I do without you?"

"There is nothing left to do, with or without me. You are finished, old man," replied Sluggia cruelly.

"Maybe so," answered Leschi. "But if your father and mother were here, they would say, 'stay with your uncles.'"

"They are not here," growled Sluggia, pulling at the reins to align his horse with Wahoolit. Several other young men joined Sluggia, including his friend Elikuka, eldest son of Yokwa Village's medicine man.

"Go then, with my blessing," said Leschi. He watched sadly as they disappeared into the cottonwoods by Chambers Lake. So many gone, thought Leschi, to death or simply blown away on the winds of change: Sennatco, Sara, Stahi, Nelson, Kanasket, the traitor dog Wyamooch, now Wahoolit and Sluggia. Had not Sara heard the howl of the *zach-ad*?

That night, the unseasonably warm weather turned cold. Leschi's few remaining people followed the White River as it snaked around Mt. Rainier's northern lava flows, abandoning it when it turned south, in favor of the Greenwater River that came down from Naches Pass. To make the best possible time they repeatedly had to ford the icy waters of the two rivers. In two day's time they forded the rivers forty times, and made nearly as many of the white man's miles. In the highlands of the pass, under the shadow of craggy Colquhoun Peak, some rode and some walked over snow frozen so solid by the chill weather that it was like stone. Then they picked up the Little Naches to the Naches River valley. The bitter cold, and crossing and re-crossing of the rivers, combined with lack of food and exhaustion, took its toll on man and beast alike. Sometimes they were lucky, and able to find a *kwiwichess* - foot log - placed across the river by the Yakama, but even then the ponies were forced to ford the chill waters. They lost several bony Cayuse ponies, which they promptly roasted and ate. They lost wounded to fever and infection, and even the unscathed to hunger and cold. When at last they descended into the broad Wenas Valley, and were able to dig adopasch roots to stave off starvation, the eyes of the survivors were dead as any cadaver's.

"My brother, Leschi, I must go with my warriors to find my people, if any are left to be found," said Owhi. Leschi and he clasped one another's forearms, then broke to pound their chests in a bitter echo of lost power.

"You, above all others, have been true," said Leschi. "Tell your father that Chief Leschi would be proud to have such a son." He watched long, as Owhi and his thirty surviving warriors climbed the undulating ridge, growing smaller and smaller, until at last they disappeared over the top in a tiny puff of dust. Leschi felt the emptiness in his heart expanding. Without Winyea and the Mashel Nisquallies, there were barely four tens of free Nisquallies left, rag-tag survivors of a once-proud tribe numbering in the thousands.

"I think that forested bluff the Governor offered would now be too big," said Quiemuth, who always seemed to see into his brother's mind.

"Do not say it," snapped Leschi. "There are many more Nisquallies in the Government camps. Whatever we may think of them, at least they are Nisqually, and they live on. Perhaps they were wiser."

"And, do not forget, there are the women and children at Mashel."

"I do not forget; I think of them every day. How I long to see my Kwahnesum again."

"And I, my little Kiya."

3

"Well, if this ain't the Gawl-darndest thing I ever seen!" exclaimed Colonel Silas Casey to his temporary adjutant, Lieutenant Angus McKibben, a gruff Scotsman with little patience for politicians. McKibben had been tapped to take Kautz's place, while Kautz recovered from wounds suffered in the charge at White River. Casey and McKibben were in the mess hall, discussing the writ of *habeas corpus* served upon Casey the previous day, when an express rider from Olympia arrived with a proclamation in the Governor's own handwriting. Casey handed it to McKibben, who read:

Whereas, in the prosecution of the Indian war, there is grave cause for suspicion that certain evil disposed persons of Pierce county have given aid and comfort to the enemy, and those persons have been placed under arrest and held under military guard; and whereas efforts are now being made to free these persons from military custody by use of the writ of *habeas corpus*; and whereas the war is now being actively prosecuted throughout nearly the whole of said county, and great injury to the public safety would accrue if these prisoners are freed; now therefore I, Isaac I. Stevens, Governor and Commander in Chief of the Territory of Washington, do hereby proclaim Martial Law over the said county of Pierce, and suspend until further notice, the functions of all civil officers in said county, and order that said prisoners continue to be held in military custody pending trial before a military commission.

McKibben exploded: "What a load of horse manure!" Then he looked to Casey for guidance. "Can he do that, Sir?"

"He can do anythin' he wants, 'til someone's got the balls to stop him. It's like the prostitute said to the preacher, son," Casey explained, his sun-flecked face squinting with amusement. "I'll stop soon as God steps through that door!"

McKibben chuckled. "So, spit in his eye, eh, Colonel?"

Casey studied the Governor's proclamation next to the writ of *habeas corpus*. The writ commanded him to produce the prisoners at the United States District Court in Steilacoom, to show cause for holding them. "Fail not," it commanded, "upon penalty of contempt, fine and/or imprisonment." Well, that didn't scare Casey; there was no way the Sheriff could outgun the Commander of a Fort of the United States Army. But he'd always been raised to believe that America was a great nation because the military served the civilian government, not the other way around. He wasn't inclined to disobey a court order.

Still, Casey had an aching scar in his scalp to remind him that it was best not to pick a fight with this particular Governor.

"Take a message for Governor Stevens," ordered the Colonel. "Hon. Governor Isaac I. Stevens, *etc., etc.* Dear Governor: I've got a court order to produce the prisoners on May 7th. It is my opinion, as I've already told the newspapers, that the Indian threat west of the mountains is mostly ended. Therefore, I'm inclined to obey, and let the court decide whether your proclamation is lawful. If you wish to relieve me of the burden of these prisoners before that date, I would not stand in your way." Casey paused, then added with a chuckle, "Sign it some way, Lieutenant, but none of that obedient servant stuff we usually use – Isaac is likely to take it seriously!"

McKibben complied, though he didn't appreciate the elegance, as Kautz would have. "Don't solve nothin'," he muttered.

"Maybe not," conceded Casey. "Like most things we do, however, it allows us to keep about our business, while we wait for God to step through that door."

4

William White, who'd left Wisconsin for his health six years previously, had at last found prosperity after a long struggle. With a wife and five children, he'd been flooded off his first claim along the Columbia; they'd all fallen ill and lost a child to the ague while in Portland; then they'd been flooded out a second time from their new claim on the banks of the Cowlitz. Moving north, the White family had finally found rich land on Chambers' Prairie, but at the war's outbreak they had fled in fear to Camp Montgomery. With spring on the wing and things quieting down, they felt it was safe to return, and attend to the clearing and repairs needed before planting.

It was a beautiful spring Sunday, although reports that Indians had been spotted in the area were making everyone a bit jittery. Church was not optional for the Whites, so they made the journey, only to find the service canceled. *Indians.* White couldn't figure it. What better time to go to the Lord?

They stopped at the home of a sick neighbor on the way back, where Mrs. White left a fragrant loaf of molasses wheat bread. They were about a mile from home, Mr. White walking by the side of the wagon bearing his wife and children, when suddenly a painted warrior on horseback rode up along side. With a quick move the warrior raised his musket, but Mr. White was quicker, catching the barrel and pulling it down as it discharged, powder-burning his forearm. The blast and the screams of the Mrs. White and her children startled the draft horse, who bolted into a lumbering gallop, everyone bouncing and hanging on for their lives. Mrs. White looked back in terror, crying to the diminishing shape of her husband, now overrun by three savages, "William, dear William!" But there was no turning back; it would have meant death or slavery, and besides, their equine savior was beyond distraction in his quest for the safety of home and stable.

It is good to be free of my uncles at last, thought Sluggia. *This is for you, Kanasket.* Sluggia smashed in the white devil's skull with a war club.

5

Kwahnesum and the other women of Mashel Village – except for Mary, who always disappeared when there was work to be done – were singing springtime songs, as they pounded laundry in the stream. It had rained; it would soon rain more. The brief let-up was enough to coax the children out for a game of shinny. Kwahnesum squeezed water from wool blankets, and hung them to dry over nettle twine pulled between branches. In the intervals between their own songs, the women were serenaded by the sounds of play and laughter, as the childrens' teams struck at the bear-bone with their curved sticks, or hooked the bone and carried it, triumphant, past the defenders.

Little Kiya was too young for the fast game. Though she stayed close to the women and the other small children, she craned her long, thin neck, eager to see the flashing sticks and darting figures of the older children. Kwahnesum looked upstream to where two old grandfathers were manning a fish weir at the outlet of the pool beneath the falls. Taking Kiya by the hand, she walked up to admire their catch. They handed out a basket writhing with silvery trout. With Sara's sharp obsidian blade, Kwahnesum began cleaning the catch, her hands working expertly as her mind wandered far away. Sometimes the war seemed like a bad dream, and she could imagine her father, and even First Mother, returning by horseback, leading her downriver to enjoy a new summer on *Whulge*. She remembered the songs that once carried everywhere over the water, and then the crack of rifle fire shattered her reverie, telling her this was no dream.

Kwahnesum leaped up, spilling fish guts and the precious catch, in time to see soldiers raining down upon the village from every direction. They fired without discrimination at old men, women and children. People screamed and ran for the woods, dived under bushes by the houses. What had been a field of play was suddenly a field of gore. Where was Kiya? Kwahnesum searched frantically for a moment, then grabbed the hand of the nearest little girl she could find, and began to flee across the Mashel by the fish weir, just as three horsemen exploded from the forest on the opposite bank.

Jimmy McAllister, one of the three Volunteers riding down upon them, recognized the girl who'd burst into their home that night. It was the beautiful girl he'd seen naked through the kitchen window; the girl with the night-sky tresses, who'd haunted his dreams ever since. Colonel Blunt, just ahead, decapitated one of the fishermen with his sword, then turned on the girl and child dodging through the streambed. Desperately, Kwahnesum pulled the terrified child into the air out of the path of the horse's hooves just as the wicked sword fell, cutting the girl's hand free. Screaming, Kwahnesum dropped the severed hand as the girl and her crimson comet's tail disappeared in the shallow rapids of Mashel River. Three men dismounted, then came at Kwahnesum from all directions. One was the fat man burned on her memory from that terrible time in Charlie's cabin. Kwahnesum had the obsidian blade clenched tight in her hand. She stabbed at the fat man's heart just as another white man grabbed him from behind. The fat man's arms flew up and deflected the blow, which slashed across his cheek and nose, but it was not a killing thrust.

"Leave her be!" cried Jimmy, pulling at Blunt, but Blunt was too strong. His elbow found Jimmy's solar plexus. Jimmy staggered to the river bank.

The fat man and the other soldier grabbed Kwahnesum. She jumped, twisted, and thrust the knife so hard, that one man fell, even as others converged upon her. Through force of will, she was able to break free for an instant. She knew what they wanted, and knew that she would never again let herself be taken like that. With a deft flick of her wrist, Kwahnesum turned Sara's beautiful blade upon her own soft belly, thrust inside and upward. The burning blackness was welcome, more welcome than any lover's touch, and with her last breath, Kwahnesum thanked First Mother for such a gift.

Jimmy knelt in the bloody river, cried over the girl whose name he didn't even remember. The rain returned. Tears, blood, rain, and river became one, washing away his ferocious craving for vengeance, leaving in its place only sorrow.

6

The Nisquallies made camp in the barren land east of the mountains, and settled down to wait for the rest of their tribe. Each day, they scanned the western horizon for a sign of Winyea. When at last he came, Leschi immediately knew there was bad news. Where there should have been at least four tens of riders, there were only eleven.

Winyea's story was so filled with horror, that at first he could not bring himself to speak. The sharpness of his grief surprised him; he thought he was numb, but putting the tragedy into words was like a fresh cut to the bone. He tried indirection. "When we arrived at Mashel, all was silent, but the river. It was a terrible silence." He paused, met his adopted tribesmen's eyes, and though they knew, they refused to allow the knowledge in; there was hope still there. Winyea's fate was to kill this hope, to spread the killing he'd uncovered, to make it real. Best do it quickly.

"We found the bodies of twenty-eight women and children, and two old men; some shot, some stabbed, many mutilated, all dead." Winyea's voice clenched in a sudden, unexpected sob. He glanced furtively from Quiemuth and Moonya, whose Kiya had been there; to Leschi and Ann, whose Kwahnesum and Mary had been there; to the shattered faces of many others, whose grandfathers, sisters, sons, daughters, and mothers, had been there. Then he looked down at the harsh, barren earth of the land beyond the mountains, so different from their beloved Nisqually bottomland. "The wolves," he said, then thought better of describing it all. "We could not always make out the faces." They understood. "We searched, but found no survivors," he mumbled.

No survivors, not even the spirit of the Nisqually people. They fell down and wailed; they rent their garments; they rued the day they chose the path of war. What had seemed to Leschi to be a simple fight for justice, now appeared as a foolish battle against death itself. All they had wanted was the river that gave them life. But nothing lives forever. Not in this world.

"REVENGE!" screamed one despondent Nisqually father.

"NO!" shouted Leschi. "We have killed too much already. Look where it has gotten us. We will mourn for three tens of suns, one for each of our fallen tribesmen. We will cleanse ourselves, and seek guidance from the spirits."

"And then what, old man?" cried the distraught father.

Leschi was beaten. "And then," his voice faltered, "and then, I do not know." The people looked away, embarrassed for their Chief. Their weary eyes scanned down the sagebrush-dotted slope to the river. After countless generations, they were back to the land that *Sah-hah-lee Tyee* dried up in punishment when their ancestors kidnapped Cloud. There was no grass by the banks of this bitter creek, and they were afraid. Not afraid of dying, but afraid that they had lived to see the time when they were the People of the River Grass no more.

Chapter Twenty-One
Habeas Corpus

1

Ezra Meeker stood in the doorway of the cramped log cabin on Fern Hill overlooking the Puyallup River. His little family had only recently returned to Fern Hill after a winter at Fort Steilacoom, to discover that the Indians had not thought their cabin worth burning. Ezra had been planning to start work on a new plank house, but now with his wide-brim hat pushed back, he just stood scratching at his head, contemplating the paper in his hand. His wife Lizzy stood on tip-toe, trying unsuccessfully to read over her gangly husband's shoulder, while balancing the new baby on her hip. Though he knew it would only upset her, Ezra also knew there was no way to keep bad news from Lizzy, so he might just as well read it out loud.

"'To the Sheriff of Pierce County, Greeting:' – well, that ain't me, so mebbe we're outa the woods on this one, Lizzy – 'In the name of the United States of America' – well, that's us sure 'nuff, at least they got the right address – 'you are hereby Commanded to Summon to be and appear at the Court House at Steilacoom' – crimminy, Lizzy, you think these-here fellers is gettin' paid by the word? – 'on Wednesday the Seventh of May, 1856, at the hour of half-past Nine O'Clock' – well, that ain't so bad, I figure to have time to milk and pasture the herd and maybe even lay in a cord or two of firewood by that lazy old lawyers' hour! – 'every white male resident within said County, above the age of sixteen years, to be and appear with such arms in hand as they can procure, to aid and assist the Sheriff in preserving Order and Peace and enforcing the Orders of the Court' – *hhhmmm*." Even Ezra couldn't think of a wisecrack for that one.

Every white man in the Territory who could read, or just understand the rants of their local barfly, knew that this was to be no ordinary session of court. The contest between the civil courts and the Governor was being pumped for all possible political capital by both sides. The opposition press called the Governor "King Stevens." The *Pioneer & Democrat* countered with the charge, "the friends of traitors, are themselves traitors."

"Let me see that court paper, Ezra," said Lizzy, and she took it from his hand. "'Fail not,'" she read, "'under penalty of law. Signed, Edward Lander, Chief Judge, and John M. Chapman, Clerk.' Oh, Ezra," she said, fading back against the doorjamb as she dropped the summons and wrapped the baby in both arms. "Ezra, you cain't ..."

"Right as rain, Missy," he replied. "I cain't shirk my duty in this matter, that's fer sure."

On a sunny May morning two days later, Ezra's simple conviction placed him shoulder-to-shoulder with thirty other men, to defend the little courthouse at Steilacoom.

"Now men," said Frank Clark, who was armed with a Colt revolver, "if the order is given to clear the courtroom, that is the signal to open fire. Me, and you, and you," he said, pointing to Ezra and another man, "are responsible to take out their leaders. The rest of you men, count how many you are from the center of our force, and pick a man that far from the center or front of theirs. I don't want everybody shooting at the same man. We may not get off too many shots, we've got to make them count." He paused. "Don't forget – '*clear the courtroom*' – if I say it, or either the Judge or the Clerk says it, that's the signal to fire. Any questions?"

A scruffy looking backwoodsman cleared his throat. "Yes, Sir, Mr. Clark, Sir. You see, I got me this beef with my neighbor, been accused of stealing his pig, 'sposed to come to court next week –"

"Done," said Frank, without a second thought. "You stand your ground and shoot straight, we'll take care of you."

The defenders were arrayed before the bench with its large pewter statue of blindfolded Lady Justice. Crouched behind upturned counsel tables, they nervously checked and re-checked their powder, licked their lips, and occasionally sprinted to the necessary house to relieve themselves.

They didn't have long to wait. The little courthouse shook to the martial rhythm of hooves, as Major Benjamin Frank Shaw rode up at the front of a column of fifty Volunteers. The big clock on the wall over the jury box showed 9:55 a.m. when Shaw burst through the doors with twenty men, arms at the ready, as the rest surrounded the building.

Shaw held up his hand, and his men spread out into a line crouched behind the back benches. The darting of his green eyes betrayed surprise at finding the court so well defended. The two forces surveyed one another, survival's tunnel vision instinct turning neighbors into targets.

At precisely ten o'clock the door to chambers opened. Mr. Chapman, the Clerk, emerged in his buttoned frock coat, willfully oblivious to the dozen fingers tightening over triggers on weapons honed in on him. Fortunately, the sight of this scrawny functionary quickly dispelled any menace. He was allowed to climb unmolested to his accustomed perch just beneath the bench.

His only concession to the unusual circumstances was that he desisted in striking the gavel, for fear it would be misinterpreted as gunfire.

"*Oyez, oyez, oyez,* the Honorable the United States District Court for the Third District, Washington Territory, is now in session. All who have business before this Court come forth and state your claims. All rise for the Honorable Edward Lander, Chief Judge."

In judicial robes, the silver-maned Judge emerged from chambers and took his place at the bench. Unlike at the Battle of Seattle, Judge Lander was not visibly armed. He surveyed the courtroom as he might on any routine motion day, though the procedural posture of the matter before him was unprecedented in the annals of American jurisprudence. "Be seated," he said, though no one had been fool enough to stand. "Mr. Chapman."

"The first matter on the docket is *In re Writ of Habeas Corpus for Prisoners Sandy Smith, John McLeod, and Henry Wren.*" With a truly inspired demonstration of his ability to affect boredom, Mr. Chapman passed a file up to the Judge.

The fellow's got guts, thought Ezra, who was sweating like a stuck pig.

"Is counsel ready?" asked Judge Lander.

Frank Clark, revolver in hand, never took his eye off Major Shaw. "Ready, Your Honor," he replied.

"You may proceed."

It was at this point that Shaw decided he'd seen enough. His orders were clear: "*enforce martial law.*" He wasn't about to allow a bunch of mealy-mouthed lawyers set free half-breed traitors in the middle of a war. He stood right up, emphasizing his own power and confidence.

"No one's proceeding here, Judge. Now you stop right there," and perhaps because his usual chirp was missing, it was clear to everybody that he meant business. "Your Honor," he said, for there was no point in antagonizing matters beyond what was necessary, "under the Governor's Proclamation of Martial Law, this session of court is illegal, and I'm here to shut it down." That ought to do it. None of that lawyer chatter. Right to the point.

Ordinarily, Judge Lander would have held the interloper in contempt immediately. But despite his cool outward demeanor, the Judge knew he was sitting on a powder keg. He remembered his wife's parting words, as she handed him a cameo of their elder daughter before he'd gone out to the stable. "Our daughter will be giving us our first grandchild next month. That little one will need a Grandpa." The Judge knew that he was target number one. He was easy to hit, sitting way up high like a clay duck at the fair. From his perch, he had an excellent view of the Volunteers sighting their muskets and pistols through the windows. No, there was no doubt about it – if he ordered the courtroom cleared, the bloodshed would be so severe that the only way this particular courthouse would ever be cleared again, would be to burn it to the ground. Beneath his august robes, the cameo beat hard against his heart.

"Major Shaw," said Judge Lander, "I appeal to you, Sir, to stand down. As you can see, any attempt to take this Court by force will result in substantial civilian casualties, as well as loss of life among your own men. While I would not venture to say which side would prevail here, I can say that only the red man could take pleasure in the sight of American killing American. So I appeal to you, Sir; send a rider back to the Governor to get further instructions. I cannot conceive that any Governor in his right mind would issue an order that results in his own troops shooting down members of the community."

All eyes were back upon the young Major. The Judge's pretty words had given him an out, but he was no coward. He'd fought the bloody campaign through Mexico in which every adobe hut was suspect, and there were times when they thought nothing of killing even women suspected of harboring the men who sniped at their camps by night. This old Judge was trying to pull a fast one on him, he could tell. *No one outsmarted Ben Shaw, no sirree!* The Governor's strong hand was the only thing between the settlers and the thousands of *siwash* still scattered throughout the Sound, just waiting for the signal to rise up and finish the job started at White River. Shaw understood that; that's why the Governor could rely on him. *Enforce martial law.* Nice and clear, not like this lawyerly double-talk from the Judge.

"Judge," said Shaw, sunlight glinting off spittle in his tangled red beard, "I've got my orders. Now, by authority of Governor Stevens, you and your Clerk here are under arrest. Either you come peaceable, or you don't. One way or another, you're comin'."

The sweat continued to ooze from every pore on Ezra's body. He sighted in on the center of Shaw's chest, blinking the salt from his eyes. Who else, right now, was aiming at his own chest? Any second now, the Judge would give the command to clear the courtroom, he knew it, and he was gonna be damn sure he got this red-bearded devil before they got him, goodbye dear Lizzy, goodbye little Emma and Ella, goodbye brother Oliver, dear Father Jacob – *and then he heard the words* –

"Stand down, men," ordered Judge Lander wearily, as he himself stood up. "Clerk will gather the files and surrender himself to the custody of Major Shaw."

Ezra, like the thirty other resurrected dead men by his side, didn't know whether to cheer or cry, as he watched the old Judge submit to the indignity of being led from his own courthouse under armed guard. *Lady Justice,* thought Ezra grimly, *must surely be thanking the Lord for her blindfold today.*

2

Charlie cooled his heels for three long days on the threadbare carpet leading up the steps to the executive offices of the President's House. An ever-shifting menagerie of office-seekers, do-gooders and fortune-hunters, cluttered the stairs, so it was no surprise that Charlie almost missed his chance, when Sidney Webster, the President's Private Secretary, called his name.

"Excuse me, Sir, did he call 'Eden'?" Charlie asked the fellow on the stair below, a heavy-set blowhard with a case of sure-fire patent cures that needed only the endorsement, "As used by the President and First Lady," to become all the rage.

"Dunno, Sir, Capt'n Wheaton, somethin' 'long them lines."

As Mr. Webster was just beginning to call the next name on his list, Charlie bounded to the top of the dim gas-lit stairway. "Captain Charles Eden, at your service, Sir," he announced. Though he'd just resigned his commission, Charlie figured he'd earned the right to use the military rank to help press his petition.

Mr. Webster, stylish in a plum waistcoat that set off the ruffled cuffs of his starched white chemise to fine advantage, scrutinized Charlie from head to foot. Charlie's plain frontiersman's buckskin fell well short of the mark. "I could place you at the end of the queue for missing your call," he announced. Charlie's face fell, until his golden curls and pale blue eyes had their effect and Mr. Webster relented. "Oh, very well, fifteen minutes, not a minute more." He took Charlie by the arm, and ushered him into a cramped shoebox of an office, with a fireplace so near the President's desk that it seemed intent on devouring it. Behind the desk sat the cleft-chinned Young Hickory of the Granite Hills himself, President Franklin Pierce. The President's perpetually youthful lock of chestnut hair kept falling across his wondrously sad, alluring eyes. To his right sat his Secretary of State, the ancient and phlegmatic William L. Marcy; to his left, the brilliant, Harvard-educated Attorney General, Caleb Cushing.

Charlie'd traveled so far and waited so long, that he'd begun to lose track of the fact that the purpose of this wild jaunt across the continent was to persuade the President of the United States to abandon a man to whom he had deep ties. The President had appointed Stevens, a fellow Mexican War veteran, after Stevens had campaigned vigorously on Pierce's behalf, helping him defeat their former Commander, General Winfield Scott. Not only that, but Charlie wanted the President to reconsider the policy of ruthlessly fighting Indians which, since the days of Pierce's earliest childhood hero, Andy Jackson, had become as essential to Presidential success as log cabin nativity. Charlie would ask all this while Bleeding Kansas erupted in open warfare between pro-slavery and anti-slavery factions, so the President had much more pressing matters on his mind. Charlie was an unlettered fellow from way out in Washington Territory, a place but dully perceived in the national consciousness, who'd had some success but mostly blundered into it, who had set out to do the impossible, and now had fourteen-and one-half minutes left to do it in, though he wasn't even sure what his first words should be.

Charlie was saved that embarrassment by the President himself, who rose and extended a remarkably delicate hand. "Captain Eden, a great pleasure, Sir. We have all followed your exploits with keen interest, especially that gallant rescue of the captive boy, what was his name?"

"King, Sir," said both Charlie and Mr. Webster simultaneously. It was obvious that the President had been fed a little synopsis by his personal secretary, and had probably just read it as Charlie stepped through the door.

"Yes, King, good job! Perhaps you will recognize Mr. Marcy, and Mr. Cushing."

Charlie mustered his deepest voice and firmest possible handshake. "Gentlemen," he said as he accepted the proffered seat. No sooner had he sat, than he was once again rescued from the dilemma of ascertaining where to begin, this time by Secretary Marcy, who also superintended nationwide Indian affairs.

"Captain, I have briefed the President on the issues presented by the Honorable William A. Wallace, Esq., in his memorial accompanying the document you produced on behalf of the Indian Chief Leschi. The President is of the view that no such grievances as are set forth in that document can be adjusted, so long as a state of war exists between the treating parties and the Government of the United States. Nor can any such grievances be adjusted outside of the usual channels established for that purpose, which in this case means working through the duly appointed Indian Agent for Washington Territory, Governor Isaac I. Stevens. Have you anything to add?"

Charlie knew this would be a tough sell, but he had not traveled for five weeks from Steilacoom through Panama to Washington City, just to listen to some bureaucratic brush-off. "With respect, Sir," he began, as he suddenly knew he must begin, no matter how angry he was, "in our neck of the woods we have a saying, 'you don't trust a snake to cure snakebites.'" In all those miles, Charlie had found time to do his homework. While he knew that the President couldn't be won over by a sob story – unless it involved the death of a child, which the President had so recently suffered – he also knew that the President was that fiercest of crusaders: a reformed alcoholic. Indeed, he'd even sponsored legislation to ensure that his own hometown of Concord, New Hampshire, went dry. "Now, I'm not saying that Governor Isaac I. Stevens is a snake; no Sir, far from it, when *sober*." He emphasized the word carefully, and the President's ears perked up. "But, Gentlemen, it pains me to tell you this, though it is my duty. Under the influence of alcohol, which happens all too often, the serpent of intoxication gets ahold of him, and he is beyond all reason."

At least now Charlie had the President's attention. "Captain," said Pierce, "I do not allow it is so, but assuming it were, what difference does it make? These savages have killed innocent American settlers, and defied solemn treaty obligations. They have made war on our troops and our towns, not without some success. Drunk or sober, certainly preferably sober, but either way, under these circumstances I'd want my Governor to fight hard, to show no mercy." Here the President paused slightly, considering his own words. "Now, I will admit, we've had some differences with Governor Stevens as to tactics – well, really, it comes down to dollars – his volunteer army is costing the Government a fortune, not to mention the cost of feeding all those peaceful Indians he's got penned up who can't fend for themselves right now. So, perhaps I'd do things a little differently, but I can't see that this is a basis for undercutting the man on the scene."

"With all due respect, Mr. President, what if the man on the scene is the cause of the trouble? The intemperance –" Charlie again chose the word carefully, knowing that both the President and his wife, Jane, were strong supporters of the Women's Christian Temperance Union – "of the man on the scene made him inflexible, which forced a war on everyone which no one wanted, not the white man or the red man. The intemperance of the man on the scene is now preventing the quick end of that very same war, even though the Indians have repeatedly made peace initiatives, offering to lay down their arms simply for a little land along their sacred river. And, mark my words, the intemperance of your chosen Governor, your chosen Indian Agent, will in this very election year, lead to your embarrassment, if he is not reined in right away. You haven't got policy in Washington Territory; you've got a barroom bully."

Had he spoken too strongly? He saw the President purse the lips of that clean-cut, firm-jawed mouth, which won him an election by having nothing to say. Charlie knew how deeply conventional this man was; how it pained him to make a decision. Now, the decision was a smile and a sidelong glance towards Mr. Webster, as the President rose and extended his hand. "Thank-you so much, Captain, for sharing these frank views with me. We shall certainly take this into account."

Mr. Webster was hustling him out the door, and Charlie knew he had failed. How wretched he felt; not even several nights defying the Temperance Union at Willard's elegant new bar could dispel his gloom. As he dragged his hangover through the stygian streets of the swampland Capitol, Charlie despaired of ever being any help to Leschi. What a fool he'd been! It was one thing for a simple Native like Leschi to believe that all you had to do was catalogue the wrongs of both races, and some magical *Tyee* would correct them. It was quite another for a white man, such as himself, to have been such a fool.

Charlie walked the gangplank to the bark that would carry him to Panama, as if it were a pirate's plank to Davy Jones' locker. He was just ducking his head, to descend the narrow passage to his berth, when his musings were disturbed by the distant sound of his own name, carried on the wind from the pier. "Cast off!" ordered the Captain. The sailors began to pull up the plank, as Charlie spun and ran back to the gunwale. "Over here, boy!" he hollered at a messenger, and the resourceful lad quickly found a stone around which he wrapped the heavy cream envelope with twine, then threw it towards Charlie, who only barely saved it from the waters of the Potomac with a scoop catch. Charlie flung back a handful of coins to the waiting boy, for which he battled a gaggle of opportunistic street urchins.

Eagerly, Charlie unwound the twine, tore open the envelope, and removed both a stiff sheet of paper and another smaller envelope. Carefully, he smoothed the paper. It was on Executive Mansion stationary.

Captain Charles Eden:

Honorable Sir. Since speaking we have received disturbing intelligence from W.T. tending to confirm your recent predictions. You are authorized to communicate to the Governor that the President expects a full report on martial law immediately. Furthermore, you are deputized by the President to carry the enclosed confidential instructions to the Governor. The President and I both feel we can rely upon your discretion to hand this envelope in its present sealed condition directly to the Governor.

I am, Sir, your obedient servant,

Wm. L. Marcy, Sec of State

Charlie exulted: he had not failed after all! Though he longed to know what was in the sealed envelope, he felt duty-bound to live up to the trust placed in him. Whatever the secret message was, it was clear that his words had helped to move the President. *There are no small men.*

3

The long days of prayer, cleansing, and fasting were over, yet still Leschi vacillated as his people grew restless. Occasional contact with small, wandering bands from other tribes, brought news of one calamity after another. The Klickitats had attacked Boston settlements at Upper, Middle and Lower Cascades; sixteen whites had been killed before Colonel Wright and the army rode in and devastated the attackers. The Colonel ordered that the leaders of the attack be hung. Their Chief was Kanasket's brother.

"I was there. Colonel Wright made us watch," said a strong young maiden, traveling by foot with her spry mother. "The Chief made a fierce war whoop from the gallows. He shouted, 'I am not afraid to die.' But when they dropped him it wasn't right, he twisted and choked, but refused to die, until at last they shot him where he hung. They tried to round us up, but Mother and I escaped by hiding in the sage."

Other news of reprisals reached their ears, until they did not know whether to believe or not – more Indians shot on sight, a whole family strangled in their beds by Volunteers. The Nisquallies became afraid that either the regular Army or – much worse – the Volunteers, would find their camp and attack. But no amount of urging could rouse Leschi, so deep was his gloom.

The sun baked the earth. There were no berries, the plants were unfamiliar. There were no salmon, no squirting clams, no cedar, no salal, nothing of the life they knew. Although the people had plenty to drink from the Naches River, they thirsted for the land they knew, for the refreshing cool of maritime mist, the shriek of the eagle and the swoop of the heron. They longed to see once again the play of snowberries, fireweed and wild carrot, against a sea of green in shades as plentiful as the bickering seagulls. Then, in the distance, a puff of dust topped the ridge, and began to grow larger.

They had nothing but flimsy shelters of tattered blankets, sagebrush and cottonwood, no real cover to protect them from what they knew was coming, and should have prepared against. Men and women both grabbed old sand-choked muskets, and took cover the best they could. Even from a distance, the force looked large and menacing – perhaps eighty or a hundred riders. Leschi whispered urgently to Quiemuth, "What should we do?"

"Be the man I love," replied Ann before Quiemuth could say a word. That seemed enough to kindle the resolution of old in Leschi's eyes. Soon, the keener eyes of the young discerned the welcome news that this was no column of soldiers, but instead Yakamas, led by Owhi and another, older Chief – Kamiakan himself.

Kamiakan and Owhi dismounted, Owhi holding back in deference to his father. The Chief wore flowing robes of fox trimmed in elaborate beadwork over his muscular back, and a feathered war bonnet, that festooned his grey-streaked tresses. Around his neck, hung a silver crucifix. His belly sagged, and his careworn face was mirrored many times in the long, ragged column.

How far the mighty Yakama have fallen, thought Leschi, as he strode forward to clasp Kamiakan in a bear hug. Then he realized that the Yakama Chief must be silently making the same assessment of his Nisquallies.

"It is good to see you, Chief Kamiakan. You are always welcome at our camp."

"And you, Chief Leschi. You are welcome here, in the land of our common ancestors."

"Here is Kitsap, of the Suquamish," said Leschi. Kitsap slouched forward, his scar now looking more haggard than fierce.

"Kitsap, I knew your father," said Kamiakan, as the two embraced.

"Kitsap has shown great courage." At Leschi's words, Kitsap straightened, proudly holding up his chin.

Owhi scanned the Nisqually camp, and registered the absent women and children. Taking Winyea aside, he heard the devastating news: *massacre, no survivors*. He whispered it to his father, who bowed his head and crossed himself in the style taught by the blackrobes at Ahtanum Mission. As the two chiefs sat in silence, passing Leschi's feathered clay pipe, Kamiakan's eyes brimmed with tears.

The Chiefs' *klootchmen* scurried about to fashion a feast out of dust. Soon, they served *adaposch* roots carefully pre-masticated to make them tender and juicy, followed by roasted quail and rattlesnake meat. Then the Chiefs began the council.

"Seeing you gives me heart," said Leschi. "Now we can join forces and fight again."

"Brave Leschi," replied Kamiakan, "do you not see what is all around you? We have fought and fought. Each time we fight, we get weaker and our people suffer more hardship. Colonel Wright's forces are now arrayed along the south bank of this very river. He has five hundred men, Leschi. Do you know how many that is? I can no longer raise more than ten tens. And he has the big guns with shells that *mox-poo*."

"Then what shall we do?" asked Leschi. "How can a man surrender the skin in which he was born?"

Chief Kamiakan shook his head. "We have two choices, my friend: surrender or die. I am not afraid of death; I have made peace with *Sah-hah-lee Tyee* and the Lord Jesus Christ. But I choose to surrender for my people, because I cannot bear to lead them to their deaths, when there is no hope of victory."

"Under Stevens' terms, surrender is death."

"Yes, I have heard this from Owhi. I suggest that you surrender to the Boston *Tyee* on this side of the mountains, Colonel Wright. He is a fair man, not like Stevens, and not like the Volunteers who slaughter our people on sight."

"A fair man?" cried Kitsap. "We have heard tales of his fairness, that ended at the hangman's noose."

"That is how he treats those who make war upon his people. He is a fierce warrior, Kitsap, like you and Leschi. That does not make him a monster."

"There was a time when I saw the distinction," said Leschi.

"Even the dog that licks your hand will bite when it feels threatened. I believe that Colonel Wright wants peace, and sees war as a last resort. In this, he is no different than any of us."

"Perhaps," said Leschi. "But Kanasket died with a call to arms on his lips. How can we betray his memory so soon?"

"I have come to discuss surrender, not war. I have come out of respect for your mother and, Chief Leschi, out of respect for you." He looked deep into the black night of Leschi's eyes. "If you wish for me to arrange for you to lay down your arms, I believe that Colonel Wright will offer his protection to you and all your people."

Leschi felt numb from head to toe. He knew this was coming, yet how completely he had shut it from his mind. Of course, Chief Kamiakan was right. He looked to Owhi.

Owhi could not meet his gaze. They had been through too much together. Like Leschi, he was grim-faced, even to the point of blinking back tears. At last he mastered his emotions to say, "Perhaps, great Chief, it is for the best."

Leschi looked to Kitsap. "What say you, fiercest of my fellow Chiefs?"

Kitsap found within his heart torments he could never erase. He had been wrong to lead an attack on the settlers, he knew that now, though he could hardly admit it to Leschi. It was on that bloody day that they had lost the good will of the spirit world. Without it, all their efforts had been futile.

"I was once a Chief," said Kitsap, "but today I have no people to lead. I have fought against you, Leschi, and fought beside you. Now, I am ready to stop fighting, if it is your command."

Leschi nodded solemnly, then looked to Quiemuth. "Brother, it is to you whom I always turn last for advice. What do you think? Shall the Nisquallies fight no more forever?"

Quiemuth studied his hands for a long time. At last he smiled, and looked his brother in the eye. "Do you remember what our father said to us? 'In fear, there is no wisdom; only death and suffering.' I am sorry to say that we have followed the path of fear, my brother. Fear of change, fear of loss. The more we feared these things, the more we brought them down upon ourselves. Our sons and daughters -" and suddenly he had to stop, overcome with the memory of little Kiya, clinging to Kwahnesum, wailing as if she could see her death in the fading faces of her parents. Quiemuth mustered his composure, and began again. "Nisqually children still live and breathe. They will have children, who will pass on the old songs and stories, and their children will pass them on, so that long after you and I and Stevens are dead, there will be a Nisqually People. What message would you send to our people, long after we are gone? Shall we pass on fear, or the courage they will need to make a new life in a changed world?"

Quiemuth fell silent. Leschi nodded. He stood and took a deep breath. "My people," he announced in his resonant, clear voice, "gather your belongings. Tomorrow we go to surrender."

4

Winyea was mistaken about survivors of the Mashel Massacre. Just before the soldiers arrived, Mary had been sitting on a boulder above the falls, enjoying the sun. She'd seen Kwahnesum come up with Kiya to help the fishermen. She'd noticed as Kiya wandered away from Kwahnesum, and something - was it foresight granted by the spirits? - had uncharacteristically drawn her down to greet the little girl. It was just as she'd lifted her in her arms that the first shots were fired. Together, they melted into the woods.

As they fled, Mary had stolen one quick glance back from the top of the falls. The scene was now etched on her memory, like a carving in stone. There was Kwahnesum, her face serene and bright, shape-shifting from temptress to *tamanous* as her sharp obsidian blade released angry snakes from her belly

257

to devour the Bostons' lust. She was smiling, not a vengeful or derisive smile, but the fulfilled smile of a daughter greeting a beloved, long-departed mother. Although at the time Mary had known nothing but fear, she now embraced the comfort of this memory. Could this have been how her own mother faced death, that terrible day when the Haida came and took her little sister, with two of her father's fingers still clutched tight to her sister's arm?

Now Mary wandered, little fingers clutched tight to her own hand, day and night. Mary would have liked to shake their grip, so much did they remind her of those severed fingers that never let go. It was a burden to drag this little girl all around the Skookumchuck River headwaters, scrounging roots, mushrooms, and an occasional trout for survival, chewing the salal leaf to suppress their omnipresent hunger. She'd grown up without a mother, so she didn't see any reason why Kiya couldn't do the same. When Kiya moaned about missing her *naha* - momma - all Mary could say was, "*Sssshhhh*, be strong, be happy you are alive."

"But I want *naha*," Kiya screamed in frustration.

"You may never see her again, so just forget about it," Mary shot back. The wailing that followed taught her it wasn't the right thing to say. "Hush," she commanded, "the Boston soldiers will hear you." That quieted Kiya, who became withdrawn, perpetually weepy and brooding. *You'll get used to it*, Mary thought to herself, *you don't need a naha to survive. Learn to still your heart.*

Gradually, their days settled into a kind of routine. They'd built a small shelter of cedar bark and fir boughs to keep dry. They spent their days gathering food, fishing, making stone tools, stripping bark, making clothing and blankets. As the springtime sun became more established, berries became available and the pinch of cold receded, leaving them more leisure. Kiya's mood improved; she began singing. They spent long afternoons laughing and playing at all the old games, with hoops, spears, and balls they fashioned themselves from whatever came to hand.

It didn't last. Mary was becoming restless. She never intended to be a mother, and this orphan thrown into her lap had not changed that. She grew sullen, and spurned play. Kiya spent long hours alone, returning to camp only late in the evening for food. "You better watch out," warned Mary, "*Seatco* will get you!"

"I'm not afraid of *Seatco*," Kiya blustered. "*Seatco* has Bostons to eat now."

Mary laughed. "So where do you wander?"

"Down to the other Native camp," said Kiya, matter of fact, as if everyone knew of this camp.

"What other Native camp? Did they see you?" asked Mary, with a mixture of hope and alarm.

"Nobody sees Kiya," said Kiya. "I am invisible, like Raven in the night."

"Will you take me there?" asked Mary.

"For something sweet," taunted Kiya, and Mary picked up a hazel switch she'd been known to use when Kiya was particularly vexatious. "Okay, okay, Grandmother," said Kiya, using the honorific Mary hated most as she scampered off to the edge of the clearing, "I'll take you tomorrow!"

5

Once again, Frank Clark made the long hard canoe trip to Whidbey's Island. This time, Judge Chenoweth refused to sign any papers. Instead, when he heard what had become of Chief Judge Lander, he insisted on leaving his sick bed to make the trip down to Steilacoom personally.

"But Francis," objected his wife, "you've had the ague for four weeks –"

"So it's high time I got over it." He sneezed, and grabbed his coat. "Let's go, Clark." Frank accepted Mrs. Chenoweth's offering of a tin packed with joints of beef, buttered rolls, and a flask of hot tea. "CLARK!" hollered the Judge, already down by the canoe.

"Coming, Your Honor," cried the beleaguered counselor, as he turned back to reassure the Judge's worried wife. "Don't worry, Missus, I'll look after him."

She smiled, blissfully unaware that a lingering chill was hardly the most imminent threat to her husband's health. Word had passed from the ferryman who leased Clark the canoe, to the Governor, that Judge Chenoweth's intervention was being sought. Major Shaw was summoned.

"Shaw," said Stevens from behind his battered desk, "enforce martial law."

"Yes, Sir!"

After a night's sleeplessness at a Tacoma inn, Judge Chenoweth arrived in Steilacoom to open court on a cloudy Monday morning. The normally bustling main street, with its expansive view of the Sound, was deserted except for a few stray dogs chasing chickens. Clark and Chenoweth turned inland, following the road to the courthouse. As they emerged from the clearing, something didn't look right. Clark wordlessly signaled a halt to the Judge. They dismounted in unison, pulled their rifles from the saddle scabbards, and crouched low in the bushes. It was too quiet.

A glint of metal. "That you, Clark?" boomed Sheriff Williams' voice.

"George?"

Out sauntered the stubble-faced Sheriff, looking every bit the Western lawman, six-guns strapped to each hip, and a rifle in his hands. "Git on in here, boys," he cried. Judge Chenoweth and Frank were welcomed inside the little courthouse, which had been transformed into an armory over the previous two days. There were forty or so men, none of whom bore fewer than two firearms. Ordinary folks like Ezra Meeker and his brother Oliver were there, and this time they were backed up by pillars of the community like George Gibbs, William Wallace, Hugh Goldsborough, and Elwood Evans. The windows had been boarded over. All the benches and tables had been upended for cover. The door was boarded shut behind them. The judicial bench had been lowered and screened with thick fir planks. Small slots had been cut in the walls for gun barrels. There was an air of tense excitement.

Judge Chenoweth donned a judicial robe hanging behind the bench, and immediately took charge. "Mr. Evans, I appoint you Deputy Clerk of the Court," he said as he strode to the bench, laying his rifle across it. The barrel nestled at the feet of Lady Justice. "I want the first matter to be Judge Lander's application for *habeas corpus*." Evans called it.

Frank Clark stood. "If it please the Court –" he began, but that is as far as he got.

"We got company, Your Honor," cried the Sheriff, peering out a crack in the boarded window.

"Motion GRANTED," the Judge ruled, and then he sneezed. "Clark, draw me a writ," he said, wiping his nose on his judicial robes. "Any other motions?"

"For the Prisoners, Your Honor."

There was a pounding at the door.

"They're granted too. Draw me two writs, and be quick about it. Will, Hugh, give him a hand." The three lawyers jumped to work on the writs.

"Open up in the name of the Governor," cried a voice from outside. More pounding.

"How many we got out there, Sheriff?"

"Maybe thirty."

"Shoot, I think we can take thirty."

Ezra Meeker stood peering through a slat on the other side of the courthouse. "'Spose we could, Judge, if the other thirty on this-here side would be kind enough to wait while we do it."

"YOU'VE GOT ONE MINUTE, OR WE BREAK DOWN THE DOOR AND COME IN FIRING!"

The big clock over the jury box showed 10:19. It didn't have a second hand. No one had needed it to be that precise before.

"Who is that out there?" cried the Judge, more snot hanging from his nose.

"Major Benjamin Frank Shaw, Territorial Volunteers."

"Well, Major Shaw, this here is Francis Chenoweth, appointed United States Judge by the President of these here United States. With me are eighty angry folks, armed to the teeth. That includes the Secretary of the Territorial Legislature, the Legislative leader of the Republicans, and a bunch of democratic lawyers who used to think your boss was slick as a lathered mare's tit 'til he started arresting Judges. Now they're ready to defend this here courthouse to the death. So if you want to break down that door, you gotta ask yourself, 'how do I stand with the Lord?' 'Cause you'll be meeting him promptly." Chenoweth wiped his nose on his robes again.

Shaw was shaken. Eighty armed and fortified? He backed slowly off, giving the take cover signal. His men drew back to covered positions. *Think, man, think.* "We kin burn you bastards outa there, Judge," he screamed, his high voice cracking.

"Yes, son, I suppose you could," replied Chenoweth calmly. "You want to go down in history as the first American officer to incinerate a United States Judge and a bunch of American citizens, you go right ahead. Then, if by some chance, we don't shoot you dead today, you get to hang for murder tomorrow." The heat of the day was still hours off, but Chenoweth's robes were soaked through.

Shaw licked his lips. His men were eyeing him, waiting for a command. His mind was blank. God damn wily lawyers, always makin' everything more complicated than need be. He was s'posed to enforce martial law, period. He wasn't s'posed to stand about and jaw. But boy, he'd sure like it if he didn't have to do this. Something told him this just wasn't such a good idea. He'd do it anyhow, 'cause his job was to fight, not think. He raised his hand to give the order.

Inside, Judge Chenoweth scrawled his signature on two freshly-inked writs of *habeas corpus*. No Judge could have a finer final duty than to issue the Great Writ, the one which commands the Executive to produce the body. Judge Chenoweth smiled at his own private gallows humor. *It's supposed to be someone else's body.*

6

A very travel-weary Charlie had the presence of mind to make sure that Mason was present when he slid the thick creamy Executive Mansion envelope across the mottled surface of the Governor's desk. He knew that, whatever the contents, it was important that it not end up in the fire.

"This is not what I'd call loyalty, Captain Eden," snapped Stevens. The Governor perched awkwardly atop a new chair, designed to jack him up six inches. It had the effect of pressing his thighs hard against the underside of his stomach drawer. He pushed the envelope about as a cat might toy with a stunned mouse.

"It's Mr. Eden, Sir. I've resigned my commission."

"Oh, yes, of course," said the Governor.

Charlie pressed on. "I am instructed by the Secretary of State to inform you that the President expects a full report on martial law immediately."

Mason licked his lips and glanced sharply at Stevens, who only smiled blandly as if they were discussing the price of butter. "Of course," said the Governor. "It goes without saying. What are your plans, Mr. Eden?" *Charlie Eden won't work anywhere in this territory*, the Governor decided.

"I – I'm not sure, Governor," replied Charlie, surprised by the question. But as he said it, he realized that he was sure. On the long journey from one end of the continent to the other, he had realized how much he missed Kwahnesum. "I suppose the first thing is to find my wife; I've got some fences that need mending."

"Your wife, oh yes," said the Governor. "That Indian girl. Well, Captain, I'm sorry to have to be the one to tell you this, but it seems she went back over to the enemy side, and she was killed in a military action up near Mashel Village. A shame, really, she was such a pretty girl – or, so I heard from Colonel Blunt." The Governor's lips slipped back to counterfeit a smile.

Every breath Charlie'd ever taken escaped all at once, leaving a terrifying void. Doubled over, he keened one loud cry, then found the will to straighten, nod, and take his leave. His mourning would not be soiled any further by the Governor's glee.

Steven's triumph was short-lived. Grasping the gold-plated letter opener that had been a thirty-eighth birthday gift from Meg just two months before, he slashed the fancy envelope, removed the elegant stationary, and perused the President's strict instructions. With each word, his scowl deepened, until he crumpled the whole page and flung it towards the fire. Mason was ready.

With a catlike stab, he caught it and held fast. The Governor did not even notice. He was already taking a long pull from the whiskey flask he kept in his frock coat pocket.

7

Though his hand was raised, Major Shaw's order to open fire on the courthouse was interrupted. Colonel Silas B. Casey, alone and wearing only his service revolver, galloped out of the woods at precisely the right moment to plant himself between the warring factions. "What's going on here, Frank?" he asked.

Shaw lowered his arm slowly. "What do you think?"

"You huntin' Judges again, young fellow?" asked Casey.

"I got my orders," said Shaw.

"Frank," said Casey, "like the prostitute said to the preacher, 'I'm open for confession.'"

"What's that supposed to mean?"

"Means you need to talk about this. Might help get your brain engaged."

"I know what I'm doin'."

"Do you, now?" asked Casey. "I recall that last time, Judge Lander saved you from shootin' yourself in the arse by being man enough to surrender. Now here you are again with your rifle buried so deep your trigger's gettin' greasy, so I figured maybe I'd give you one more chance not to do the dumbest thing a military man's done since Benedict Arnold."

"I don't need your advice," spit Shaw. "I take my orders from the Governor, and God."

"Reminds me of the story of the preacher in the rainstorm, Frank," said Casey. "Raining like the dickens, it was up around the preacher's waist when a feller comes by on a horse and says, 'hop on,' but the preacher says, 'no thanks, God'll save me.' Well, it rains and rains and the water's up to his neck when a rowboat comes by, and the feller says, 'hop in,' but the preacher says, 'no thanks, God'll save me.' Well, next thing that preacher knows, he's drowned, and when he gets up to heaven he asks God, 'why didn't you save me?' God looks at him kinda funny, and says, 'What do you mean, preacher? I sent you a horse and a rowboat, what more could you want?'"

"That's a good one!" cried Judge Chenoweth, as laughter spilled around rifle barrels peeking through the chinks in the courthouse ramparts.

"You laughin' at me?" demanded Shaw.

"No, Major," yelled the Judge. "I'm laughin' at the joke."

"What's yer point, Casey?" asked Shaw.

"My point? I'm yer heaven-sent rowboat, Frank. Climb aboard. It's your second chance not to make a big mistake. Don't count on getting a third."

Shaw didn't like it one bit. His job was to fight, not think. But it wasn't to shoot American citizens; he had to admit, that put him on edge. Maybe it wouldn't hurt to go back and seek clarification of his orders. He sure hoped the Governor wouldn't take it wrong. He could always blame it on Casey.

"Stand down, men," ordered Major Shaw.

The sound of sixty muskets un-cocking can be prettier than the song of the nightingale to a man on the muzzle end. Smiling, Colonel Casey dismounted and pounded Major Shaw on the back. "Good man, Major," he said. "You just went a long way towards becoming a real commander."

The door to the courthouse creaked opened. It was Judge Chenoweth and the Sheriff. "These are for you, Major Shaw," said the Sheriff, as he handed him the two writs. Shaw looked to the parchments in his hand. *You are Hereby Commanded ....* The ink was not even dry when he tore them up, then stomped the pieces into the dirt beneath his boots, laughing the whole time.

"You laughing at me?" asked Judge Chenoweth.

"Nah," replied Shaw. "I'm laughing 'cause we was all about to get ourselves kilt over a coupla pieces of paper. Just as easy to tear 'em up!"

It was then that a red-cheeked, winded Secretary Charles Mason galloped into the clearing, his spectacles askew. "Oh, thank God," he cried, "Shaw, I'm glad I got *heah* in time. Take this." And he thrust forth a freshly inked order from the Governor's office.

Martial law is hereby rescinded.

Shaw stopped laughing. *If I hadn't listened to Casey, I'd be a murderer right now.*

"Will I be holding you in contempt," the Judge asked Shaw, "or do you want to dig them writs outa the dirt and stick 'em back together?"

8

Shaw, Blunt and Mason all shifted uncomfortably in the chairs the Governor had ordered them into, watching as the Governor paced in fury. Stevens could not believe that a few Judges could stir up so much trouble. All he'd tried to do was protect the public from traitors, yet now an arrest warrant was out for Shaw, and even some of Stevens' strongest supporters were whining as if he'd turned over Olympia to the *siwash*. Stevens knew he had to do what Old Hickory had never done – give ground, while he still had some to give. But he didn't have to like it.

"Shaw, you're dispatched to the east side of the mountains to hunt down Leschi," barked Stevens, standing with his back to his men, looking out his office window at the kelp and driftwood tangled like witches' fingers at the edge of the surf.

Shaw leaped like a salmon. "Yessir!" he chirped, already half-way out the door. He couldn't get out of there quick enough.

"Blunt, as head of the military tribunal, issue an order stating that because the further prosecution of the traitors would pull too many valuable officers out of action, the tribunal releases the traitors to the proper civilian authorities. Got that?" Blunt, a deep scar creasing his cheek and double chins, offered a lugubrious nod of assent.

Stevens gave him three beats to respond, before spinning and bellowing, "Blunt, are you still here?"

"Yessuh," replied Blunt. Silence, as the Governor's eyes bored through him with barely contained fury. "I mean, I mean," stammered Blunt, standing hastily, knocking over his chair, "No, Sir!" and he was gone like a cherry-red, forge-heated three-hundred pound shell.

Now it was Mason's turn to squirm. The Governor walked slowly around his desk until he was standing directly over him like a headmaster about to apply the ruler to a pasty-faced schoolboy.

"Charles," began the Governor, his voice high and soft. "Charles, you did the right thing."

What?

"Yes, Charles," cooed Stevens, "you did the right thing, rescinding martial law."

Mason relaxed; allowed himself a faint smile. Suddenly Stevens' voice turned to ice. "And if you ever do it again, if you ever even think of acting in my name without my consent again, I'll have every ball in your body, from the balls of your feet to your eyeballs, and yes – every ball in between – nailed to my wall within the hour!"

Mason crossed his legs.

"Get out of here!" Mason tried his best, but suddenly the doorway was blocked by armed men. It was Sheriff Williams, with a posse of thirty citizens.

"Gentlemen. What can I do for you?" bluffed the Governor.

"Isaac I. Stevens?" asked Sheriff Williams, with stiff formality.

Stevens didn't play along.

"Isaac I. Stevens, by authority of the United States District Court for the Third District, Washington Territory, I hereby arrest you for contempt of court."

"Arrest me?" cried Stevens, backing into his blood-stained desk, then around it. "ARREST ME," he screamed, "your Governor, in time of war?" Stevens fumbled in his desk drawer for a revolver, but the Sheriff was too quick for him, launching himself directly over the desk in a flying tackle. The pistol fell to the floor and discharged up through the desktop, the slug imbedding itself harmlessly in the ceiling. Other men quickly surrounded the Governor, who saw the futility of further resistance.

As they marched Stevens past the flummoxed Mason, the Governor hissed, "Act like a man, Mason. Don't go crawling to Meg."

Chapter Twenty-Two
Surrender and The River

1

The day dawned warm and breezy, clouds puffed like dahlias against the sky. Mary followed Kiya downriver, to a point where it was joined by a fast-running creek off the south ridge. Gripping her knife, she edged up to the clearing, and peered out. Mary immediately recognized the sun-dried, hawk face of Wahoolit, by the fire. Several other Nisqually braves were there. Her heart leapt with gladness. Could it be? That powerful, slim build was unmistakable – Sluggia! Pushing the brush aside, she threw her shoulders back and breasts forward, revealing herself to them.

That evening around a blazing fire, Mary and Kiya feasted on pork pilfered from a white man's ranch, the grease rolling down their chins. Then Mary told the men the tale of the Mashel massacre. The former warriors were overcome by rage and helplessness. Sluggia vowed to seek revenge.

"Calm yourself, my firebrand," whispered Mary to Sluggia. Covertly, she stroked his back down to his firm buttocks. The sweetness of the meat and the smell of the men stirred her desire. That night, long after the fire died down, she went to Sluggia's blanket. He was waiting, hard with anticipation, each thrust of his hips a homecoming.

Later, his softness still pressed to her thigh, she dozed in the crook of Sluggia's arm, as he confided his plans. It was not Stevens he blamed for the deaths of their people. It was her husband, his uncle, their Chief. Or did she dream it? Mary startled awake. All was hushed, Sluggia's breaths even and rhythmic, Sky Women watching wistfully from above. She slipped back into a deep and dreamless sleep, the kind she liked best of all, the kind that bordered on death.

The next morning, as she knelt feeding twigs to the coals of last night's fire, she felt a presence looming overhead. Turning, she found Wahoolit's unsmiling face glaring down at her. "You are the wife of our Chief; you should be ashamed."

"He may be dead," she replied, meeting his gaze without modesty or regret.

Wahoolit brushed aside her words. "You will be nothing but trouble here," he said. "You must go."

"Go where, old woman?" It was Sluggia, across the fire pit, holding a musket.

"To *Otlas-Skio*, for all I care," replied Wahoolit as a silver coffin knife appeared in his good right hand out of nowhere, and he yanked Mary to her feet with the shining blade at her throat. "Drop the gun," he commanded. Sluggia did as he was told, and Wahoolit shoved Mary forward. She stumbled through scattering sparks, landing at Sluggia's feet. "GO!" The other braves now ringed the trio. There was little doubt where their loyalties lay. Kiya watched too, wide-eyed and silent.

"You'll regret this," was all Sluggia could muster.

"One more word, you'll see how much I regret it." Wahoolit's *tamanous*, the hawk, folded its wings back, ready to strike. Sluggia remembered well Wahoolit's prowess with a thrown knife, from their many friendly contests in days past. Slowly, the two outcasts backed away. Kiya slipped her hand into the stiff, curled fingers of Wahoolit's left hand, and squeezed as she watched Mary disappear from sight.

2

On a warm July Monday in 1856, a few weeks after the Governor's arrest and release to his own recognizance, Stevens stood trial for contempt before his former captive, Chief Judge Lander. By the Governor's side stood a squirrel-faced little man with jowls, and thin grey-black hair, combed with hair oil into distinct lines. It was Mr. Dandy Pritchard, a lawyer selected by the Governor for his short stature and easy corruptibility.

"How do you plead, Sir?" asked the Judge.

"Not guilty, Your Honor," replied the Governor.

Stevens had advised Mr. Pritchard that he could not endure a slow political roasting from the witness stand. "With all due respect, Your Honor," added Mr. Pritchard, thrusting his diamond stick-pin towards the bench, "there is no need to take evidence. Rather than open the executive cabinet to abuse by the courts in time of war, my client will stipulate to noncompliance with Your Honor's writs."

The Judge glanced at Frank Clark, who had donned his County Attorney hat. "Your Honor, the People are entitled to present their case," objected Clark, who had lived and relived his withering cross-examination of Stevens dozens of times in the past week. Cases he couldn't lose ordinarily bored him, but not this one.

Judge Lander was determined to approach the matter without any hint of partiality. "No need to waste the Court's time or the People's money," he said.

"If it please the Court," said Pritchard, "our defense is a legal one: military necessity, and martial law when Your Honor's *habeas corpus* writs were issued."

"Martial law which had no necessity, because there were not sufficient hostilities to displace the ability of the civil courts to function," countered Clark.

"Mr. Clark is correct," said the Judge. "Have you got anything else for us to consider, Mr. Pritchard?" The squirrel gave his little head a jowly shake. "Very well. Inasmuch as the prisoner has waived trial, and having rejected his legal defense, I find the defendant, Isaac I. Stevens, guilty of contempt of court, which he may purge by payment of a fine of fifty dollars."

"If it please the Court." This time it was not Pritchard.

"Yes, Governor?"

"In this time of war, it can only be the savages who take pleasure in this proceeding, which has diverted my attention from the one task I place above all others: protecting the safety of the people of Washington Territory. To that end, I have a document to present to the Court."

"It's a little late for taking evidence, Governor," said the Judge.

"It is not offered as evidence, Your Honor, yet it is quite germane."

"Very well," said Judge Lander, "out of respect for your office." He nodded to Mr. Chapman, who took the document gingerly between thumb and forefinger as if it were a dead wasp, then passed it up to the Judge. In the Governor's own hand, was written:

> I, Isaac I. Stevens, Governor of the Territory of Washington, by the authority vested in me as Governor by the President of the United States, and in order that Isaac I. Stevens may continue in the uninterrupted discharge of his Constitutional duties as Chief Executive of the aforesaid Territory, do hereby PARDON the said Isaac I. Stevens, defendant, from any and all judgments and/or executions, and all proceedings for the enforcement and collection of fines and costs, in connection with a certain contempt proceeding in the United States Court for the Third District of Washington.
>
> By Order of the Governor,
>
> Signed, ISAAC I. STEVENS,
> Governor, Washington Territory

As the Judge read this remarkable document, his eyebrows burrowed together until they appeared to join. He handed the document down for Mr. Clark's perusal. Frank read it with glee. *Now here's a feller who really understands the fine art of fighting dirty.*

"So, Governor," asked the Judge, no trace of amusement in his voice, "as I understand it, you claim to have pardoned yourself?"

"The Governor has pardoned me," corrected Stevens.

"Well, then," said Judge Lander, "tell the Governor this: if both of you do not pay to the Clerk fifty dollars, you're both going to jail."

Pritchard tried to say something, but Stevens brushed him aside. "Your Honor, I will never pay one nickel of your unjust fine."

This was exactly what Lander had hoped to hear. "Sheriff," he said brightly, "take him away."

Just as Williams laid a strong hand on Stevens' arm, a voice from the gallery cried, "Your Honor, if I may be so bold."

"The Court recognizes Secretary Mason." Charles stepped forward and counted out fifty dollars in gold coin into Mr. Chapman's dry palm. "On behalf of the Governor," said Mr. Mason. *Govenah.*

"The prisoner is discharged." The crack of the gavel ended the session.

Afterwards, Frank Clark was chatting with Mason in the clearing in front of the courthouse, when the Governor emerged. "Mason," said Stevens, "I hope that wasn't Territorial funds you just expended."

"Your special fund, Sir."

"Disgraceful. You shall pay back every penny from your own purse. Now go!" Mason's face fell, but he went.

"You shouldn't treat him like that, Governor," said Frank. "With the Legislature meeting in emergency session to investigate your little martial law fiasco, you need your remaining friends – all three of them."

"A great man has no friends, Clark," replied Stevens. "You of all people should understand that."

"I'll take that as a compliment, Governor."

"Take it however you wish," said Stevens. "And tell your friend, Will Wallace, that if he doesn't want to spend the rest of his life as the minority leader on the committee for protocol, he'd better realize that the voters will always prefer the man who stands up to protect them, over the man on the side of savages, half-breeds, and lawyers."

"What about the man on the side of justice, Governor?"

"Go sell that line of feathers to the kin of the White River folks. You know what they'll tell you?" Stevens stepped right up to Clark, and poked him in the chest with each word. "*Revenge – is – justice.* Got that?"

Clark mounted his waiting bay mare. "Thanks for setting me straight, Governor," he said. "I always thought it had something to do with law."

When the Governor arrived at his office that evening, he found a Joint Resolution lying on his newly-patched desktop:

Be it resolved by the Legislative Assembly of the Territory of Washington that, in attempting to suspend the writ of *habeas corpus*, the Governor undertook to exercise a power conferred by the Constitution of the United States on Congress alone.

That, in the Governor's attempt to interfere with our courts of justice, or to try citizens before a military tribunal, he acted in direct violation of the Constitution and Laws of the United States, and that any such attempt to exercise unconstitutional power, tends to the subversion of our institutions, and calls at our hands for the strongest condemnation.

Cursing, Stevens tore up the document and threw the pieces into the trash. Mason, surreptitiously watching from the antechamber, filed away the original, from which he'd had a copy made for the Governor.

More than ever I must get Leschi, thought the Governor. How could it have come to this? The shining star of the West, the great Isaac I. Stevens, the man who would ride his triumphs in the West right into the President's Mansion, now depended for his political survival upon the capture and execution of a broken-down old *siwash.*

3

It was supposed to be a sad day, yet Leschi's people were smiling for the first time in months. From some unknown reservoir of hope, a few tattered brightly-colored rags and ribbons had been salvaged to festoon foreheads, necks and waists, or to be tied as fluttering banners onto spears. As the Nisquallies topped Manastash Ridge, they paused to draw a last breath of freedom. Looking back and up, the ice and rock spires of the Cascades glimmered against a cloudless cobalt sky. Before them, ancient lava flows sculpted by glaciers and floodwaters, left a wide-open sagebrush steppe falling away to rocky meadows painted with lupine, sunflowers, buckwheat, and bright pink bitterroot. Below was their fate: the Kittitas Valley and Colonel Wright's encampment along that other festive ribbon, the shimmering Yakima River.

Ann had conjured an otter headdress from her satchel. Heedless of the heat, Leschi wore it proudly over his neatly trimmed greying locks. Around his neck, he wore the tortoise shell and bear tooth necklace, Sara's parting gift. *Wise and strong,* she had said. He needed all his strength and wisdom for what was to come. In his big, weathered hands, he gripped a clunky fusee musket, its burnished dragon plate glinting in the sun. The rifle he'd taken off Jackson Moses was well hidden in a cave above Wenas Creek. Only a fool leaves himself no contingency plan.

Colonel George Wright, a West Pointer who was nursed on tales of the exploits of Ethan Allen and the Green Mountain boys, sat erect at the head of a small honor guard, watching the distant dust cloud form itself into distinct riders. Negotiations that had drawn into weeks culminated in this moment. It was hot, and the Colonel's wool dress uniform stuck to his skin, itching like poison oak. He betrayed discomfort only by the barest trickle of sweat off his slightly receding hairline, down past his doleful eyes, prominent nose, and clean-shaven cheeks. Erect in dress blues, he was measured and perfectly controlled.

The Indians rode to within a few dozen yards of Wright's men before Chief Leschi called a halt. As the dust swirled up from their hooves to envelop the vanquished army, Wright noted how few and weak they truly were. This was the force that terrorized the western settlers? Then Leschi emerged out of the dust cloud, and Wright knew why it was so. The two men were nearly the same age and of similar bearing, but it was more than that. Each immediately saw in the other a kinship that transcended the accidents of race and birth.

"Greetings, Chief Leschi. You and your people are welcome at my camp."

"Greetings to you, Colonel Wright. On behalf of the Nisqually people, and Chief Kitsap of the Suquamish, I thank you for your hospitality." Kitsap, mounted slightly behind Leschi, merely inclined his head, so that his scar glowed a deeper red to the ranks of white soldiers behind the honor guard.

Colonel Wright asked the question to which he knew the answer, though he keenly anticipated hearing it. "What business have you here today, Chief Leschi?"

What business indeed? Leschi saw Kanasket's face, towering and open to the sky. There was Old Nelson by his side, giving his life that Leschi could survive. There was Sara, who heard the *zach-ad.* There was Stahi, who sobered up and became a man. And his dear, martyred Kwahnesum, her high, clear voice carrying a song of love across the waters of *Otlas-Skio.* For a moment, with the weight of the dead on his tongue, he could not speak the words.

He owed them the courage to follow his own fate. "Colonel," said Leschi. "Upon your assurance of protection, I have come to offer the surrender of the Nisqually people, and Chief Kitsap."

The Colonel nodded. "My terms, on behalf of General Wool and the President, are as follows. First, a complete renunciation of the use of force against all Americans, now and forever. Second, your arms and your ponies. For that, you shall have my protection. Your people will be fed and shielded from harm and arrest. You shall have safe passage to a suitable reservation of the Government's choosing."

"It is so," said Leschi. He poured the powder from the pan of his musket, and handed it stock first to Wright. He dismounted with his spear, held it high for all to see, and then with one powerful downward thrust, shattered it across his knee. He handed his pony off to be led away by a military groom. At a signal from Leschi, his people dismounted, and filed by a waiting wagon, dropping their firearms and spears onto the bed.

"Come now," said Wright, smiling. "Your people must be weary and hungry. Make a camp by ours, and our quartermaster will bring provisions for your women to prepare."

Leschi bowed, and turned to lead his people for the last time. At that moment, a second dust storm rose atop Manastach Ridge. They watched as it grew bigger, forming within the minute into riders, then into a hundred troops, riding under the banner of the Territorial Volunteers.

"Deploy!" ordered Wright. His men quickly formed a protective ring around the helpless Nisquallies. As they were pressed together between horse rumps, they felt the first bitter taste of dependence upon the power of one set of white men against another. Leschi caught occasional glimpses of Colonel Wright gesturing as he argued with the Volunteer Commander, a young skinny man with a long, tangled red beard. At last, the Volunteers rode off.

"Leschi," warned Wright, as he pulled up on the reins of his chestnut mare, "stay close to our camp. Those fellows want your blood, and they were pretty mad at me for not just handing you over. Their commander, Shaw, said he didn't care about anyone else, he only wants you."

Leschi was despondent. The moment they found peace, the long hand of the Governor found them. He surveyed the anxious eyes of his beloved people. How could he bring back the joy of that morning?

4

For seven days the Volunteers remained camped just above Colonel Wright's force. Each day, Major Shaw appealed for the release of Leschi to his custody, and each day he was rebuffed. At night, Shaw's men taunted Leschi in Chinook and *Whulshootseed*, each taunt an increasingly graphic description of torture and death. Finally, they rode off to the southeast. Their departure did not end the disquiet in Leschi's heart.

In the desert, the summer sun relentlessly beat down. The long days of purposeless captivity began to take their toll, as men and women bickered and softened in the sun. All hope seemed lost, until - a miracle occurred. Out from the shimmering heat came a lone horse, bearing a hot and tired Nisqually, who clutched the reins with one shriveled hand, and a child with his good hand. Leschi, Ann, Quiemuth and Moonya rose to welcome the rider, who was led him to their camp by a sentry. It was then that Moonya beheld what she had dreamed a hundred times, yet knew to be impossible. Tears streamed down her face as she ran to greet the horseman, Quiemuth close on her heels, arms pinwheeling like a duck launching from a pond. It was Wahoolit! Leschi laughed to see his taciturn face break into a rare, spare smile. Did his eyes deceive him? The precious burden he was handing down for kisses and loving strokes beyond counting was Kiya! *Alive!* Kiya!

Leschi, swooning with happiness, was not too overcome to ask the question that he dared not ask. "And Kwahnesum?"

There was no need for Wahoolit to speak; the tightness returning to his cheeks told the story. Leschi nodded, biting down on his lower lip. "Your Mary says that she was very brave," said Wahoolit.

"Mary!" cried Leschi, breathless as he careened from joy to sorrow to joy. "Mary is alive?" Again Wahoolit's face grew clouded, but his words allowed it was so. Later, when they were alone, Leschi heard the bitter side of that tale. It scratched him inside. To be held helpless, a prisoner, while Sluggia and Mary .... He clenched his teeth, balled his fists. He could not even finish the thought. Yet it was always there, indigestible and bitter as a black-cap mushroom.

One moon after the departure of Shaw, straggling refugees began to arrive, seeking protection from Colonel Wright against the Volunteers. At first, the stories were garbled and incomplete - an isolated atrocity here, the third-hand rumor of some great tragedy across the river in Oregon. Too soon, however, the heavy fragments congealed into an unmistakable tale of brutality.

Shaw's men had scoured the land of the Walla Walla and Nez Perce in a vain search for hostile Indians to fight. Despite finding only pockets of peaceful refugees, Shaw had promised his men that they would not go home "without striking the enemy." Abandoning the sweltering Walla Walla Valley for the cooler Blue Mountains of Oregon, Shaw's force tracked the shattered Walla Wallas to the valley of the Grande Ronde River, where they had sought refuge with their cousins, the Cayuse and Umatillas. The Walla Wallas had squatted there for many months, in a large encampment of over one-hundred tents, cabins, and makeshift lean-tos. They were dwelling in peace, trying to forget the terrible time when Volunteers had attacked their village, and killed Chief Peopeomoxmox.

"We were afraid," said a young Native maiden through split and swollen lips. She had been welcomed into the Nisqually camp two days before, too bruised and exhausted to speak. "We had many, many people, but only a few braves. Mostly, we were women, children, elders."

Ann held her hands. She did not inquire. She knew that the full story would come when the girl was ready. Tense silence circled the cooking fire.

"We sent a messenger to tell the white soldiers that we were no threat. That we were not warriors, only families. That our chiefs were gone, or dead, and that no one could parley with them. That we had but few guns, and used them only to hunt game. The messenger came back and said that the red-bearded officer was angry. He insisted on seeing our chiefs. But we had no chiefs. No head men. After what happened to Peopeomoxmox, we decided it was best to live without chiefs. We thought if we had no chiefs, they would leave us in peace. That's what we thought," she said to the fire. "That's what we thought." Her voice trailed off. Ann pressed her limp hand.

"Because the red-beard was angry, we decided to run away. As we were preparing to flee, the white soldiers attacked. We did not fight back. We never wanted to fight. I tried to run, but I was carrying my baby, so I was too slow. A man with a hairy face caught me. He smelled so bad. We had but a few men. We had no chiefs, no head men." She looked to Ann. "What did they want, Grandmother?"

Ann took her into her arms, and held her. She did not need to ask what had happened to the baby. The girl had come empty-handed, her eyes as wide and barren as the broad steppes she had crossed on bleeding feet to get to their poor camp.

What did they want, Grandmother? Leschi knew what they wanted: *him.* He'd been a fool to think he could hide away here, burying his head in the sand while the Governor's fury broke all around him. He'd have to cross back over the mountains, stealthily, alone. He had to find a way to reach the Governor, to speak with him face to face, man to man. Otherwise, their enmity would drive all the Native people of the Northwest to their graves.

He would leave that very night.

5

Mary could get used to this kind of life. After months of sleeping on the hard, cold ground, the feather mattress under her back and the cotton sheets over the swell of her hip, felt like the caress of *Laliad*. As sleep dropped from her eyes, her dreams were replaced by images no less fanciful: gauzy curtains undulating in the breeze, a porcelain washbasin, smooth, sky-blue papered walls, hung with exotic paintings of mounted men in strange hats and tight scarlet jackets, blowing horns and hunting behind packs of dogs.

Mary rolled over to find Sluggia's side of the bed already empty. Donning a dressing gown made from some mysterious skin, and unfamiliar cloth moccasins that Mrs. Simmons called *slippers*, she padded to the landing and half-way down the stairs. From there, she could see across the broad living room with its overstuffed chairs and sofa, to the dining room where Sluggia was standing with Mike Simmons, shaking his hand. Mike's sister, the widow Martha McAllister, looked on eagerly.

"Then it's settled," said Mike in Chinook, patting Sluggia on the arm with his other hand. Martha spotted Mary and shot Mike a warning look, causing him to drop Sluggia's hand, and turn to face Mary.

"Good mornin'," he boomed overloud in English, and he grinned his crooked-toothed grin like a boy caught licking the frosting. "Did you sleep good, Mary?" he inquired. Martha translated into *Whulshootseed*.

Yes, she had slept very well, and they had no need to keep secrets from her. She resented it, but she knew enough to bide her time. She had little doubt she could wheedle it out of Sluggia. Meanwhile, the big grey-bearded bear, Simmons, was prattling on about what a great day it was for the Nisquallies. Mary just had time for a cup of the white man's bitter coffee with some bread and jam, before she and Sluggia were swept along with Mike, his wife Lizzie, and sister Martha, out the door and into canoes.

They ran the quick-flowing Little Deschutes into Budd Inlet, where they joined bewhiskered white men in frock coats aboard the steam-belching canoe, *Active*. Mary stood in the bow to feel the wind whip her long black hair. They outpaced the orcas playing off McNeil Island, steamed at breakneck speed around the horn of Fox Island through Hale Passage, and into the little inlet in front of the temporary Nisqually Reservation.

All this fanfare just to dump us in the prison camp? That didn't seem quite right, as Sluggia led Mary up to a small speaker's platform decked out in red-white-and-blue bunting, in front of which sat the several hundred remaining members of the Nisqually tribe. It seemed from their settled expressions that the tribe had been waiting for a long time. The faces in the crowd were familiar, yet alien, drained by long months of captivity.

Mary was shown to a chair next to a small fidgety man with hazel eyes, that flitted about like honey bees in clover. "What is all this?" she whispered to Sluggia.

"You'll see," said Sluggia.

Mike Simmons pressed his gut to the small podium, and gripped it with massive arms, until his dominating presence quieted the crowd. "Nisqually people, listen real good!" cried Mike in English. A young Volunteer translated into *Whulshootseed*. "Governor Stevens has come to bring you great news. Governor."

Mary jumped right along with the little man beside her, who took the podium. *This runt is Stevens?* She'd barely recovered when she heard her own name called in the Governor's ringing countertenor. Before she knew what was happening, she was at the podium, sandwiched between Sluggia and Stevens, gazing out at the crowd.

"Mary, wife of your Chief," the Governor was saying. "Not the old Chief, who led your friends and family to destruction. Here, by her side, is your new *Tyee*, Chief Sluggia. Sluggia and Mary are here to welcome this glorious day with you, and to lead you, their people, to your permanent reservation."

Mary followed the translation carefully. So this was the big secret. No need to keep it from her. Now she admired Sluggia's wiles almost as much as his strong, hard body. She slipped her arm around his waist, and together they waved to their people, who stared blankly back.

"The war is over," the Governor was saying, "the renegades have been defeated. You were wise to stay out of the fight. You were wise to trust me like a father. *Tyee* Stevens always takes care of those who are loyal to me. And so, I have decided that you Nisquallies who stayed loyal should be rewarded. That is why I now grant you a new reservation, one so large that it could fit four of the old reservations inside it. And because I want the loyal Nisqually people to live in peace and prosperity, I have decided that your new reservation should be along the Nisqually River, by Muck Creek."

As the words were translated, slack jaws firmed with wonder, dulled eyes rekindled, spines straightened and shoulders unfurled. The people stood, their cheers building louder and louder. The people hugged one another, danced about, raised their fists, cried to the heavens with joy. Victory! Victory at last! Even as they'd given up, *Sah-hah-lee Tyee* had not abandoned them.

Then one man who'd sat way to the back and never stood to cheer, called out in a voice deep and clear: "What about Chief Leschi?" The cheering died, as the question was translated back to the Governor. For a moment, many feared that with this impertinence, the Governor might change his mind. Instead, Stevens turned the question over to Sluggia, who spoke his first words as Chief.

"My Uncle had his day. He led our people to ruin, then crossed the mountains with his tail between his legs. I offer you and your children a good life on the river. Those who prefer poverty and disgrace, go follow Leschi, if you can find him. The rest, follow me!"

There was not one who chose to follow Leschi. Still, Mary was not blind to what every Nisqually whispered: had Leschi not fought for them, they would not be returning to the river they loved.

In Mary's dreams that night, Kwahnesum opened her stomach yet again, releasing snakes that struck at Mary with bared fangs, until she managed to scream herself awake. She lay panting, safe beside Chief Sluggia in a camp on the Nisqually Delta.

"*Ssshhhh*, be quiet woman. Are you not the wife of a Chief?" scolded Sluggia, half-asleep.

Yes, I am.

6

Leschi kissed Ann so lightly, his lips were like the wash of moon on her forehead. Even so, her eyes popped opened. "You are going away," she said, before he had a chance to lie.

He nodded. "I have no choice. It is for all our people."

All our people, or Mary? thought Ann, who'd seen the look in Leschi's eyes when Wahoolit brought news that Second Wife was still alive. She rose silently, checked Leschi's bags, produced pemmican cakes, Boston salt pork, and biscuits, to add to his meager stores. She made sure his skin was filled with fresh water. Then she began to pack her own gear.

He stopped her with a hand on her shoulder. "It is too dangerous," he whispered.

She turned her face to his. Her ruddy cheeks and the lines spreading from her eyes and mouth, were a map of all their travails. How could men be so foolish? "Will it be safer to leave me to sneak along behind, alone?"

As Ann made the final hurried preparations for their departure, Leschi took a moment to memorize the familiar broad nose, and friendly wide mouth, of his brother, deep in sleep. It was hard to leave Quiemuth without saying farewell, but Leschi knew that if he woke him, he would insist on coming. Leschi did not have the heart to quell Moonya and Kiya's newfound joy. "I am no longer afraid," Leschi whispered to his brother. "Please, forgive me for going without you," he added.

It would be difficult to obtain horses. The stable gate was guarded all night, and therefore out of the question. They decided to go after the big military Morgans ridden by the sentries, who tied up their mounts outside the guard house whenever they stepped inside for a break. It was audacious, but in a way perfect. The horses were saddled and easily spirited away, and it gave them a head start while the sentries sought fresh mounts. True, there were always other sentries out on the perimeter, but they would have to take their chances with that. The sentries' main focus was keeping people out, not in.

Leschi and Ann waited in the sage as two sentries tied their mounts, and stepped inside the guard house. Moving quickly, they unwrapped the reins and slipped into the stiff, uncomfortable Grimsley saddles with the ostentatious brass pommels favored by the War Department. Whispering softly, they walked, then trotted, then cantered the beasts away into the night.

They didn't dare break into a full gallop in the moonlight on such uneven terrain. They feared a stumble or worse, a broken leg. As the first taste of freedom shocked the heavy breath of captivity from their lungs, they heard a sharp call: "Who goes there?" It came from off to their left; Leschi pulled up the reins, straining in the darkness to make out a man-horse-rifle silhouette of deeper darkness. Leschi was on the verge of risking a wild gallop, when to his astonishment Ann spoke in a deep voice: "Chief Leschi."

"Go on, I'm takin' a break," said the shadow man, who passed within thirty yards on his way in.

They had topped Manastash ridge by the time the alarm sounded. Quickly, they disappeared into the vast spiderweb of ridges leading towards the Cascades. They rode through creeks and doubled back to throw trackers off their trail, then made camp just before sunrise at Wenas Creek, where Leschi recovered his rifle. Snuggled together in one blanket against the chill of a late summer dawn, Leschi asked the question on his mind for the whole night's ride: "How did we got past that sentry?"

"At night, while you sleep, I listen," replied Ann. "I like the song of the coyote. Like us, he is a wolf driven from his home, who cries all night, remembering. Each night, I have heard the sentries exchange their passwords. Some nights it is '*wool socks*,'" she said, stumbling a bit on the English. "Most recently, they have chosen to honor you; or perhaps it is no honor."

"I am lucky to have you along."

"It is not luck, my husband. It is what *Sah-hah-lee Tyee* wishes."

"It is what I wish, too," said Leschi. He kissed her for the second time that night, this time more deeply. He pulled her close, and with wonder their bodies followed the long-abandoned path to passion, as if they'd walked it only yesterday.

They slept until the sun set behind the mountains, then began the arduous re-tracing of their steps back across the Naches Pass. Unlike before, they were fed and rested, and hard cold and snow did not lie on the land, except at the highest elevations. The rivers were icy as always, but the days still held warmth. Roots and berries were plentiful, and Leschi shot rabbits and a buck for their dinners. When at last they reached the White River, they were delighted to find the big, dark spotted Grandfather Chinook, waiting there to greet them. That far from *Whulge*, the salmon were too far gone to eat; they were hook-jawed spawners, whose rotting flesh fell off in chunks, as they died for the coming generation. These ancient Chinooks brought the promise of fresher fish below, and by the time they reached Mud Mountain, they had feasted again on the bright pink flesh that reminded them why they were still struggling for their way of life.

Had that way of life already died? The familiar lands between the White and Nisqually Rivers were all empty. Everywhere they wandered, over paths they knew like their own heartbeats, the people were gone. The rivers and meadows were deserted. The hunting camps were rotting, the longhouses burnt or overgrown, the fishing weirs tangled in weeds, or washed away.

Ann and Leschi exchanged their incriminating military mounts for dark Mustangs they found running free on South Prairie. Leschi hid the rifle again, so that anyone who spotted them would see just a broken down old Indian couple, wandering lost in the wilderness. But they could never be lost on this land; it was their spirits that were lost, as their horses headed straight for Mashel Village.

The Mashel River still played joyously in quick-running shallows. The falls still sang day and night. But there was no one to hear the song. The longhouses were burned to the ground. The bodies were gone, hoisted to the trees by Winyea, or eaten by wolves and bears. It was the terror that lingered; they could sense screams suspended in the air like an angry swarm of ghost bees that stung to the bone. In the small clearing where the children had played their last game of shinny, Leschi and Ann fell to their knees, and when that was not deep enough, to their bellies, dislodging beetles, millipedes, and spiders. They scraped at the loam, as if they could burrow their way to *Otlas-Skio* to pull back their children, hand by tiny hand.

Weeping, Leschi and Ann followed the path across stepping-stones, beneath the falls. Since time immemorial, the village had kept canoes hidden beyond the falls, for escape against surprise attack. As they crossed the stepping-stones, Ann doubled over, her stomach clenched in the grip of a sudden cramp. Leschi held her tight from behind, pressing the warmth of his hand into the spot. As she stood hunched over, Ann saw in the ripples of the stream a whiteness like the underbelly of a fish, but stationary, wedged into the rocks. She plunged her hand into the water, and brought up the mother-of-pearl handled obsidian knife Sara had given to Kwahnesum. They gazed upon the knife with reverence.

"This is where she died," whispered Leschi.

"We are on the right path," replied Ann. "She guides us."

"We are on the only path we could possibly follow," said Leschi, tucking the knife into his belt. "Men follow the river; the river follows no one."

They found the hidden canoes, selected a small one, and set off down the Nisqually. The beauty was heart-rending, bittersweet – and short-lived. Just above Muck Creek, their voyage ended a volley of gunfire. Bostons on the opposite bank had spotted their canoe, and cast aside their fishing poles for muskets. Balls slammed into the side of the canoe, capsizing them away from the shots. Leschi surfaced just in time to see Ann bobbing in the water a canoe length behind him. "GO!" she cried, then disappeared under water as lead from a second volley spit and splashed at her long, white hair. Like ancient bleached seaweed, Ann's hair whirlpooled with bright red blood, as it was sucked down. Leschi splashed frantically back through another hail of musket shot, but Ann was gone. The fishermen laughed as they reloaded. At the last moment, Leschi dove down under the next volley and swam hard underwater to catch the overturned canoe. Taking an occasional breath in the shelter of the killed canoe, Leschi drifted downstream, his tears salting the fresh waters of their beloved river.

Chapter Twenty-Three
Capture

1

Stevens stabbed at the cream envelope with his gold-plated letter opener. He'd been drinking heavily to blot out the memory of his disgrace before the Nisquallies. While the *Pioneer & Democrat* had been able to sell the change of policy to the public as an act of statesmanship, men of consequence understood perfectly well what had happened. Will Wallace, Frank Clark, and that turncoat, Charlie Eden, had seen to that.

Now the Governor held in his hand a new missive from his fair-weather friends in Washington City.

Sept. 12, 1856

His Excellency, Isaac I. Stevens, Governor, W.T.

Sir:

After careful consideration of your defense of martial law, the President cannot find a justification for that extreme measure. Nothing but direful necessity, involving the probable immediate overthrow of the civil government, could be alleged as excuse for superseding that government temporarily and substituting in its place an arbitrary, military rule. The recognition of such an inherent power in any functionary, even the Chief Executive, would be extremely dangerous to civil and practical liberty. Martial law can never be excused where its object is to prevent other officials from properly discharging their duties. This seems to have been the principal grounds on which you acted, and the President's imperative sense of duty is to express his distinct disapproval of your conduct.

I am, Sir, your obedient servant,

Wm. L. Marcy, Secretary of State.

"Mason!" cried Stevens, as Mason stepped into his office. "File this under 'T' for 'treason.' And take a message to our friend, Sluggia."

"Yes, Governor," said Mason, tucking Marcy's letter into a folder.

"Tell him I'm offering a fifty blanket reward for any information leading to the capture of Leschi – alive. You got that? I want him alive."

"Alive, Sir?" asked Mason, puzzled.

Stabbing his finger in the general direction of Mason's folder, the Governor exploded. "It says right there that we've got to live under the rule of the blasted Judges." Stevens looked down, wobbled a bit, then belched. "Well, all right. From this day forward, the Judges work for me."

2

There was something about the scraggly old Indian snooping about the store at Fort Nisqually, that triggered a spark of recognition in Edward Huggins. The old Indian was barely covered with tattered rags inadequate against the late October chill, his ribs stood in sharp relief against his chest, and his hair was long and matted. Nonetheless, there was a clarity to his dark eyes, an innate pride in his high brow and strong shoulders, that bespoke some inward grandeur. Huggins remembered that time long ago, when he and Dr. Tolmie introduced two strong Nisqually brothers to a skeptical crowd. He placed a young clerk at the till, then hurried out to fetch Dr. Tolmie.

By the time they returned, the Indian had persuaded the young clerk to trade a musket with balls and powder for a half-dozen pelts, though selling firearms to the Indians was now forbidden. "That will be all," Dr. Tolmie said to the clerk, who jumped six inches to realize it was the Chief Factor's hand on his shoulder.

"Sorry, Sir, I told him that it wasn't permitted, but ..." Meanwhile Leschi was stepping back, lowering his head so that his tangled hair covered his face.

"That's all right, son," said Dr. Tolmie. "Greater men than you or I have been hornswoggled by this bloke." He stepped around the counter and laid a hand on Leschi's arm. "I'll see you in my private quarters, old fellow," he said, guiding Leschi out of the store, across the grounds, and through the white picket fence to the Chief Factor's house. They settled in the parlor, at a table in front of a brick hearth set with a blazing fire. Leschi was so exhausted that he nearly fell asleep the moment he hit the chair. He had spent months skulking in the forest, mourning Ann. The exposure and anguish had taken a severe toll. Dr. Tolmie asked Jane for some soup, which Leschi devoured. Then he laid him on the leather settee, covered with a red wool blanket. "Don't worry old mate," said Tolmie, "you are safe here. We'll talk tomorrow."

How long Leschi slept, he did not know. He awakened briefly in utter darkness; again in the meager dawn of a rainy day. In his dreams he heard the happy voices of children, and the comfortable domestic chit-chat of another lifetime. Then he was in the twisting river, shots spraying about, as he reached for Ann but she went down, down, beyond reach, her slippery hand lost, as weeds entangled him, pulling him away.

When Leschi finally woke, he thought for a moment he was looking up at *Ta-co-bet*, but it was only a familiar halo of honey hair as Charlie helped the Chief into a steaming bath. Rested and clean, Leschi donned the fresh set of white man's scratchy wool pants, and the collarless cotton shirt laid out for him, over which he added a stiff fringed buckskin jacket. "You look like Daniel Boone," laughed Jane Tolmie. Leschi had no idea who Daniel Boone was.

After a dinner of blood pudding, beefsteak, and sugared turnips, the three men turned to business. "I never thought I'd see you again, Leschi," said the doctor, puffing on his pipe. "I should have known better."

"I am not so easy to get rid of, right *Challie?*"

"No, my Chief," said Charlie, smiling the golden smile which first captured Kwahnesum's heart.

"Tell me, *Challie,* did the Great *Tyee* in Washington City see our talking paper?" Eagerly, Charlie told Leschi the story of his meeting with the President, how at first it seemed a failure, then sowed the seeds for a welcome change in policy.

"I returned bearing secret orders from the President to the Governor. Within a few weeks, Stevens gave your people a new, bigger reservation by Muck Creek, along the river. It is the reservation for which you fought."

Leschi stood bolt upright, knocking over his chair behind him. Pulling Charlie up into his arms, he embraced him in a great bear hug. Though crying, Leschi's careworn face looked lighter than it had in years. For a moment, he was more the confident young man of the defense of Fort Nisqually, than the burdened statesman and warrior of recent times.

At length, Leschi found his voice. Holding Charlie in front of him, he said, "Kwahnesum would be proud, my son. You have become a big man."

Charlie, too, was overcome. "You know about Kwahnesum?"

Leschi nodded sadly.

"I only wish I had your powers of persuasion, Chief –"

"Father," corrected Leschi.

"Father," said Charlie. "That last night, at Kanasket's hideaway, I begged her to come home with me. But she would not."

"Do not blame yourself, my son," said Leschi softly. "I know too well where that path leads. Kwahnesum was a brave warrior for her people. She could no more run from who she was than a snake, shedding its skin, could become a salmon. Her ancestors have welcomed her to a land where there are no reservations."

When the two men sat down, Dr. Tolmie took up more immediate concerns. "Leschi," he said, "though I admire your courage, still I must ask, whatever possessed you to return to this side of the mountains?"

"Steven's Volunteers hunt me everywhere I go, my friend. When they cannot catch me, they take out their bloodlust on my cousins. I must speak with *Tyee* Stevens. I will flatter him with thanks for the return of our river, try to bury the hatchet of war once and for all. It is the only way that my people can live again in safety. Can you help me?"

"I want to help you, Leschi, of course," said Dr. Tolmie. "But I don't think meeting with the Governor will do any good."

"Maybe not, but I must try." Leschi laid a hand on his old friend's sleeve. "Even a vanquished foe is entitled to some dignity."

"Father, please, listen to Dr. Tolmie," pleaded Charlie. "If you go see Stevens, he'll take you prisoner. He still fears you above all others."

Leschi grabbed a large iron blade from the discarded tray of beef, and held it over his wrist. "I will cut off my right hand this very moment for the Governor, to prove that I will fight no more." His eyes shone with intensity.

"That is exactly what he fears," replied the doctor, as he gently removed the knife from Leschi's hand. "Not your power to fight, Leschi, but your power to move men. That's why it is no longer merely a question of killing you. He must discredit you first; then he will kill you."

"If it is my voice he fears, I will cut out my tongue," said Leschi, so intently that Dr. Tolmie believed it might be true. "I want nothing more of being Chief. I am ready to die." Then he told them of losing Ann, and his face emptied as if she had taken all light with her to the bottom of the river. "Tell Stevens he may take me if he wants. All I ask is that he call back his Volunteers, and let the red man live in peace."

The doctor ran his hand over the barren plain from which his hair had long since receded. "You have money that I hold here for you, credits against horses recovered by my agents from your lands. You could take it and go far away from here."

"No," said Leschi. "A man cannot outrun his own heart."

"All right," said Dr. Tolmie. "I will go speak to the Governor on your behalf, Leschi. I will see if I can arrange safe terms for a meeting. Meanwhile, I suggest that you lay very low. If Huggins could recognize you, others can too."

"Let me go with you, Father," begged Charlie. Leschi would not endanger him. The old Chief thanked then both, told them where he was camped, and slipped out that night under cover of darkness.

3

Leschi made his way back up the Nisqually to an old fishing camp near Horn Creek, where he and Quiemuth had fished with their father when they were boys. In later years, the brothers had sometimes taken their families to this place. As Sennatco had taught him, Leschi sat by the eddy on the bend of the river, his small sapling weir impeding a few salmon just long enough for him to snag one in a net of willow twine. His hands gutted the fish and prepared the fire of their own accord, while his mind relived the many stories his father had told them on this river bend. His favorite was the tale of how Coyote defeated the monster *Nashlah*, who had been eating all the animal people. Coyote bit the head off a snake, snuck up on *Nashlah* when he was sound asleep, and tied the head to *Nashlah's* own tail. When *Nashlah* awoke and saw the snake, he gobbled him down, swallowing himself in the process. As he turned inside out, all the animal people he'd eaten jumped to safety on the riverbank. "The very same riverbank you're sitting on right now," is how his father had always ended the tale, transforming the ordinary bear grass and alders along the shore, into the stuff of legend.

Leschi was pondering Coyote's strategy when he heard the snap of a footfall in the woods nearby. With one motion, he threw dirt on his little campfire and rolled under a nearby fir, gripping Kwahnesum's obsidian knife in his hand. Two men stepped into the clearing and crossed quickly to the fire pit, where one knelt and extended his hand, feeling the hotness of coals beneath the dirt. He kicked the dirt aside. The glow illuminated the familiar oval eyes of Leschi's departed sister.

"Uncle," called Sluggia, scanning the outer ring of trees, "it is only me, your nephew, with my friend, Elikuka. You remember Elikuka, eldest son of the medicine man?"

Leschi waited until the two young men were facing away before he rolled out from under the fir tree and stood, his hand still holding the knife. "Sluggia!" he shouted, and they jumped and spun, drawing knives of their own. Then Sluggia relaxed. He sheathed his knife, and smiled. His friend, Elikuka, followed suit.

"Uncle," cried Sluggia, extending his hands as if to slick him down. Leschi did not withdraw his blade. Sluggia's hands dropped, but he maintained his good humor. "I can understand your wariness, Uncle, but I assure you that I mean you no harm. I have come to help you. I heard that you wish to speak with the Governor, isn't that so?"

Leschi nodded.

"Well, then, I can arrange it." Sluggia paused, but seeing Leschi was determined to remain silent, he continued. "I have influence now. I am Chief. Did you know that?"

"Our people chose you?" asked Leschi, pointedly.

Sluggia ignored the question. "I speak often with the white *Tyees*. I have spoken with Dr. Tolmie and the Governor. The Governor says he is willing to discuss terms by which you could surrender yourself, and live in peace."

Despite the mention of Dr. Tolmie's name, Leschi remained cautious. "Show me I can trust you," he said. "Are you the same man who tried to cheat your cousin Owhi, when the stakes were much lower than they are today? What would you do to be rid of a rival to the title of Chief of the Nisquallies?"

Sluggia shrugged his shoulders, as if the whole thing were a matter of complete indifference to him. "If I wanted you out of the way, Uncle, I could kill you on the spot. You were justly praised for strength in your day, but we are two in our prime, and you are only one." Sluggia looked him over. "Not so prime, I might add."

Bristling, Leschi tightened his grip on the knife. "Prime enough to kill you first," he spat.

Sluggia gave him a nervous smile. "I mean no offense," he said. "I only wish to set your mind at ease. The fact that we do not attack must count for something, Uncle." He paused. "If you will not believe me, believe another." At a signal, Mary stepped forth from a grove of hemlocks at the far side of the clearing. Her smooth high cheekbones and oyster eyes caught the light of the coals, reflecting warmth and comfort. She was still the lithe salamander she'd been the first day he'd ever set eyes on her, yet she had grown too, for now she was a woman.

"Mary!" cried Leschi, overcome by the passion her proximity always stirred, despite knowing that she had broken her vows as a wife. She ran to him and kissed his cheek.

"I heard that you survived," said Leschi, stroking her long, soft hair with one hand, while still brandishing the obsidian knife with the other.

"I escaped, my Chief," she whispered. Then she told him the details of Kwahnesum's courageous death.

"With this very knife," marveled Leschi. "Then it must never draw blood from our own people again." He kissed the black blade before sheathing it.

Sluggia smiled, stepping to within arm's length. "Tell him, Mary. Tell him of the Governor's offer."

Leschi took Mary by the chin, guiding her eyes to meet his. "If this is so," he said, "it is everything I could wish."

Mary forced a tight smile across her lips, but her eyes were crying, *beware! beware!*

"Go ahead, Mary, tell him!" commanded Sluggia.

She shook her head free, cried, "Run husband! It's a trap!" Leschi stood his ground long enough to block the blow aimed at her head, and in saving Mary he lost the moment of escape. In an instant, Leschi was tackled by the two young men. Though he managed to blacken Sluggia's eye and bloody Elikuka's nose, he was kicked and battered, hog tied, then thrown across the saddle of a waiting horse. Though Leschi's bruised ribs cried out after an hour of bouncing against that saddle, the pain was nothing compared to the revulsion he felt when he was dumped at the feet of Mike Simmons.

"Well, lookee-here what the cat dragged in," cackled Simmons with glee. He slapped Sluggia on the back, eliciting a grimace of pain. "You'll getcher fifty blankets tomorrow, Sluggo." In the hollow pit of his stomach, Sluggia knew that even if it were a hundred hundred blankets, he'd never be warm again.

4

The three Stevens sisters watched the captured Indian chief through early-morning eyes, wide with wonder. Though Hazard had seen him at Medicine Creek, for the girls this was their first glimpse of the monster, Leschi. Sue clung to Kate's hand; though Kate was now four years old, Sue still considered her the baby. Maude, a robust and fearless six, walked right up to Leschi, whose hands were bound behind him. Leschi's lip was swollen and cracked. A bit of dried blood clung to his chin.

"Does it hurt?" she asked in English.

"He can't understand you," said Hazard.

The big Indian Grandfather looked down at her with kindly eyes, and shook his head, no.

A hastily dressed Governor stumbled down the stairs. "Hazard, would you please take your sisters to the kitchen?" he asked in a mild voice. "I think you'll find mama there, fixing porridge."

Meg peeked out from a doorway at the far end of the hall, gave a little cry, and ran out to shoo her children away. But Maude hung back, eyes glued to the Indian Chief. Stevens knelt and tenderly took Maude's hand. "What's the matter, Pumpkin?"

"Is this the bad man who hurt everyone?"

The Governor nodded gravely. "Yes, Pumpkin."

"He's hurt, Daddy."

"I'll take care of him, Sweetie, don't worry." He smoothed her hair absent-mindedly. "Now go to your mother. Mama might need help with breakfast." He kissed her on the forehead where she often held worry. With a little sigh, it drained away. Stevens watched protectively as she padded down the hall. Even though he'd anticipated this triumph for many long months, he delayed it the extra few moments it took for Maude to get all the way out of sight.

Then the Governor stood, glowing with exultation. "Great job, Mike, I won't forget this." Mike puffed out his chest. "They're still working in there," said Stevens, pointing back at his new office, half-papered in blue and gold stripes. "I'll see the prisoner in town. Get Mason to interpret." Then he remembered his promise to Maude. "And Mike," he added, laying a hand on the sleeve of Simmons' wool greatcoat, "help him clean up his lip."

Mike shot Stevens a quizzical look, then nodded and yanked Leschi away from the door of the Governor's grand mansion. With a small detail of Volunteers commanded by Colonel Blunt himself, Mike led the prisoner past the tattered luminaria, remnants of the previous night's housewarming party, down the hill and through the town, to the smelly warren of Territorial offices on the shore. Although it was barely past dawn, word of Leschi's capture had electrified the town. The muddy streets were lined with gawkers, eager to catch a glimpse of the notorious enemy Chief.

Stevens giddily set in motion plans that had been in place for weeks, only awaiting the protagonist. Though it was already Friday, he dispatched Simmons to notify Judge Chenoweth that he wanted Leschi tried for murder at a special session of Court, that very Monday, November 17, 1856. The Grand Jury would convene on Saturday, with Tony Rabbeson as its foreman. Nothing would be left to chance.

This interview, with himself as victor and Leschi as the vanquished, had been the Governor's fondest wish, his nightly dream, for months. Stevens had not seen Leschi face-to-face since Christmas Day, 1854, at Medicine Creek. At last, here was Leschi, hands bound, standing directly across the Governor's patched, dented, blood-stained desk. The office was littered with half-filled crates.

Stevens glared in silence, Mason to one side, Blunt to the other. Blunt was just menacing enough to ensure that Leschi would not try anything foolish. Stevens meant his silent contemplation of the prisoner to be intimidating, but Leschi foiled him by speaking first. "You have a beautiful family, Governor," he said in *Whulshootseed*. "Bright, healthy children, and a woman with skin like the snow lily." Mason interpreted, blushing slightly at the description of Meg.

"It is kind of you to say so," responded Stevens, diplomatically. "I have recently had the pleasure of meeting your former wife, Mary. As native women go, she is a beauty."

Leschi chose to ignore the barbs, inclining his head slightly. *How straight he holds himself*, thought Mason. *As though he were not the captive.*

"And the rest of your family," pressed the Governor without mercy, "I trust that they are well?"

Leschi's eyes were cool. He was determined not to betray a hint of the fresh pain in his ribs, or the loss in his heart. "My brother is well, thank-you," he responded in a businesslike tone. "But many in my family, in my tribe, amongst all the tribes on both sides of the great mountains, have lost loved ones. We have paid a heavy price in this war."

"It is not only your people who have suffered, Leschi," said the Governor. "Every week I have to comfort the families of those who will never return."

"It is a burden we share as leaders," replied Leschi. "A burden we might yet atone for," he added, with a hopeful rise of a brow.

"You and your people signed a solemn treaty, Leschi," said the Governor, his voice hard. "Then you struck first, killing your own friend, Jim McAllister, killing hapless express riders, slaughtering innocent settlers, including women and children." Stevens paused, giving Leschi a chance to dispute these plain facts. When Leschi said nothing, the Governor continued. "I bear no burden. I have nothing to atone for. I did only what was necessary to defend my people. Look to your own conscience, Leschi. You should never have torn up that commission. You should never have renounced the treaty. Had you trusted in me, you could be living in peace with your people on the river, instead of sitting here, a prisoner, awaiting trial for murder."

Stevens and Mason expected the flow of eloquence they had heard at Medicine Creek. Leschi surprised them both.

"You are right, *Tyee*, I should have trusted you," he said. "I should never have torn up the commission. I acted out of anger and fear. Nothing good could come of it."

Stevens wasn't satisfied. He wanted a fight; he wanted to gloat. For all Leschi's meekness, it did not feel like he was beaten. Stevens rose in anger, determined to make Leschi see the utter hopelessness of his situation. "That's right, Leschi. Many are dead because of your foolishness, including your own daughter." Blunt watched Leschi intently. Mason balked at the translation, but after a nasty glance from Stevens he spoke the words, giving them a gentler tone.

"Yes," replied Leschi mildly. "We both know how painful it is to lose a daughter."

How could he know of Virginia? The Governor dropped into his seat, knocked back by the vision of the eyes he loved trapped in that fevered body, trusting him to make everything better.

"*Govenol*," said Leschi, "what happens to me now is unimportant. I am finished. What is important is your heart, because you are still a powerful man. I wish to thank you for giving back to my people a piece of our sacred river. That river is our mother and our daughter. Thanks to you, our tribe lives again."

Stevens nodded blankly. Leschi was mocking him. He would not sit here and suffer Leschi's thanks for giving the enemy back their life. Who could bring Virginia back? Or his mother? No one, not this old fool across the desk, not Meg, not the President nor any office or honor he could win. Surely not any of this *siwash* hocus-pocus about spirits in the river.

Leschi was still talking, but Stevens barely listened. "Now your Jesus and our Great Spirit call upon you to stop hunting my people," he was saying. "We are not wolves. We are men like yourselves, women like your beautiful wife, children like your fine children. Take me, do as you will with me, but spare my people."

How quickly Stevens had tired of this interview. It had not gone as planned, and he was determined to wrap it up. "I don't need to take you, Leschi," snapped the Governor. "I've already got you. I don't think you're in any position to bargain. Tomorrow, you will be charged with the murder of A.B. Moses. You will be taken to Steilacoom, and tried on Monday – that's three suns. After you are found guilty, you will be hung like the common criminal you are. Do you understand?"

"Yes," said Leschi, "I understand. You explained it to me at Medicine Creek, when you said, 'the Great Father does not bargain with his children.' Has all the suffering not convinced you that this was a mistake, that it is still a mistake today?"

"GET HIM OUT OF HERE!" cried the Governor. Leschi was yanked roughly from the room by Blunt.

"Why Ben Moses?" asked Mason, as soon as Leschi was out of earshot. "Why not the White River settlers?"

"Witnesses. There aren't any reliable ones for the massacre."

"What about Jim McAllister?" asked Mason.

"Jimmy got cold feet about testifying," replied the Governor. "Besides, you will find on your desk a nice contribution to my campaign fund from Ben's brother, Jackson. Now, get moving on this trial!" Mason departed with his most maddening smile, the one that managed to be simultaneously unctuous and bemused. Though it was barely nine in the morning, Stevens took a pull on his pocket flask.

Then a shot rang out.

The driftwood casement over the door shattered inches above the heads of Blunt and Leschi. Blunt grabbed Leschi by his bound arms, using him as a shield while he swept the crowd with his pistol. Blunt raised the barrel and fired a warning shot in the air. "DISPERSE!" he commanded. All but one did – a woman across the street, who calmly loaded a fresh charge in her breech-loading rifle. Blunt pulled Leschi back inside, peeked out the doorway to be sure his eyes were not deceiving him, then pulled his head back inside quick as a turtle under a horse.

The Governor came roaring out of his office. "Who's that shooting?" asked Stevens.

"A McAllister, Sir," said Blunt.

"Jimmy?"

"No, Sir; Martha."

"Martha?" said Stevens.

"She's right out there, plain as day. Should we arrest her?"

"Are you crazy?" barked Stevens. "That's Mike's sister." The Governor stepped into the doorway. There was Martha McAllister, sighting down the barrel of a smoking Sharp's rifle.

"Mrs. McAllister."

"Step aside, Governor."

"Look, Martha, I can understand –"

"No, you cain't."

"Well," allowed Stevens, "you're probably right. But why don't you let us handle this the right way? We have to give him a trial, you know that."

Martha said nothing, but she lowered the rifle to her hip. "Cain't believe I missed the bastard," she confided.

"It's a good thing," said Stevens. "Now, go on up to the new house. Meg'll give you something to eat."

Martha nodded. "I'll see you at the hangin'." She shouldered the rifle, turned and walked away.

V

Justice & Mercy

(November 15, 1856 – February 19, 1858)

Chapter Twenty-Four
Trial

1

The little Steilacoom courthouse so recently under siege by its own troops, was now packed to the rafters with excited spectators, eager to watch the dreaded Chief of the renegades receive the full measure of American justice. Some were merely curious; others sought revenge for the loss of loved ones or friends in the recent war. Two Sheriff's deputies policed the doorway, collecting firearms. Though word had only just gotten out on Saturday that this trial was to be held, already there were twice as many spectators outside, as fit within the confines of the courthouse. Food and trinket hawkers, intermixed with spontaneous games and fiddle music, lent a county fair atmosphere to the scene.

The front row behind the prosecution was reserved for prominent victims. To the far left, by the wall, sat Mary Slaughter, her little fatherless boy, Will Junior, dozing at her breast. To her right sat Martha McAllister, her face drawn tight as a bear trap, a blood-stained hankie balled in her fist. Next was Jimmy, glum and pale, and his sister Ainsley – now officially Mrs. Joseph Bunting – looking smart, yet duly mournful, in a black wool cape over a gown trimmed with lingerie collar and cuffs. To Mrs. Bunting's side sat Mr. Bunting, in silver-trimmed black from head to toe. To his right and therefore immediately behind the prosecutor, sat the family of the alleged murder victim, Jackson Moses, his wife and two children. Jackson, wearing Ben's favorite knit blue and black yarmulke, toyed absent-mindedly with the stub where his left ear used to be. On the central aisle next to Jackson sat Governor Stevens himself, tucked into a smart frock coat that accentuated his broad shoulders, muscular arms, and tight hips. His bright hazel eyes were pivoting every which way, flashing triumphant greetings around the room.

"*Oyez, oyez, oyez,* the United States District Court for the Third District of Washington Territory, holden at Steilacoom, is now in special session, the Honorable F.A. Chenoweth, United States District Judge, presiding. All rise!" cried Mr. Chapman. Leschi felt himself lifted from his seat by his attorney, Frank Clark. The buzz of strange words confused him; though he was comforted to have Dr. Tolmie immediately behind him, interpreting the proceedings, there simply were no words in *Whulshootseed* for much of what was going on. Leschi turned for a minute to nod at Charlie Eden, who gave him a friendly golden-haired smile and wink. Behind Charlie stretched a vast desert of hostile white faces.

Dr. Tolmie had read Leschi the indictment, a nearly incomprehensible document that spit words as plentiful as stars in the sky, and seemingly as isolated from one another. Leschi had gleaned this much: he was charged with shooting Abram Benton Moses *feloniously* and with *malice aforethought*, which were magic incantations. The incantations were repeated at key moments, like when he was accused of loading the gun, or aiming it, or pulling the trigger, or causing a leaden ball to fly through the air and penetrate the skin of Mr. Moses, causing him to die. He didn't remember Mr. Moses from the wedding; wouldn't have recognized him if he was alive and walked into the courthouse. He was sorry Mr. Moses was dead, especially since he'd been Charlie's friend. He knew he'd pointed his gun at various soldiers during this war, and he'd managed to kill a few of them. Based on where they said Moses had been killed, however, Leschi was sure he hadn't killed him. Besides, any killing he'd done was no different from the Boston soldiers. It wasn't with *malice aforethought* unless that meant trying to kill the enemy during war. If that was *malice aforethought*, then sure, he had it, just like the Governor, and every soldier from Colonel Casey on down the line.

"Mr. Clark," said the Judge, when everyone was seated. "Aren't you supposed to be at the prosecution table?"

"Your Honor," said Clark, rising, "I have a conflict in this matter, as I was previously engaged on behalf of Mr. Leschi. The prosecution is in able hands with Mr. Dandy Pritchard, I believe."

The well-fed squirrel stood, and inclined his hair-oiled widow's peak towards the bench. For the occasion, Mr. Pritchard was sporting a tight frock coat, velvet waistcoat, and yellow silk jabot with a diamond stickpin. "I am honored to do this duty for the People of Washington Territory," he said.

"Very well," said Judge Chenoweth. "We are convened to hear an indictment whereby the Indian Leschi is charged with felonious murder with malice aforethought on the person of Abram Benton Moses, late sheriff of Thurston County. Are there any objections to the jury panel, Gentlemen?"

"May I inquire?" asked Mr. Pritchard. At a nod of Judge Chenoweth's pink dome, he sidled up to the railing of the jury box. "Gentlemen, thank-you for your service," he groveled. *Like we had a choice*, thought Bill Kinkaid, easily the most senior of the twelve men who'd been summoned on the Lord's Sabbath to travel to Steilacoom. "I have only one question for you, but it is of the utmost importance," said Mr. Pritchard, his stick-pin glowing. "This is a capital case. Are there any amongst you who harbor any religious or other scruple against the provision of the law which sets the penalty for murder as hanging by the neck until dead?" He pounded the railing at the word "dead," so that it lingered in the ensuing silence. Not a man flinched from his glare.

"Very good," said Mr. Pritchard, "this panel will do for the People."

"Mr. Clark?" said the Judge. Clark scanned the faces on the box, lighting particularly upon the earnest woodsman, Ezra Meeker, who'd stood shoulder-to-shoulder with him in defense of this very courthouse. "Any of you gentlemen feel that an Injun ain't entitled to American justice, same as any white man?"

Well, no, now that you mention it, they wouldn't own up to that.

"Any feel that a soldier in time of war who shoots the enemy is guilty of murder?"

Of course not.

Clark looked back to the bench. "These good folk'll do just fine, Your Honor."

"Call your first witness, Mr. Pritchard."

"The People call Mr. Antonio B. Rabbeson."

Tony stepped to the witness box in his best starched white shirt, and creased black trousers, looking like a corpse sprung from the casket. Clark was on his feet. "Now wait just a minute, Your Honor," cried Clark. "This Gentleman's the foreman of the Grand Jury that indicted my client. I don't rightly see how he could testify."

"Why not?" asked Chenoweth.

Why not, indeed? "Well, maybe he can, but then the whole pig-headed indictment is no good, 'cause he must have voted it out based on his own testimony."

Mr. Pritchard rose slowly as if the burdensome task of explaining the a-b-c's of criminal procedure was almost too painful to endure. "What transpired before the Grand Jury is secret," he said, looking down his nose. "Defense counsel was not present, and has no knowledge of it. The indictment is good on its face, and cannot be examined here. There is no rule of evidence disqualifying this witness."

Chenoweth looked out across the stern faces of the spectators, already half lynch mob. "I agree," said the Judge. He had no intention of allowing this trial to be derailed over a technicality.

Tony shot a quick smirk at Clark, which he wiped off his face as he put his hand on the Bible. "Do you solemnly swear that the evidence you are about to give shall be the truth, the whole truth, and nothing but the truth, so help you God?" droned Chapman, in a manner that drained the words of all import.

"Yes, Sir," said Tony in his best Sunday-school voice. As he spoke the oath, he looked past Pritchard to Governor Stevens. He didn't quite nod, but the greeting was plain to anyone with eyes to see it.

Tony was seated. "State your name, please, Sir," began Mr. Pritchard.

"Anthony B. Rabbeson."

"Where do you stake your claim, Mr. Rabbeson?"

"By Union Mill, on Long Lake."

"Prior to the recent disturbance with the Indians, were you familiar with an Indian known as Leschi?"

"You mean the feller sittin' over there?" asked Tony, pointing at the defendant. "Yes, Sir, he didn't live but six or seven miles from my claim. I'd seen him about. Didn't know his name, then. Called him Staub."

"Did you have occasion to be up at Connell's Prairie, October 31 of last year?"

"Yes, Sir."

"Could you tell the jury what happened when you first got to Connell's Prairie?"

"Well, Sir, there was seven of us ridin' down from the east on the Military Road. We come out to the clearing and first thing we see is Connell's house and barn burnt down, still smolderin'. Then we see a bunch of redskins milling about, so we figure there's trouble."

"Did you recognize any of those redskins?"

"Leschi was there. I'm not sure 'bout the other ones."

"Was anything said?"

"We just chewed the fat, that's all. They claimed to be peaceful, and we warn't eager to put it to the test, seein' as how they outnumbered us pretty good. So we trotted off down the road, and quick as we got out of sight, we skee-daddled."

"Who was 'we'?"

"Well, let's see; Bill Tidd was there, prob'ly up front with Doc Burns, Andrew Bradley, and a young feller name of Bright; and Mr. Ben Moses was right in front of me; and Mr. Miles behind me."

"What happened next?"

"We made a pretty good gallop across the meadow, maybe three-quarters of a mile or so, before we hit a swamp. Now, them buggers took one of them Injun shortcuts. I seen 'em plain as day, off to the right, they stepped right out of the wood, leveled their muskets, and fired on us."

"You saw who?"

Tony pointed at Leschi. "That man, right there. He was wearin' a big felt hat, same as when we first seen him."

"What happened next?"

"I returned fire, then saw that Mr. Miles was down, so I went back to help him. Warn't no use, he was already dead. So I turned and rode like the dickens 'bout another mile before I seen poor Ben Moses, slumped in his saddle, up ahead."

"What had happened to him?"

"Leschi'd shot him clean through," said Tony. "He told me to go ahead, save my skin, but I ain't that kinda feller. I helped him off to the side of the trail, hid him good, made him as comfortable as possible. Then I had to go, 'cause I figured the other boys needed me; but I promised him I'd come back fer him."

"Then what?"

"We kilt us some Injuns, that's what," bragged Tony, though he'd arrived only after the deed was done. A murmur of approval spread across the room. "Then we went back fer Ben, but he was too far gone. They brought him back in later, dead."

"Anything else?"

"No, Sir. His last words were, 'Boys, if you git outa this alive, remember me!' I'm sure gonna remember him. He was a good man."

"No further questions."

Ben's sister-in-law and two nieces were weeping softly. Jackson's head was bent, jaw rigid, Ben's Star of David locket gripped between thumb and forefinger. There was a hush in the courtroom. Ben Moses would get his wish. He would be remembered.

2

Frank Clark looked relaxed in a loose-fitting cutaway jacket and drooping bow-tie, as he stood to begin the most important examination of his career. Everyone knew what he was capable of, for which they despised and adored him like lovers at the end of an affair. On this day, however, the desire to see him fail trumped the craving to see a witness humiliated.

Great lawyers are like squid; blind to much of the world, they nonetheless exquisitely sense the medium in which they swim. Clark was no exception.

He knew that Rabbeson was lying, but that no one cared. Impeachment was not his strategy as he sauntered up to the witness.

"Morning, Mr. Rabbeson," he said.

Tony nodded. He wasn't about to utter one unnecessary word.

"Or should I say, Captain Rabbeson?" Clark raised an eyebrow.

"Yes, Sir."

"You are a Captain of the Washington Territorial Volunteers?"

"Yes, Sir."

"You were a Captain on October 31, 1855?"

"Yes, Sir."

"And Abram Benton Moses, the deceased; was he also a member of the Volunteers?"

"Yes, Sir."

"At what rank?"

"Corporal, Sir."

"And Mr. Miles as well – also a Volunteer?"

"Yes, Sir. A Lieutenant."

"And Mr. Tidd?"

"Regular Army, Sir."

"In fact, all seven of you were either U.S. Army or members of the Washington Territorial Volunteers back on October 31st last year?"

Tony nodded affirmatively.

"I'm sorry," said Clark, putting a hand to his ear, "I didn't get that."

"Yes, Sir," growled Tony, twice too loud.

Clark smiled innocently at the jury. "Captain Rabbeson, though you've got a nice white shirt on today, you were wearing something a little different that day, weren't you?"

"Yes, Sir."

"You were wearing the tan uniform jacket of the Volunteers, weren't you?"

"Yes, Sir."

"All of your party were wearing that uniform, or army blues, isn't that right?"

"All 'cept Doc Burns, yes, Sir."

"And why not Doc Burns?"

"Too fat; he popped his buttons clear off." A few laughs.

"But Corporal Moses and Lieutenant Miles were in uniform, right?"

"Yes, Sir."

"They were in uniform when they were shot, correct?"

"Yes, Sir."

"Were you boys out for a pleasure ride?"

Pleasure ride, hell no! "I don't get your meaning."

"Why were you up to Connell's Prairie, Captain Rabbeson?"

"We was detailed to ride under the command of Lieutenant Slaughter, regular Army, to join up with forces engaging the Yakamas. When we heard that there was some problem over there, the Lieutenant ordered me'n the other boys to carry dispatches back to Fort Steilacoom."

"So you boys were fightin' Injuns?"

"Yes, Sir."

"And at the time that Corporal Moses and Lieutenant Miles were shot, you were carrying military dispatches from one regular Army officer to another?"

"Yes, Sir."

"Dispatches about the war with the Indians?"

"Yes, Sir."

"Nothing further."

"Redirect, Mr. Pritchard?" asked the Judge.

Pritchard rose. "What war against what Indians?" he asked.

"The war against the Yakamas."

"On the east side of the mountains?"

"Yes, Sir."

"Nothing further."

"The witness may step down," said the Judge. Tony looked relieved as he scampered away from the witness box.

"That'll do it," announced Pritchard. Quick and easy, the Governor had instructed. They were confident that there wasn't a jury in the Territory that would acquit Leschi, no matter what the evidence. "The People rest."

"Mr. Clark?" asked the Judge.

Frank Clark was enjoying himself. Mr. Dandy Pritchard wasn't as dumb as he looked. He'd have to play his trump card.

"Defense calls Isaac I. Stevens to the stand."

3

As Ann went down under the water, she summoned her *tamanous*, the mighty Chinook, to guide her. With efficient strokes, she propelled herself into the weeds along the far side of the river. She was well hidden when she came up for her first breath. She peeked out just in time to see the overturned canoe bearing her husband to safety – she prayed – around the bend. Patiently, with the stillness and invisibility of the wary salmon, she drifted among the cattails and river rushes, embodying her Nisqually heritage. The Bostons scanned the rippling currents a minute longer. Satisfied that the Indian had been shot or drowned, they returned to fishing, drinking, and pissing in the river, occasionally throwing in an empty bottle and shattering it with musket fire. Ann stealthily crept out of the cold water, to lay shivering in the thin late afternoon sun. She touched her hand to the top of her head, and was surprised to find that it came back bloody. Finally, the Bostons packed up their belongings, dumped the rest of their garbage, and disappeared into the brush. After waiting a cautious interval, Ann stood, wavering unsteadily as the blood dripped down her face.

Betsy Edgar was taking in the wash when she sensed a presence, turned, and thought for a moment she'd come face to face with a *Zugwa*. It was only Ann, white as a Boston, dripping red deep as Devil's paintbrush. Dropping the clean sheets in the dirt, Betsy ran to catch Ann's fall.

The next few weeks were a blur, as Ann fought off the effects of the lead ball that had grazed her scalp. The fever passed thanks to Betsy and Alala's tender care, until the day came at last when Ann drifted comfortably in a copper tub, inhaling the steam of healing herbs and, after her bath, the tantalizing aroma of roast mutton. How wonderful to be hungry again. As she dried herself, marveling at the skin hanging slack off her bones, she was amazed to hear the sound of voices carried on *Laliad* – not just one or two, but many voices – singing one of Sara's old favorites:

> *The sun shines in your eyes, my dear,*
> *The moon glows in your breast,*
> *Sun and moon will still be here*
> *When we've gone to our rest, dear,*
> *When we've gone to our rest.*

It was the tribal women, returned to the new reservation on Muck Creek. Ann was so overjoyed that she could hardly believe it. Immediately she went out to join her friends, insisting on helping in everything – all the rebuilding, and restocking of foods for the winter – so much in a single day, that soon she collapsed with the effort.

Within another few weeks of careful nursing, Ann was closer again to momma bear than river sprite, having regained a good layer of fat to protect against the growing chill. She enjoyed the quiet domesticity of grinding the dried berries for pemmican, smoking the salmon, and weaving mats in preparation for winter. She enjoyed playing with John McLeod's daughters, Jane and Tupso, guiding them in the ancient art of basketry, telling them old tales, teaching them tribal songs. But as she sat in the new longhouse with her people, she knew her time of rest was drawing to a close. She had to find Leschi.

It was then that, as if by magic, the forest shadows yielded up the familiar faces of Quiemuth and Wahoolit. Though Quiemuth was ten summers Leschi's senior, he had never looked so old. Ann held him all the tighter for that, then fondly slicked down his once-powerful arms. Her face must have spoken the many questions she held inside, for Quiemuth laughed and began to explain. "After you and Leschi escaped, dear Sister, Colonel Wright marched our people down to the Columbia, and accompanied us on barges to Fort Vancouver. Stevens' Indian Agent refused to take us if he could not arrest the head men. Colonel Wright, who is an honorable man, would not permit this, in light of his pledge of protection."

"There's a Gentleman," said Sandy Smith, relieved at last to locate the once-familiar species in the wilderness. "A Gentleman always keeps his word."

Quiemuth continued his narrative. "Colonel Wright turned our people over to the Indian Agent to be brought to the new reservation, but he withheld the marked men, Wahoolit, Kitsap, Winyea and me. He told us he would bring us back to the Yakama reservation over the mountains, but we said we did not wish to live there, where it is too dry and hot and cold. He said we had no choice; we would leave in the morning. That night, as we were camped outside the walls of the fort, he placed only one guard on us. Speaking loudly so we could hear, he gave the guard strict orders to watch for shooting stars. And so, we escaped."

"Ah yes, a Gentleman and a Scholar," marveled Sandy.

"But where are Kitsap and Winyea?" asked Ann.

"They have gone to join the Suquamish at their reservation."

"May they always walk in peace."

That night, they all slept a sound and grateful sleep, feeling that at last their troubles might be drawing to a close, that *Sah-hah-lee Tyee* might still have a purpose for the People of the River Grass. Early the next morning, Moonya herself arrived at the new reservation, with George and little Kiya in tow. Kiya ran to embrace her father.

Betsy offered George a plate of scrambled eggs and bacon. "It was my husband's favorite breakfast," she said, smiling as the boy wolfed it down.

"He would eat the rocks themselves, if you put them on a plate," said Moonya, looking in the doorway. Then she called the adults outside, away from the children, to break the news of Sluggia's betrayal of Leschi. "Leschi is on trial today in Steilacoom. They say they will hang him."

Ann gasped. Wahoolit cursed. Ten minutes later, Betsy's Muck Creek cabin was near-deserted, the dishes left for Sandy Smith to tidy up, as the others headed for Steilacoom. "That Governor's no Gentleman," he confided to Miss Buttercup, as he picked out the bacon before feeding her the scraps.

4

A dead silence fell over the courtroom as people held their breath, stifled tickles in the throat, endured aches rather than shift their weight. The Governor was as surprised as anyone to find that he was to become the star witness for the defense. There'd been no subpoena, no warning of any kind; indeed, it was only happenstance that he had attended. Well, perhaps not happenstance – with such rich veins of revenge and political capital to be mined, he could not stay away, and apparently Mr. Clark had gambled on that.

Stevens sprang to attention, pulled his frock coat down, thrust his waxed goatee forward and shoulders back, then marched like a Crusader into the breach. He was a soldier and a great leader; he'd be damned if some dandified pettifogger was going to rile him. He was determined to prove that calling Isaac I. Stevens to the stand was the biggest mistake Frank Clark would ever make.

Formalities out of the way, Stevens perched on the edge of the witness chair, making himself as tall as possible. Clark was standing far away, behind the defense table, casually shuffling a few papers before looking up, as if mildly surprised to find the Governor there. Stevens liked the way the box was raised, so that although he was seated, he was even with Clark's insouciant blue eyes. Clark blinked twice; Stevens not at all.

"Thank-you, Governor, for taking time out of your busy schedule to testify today," said Clark. Stevens inclined his head slightly, then realized he'd just been duped into appearing as if he'd deliberately come to court to aid the defense! He scowled, but Clark was already on to his first question.

"In your role as Governor of Washington Territory, are you Commander in Chief of the Washington Territorial Volunteers?"

"Yes." No 'Sir' from him, by God!

"And are you also Superintendent of Indian Affairs for this Territory?"

"Yes."

"Appointed by the President of the United States to both positions?"

"Yes."

"Now, the United States entered into a treaty, called the Medicine Creek Treaty, with a group of Indian tribes, including the Nisquallies, correct?"

"That's right."

"The United States views these Indians with whom it made this treaty to be sovereign, like a foreign power?"

"They are Indian tribes."

Clark gave the jury a very small, indulgent smile. "Yes, Sir, I'm sure we all know that; but that's not my question. Are they considered by the United States to be sovereign, like a nation?"

"They are our children, dependent upon us for survival," said the Governor. "If that is sovereignty, it is a very degraded kind of sovereignty."

Clark snatched a document from the table and scurried up to the witness box, where he shoved it under Stevens' pointed nose. "Governor, I show you what has been marked as Defendant's Exhibit A. Isn't that a copy of the Medicine Creek Treaty?"

Stevens examined it as if he'd never seen it before. The longer he was silent, the worse he looked. At last, he conceded, "Yes."

"Doesn't it say that the tribes, for the purposes of the treaty, are to be considered one sovereign nation?"

"Yes," replied Stevens, "but that is only for purposes of the treaty."

"Is it the custom of the United States Government to make treaties with private parties?"

"I wouldn't know."

Clark spun to share a look of wonder with the jurors.

"You, Governor of this Territory, Superintendent of Indian Affairs, wouldn't know?" he needled. "Can you give me an example of any private treaty?"

Stevens sat stone still and silent.

"I thought not," said Clark. "Do you concede that the act of treating with the Indians demonstrates that they are viewed by the United States as a separate nation?"

"Well," huffed the Governor with a vehemence that he hoped might turn the tables, "the savages certainly aren't Americans."

"And in fact the defendant, Leschi, was a Chief of the Nisqually nation?"

"I made him a Chief. He tore up his commission on the treaty grounds. From that moment forward, he became a mere renegade, an outlaw."

"After which time you had your sub-agent, Mike Simmons, solicit Leschi's signature on the treaty?"

Stevens glowered.

"Or was his mark forged?"

"Objection!" cried Pritchard, his jowls shaking. "Pure impudence! The Governor is not on trial here."

"Your Honor, the point is to show Leschi was a leader of a sovereign nation without the Governor's say-so. But I'll withdraw that question, if the Governor will do us all the favor of answering my first question. After tearing up the commission, did the Governor still ask Simmons to get Leschi's mark on the treaty?"

Judge Chenoweth had enjoyed the whole spectacle. "Well, that seems fair enough," he said. "Governor, what about it?"

"Yes."

"So even after Leschi tore up his commission, you treated him like a Chief, not a renegade?"

"Objection! Argumentative."

"Sustained."

"Isn't it true that during the recent war you put a price on the head of any hostile Indian, setting especially high prices for the Chiefs, and the very highest price for Chief Leschi?"

The Governor knew Clark's game. He thought he was so smart, but he wasn't smarter than Isaac I. Stevens. "There was no 'war,' Mr. Clark, though it was clever of you to try to slip that into your question. Washington Territory suffered criminal attacks by lawless bands of renegades who never represented their tribes."

Clark leaned across the witness box, sticking his face right into the Governor's. "Excuse me, Sir," he said, "but did I hear you correctly? There was no war?"

"There was no declaration of war," countered Stevens, already a bit nervous with the position he'd staked out for himself.

"So you're testifying, under oath, that what we all just went through wasn't a war?"

Stevens' head spun from side to side as if his collar had just shrunk. "Yes."

"You went to West Point, did you not?"

"Yes, Sir." Dammit! At the mention of the Academy, he'd reflexively let a 'Sir' slip out!

"Don't they teach there, that a formal declaration of war is not required for the existence of a state of war between nations?"

Well, yes, they did teach that. How could this scrivener know that?

"I have heard it said."

"You have heard it said? For example, the Barbary Wars were never formally declared, but arms were fired, ships and men were lost in battle, national interests were in conflict, correct?"

"So it is said." Stevens strained to raise himself another half inch in his seat.

"In other words, we were at war?"

"I suppose so."

"The United States has been at war with the Nisqually nation over the past two years, correct?"

"We have engaged in military action to subdue lawlessness." Stevens picked up the Medicine Creek Treaty and waved it at Clark. "That lawlessness defied the official policy of the Nisqually nation, as expressed in your own Exhibit A."

Clark hadn't had this much fun since he'd finally gotten under the skirts of the Sheriff's daughter. "While we're waving exhibits, Governor," he said, approaching the witness again, "let's try this one, marked Defendant's Exhibit B. Would you identify it please?"

Stevens gave it the barest glance. "It is a declaration of martial law."

"It is in your hand, signed by you in your capacity as Governor, correct?"

"Yes."

"Please be so kind, Sir, as to read it."

Stevens began reading to himself, the veins on his neck throbbing.

"I meant, Sir, please read it out loud," prodded Clark.

Stevens glared at Clark, but this time the insouciant blue eyes did not blink. "Whereas, in the prosecution of the Indian war –" Stevens read, too quickly and half garbled.

"What was that last word?" probed Clark, merciless.

"WAR!" shouted Stevens.

"Ah," replied Clark, "I thought so. And down a little further, after the word 'custody', what does it say?"

"—and whereas the," Stevens cleared his throat, "war is now being actively prosecuted throughout nearly the whole of said county –"

"That's enough," said Clark. "Do you still maintain that there was no war between the United States and the Indians on our side of the mountains?"

"I suppose you could call it that."

"And you did?"

"I did. But it doesn't change the fact that Leschi's an outlaw."

Clark turned to the jurors. "Why don't we allow these gentlemen to decide that, Governor." He turned back. "On October 24, 1855, you ordered Eden's Rangers, a company of Volunteers under the command of Captain Charles Eden, the gentleman seated over there –"Clark pointed to Charlie, as the Governor scowled at him – "to capture Chief Leschi and his brother, correct?"

That Injun-lover Eden is sitting right there and knows the truth of it. Still, the Governor was determined to tough it out. "To escort Leschi and Quiemuth to the reservation, for their own safety," he said.

"Was it for their own safety that you ordered Captain Eden to bring them back, dead or alive?"

"Alive if possible, is what I said."

"Dead if not?"

"They had to comply with the treaty."

"So, pursuant to your orders, Eden's Rangers exchanged gunfire with Leschi's Indian forces on Connell's Prairie, the night of October 27-28, each side killing men on the other side?"

"The Injuns started it. They killed McAllister and Connell in cold blood."

"But what I described did happen, right?"

"There was an engagement, yes."

"And as for who started it, two days prior, Eden's Rangers had burned Leschi's village to the ground, correct?"

"That wasn't part of the orders I gave –"

"You were shocked? Distressed?"

"Well, no –"

"You ordered disciplinary action?"

The Governor pursed his lips and shook his head, no.

"In fact, you congratulated Captain Eden for this action, correct?"

"I felt that strong measures needed to be taken to enforce the treaty."

"You congratulated Captain Eden for burning Chief Leschi's village, correct?"

Stevens glared back. If he couldn't win the legal battle, he'd damn well win the political one. "You bet I did, Mr. Clark. While you and your weak-kneed ilk have been cheating the people out of their farms from the safety of town, me and my boys have been risking life and limb to protect our way of life against the savages – even to protect people like you, who live off the sweat of others."

"*Bravo!*" cried a man in the gallery, and suddenly a dozen, then two dozen, then a hundred men and women were on their feet, cheering for the Governor, hooting down the Judge's gavel, hurling curses, threatening to tar and feather the apostate Clark, and lynch his client from the nearest cottonwood.

"ORDER, ORDER IN THE COURT!" cried Chenoweth. When no order could be restored, the Judge called a recess, and the Sheriff with a posse of ten armed men were forced to spirit Clark and Leschi into the Judge's chambers for their own protection.

5

Mr. Clark rested his case in chambers. He'd gotten all he needed before the ruckus arose. He had no desire to get himself killed for his client.

Judge Chenoweth ordered the courtroom cleared of all but essential personnel. Closing arguments were terse and to the point. The Judge instructed the grim-faced jurors on the legal definition of murder, adding, "If you find that the killing of A.B. Moses arose from lawful combat between soldiers in a war between sovereign nations, the law does not regard such killing as murder."

Twelve men huddled around one heavy slab of maple in the cramped jury room adjacent to chambers, at the back of the courthouse. The dark room had only one small, high window. It was lit by the glow of a pot-bellied stove and a few smelly whale-oil lanterns. At three-thirty in the Pacific Northwest November afternoon, it already felt like midnight.

There was no need for introductions – these men all knew each other, or at least, of each other. They settled on "Father" Bill Kincaid of Sumner for jury foreman. Father Bill was a craggy-faced old farmer, with great white bristles sprouting from nose and ears, who was well respected for his even temperament and fourteen children. "Gentlemen," said Bill, all business, as he tore up a sheet of paper and passed out the pencils. "We'll take a secret ballot. Write 'Guilty' or 'not Guilty.' That's all."

"Um, Father Bill?" asked young Isaac Wright, "what if'n we, uhh ...?"

"Yeah, all right son, don't worry. You can mark 'X' for Guilty, and 'O' for not guilty, got it?"

"Yes, Sir." Isaac licked the nib of his pencil, and went at it.

Soon, there was a small pile of slips before Father Bill. He handed Ezra Meeker a sheet of paper. "You keep a tally," he instructed. Then he began opening the slips.

"Guilty." Ezra marked a slash in the first column.

"Guilty."

"Guilty."

"O." Men glared at Isaac Wright, who dipped his head and turned beet red. "That's 'not Guilty,'" added Father Bill just to get the attention back off of Isaac, though Ezra had already marked one lone slash under the second column.

"Guilty."

"Not guilty." A few eyebrows shot up. One man muttered a curse.

"None of that, boys," chastised Father Bill. He opened another slip of paper. "Not guilty," he said, with a touch of extra emphasis. By the time he'd finished, the count stood, eight to four for conviction.

"Well, there you have it boys. I guess we'll just go around this table, and anyone who's got somethin' to say will have their say, and then we can take another vote."

Abe Woolsey, a big man with only one dark eyebrow that slashed the whole distance across his forehead, spoke up immediately. "I don't see what in tarnation this is all about!" he cried. "I coulda sworn we'd have this devil convicted on the first ballot, yew-nanimous." He pounded the table to emphasize the last word. "What the hell's wrong with you people?"

A few of the other jurors nodded and grunted, but no one saw fit to add anything very articulate, so Father Bill stepped in. "Maybe one of the gentlemen who voted 'not guilty,' wants to respond?"

Ezra Meeker cleared his throat. "I'll own up to that, Sir," he said. "I just don't see how a man fightin' a war can be guilty of murder, that's all. I'm a plain sort of feller; I don't go in much for fancy reasonin', so maybe I can't follow the Governor on this. Near as I kin tell, we was at war with Leschi when they say he shot poor Mr. Moses."

"So you're just gonna let him get off scot-free?" cried Woolsey. "Criminy, he kilt all them kids and women up to White River, and you want to let him go free?"

"Them kids and women was friends of mine," replied Meeker, his face pinched in sorrow. "I'm the one commended that spot to them fer settlin'. There ain't one night since that massacre that I ain't asked myself whether they'd be alive today if not fer me." There was silence around the table. "But, last time I checked, that ain't the case in front of us. We're here to try the killing of Mr. Moses."

"Who was a friend of mine," chimed in Burleigh Pierce. "He saved my farm from that weasel Clark back when he was Sheriff. I say Leschi's guilty."

"Well, that's real nice about your farm," said chubby Albert Balch, whose sea captain brother had first settled Steilacoom, and whose other brother published the *Puget Sound Courier*, placing him square in opposition to everything Stevens. "But it doesn't amount to a reason to find Leschi guilty of murdering him. We're here to uphold the law; we oughta leave the lynching to the fellows outside."

"Ask yourself, Mr. High and Mighty, who'n hell you'd rather have 'em lynch?" hollered Woolsey, leaning across the table threateningly, "some *siwash* sonafabitch, or the jurors who let him go free?"

"Now, gentlemen," said Father Bill, "calm yourselves. We're here to try Leschi, not each other. Why don't we take another vote to see if anyone's mind has changed."

"Can I just say one thing?" asked Peter Wilson, a thin rheumy fellow.

"Sure, Pete, you go right ahead," encouraged Father Bill.

"I think we were at war with the Yakamas, but not with Leschi's band yet. The Governor was just trying to enforce the treaty. A lawless ambush is just that – a crime, not a military action. Sure, we were at war later, maybe after they engaged Lieutenant Slaughter or attacked Seattle. But not when Leschi murdered Ben Moses."

"Okay," said Father Bill. "We vote again." He distributed the slips of paper, and everyone bent to the task. They came back. This time, there was an "X" in place of an "O". Nine to three for conviction.

"So we know it's Meeker and Balch; who's that third vote fer the *siwash* bastard?" boomed Woolsey. No one spoke up. "That's what I thought. Coward."

They argued some more, then took another vote. Nine to three for conviction. Everyone ganged up on Balch and Meeker. "You jest keep it up,

Injun lovers," cursed Woolsey at last. "We know where your cabins are; we know yer kin."

Meeker stood up, and Woolsey stood to face him, the two men glowering. "When it comes to threats agin my family, Mr. Woolsey, I don't take to it kindly. You try anythin', you'll be breathin' out yer belly."

"Gentlemen!" cried Father Bill, inserting himself bodily between the two men. "Please! This won't get us nowhere." They voted again. Nine to three. And again. Nine to three.

"I am afraid this is hopeless, Gentlemen." They sent a note out to the Judge. They were deadlocked.

Judge Chenoweth scowled as he read it. He stuck his head into the jury room. "Listen to the other fellow, Gentlemen. If ever a case needed a verdict, this is that case. We need to get this thing behind us one way or another, so Washington can go forward."

They were chastened; they were energized; they locked horns in another hour of vicious debate. Then they voted again. Nine to three.

"Look," said Burleigh Pierce, the only man among them who still appeared fresh, though inside he was boiling, "it's not that any one of us is going after the other, right Mr. Woolsey?" Abe Woolsey said, "No," in such a way that it wasn't clear whether he was agreeing or disagreeing, but Pierce pressed on. "It's that we represent the whole community here. And if we don't do what the people of Washington Territory want, how are we ever going to live with our neighbors?" He looked Balch and Meeker in the eye. "I mean, really, you fellows might just get off with tar and feathers, but ten or twenty or forty or however many years from now, at your funeral, you're still going to be known as the man who refused to convict the leader of the White River massacre. Is that what you want? Is that the burden you want to lay on your children, to be the sons and daughters of a marked and hated man?"

They voted. Ten to two. A small cheer went up. "Balch, Meeker?" asked Pierce.

"It sure warn't me who switched," said Meeker, proud of his conviction not to convict.

Woolsey slapped a very shaken Albert Balch on the back. "We won't forget this, Albert," he said. Balch wouldn't meet Meeker's eyes.

"So now it's just you, Meeker," continued Woolsey. "You and the coward." Everyone's glanced around the room, suspicious and defensive at once.

"I am no coward," said a strong voice. With a collective shock, everyone realized it was Father Bill speaking. "I will never vote to convict that man."

And he never did, through six tense hours, ten more ballots, and three fistfights. At last, just after midnight, bloodied and bruised, they stumbled into chambers. "Your Honor," said Father Bill, his left eye swollen shut, "we cannot reach a verdict."

The Judge entered the near-deserted courtroom unannounced. Mr. Chapman and the Sheriff were sharing a bottle and swapping lies with the attorneys and Charles Mason. They stopped and looked up expectantly. The Judge's weary steps echoed all the way to the bench. "Hung jury," he muttered. "I declare a mistrial." He looked for his gavel, couldn't find it, so he settled for a pull on the whiskey bottle instead.

No one was cheering. Frank Clark slipped out quietly under the Sheriff's protection, and accepted his hospitality for the night. It was a wise choice; that night, as he took comfort in the daughter's bed, an angry mob burned his house to the ground.

Chapter Twenty-Five
Quiemuth

1

At a steady trot, Quiemuth, George, Wahoolit, Ann and Betsy, skirted the outer perimeter of Fort Nisqually, then headed northeast towards Steilacoom. It was well past midnight when they reached the first outlying cabins along the shores of Sequalitchew Lake, known to the Bostons as the site of the first celebration of American Independence in the Pacific Northwest. A chill wind blew in off *Whulge*. The distant *pop-pop-pop* of gunfire, and a cacophony of voices, made it sound like the Fourth of July all over again. Fearing it was a celebration of Leschi's conviction, they squatted by the old footpath, listening for clues to decode the disturbances. It was then that they heard the approaching sound of runners. By distant firelight, they made out the shapes of two men, briskly striding along the old Indian path.

Wahoolit sprang out, brandishing his silver coffin knife, pinning the lead man against an alder trunk. "Well, well," he snarled in *Whulshootseed*, "if it isn't my new Chief."

Sluggia reached for his weapon but Wahoolit was too quick for him, knocking it away as he pressed the knife blade under Sluggia's chin. Elikuka jumped back in his tracks and reached for his own knife. His hand was caught and pinned back by Quiemuth's strong grip. Wahoolit thrust his jagged brow against Sluggia's. "I heard a strange tale back at the reservation," he hissed. "Seems like you have come into great wealth so quickly. Fifty new company blankets! You must have clubbed many fine otters for so rich a payoff."

Sluggia looked with hatred from man to man, then beyond, where Ann, Betsy and George, watched his humiliation. "You would do well not to make a commotion and attract the Bostons," Sluggia said. "They are hungry for our blood tonight."

"*Our* blood?" cried Wahoolit, loudly defying Sluggia's warning. "What do you know of our blood? You who betray your own blood for a few trinkets."

"The jury refused to convict Leschi," cried Sluggia. "I was there to testify for him, but they would not let me."

"You lie!" cried Wahoolit, scraping the blade against Sluggia's trachea.

"No!" said Elikuka, "it is the truth. Listen to the voices of the Bostons. It is anger, not rejoicing, that you hear."

They listened again. It did seem that the voices were filled with the rage of vengeance denied.

"This good news makes you no less a traitor, Sluggia," said Wahoolit. "Though you are not fit to lick his boots, your fate is now linked to Leschi's. If he is freed, you are free. If they find him guilty, you are a dead man." Wahoolit lowered his knife. "Now, go," he commanded, shoving Sluggia into the night.

Soon afterwards they came upon the camp of more trustworthy Natives, who confirmed the amazing news. Leschi had been tried; the Governor himself had testified; but the jury refused to find him guilty! Ann fell down upon the ground and gave thanks to all the spirits, Raven, Chinook, *Ta-co-bet*, Jesus, *Sah-hah-lee Tyee*, and *Doquebulth*. Then she and Wahoolit joined the camp, to sleep before greeting their victorious Chief.

Quiemuth had other plans. "I am so grateful to hear that the white man's justice is real," he said. "I am tired of running. Today, I will surrender."

2

"*Hung jury!*" Stevens glared from behind the same old battered desk, relocated to the freshly papered home office behind the downstairs parlor. No more would the stink of rotting fish corrupt the business of the Territory. "*Hung jury!*" he cried again, as if the words themselves could undo the unthinkable. "Hang the God-forsaken jury! Who's responsible?" he barked.

Mr. Pritchard looked to his shoes; Mason returned the Governor's glare with a practiced air of mild servility; Rabbeson looked to Abe Woolsey, who fingered the culprits. "Ezra Meeker and Bill Kincaid."

"Kincaid? Father Bill?" exclaimed the Governor. "Meeker, right, he's probably taking cash under the table from Clark, but Father Bill? Since when did he become an Indian lover?"

There was no answer to be had, so everyone's shoes grew suddenly more interesting. Finally, Pritchard mumbled that he'd been surprised, but Pierce County juries just weren't reliable.

"Gentlemen," announced the Governor, "Mr. Pritchard has a point. It's time for a little judicial redistricting."

The strategy session went on late into the night. Meg and little Maude carried in dinner. Later, they carried out the empty platters, and closed the French folding doors. The big brick fireplace devoured log after log. Mason tossed back his auburn hair, intently taking notes, his brown eyes soft with adulation. This was why he served this maddening man. When it came to the fine art of politics, nobody played the game better – and he was the one who got to translate the man's vision into action. It was exhilarating, like playing chess with live chessmen. The hung jury was check, but far from mate.

Finally, after every detail was in place and everyone had gone home, Stevens trudged up the stairs. Meticulously, he hung his jacket, folded his clothes, and knelt to pray beside his sleeping wife. "Dear Lord, hear my plea."

From downstairs, there came a sharp rap at the door.

Stevens threw his trousers on over his nightshirt, picked up a pistol as a precaution, and hurried down. Through the peep-hole he spied a familiar-looking young white man in the company of Shaw and Simmons. They were holding two Indians – a *klootchman*, and a short, stooped, shivering old man, wedged between them, his hands bound behind his back.

"Quiemuth!" cried Stevens, throwing the door wide. The Governor ushered his guests down the hall and into his office, holding back Simmons as he closed the door. "How'd you get him?"

"Damned fool surrendered himself to Dr. Tolmie at the same time my sister's boy was in the store," said Mike Simmons. That's it, thought Stevens. The young man was Jimmy McAllister. "Me'n Ben Shaw got there just as Martha an' Joe Bunting was looping the noose over a limb. We struck a deal. They turned the *siwash* over to me, and Jimmy comes along to protect the family interest."

"You think Joe knows where he is now?"

"Don't take a genius," replied Mike.

"Who's the squaw?"

"That there's Betsy, John Edgar's widow. Insisted on tagging along so's the old Chief stays safe. She's a Puyallup; I wouldn't trust her to tell my cock from a turkey neck."

The Governor slapped Mike on the back. "Nice work, Mike." He was in a good mood; once again, Providence smiled upon him. "Alright, we can't do anything with him 'til morning. Tell Shaw I want him to escort Mrs. Stevens and the children to your place. Send the squaw upstairs to the children's room; it ain't decent for a woman, especially a widow, to be spending the night in a room full of men. We'll let Quiemuth sleep in my office. You and Jimmy stick around; help me keep an eye on him."

"Sure thing," said Mike. "I'll lock up."

"You've done enough," replied the Governor. "I'll take care of that. Send Shaw out here."

The Governor put his arm around Shaw, and whispered a few special instructions. Then they went upstairs to rouse Meg and the children.

The men settled in for the night, Mike Simmons on a blanket on the floor, Quiemuth on a blanket across Stevens' big desk. At first, Betsy refused to leave the room as long as Jimmy was there. They struck a deal: Jimmy would bunk down in the hallway outside the office, and she would sleep on the landing at the top of the stairs. As Jimmy was gathering up his bedroll, Quiemuth sat up and smiled at him. *"Mamook mika mitlite tumtum, tenas man?"* – Do you remember, young fellow? he asked in Chinook.

Jimmy froze at the doorway. He remembered plenty, and didn't take kindly to being reminded. Quiemuth maintained his friendly smile. "You were just a boy," he said. "Leschi and I had come to find your people, lost in the forest. You were scared; you ran away. I was the one who rescued you. I lifted you up over my shoulder, and brought you back to your mother."

Jimmy strained to match the story to memory. Yes, there was something ...

"You have grown into a fine man. Your father would be proud."

Jimmy nodded once, turned, and left the room. Betsy squeezed Quiemuth's hand. "It is good," said Quiemuth. "I have known Mike Simmons a long time. Get some rest."

Wind-whipped rain splattered the walls and windows, an insistent drumming of tense fingers. The brothers, *Enumclaw* and *Kapoonis* – thunder and lightning – wrestled in the sky. Betsy could hear Simmons' great snorting snores from inside the office, his oblivion reassuring. Jimmy tossed and moaned at the bottom of the stairs, but he, too, was asleep. Still, Betsy was determined not to allow herself the luxury of sleep. Someone had to guard the guards.

Everything was dark and close, except for one flickering gas lamp in the hallway, turned down low. The house was situated on the top of a bluff. It was the hubris of the white man to place a house where *Laliad's* full fury breaks upon the land. No Native would ever build here, and to lie in such a house was not restful. The glow of lamplight made the rain-spattered windows look like totem faces crawling with maggots. As time went on, the dead seemed more alive than the living. Betsy could feel them all around her, and she grew afraid. For whom had they come?

Betsy heard nothing as the man in the black mackinaw gently opened the unlocked back door, but she felt the cold air. She sprang up and dashed down the stairs just as a shot rang out, shattering a pane of the French doors. She was on the assailant's back, tearing at his neck with her long fingernails, before he could get off another shot. He spun and dove backwards. Together they smashed through the lattice window panes, scattering glass all over Mike Simmons as they fell. Quiemuth rose up off the desk and staggered towards the jagged opening in the smashed doors before he faltered, his hand rising to above his breast, below the right shoulder. "I'm shot," he said in *Whulshootseed*, just as Betsy sunk her teeth into the gunman's wrist, causing his hand to lose its grip on the pistol. The man's other hand grabbed at the pistol but Mike got it first. With his knee, the gunman delivered a crushing blow to Betsy's gut. He leaped up, drawing a gruesome Bowie knife that glittered faintly in the low lamplight.

Betsy sucked desperately for wind. "Shoot him!" she gasped in English. There was a moment of perfect equipoise, as the fury froze, brittle as new ice over rapids. Something unspoken flashed from Mike Simmons to the man. Mike did not shoot. The man drove the long blade deep into Quiemuth's heart.

"No!" cried both Betsy and Jimmy, but it was too late. Without another word, Quiemuth dropped first to his knees, then off the dripping blade onto the floor, dead.

Jimmy, stilled by shock, watched as his brother-in-law dashed down the hall and out the back door, leaving it to bang in the wind. The Governor ran down the stairs, his nightshirt flapping around his ankles. He looked at the shattered French doors, the wailing *klootchman*, the corpse that had been Quiemuth, centered in a rapidly spreading pool of blood. "Who did this?" Stevens demanded.

Mike looked to Jimmy, who looked down. "Cain't rightly say," said Mike. "It was so dark."

3

Leschi was dozing on the rough-hewn cedar plank floor of the Fort Steilacoom prison shed, half-dreaming to the *rat-tat-tat* of steady rain against the walls. A sharp rap, followed by the sound of keys scraping the lock, awakened him. He sat up, dazed from another restless night filled with distant angry chants of, *"Les-chi Must Die."* No one had visited him at all, other than the young soldiers who removed his slops and brought him strange, indigestible food. It had been several suns since the trial ended – two? three? – and still nobody had bothered to tell him the outcome. In his heart, he knew he was a condemned man. He only hoped he would get a chance to say goodbye to his few remaining loved ones, Quiemuth, Moonya and the children, perhaps even Mary.

Leschi blinked, clearing sleep from his eyes. He tried to focus in the dim light on the stiffly upright figure who'd entered. An officer, that was plain.

Young, smooth skin, bright blue eyes, short-cropped, wheat-colored hair. And respectful, thought Leschi, as the man executed a clipped bow, then turned away to allow the Chief a moment to compose himself.

Leschi's visitor bowed at the neck. "I am Lieutenant Augustus Kautz, at your service, Sir," he said, in strangely-accented Chinook. Leschi noted a slight limp as Lieutenant Kautz closed the distance between them, and Kautz saw him notice. "It is nothing, a mere scratch," said the Lieutenant. "Perhaps if you had been a better shot?" he added, his face stern, but his blue eyes hinting mischief.

"I am sorry to have disappointed you, Lieutenant," replied Leschi. "This was?"

"At White River." The bold charge at the swamp came rushing back to Leschi, along with the officer leading the assault, whom he'd knocked from his mount.

"You showed great courage that day," said Leschi, with genuine admiration.

Kautz waved off the compliment as he surveyed the bare room. "We will get you a chair," he said in English, "and a bunk, *ja?*" Leschi shook his head and shrugged. The Lieutenant repeated the same message in his clipped Chinook.

Leschi smiled. "*Mahsie,*" he said – thank-you. *Why would he need such things, if they were going to hang him?*

The young officer clicked his heels and inclined his head. "I have news," he continued. "The jury could not agree. The Governor sends word that he wishes to make you have another trial. So, you will be here a while, waiting."

The jury could not agree! Leschi was astonished. So focused had he been on sacrificing himself, that he had not permitted himself a glimpse at a possible future with him alive. Now that future rushed in, unbidden: he saw himself and his brother in the bosom of a reunited tribe, fishing the shallows and deep eddies by the river bends, singing songs that came easy as breathing, passing his father's tales to the next generation of Nisquallies. It was hope; dangerous, delicious, hope, that caught at his breath.

Lieutenant Kautz limped two steps back to the door. "As a fellow soldier who admires your courage," he said with careful emphasis, "the jury result I take with pleasure." He bowed, and was gone.

4

Like everyone else in Washington Territory, Lieutenant Kautz knew of other, much darker news, concerning Leschi. Kautz was not willing to be the one to break it. The death of Quiemuth had instantly wiped the failure to convict Leschi from the headlines. The Governor was not an official suspect, though everyone had a theory on his possible role. Some said that the whole affair demonstrated his recklessness, while others lauded his resolve against the *siwash*.

Though it was common knowledge that the McAllisters, especially the son-in-law, were responsible, no witnesses would step forward to identify the killer. Indeed, just that morning, Joseph Bunting had been released for lack of evidence, after spending only one night in jail. As soon as he got home, Ainsley and Martha tenderly applied healing comfrey salve to the scratches on his neck, and the nasty bite mark on his wrist.

The day after Kautz's first visit, Leschi was sitting at one of two chairs, watching a small patch of fluctuating grey framed by his barred window, when the Lieutenant again presented himself with a polished half-bow. "You have a visitor," he announced. "Your *klootchman*."

Leschi rose. "Mary!" he cried before the Lieutenant stepped aside to allow an older woman to slip by. Leschi was astounded. His mouth hung open, trying to say something to cover his gaffe, trying to apologize for leaving her for dead, but his tongue was like the pump handle on a dry well, flapping and useless. Ann did not care; she ran to his embrace and squeezed back with all her strength. "Ann, dearest Ann, forgive me," cried Leschi. He moved to kiss her head, but seeing the new scar there, he took her doughy cheeks in his palms, kissed her brow, then slicked her arms.

"Between us, husband, there is nothing to forgive," she said. "I am overjoyed to find you alive."

Leschi kissed Ann's lips, then knelt before her, bowing his head. "First Wife," he said, "our departed First Wife used to call me a fool, even when others marveled at my wisdom. I am only wise enough to know that she was right. Any pain I have caused you, now I feel many times over."

Ann dropped to her knees in front of Leschi, clasping his hands in a vise grip. He trembled to see something unspeakably dark, seared deep in her sunken eyes. At first he feared he had caused it.

"Husband," she choked out, "I love you. I will always love you." He tried to embrace her. She resisted, so he waited, sensing a horror beyond understanding, welling up from her core. Ann's throat had constricted. Little sobs heaving from the belly shot gusts between her teeth. He tried to comfort her. Again she slipped his grasp, fell away with the look of a rabid wolf, then she keened a sound with each guttural pant, "Quie, hhhh, Quie, hhhh, Quie ...."

He saw it. "QUUIIEEMMUUTTHHH!" he shrieked, knowing what an instant before was unknowable. It was too painful; not stone, nor diamond, let alone mortal flesh, could endure recovering a wife and losing a brother in the space of a single breath. The earth gaped wide, as Leschi's whipsawed spirit fell farther than it had ever fallen, deep into *Ta-co-bet's* burning crater, beyond the place to which he'd fallen after losing his mother, beyond the foul place he'd dwelled after losing Sara, below even the pit in which he'd wallowed after losing Kwahnesum. He tore at his hair and skin and knew nothing of suns or moons or storm clouds for many days or weeks. Or perhaps it was only for the interval between one icy raindrop and the next, as if his whole lifetime with Quiemuth was just one of the countless drops of water hurled from heaven each moment, only to shatter against the white man's glass pane, then run off into nothing in the cold dirt below.

Chapter Twenty-Six
Unfriendly Fire

1

New Year's Day 1857, dawned considerably brighter for the Bostons than had the previous New Year. No longer a bold force to be feared, the Nisqually Chief languished in the prison of his own melancholia, as much as behind the bolted door of the Fort Steilacoom stockade. Normalcy crept back into daily life. The harvest had not been good, but at least there had been one. The price of staples had fallen, confidence was rising, and those who had toughed out the hard times were poised to profit from the influx of newcomers.

Nonetheless, there were political storm clouds on the Governor's horizon. In February, the Republicans nominated Alex Abernathy to oppose Stevens in the July election for Territorial Delegate to Congress. A farmer from Whidbey's Island, who'd served in the legislature and in the war, Abernathy had all the right credentials. There was no shortage of campaign ammunition. Soldiers' scrip remained unredeemed, the Governor's drinking was an open scandal, Leschi was captive but not convicted, and the blade that killed Quiemuth hung proudly over the mantel at the McAllister homestead, a symbol of vigilantism and cronyism under Stevens.

The whole Territory held its breath, awaiting Leschi's re-trial. The wheels turned slowly, as the Governor's master plan to redistrict the Territory and move the trial to Olympia, worked its way through a surprisingly resistant Washington City. The murder of Quiemuth in the Governor's own office led to Stevens' removal as Territorial Indian Agent, and cost him credibility. He was one misstep short of immediate firing by Pierce's successor, James Buchanan. The instructions from the Executive Mansion were terse: *Leschi must have a fair trial, or else.*

"Isaac," said Martha, twisting his name so it dripped like molasses off her tongue, "you know my husband was loyal to yew, right down to th' end."

"Yes, M'am," responded Stevens, in his best counterfeit of a polite Kentucky beau.

"You promised me that murderin' *siwash* would be hung quick as can be."

"Yes, M'am. But –"

Martha cut him off with a wave of her hand. "You remember my rifle?"

"Yes, M'am." Stevens' quick glance implored Mike Simmons to come to his rescue. Mike leaned back, folded his arms, and smiled.

"Well, I ain't gonna make that mistake twice," said Martha. "Next time, its me and my whole brood, all totin' double-barrel twelve gauges, and everythin' within thirty feet of that murderin' *siwash'll* look like ground chuck."

"Now, Martha –"

"One thing I hate, it's excuses." She leaned across Stevens' desk. "Yew get that sonnuvabitch to the gallows quick now, or we're comin' after him."

"I wouldn't advise that, Martha," said Stevens, envisioning the adverse effect on his Congressional campaign.

Martha just laughed in his face. "Or what, Mister Gov'nor? You gonna arrest yerself for conspiracy to murder?"

Stevens blanched. Martha smiled her best Sunday-school smile, as she stood and offered her arm to Mike.

"You know, Mr. Simmons," she said loudly as they left, "you'd make a purty good Congressman."

"So would you, Mrs. McAllister, so would you."

2

At last the much-awaited legislation came through. Leschi could now be tried in Olympia, where the Governor controlled the Sheriff, who in turn controlled the jury pool. On a cloudy Wednesday, March 18, 1857, the banquet room of the Washington Hotel doubled as a courtroom. What it lacked in majesty it made up for in capacity. Nearly three hundred spectators overflowed the chairs, and stood, leaning against the undignified fruit and floral motif of the wallpaper, intoxicated by a heady mix of drama and vengeance. Many of the same folks who had attended the welcoming party for Governor Stevens in that very chamber two and one-half years before were in attendance. Indeed, the master of ceremonies from that occasion, Chief Judge Lander, presided yet again from atop a hastily cobbled bench. The war's widows and orphans were present in force, a belligerent and impatient crowd.

Ann led a small, courageous contingent of Nisquallies, who sat way to the back of the room with heads bowed, for fear of provoking taunts – or worse. Moonya and George were present, as were Mary, Betsy, and even Chief Sluggia, exiled to a seat on the end of the last row, away from the other Natives. Neither Winyea nor Wahoolit dared show their faces, for fear of arrest or lynching.

Leschi missed the comforting support of Charlie Eden, who'd been sent with Lieutenant Kautz on an important mission for the defense. Just the week before, Frank Clark had heard from John McLeod that Rabbeson's so-called "Indian shortcut," was in fact twice as long as the route taken by the express riders, "or I'm a snake's left leg." Whether McLeod was or not, he was unquestionably a half-Algonquin accused traitor, and therefore not fit for the witness stand. So Clark sent Charlie Eden and Lieutenant Kautz, who had been taught to survey by the Army, to check out the story. Although Charlie knew the area up on Connell's Prairie well, he reminded Clark that he hadn't been there the day of Moses's death, so for complete authenticity they had to find someone who had.

They found Doc Burns haunting the tavern in Steilacoom. Doc graciously agreed to join the team, to show them exactly where, "That rathscal Lethi was first encountered, and where he stood when he shot poor Ben. But first," added the good Doctor over a shot of sour mash, "I've got a baby to deliver." They waited impatiently another day while Burns visited a happy home just outside Olympia, so they didn't get on the road until Saturday. With two days' hard ride each way, and at least a day to do the job, whether they'd be back in time to testify was an even money bet. If Frank Clark stalled the trial, maybe they'd make it.

Leschi sat at the defense table, erect and impassive. Since that day so long ago on the shore of Lake Sammamish, where Dr. Tolmie first told Leschi about the white man's "trial," Leschi had wondered at the powerful magic of this ceremony of guilt and innocence. He had no illusions; he'd seen how quick the whites had been to hang poor innocent Kassas for the death of the Sandwich Islander. Nor could he help but wonder whether his brother's death was not somehow related to his own good fortune at the first trial. But such ruminations were a luxury he could no longer afford. Leschi would fight to live. He would live for Ann, for Moonya and her children. He would live for the Nisqually people, who were languishing on the new reservation under the strong hand of the Bostons. He would live for Quiemuth – yes, for his dear brother, most of all – who had never wanted more than a plot of fertile land to till, but who had followed and guided him with uncomplaining loyalty, every hard step of the way.

"Call your first witness, Mr. Pritchard," said Judge Lander, his great snowy mane adding a special majesty to the proceedings.

"The People call Mr. Antonio B. Rabbeson."

The pock-marked Tony Rabbeson rose up, a revenant in search of a silver stake. He gobbled down the oath and regurgitated his well-worn tale of the gallant All Hallow's Eve ride into the swamp near dusk, and the shots fired by Leschi, that felled Mr. Miles, and his dear friend, Ben Moses.

Then it was Frank Clark's turn. Frank, just a regular guy with blue eyes, a square jaw, and a quick smile, flowed smooth as water over stone to the front of the defense table. Tony licked his lips, swiveled his shoulders, cleared his throat as his eyes slipped off one gaze after another and finally into his lap, so shiftily that, without a single question having been asked, everyone got the feeling that he was lying.

"So you saw Leschi at the clearing?"

"Yep."

"And you knew it was Leschi 'cause you'd seen the same fella around your homestead, by the name of Staub?"

"Yep."

"So for all you knew, it was a feller named Staub."

Tony slunk down in his seat. "Nope. It was that feller there." He pointed at Leschi.

"Did this feller have a scar on his face?"

Tony licked his lips as he studied Leschi at the defense table. No scar. "Nope."

"You sure 'bout that?"

"He was wearin' a Mexican hat. Mebbe it was covered up."

"Maybe you didn't really see his face?"

"Oh, I seen it. It was Leschi, all right. I'd know them murderous eyes anywhere." His small smirk was well received by the crowd, but Frank Clark's retort erased it lickety-split.

"*So the hat that maybe covered the man's maybe scar wasn't big enough to cover his eyes?*"

"It was Leschi," said Tony weakly.

"Answer the question."

Pritchard rose. "Your Honor, he did answer the question."

"Move on, Mr. Clark," said Lander.

Clark's eyes registered surprise at the Judge's ruling, but never left Rabbeson's. "All right. So you're positive Leschi was one of the Indians who met you when you first rode into the clearing?"

"Yep."

"Was he mounted?"

"Cain't say."

"You saw his eyes but missed an entire horse?" shot back Clark.

"Objection!" cried Dandy Pritchard, who wasn't about to allow Clark ridicule his only eyewitness.

"Sustained as argumentative," said Judge Lander. He leaned over the makeshift dais, nearly toppling it before he caught himself. "Save your speeches for the summation, Counselor." It seemed that even Judge Lander wanted a quick conviction.

"You testified on direct that it was Leschi who fired the fatal shot. Isn't it true that two days after the shooting, when this was all fresh in your mind, you told Dr. Tolmie that there was too much smoke to see the Indians' faces?"

Tony's head twitched towards the right, as if he were cocking an ear to a faint conversation. He pursed his lips, furrowed his brow, and shook his head. "Nope," he said, "couldn't a been me."

"And if there was too much smoke," said Clark, "then your claim that Leschi pulled the trigger goes up in smoke too."

"No, Sir. Shooter was wearing the same big beaver coat as Leschi, and the same Mexican hat we seen when we first got out to the clearin'."

Frank took one quick bite of this story and spit it back. "So you didn't really see his face, only the hat and coat?"

"Well, that was the main thing."

"So that feller you saw from the start, was a scar-faced man in a floppy hat, and a big beaver coat?"

Now Tony's seat had become uncomfortable, and he shifted his whole bottom. "Coulda been."

"Whose face you didn't see when he fired the shot?"

Tony considered this. "I saw it some."

"You saw it some?" pressed Clark. "But you couldn't've identified him if it warn't for the hat and coat, right?"

You could see in his squinched-up face that Tony didn't like this. "That was the main thing," he said again.

"And the feller with the hat and coat had a scar on his face?"

"I guess."

"Did he or didn't he, Captain Rabbeson?"

"I'm thinking he prob'ly did."

"Leschi here, he doesn't have any scar on his face?"

Finally, Tony remembered what Mr. Pritchard had said when they'd discussed this. "No, come to think of it, mighta been paint. Them *siwash*, they're always paintin' up their faces."

"Mr. Rabbeson, before you change your testimony, let's go back a minute. You said before it was a scar. If it was a scar instead of paint, then it couldn't have been Leschi?"

Mr. Pritchard had also suggested an answer for when he was in a jam, and now seemed like the right time. "It was Leschi. You look down the barrel of his gun, Mister, you don't fergit them murderous eyes. You wouldn't know that, having sat out the whole dang shootin' match. Ask yer partner there, Captain Wallace. He'll tell ya."

Frank knew he'd been hurt, so he moved quickly to his best issue. "How far was it from Connell's place to the swamp, where the shots were fired?"

"'Bout three quarters of a mile."

"You galloped the whole way?"

"You bet your farm we did." Then he got cocky. "Or someone else's farm." The crowd roared with derisive laughter.

Ignoring the jibe, Clark pressed on. "You galloped along the Military Road?"

"Yep."

"Leaving Chief Leschi behind."

"Uh - hhnn."

"And yet the amazing Chief Leschi somehow got himself ahead of you, and was waiting in the swamp in ambush?"

"Yes, Sir, he was. Like I said before, he took a shortcut."

"Oh, yes, a shoorrrtt-cuuutt," said Frank. "How long's that shortcut?"

"I been back up there," said Tony defensively. They were ready for this one, too. "I walked it. It's mebbe three or four hunnert yards to the spot they shot from."

"Maybe?" said Frank Clark, his voice scornful. "Didn't you measure it?"

"Not exactly. But it's three or four hunnert yards, is all."

"Well, then, if someone were to testify that they'd measured it, and that that so-called shortcut was a rough track twice as long as the smooth wagon road you followed, you wouldn't have any basis in fact to disagree, now, would you?"

Tony stiffened. "Objection!" cried Pritchard. "Counsel is confusing the matter with speculation that is not in evidence."

"It's a fair question, Your Honor."

"Do you intend to bring in such evidence?" asked Judge Lander.

"Yes, Sir," answered Clark without a breath of hesitation. He certainly intended to; whether he could or not was another matter.

"Overruled." Before Clark could repeat the question, the Judge leaned way over, again threatening to topple the rickety bench. "But Mr. Clark," he said, "don't make me regret this ruling. You've made a representation that you will tie this in, on your honor as an officer of the Court. I won't forget it."

Clark, who'd so often been at the center of rumors – unproven, of course – about bribed jurors, waylaid witnesses, and other shenanigans, flashed his brightest choir-boy smile. "Of course, Your Honor," he said. Then he turned to Rabbeson, who'd failed to melt into the woodwork. "Since you never measured the so-called 'shortcut,' if a witness were to testify that it was in fact twice as long as the route you took, you'd have no basis to disagree, would you?"

"It ain't."

"But you didn't measure."

"It don't seem it."

"But you don't have any hard facts to prove that, do you?"

Tony squirmed. "Mebbe not."

"And if it in fact proves to be twice as far, then your story that Leschi was the shooter can't be true?"

"I dunno."

"You sure you saw him when you first entered the prairie?"

Be positive. "Yep."

"Then he couldn't be at two places at once, could he?"

"Objection!" cried Pritchard.

"That's all right, Your Honor," said Frank Clark. "I'll withdraw the question." It lingered unanswered as Clark sat down. Now all he had to do was tie this in with Lieutenant Kautz's testimony – if he arrived in time.

What Clark didn't know was that the "baby" Doc Burns delivered was the defense's new strategy, laid out for the Governor's enjoyment. Nor did they know that the Governor's jack-of-all trades, Colonel Jack Blunt, had added a new skill to his repertoire. "Yes, siree," he told the Governor proudly, when he and Burns returned from Connell's Prairie that morning, "I rustled their horses while they slept."

"With my help, Gov'nor Thevens!" cried the harelipped surgeon.

Stevens surveyed Kautz's military Morgan and Charlie's bay mare. "Excellent," he said. "Doc, present your invoice for services rendered to Mr. Mason, who will see that a warrant for payment is issued promptly. Colonel Blunt, let these fine animals loose up near Fort Steilacoom. We don't want anyone to think we're horse thieves."

2

Pritchard chewed through a few witnesses to bolster Tony's bogus story that he could actually have recognized Leschi. It was barely noon when the prosecution rested, and still no sign of Kautz and Eden.

After a short lunch break, Frank's partner, Will Wallace, called Andrew J. Bradley to the stand, to testify that there was too much smoke to identify the Indians who shot at them in the swamp.

Frank called Mr. Mason, who firmly established that all the men fired upon prior to the death of Ben Moses were soldiers engaged in actions against Indians, including the western tribes. "But we were not at war with them yet, on *Octobah* 31st," claimed Mason.

"What d'ya mean, not at war? Hadn't our Volunteers fired on them, killing some of Leschi's men?"

"Maybe in self-defense," conceded Mason, "but they were not under orders to mount a military campaign against the Nisquallies."

"They were under orders to capture the Nisqually Chief."

"To escort him to the reservation for his own protection," corrected Mason.

"For which purpose they burned his village?"

Mason tossed his hair back. "Not everything troops do is planned, Mr. Clark," he said. "You couldn't know that, of course ..." His words trailed off into a thin, mocking smile.

Still no sign of Kautz and Eden. It was only two o'clock, and Clark was running out of witnesses. He called Mr. Gorich, the man in the canoe with the potatoes, to explain how Leschi had spared his life the day of the daring raid on the Fox Island reservation. He called a young boy who, with his friends, had thrown seed pods at Leschi's men, and been treated as the mischievous boys they were, allowed to live to tell the tale. Three o'clock, and Frank was down to only two witnesses: Dr. Tolmie and Sluggia. He called Tolmie first.

"Doc," asked Frank, "did Captain Rabbeson and his company ride in to Fort Nisqually on November 2, 1855?"

"Yes, Sir," said the doctor in his best Queen's English, despite more years on the Sound than any American who called the land his own.

"Did you speak with him about what had occurred?"

"Yes, Sir. Captain Rabbeson gave me a detailed narrative. He informed me that his company had encountered Indians near where Connell's barn had been burnt. He told me that they'd been fired upon by Indians when they reached the swamp, and that Lieutenant Miles and Corporal Moses had been killed. He also told me that they'd managed to kill a few Indians in a fight on Elhi Hill."

"Did you ask him if he recognized any of the Indians by Connell's barn?"

"Yes, Sir. He told me they were Nisquallies or Puyallups. He said he knew a few of them by sight. He said one of them was Staub – he called him that. He said there was a scar-faced Indian there too, but he didn't know his name."

"What about the Indians that shot Miles and Moses?"

"I asked him if he recognized any of them. He said no, there was too much smoke and it all happened too fast."

Frank was pleased. "No further questions."

Darby Pritchard scurried around the table quickly, before the words could sink in too deep. "Did he tell you anything about what Staub was wearing, Dr. Tolmie?"

"Yes. He mentioned a *vaquero* hat and a beaver coat."

"Did you tell him anything about that outfit?"

Dr. Tolmie glanced at Leschi apologetically. "Yes," he said, shifting a bit in his seat. "I said, sounds like some clothes I'd sold to Chief Leschi."

"Objection!" yelled Clark. "This is hearsay."

"Overruled."

"Did you in fact sell Leschi a beaver coat and *vaquero* hat?" pressed Pritchard.

"Yes, Sir," said Dr. Tolmie.

"When?"

"'Bout two weeks earlier."

The smartest guy in the room suddenly didn't feel so smart. How could he have put Tolmie on the stand? He'd fallen into a trap. Now, unless Kautz and Eden appeared in the next few minutes, there was only one witness standing between Leschi and the gallows: the very man who'd betrayed his own uncle to the Governor.

3

"Call the Indian known as Sluggia," said Mr. Clark; Mr. Chapman repeated, "the Indian known as Sluggia, take the stand." Major Shaw, who was acting as interpreter, echoed the words in *Whulshootseed*. Sluggia rose from his seat in the far back corner, as all the spectators' heads swiveled to fix on him. Head down, Sluggia pressed slowly towards the witness stand, like a man leaning into a stiff wind.

Sluggia, professing a faith in Jesus Christ as Lord, was sworn on the white man's bible. From the witness chair, he surveyed the jury with his delicate oval eyes, being careful not to look at his uncle. Frank Clark took him easily through the introductory portions of his testimony, establishing who he was in relation to the defendant. Then he established that, although kin, he was no friend of Chief Leschi.

"Yes, it was I who captured Leschi, and turned him over to the Governor's man, Mike Simmons," said Major Shaw, translating Sluggia's words back into English for the Court. Sluggia's eyes were downcast.

"Why did you do it?"

"My uncle was once a great leader," said Sluggia through Shaw. "It was he who laid the trap for McAllister. It was he who saved us from the Boston rifles a few days later, by suggesting we hold up sticks with clothing. But in the end he was too soft. He would not let us fight the only war we could win; the war of terror. You won the war of terror when you killed our children at Mashel Village. For that I blame Leschi."

Frank Clark stepped close. "Is that why you betrayed him, Sluggia?" he asked.

Sluggia pulled back and answered angrily, "It was he who betrayed me. He took a white man as his son. I was the son of his sister; I should have been as a son to him. He preferred the man with the honey hair to his own kin; the very man sent to capture him, the man who drove my cousin to her death."

"That would be Captain Eden, who was married to Leschi's daughter?"

Sluggia nodded, tight-lipped.

"It is common among your people to exchange items of clothing freely, such as coats, and hats, and the like?"

"It is common." Sluggia stared at his own feet.

"So," continued Frank, "if it is true that Leschi obtained a beaver coat or *vaquero* hat from Dr. Tolmie, that does not necessarily mean that he was the one wearing them a few weeks later?"

Pritchard hopped up. "Objection – leading."

"Sustained."

"Was Leschi wearing that beaver coat and Mexican hat when Moses was shot?"

"*Halo*" – No.

"Who was?"

A long pause. "I cannot recall." But he could recall. He simply refused to incriminate himself.

"You are sure it was not Leschi?"

"Yes."

"Were you present at Connell's Prairie on October 31, 1855?"

For the first time, Sluggia met Frank Clark's eyes. "Yes."

"Did you see the Indians fire on the express riders?"

"Yes."

"Was Leschi among those men?"

"No. Leschi was far away, over the mountains, in the land of the Yakama."

Why did he have to say that? thought Frank. Sluggia was convinced he'd just saved his uncle for certain, thus saving himself from Wahoolit.

"Your witness," said Clark.

Mr. Pritchard stood. "So Leschi set the trap for Lieutenant McAllister?"

"Yes."

"Leschi was present?"

"He did not shoot McAllister."

"That's not the question, Chief," said Pritchard, stepping right up to Sluggia's chair. "Was Leschi present?"

A very sullen, "*Nawitka*" – Yes.

"And Leschi was at the first battle of White River, against Lieutenant Slaughter – that time you Injuns held up your hats on sticks?"

Sluggia dropped his head and shook it. He saw his mistake – how could he have been so stupid? Pritchard pressed his advantage. "You just said yourself that it was Leschi who came up with the idea of holding up clothing on sticks to draw fire?"

Sluggia just sat. The Judge spoke up. "Mr. Sluggia, you have to answer."

Sluggia nodded. "Yes," he whispered.

"The court will please take notice of the military record admitted by consent of the parties," said Pritchard. "The record shows the death of McAllister on October 27, and the White River Battle on November 4."

"The jury is instructed that those dates are accurate," replied Judge Lander.

"Sluggia," said Pritchard, "that means that Leschi was present near Connell's Prairie four suns before and four suns after the shooting of Corporal Moses. Do you agree with that?"

Sluggia stared at his feet.

"What was that?" prodded Pritchard, like a squirrel gnawing at a stubborn acorn.

"I suppose."

"Right after McAllister was shot, there was a shooting match with Captain Eden's men, right?"

"Yes."

"Did Leschi run off, or was he there for that?"

"He was there."

"And that didn't end 'til around midnight, right?"

"Yes."

"So you want these gentlemen to believe that, right after his tribe was involved in exchanging gunfire with Captain Eden, by which time it was early in the morning of the next day – October 28 – Leschi got it in mind to ride about a hundred twenty miles over rugged mountains to see the Yakamas, and then turn around and head right back? That's some two hundred forty miles through mountains and snow, all in seven days?"

Sluggia raised his eyes to the jurors. Ignoring the question he simply pleaded, "You have to believe me, he didn't shoot the man called Moses." Major Shaw interpreted his words; the jurors folded their arms and stared back, no hint of sympathy.

"Nothing further."

Clark shot up on pure inspiration. It was only three-thirty; there was no way he could stretch this out until adjournment. Sluggia was Leschi's only hope now. Frank didn't know how, but his squid sense told him that Sluggia was telling the truth when he insisted that Leschi did not shoot Moses.

"Who did it, Sluggia?" he prodded. "Who shot Corporal Moses?"

Sluggia looked from Clark to the jury and back to Clark, but he remained sullenly silent. Judge Lander leaned over. "Answer the question," he commanded.

Sluggia returned to the study of his feet. "If I answer that question," he said, "no one will believe me. They will come to kill me and my people."

"If you do not answer the question," said the Judge, "I will put you in jail." Major Shaw translated this. Sluggia sank even deeper into himself.

Frank crossed quickly to just in front of the witness. "Please, Sluggia," he said, speaking in an avuncular, almost tender voice. "We need to know what you saw."

Silence.

Frank backed off for a moment. "You were there?"

"*Nawitka.*" Yes.

"You saw it?" said Frank in an urgent whisper, so like a spiritualist at a seance that it immediately transported all the hundreds of listeners back to the greenish half-twilight of that lonely All Hallow's Eve swamp.

"*Nawitka.*"

"Then you must tell who shot Abram Benton Moses, and let the jury decide who to believe."

Silence.

"Was it you?"

"*Halo!*" No!

"The law will protect your people," said Frank, though it hadn't saved Quiemuth, or even Frank's own house. "Who killed Abram Benton Moses?"

For the first time that afternoon, as the light of a blood-red sun slanted through the small windows, Sluggia dared to look Leschi in the eye, then closed his own. On the dark screen of memory, Sluggia watched himself, a cold boy on that cold late afternoon, wrapped in his uncle's new coat and hat, firing the volley that felled the soldier called Miles, who rode at the back of the column. Sluggia watched the desperate thrashing of the second soldier whose horse spun with fear as he drew his musket and fired too soon, right into the back of the soldier ahead in line, the man called Moses, knocking him forward and spooking his horse into a mad gallop down the trail. Sluggia watched the second soldier see what he had done, then see that Miles had seen it too, as he rose from the ooze where Sluggia's shot had knocked him, reaching up for a helping hand. Sluggia watched as the second soldier galloped away, leaving Miles still reaching up, an easy target taking a few halting steps before a volley from Wahoolit finished him, and he fell senseless back into the brackish swamp, carrying what he'd just seen to the grave.

"Lrobb - be - son," Sluggia answered, and at first it came out broken up like *Whulshootseed,* and most people awaited Major Shaw's translation. Shaw sat silent and white as a ghost. Sluggia said it again, more distinctly: "Lrabb-be-son." The lawyers and jurors and the big crowd struggled to put the sounds together in their own minds, "*LRab – bes – son,*" "*Rabbes - son,*" "*Rabbeson!*"

4

Frank Clark rested the defense, brimming with confidence. Of course, Tony Rabbeson had taken the stand to deny the "heathen's lies," but Sluggia had nothing to gain by lying so dramatically and, as Frank pointed out in closing argument, everything to lose: his position as Chief, the Governor's favor, and even perhaps his life at the hands of vengeful veterans of the Territorial Volunteers.

"Counsel," barked Judge Lander. "I noted a distinct lack of evidence regarding measurement of the Indian shortcut." Frank realized with a start that he had forgotten his pledge to the Court. Judge Lander had not forgotten, and he was angry.

"Gentlemen of the jury," said the Judge. "Regarding the matter of whether Leschi was present at the scene of the shooting of Corporal Moses, you may consider all the testimony that you heard from the witnesses on that point, but you may not consider the speculative assertions by counsel for the defense that the so-called shortcut was longer than the wagon road, since Mr. Clark has failed to tie in that claim with sound evidence." The Judge glared at Clark; the jurors smirked at Clark; Mr. Clark felt it necessary to dip his head in a show of contrition.

"Very well," continued the Judge. "Now for the general instructions on the law. Murder is the unlawful killing of another human being with malice aforethought, which means with intention to kill. 'Malice' in this context does not require anger. If you find beyond a reasonable doubt that Leschi committed this crime against Abram Benton Moses, or acted in concert with one who did so, then you shall return a verdict of guilty. Otherwise, not guilty. One other thing – counsel for the defense argued that Leschi could not be guilty because he was acting as a soldier in time of war. You should not consider that defense because I have determined that there was no war on this side of the mountains with the Nisquallies at that time. Now go, gentlemen, do your duty."

Frank heaved a sigh of relief. A scolding and a bad ruling on the military necessity defense was a small price to pay for the bombshell that the prosecution's star witness probably killed Moses in his panic to shoot back. Frank was convinced that the Territory's case was in tatters. Evidently, others agreed. A few members of the bar sidled up to congratulate him. Will Wallace winked at him.

It was then that Charlie Eden and Lieutenant Kautz rushed in, covered in mud, stinking with the sweat of long days of labor. Breathlessly, they told their tale of horse rustling and betrayal. "But we completed the survey," said Lieutenant Kautz proudly, as he spread a map on the defense table. "See, it confirms what *Herr* McLeod said; sixty-eight chains over the Military Road, versus one-hundred-four chains over the rough Indian path Rabbeson calls a shortcut."

"Which is what in miles?" asked Frank Clark.

"Almost nine-tenths of a mile for the path Leschi was supposed to have followed, while Moses and Rabbeson galloped four-tenths of a mile!"

"My God," said Will Wallace, "we've got to get this to the Court's attention right away." Frank agreed; quickly they sent a note into the Judge's chambers. The response was immediate and terse.

"You had your chance. The case is submitted."

Then the Clerk appeared. "We have a verdict!"

So soon? Barely long enough to elect a foreman and take one ballot. No one in the crowd had left their seat. The jury strode back in, heads high, faces blank as fog.

"Have you reached a verdict?" asked Judge Lander.

"We have, Your Honor," replied the foreman, whose wax mustache was drooping.

"Will the defendant please rise and face the jury?" Frank and Will guided Leschi to his feet.

"On the charge of murder of Abram Benton Moses, what is your verdict?"

"We find the defendant guilty," said the foreman. Leschi flinched almost imperceptibly, for he had learned well the difference between the words "not guilty" and "guilty." Frank Clark was speechless. Most were not; a thunderous cheer rose up and rattled the windows of the Washington Hotel.

After allowing a few minutes for the cheers to subside, Judge Lander gaveled the room to silence. He turned his craggy face towards Leschi, who held his head high. "Prisoner at the bar, you have been found guilty by an impartial jury of the crime of murder, one of the most heinous offenses known to our law."

"Your Honor," said Clark, finding his tongue. "We move for a new trial based on newly discovered evidence. Lieutenant Kautz has just returned a survey, showing that the so-called shortcut was twice as far as the road followed by Mr. Moses."

"I think this evidence could have been produced at trial, Mr. Clark."

"Their horses were stolen, Your Honor, to prevent their prompt return."

"Connell's Prairie has been up there ever since the first trial, Mr. Clark. The fact that you waited until just before this trial to examine it, is your own failing, no one else's. Motion denied."

Clark dropped into his seat, a beaten man.

"Prisoner at the bar," resumed Judge Lander, "I hereby adjudge you to be a murderer. Have you anything to say before the Court pronounces sentence upon you?"

As the Judge's words were interpreted to him, Leschi broke into a very incongruous smile, as if an old friend had hailed him. "Yes, thank-you, Judge Lander," he began. "I do not know anything about your laws, but I was hoping I would get a chance to speak. Thank-you. I wish to say to you, and to the Boston people, that I did not kill the man Moses. As God sees me, this is the truth. But I did kill others of your soldiers. They fought bravely, and I honor their spirits. I supposed that the killing of armed men in time of war was not murder; if it was, then the soldiers who killed my people are guilty of murder too. I never killed an unarmed man, or a woman or child. I ordered my people not to do so, and controlled them as best I could. I fought to defend my home, the same as you. Before God I am not guilty. I accept your judgment with a clear conscience."

When Leschi stopped speaking, the silence was palpable. The old Judge's lip began to quiver. He was determined not to be deterred by his heart, from the duty his position imposed. "Your case," he began, but he had to pause a moment to clear his throat. "Your case has been patiently heard by a jury of the neighborhood, and by this Court. It is now my painful duty to pronounce the sentence of the law upon you, for the crime whereof you stand convicted. I shall do this in as brief terms as possible, being conscious of the difficulty of addressing you through an interpreter.

"The sentence of the Court is that the Sheriff of Pierce County, or his deputy, shall, on the 10th day of June, 1857, take you from your place of confinement, to a place of execution nearby, and between the hours of ten o'clock in the forenoon and two o'clock in the afternoon on said day, shall cause execution of the sentence of this Court, which is that, for the crime of murder, you shall be hanged by the neck until dead, and may God have mercy upon your soul."

There was a deep hush as the entire banquet hall drew a breath. A blood-curdling war cry from the very back of the room shattered the silence. In the back row, Sluggia fell dead to the floor, the silver blade of a coffin knife imbedded to the haft between his shoulder blades.

Chapter Twenty-Seven
To *Tenalquot*

1

Now was the time of vindication. Everywhere Stevens went, boisterous crowds sounded their welcome. He was no longer just their Governor; he was their general, their protector, their avenging angel, their Great White Father. Alex Abernathy, Stevens' opponent in the Congressional race, was a plainspoken farmer whose quiet call for an end to corruption and drunkenness in Olympia fell on deaf ears. Stevens did not even have to mount a defense. All he had to do was smile, as the poor fellow stumbled over attacks, tempered by apologies. Then Stevens patted Abernathy on the back, and winked at the crowd. "Well, Farmer Abernathy," he'd say, "if Leschi had been as nice a feller as you, there wouldn't have been any massacre, and we wouldn't have had to bring him to justice."

The *Washington Republican*, successor to the *Puget Sound Courier*, maintained a steady drumbeat of ridicule against the Governor, but it rolled off like rain from a duck. Stevens, it said, "suffered from a disordered imagination," envisioning himself "a great man with the military genius of an Alexander," when in fact he was just "a tin-pot Napoleon." When Stevens showed up stone cold sober in the opposition stronghold of Steilacoom, his weak effort on the podium was ridiculed by the *Washington Republican*:

> It seemed to lack the infusion of Spirit, which has made all the gentleman's past speeches in the territory so intoxicating.

The Governor's partisans procured a signed statement from Stevens' neighbor, a clergyman, who averred that he did not believe Stevens to be in the habit of abusing strong drink. Two days before the election, the *Republican* responded with the headline:

GOVERNOR DESISTS FROM WHISKEY IN CHURCH!

over an editorial charging that intemperance made Stevens unfit for office. The *Pioneer & Democrat* responded that the *Republican* was written "by dirty dogs."

They needn't have bothered. The more drinking became a campaign issue, the more the hard-drinking pioneers along the campaign trail offered to buy rounds for the Governor. Stevens won more votes in the saloons than he could ever lose on the podium, and outpolled the teetotaling Mr. Abernathy, two to one.

"Nobody likes a scold," Stevens confided to stone-cold sober Secretary Mason, as he appointed him acting Governor on August 11, 1857, pending the arrival of his successor. Charles smiled his tight smile and flicked back his hair. He understood well why Stevens was refusing to take him along to Washington City. It had nothing to do with Mason's parsimonious temperament. It was the way Meg's eyes softened whenever he came near.

Meanwhile, the wheels of justice ground forward in their ponderous way. Motions were made and denied; appeals filed, stays of execution granted. At last, on December 18, 1857, Chief Leschi, flanked by Frank Clark and Charlie Eden, appeared at the Supreme Court of the Territory of Washington. Judge Chenoweth was there, sitting up high like a bald eagle perched on a dead snag. To his left was his fellow Judge, Obadiah Benton McFadden, the forty-two year old Pennsylvania prothonotary who'd read a little law on the wagon train, and reinvented himself as a Judge in the Oregon Territory.

Leschi, a man raised to listen for the spirit of the mountain or the salmon leaping against the rapids, was treated instead to a two-hour colloquy on the effect of court consolidation on pending charges, and the sufficiency of the indictment to distinguish between degrees of murder under statute versus common law. This abstruse argument was rendered even less comprehensible by the halting interpretation of Ben Shaw, the man who'd told the Governor he could get the Indians to sign their own death warrant.

Leschi did understand the argument on one point. Mr. Clark contended in the strongest possible terms that it was error for Judge Lander to refuse to permit a new trial based on the evidence uncovered by Lieutenant Kautz's survey of Connell's Prairie. That seemed but simple justice – to take a man's life for murder, the jury must hear the evidence.

Judge Chenoweth asked Leschi if he had anything to say. Leschi stood and shifted uncomfortably from foot to foot. There were so many books and papers piled all around, so many words and so little sense, the whole courtroom was like a dead forest. In a quiet but firm voice, Leschi repeated what he had told Chief Judge Lander: he did not kill Moses, he fought only to protect his home, he believed that the killing of a soldier in time of war was not murder. Then he knelt, made the sign of the cross, and said, *"Ta-te mono, Ta-te lem-mas, Ta-te ha-le-hach, tu-ul-li-as-sist-ah."* The Judges looked quizzically at Shaw, who stood silent.

"Mr. Shaw?" pressed Judge McFadden.

Shaw repeated the words he knew so well, the words he himself had used a thousand thousand times, since his first catechism. "This is the Father, this is the Son, this is the Holy Ghost, these are all one and the same, Amen."

"Yes, well, this is a court of law, not a confessional," said Judge McFadden irritably. Then he began to read the handwritten opinion the Court had agreed upon, even before the arguments were heard.

> The case comes before us on a writ of error to the Second Judicial District. The prisoner has occupied a position of influence, as one of a band of Indians who sacrificed the lives of so many of our citizens in the war so cruelly waged against our people on the waters of Puget Sound.

> It speaks volumes for our people that, notwithstanding the spirit of indignation and revenge so natural to the human heart incited by the ruthless massacre of their families, at the trial of the accused deliberate impartiality has been manifested at every stage of the proceedings.

> It is to be regretted, for the sake of the accused, as well as the future peace of the Territory, that a more summary mode of proceeding had not been adopted. This case, however, now comes to this Court, and we are not disposed to shirk our duty.

"What is he saying?" asked Leschi of Charlie. "I am told the words, but I cannot understand how they go together."

"Near as I can tell," whispered Charlie, "he is saying that you are a savage monster, and the white men are angels for giving you a trial instead of just taking you out and having you shot."

"All those fancy words to say this?" asked Leschi, and he smiled. Judge McFadden paused in his recitation.

"The prisoner will remain silent!" he barked. Then he returned to his explanation of why the forms of law permitted Leschi's execution.

The Court's ruling on Lieutenant Kautz's survey was totally beyond the ken of Leschi, or even Charlie, who had thought he understood the English language. Frank Clark interpreted: "The Judge just ruled that Kautz's map would not have changed the jury's mind, so there is no error in refusing a new trial." Charlie's jaw tensed in fury.

"He's right," whispered Leschi. "That trial in the Governor's town was over before it started. Do nothing foolish, my son. Men are men, after all."

"If I have to warn you again," said Judge McFadden, "I will have the prisoner bound and gagged." Then he finished reading the Court's decision, affirming Leschi's conviction. Leschi was forced to stand, and suffer a second sentence of death, this time to be carried out "between the hours of ten o'clock in the forenoon and two o'clock in the afternoon of Friday, the 22nd day of January, 1858."

As Leschi was led out of the chamber in shackles, a distraught Charlie turned to Frank Clark. "Is there anything left for us to do?" he pleaded.

"There's always something," said Frank.

"Anything!"

"Let's see if the new Governor has a heart buried under all those layers of political pork."

"Of course," said Charlie, "a pardon."

"Yes," said Frank. "A pardon for his damnable innocence."

2

The crescent moon hung like a cat's smile out the window of Colonel Casey's residence on the grounds of Fort Steilacoom. By the time Frank Clark had been able to arrange a meeting between the new Governor and Leschi's supporters, it was the evening of Tuesday, January 19, only three days before the appointed execution.

The horse-faced Governor, Fayette McMullen of Virginia, went around the room twice shaking hands, and would have made a third circuit had Secretary Mason not intercepted him. A pleasant enough former stagecoach driver, Governor McMullen liked nothing better than to "slap hams," as he called it. His spoils for managing the Virginia delegation to the Democratic National Convention for Buchanan, was this odd job of Governor of a God-forsaken wilderness. He was determined to make the best of it.

After everyone had been seated, Dr. Tolmie rose up like a biblical prophet, his few remaining locks curling into his fog-tangled beard. His job was to fill in the Governor on the background – how Leschi had been a friend to the white man, helping new pioneers, even fighting to protect Fort Nisqually against Patkanim's attack.

"You have doubtless heard Leschi blamed for many deprivations committed during the late war, but the truth is very different. In fact, Leschi tried to restrain his warriors from attacking women, children and unarmed settlers – often successfully – at the risk of his own authority over the more bloodthirsty members of his tribe. The terrible massacre at White River was the product of insubordination among younger warriors, which Chief Leschi condemned."

"Now, Doctor, how can we really know this-here sort of thing?" asked the Governor. "I mean, it would be natural for his kinfolk to cover up for him, wouldn't it?"

"I have been a friend to many of these people for years. I have provided them medicine, blankets and seed; I have tended to their sick, taught them farming techniques, celebrated their births and marriages, mourned the passing of their dead. I am fully within their confidence. What I am reporting to you now, I have heard from many reliable sources at widely separated times." The Governor washed down a grunt with a pull on his whiskey, but at least he was listening. "Also, we have many examples during the war when white folks came under Leschi's power, and he let them go without harm. Most notable was the young hostage, George King, whom Leschi returned unharmed."

Governor McMullen ducked his neck, like a turkey swallowing, which seemed to be his way of nodding. "Well, Doctor, what of this war he started? You can't argue with that, can you? He did start the war?"

Dr. Tolmie told McMullen about the inadequate land offered under the treaty Leschi refused to sign, which was signed for him by trickery. "Its inadequacy was recognized even by your predecessor, who ended up giving the Nisquallies a better reservation on the river after the war."

"Well, slice this toad up however you want," replied Governor McMullen. "Leschi's people fired the first shots, and therefore they started the war."

"I am convinced, Governor, that Leschi would never have gone to war had Governor Stevens not ordered troops out to his village to capture him – dead or alive."

"I see," said the Governor.

"The plow was left standing in the field," added Charlie. "They were planting winter wheat, Governor. Not what one would expect of a man who plans to go to war."

"Leschi's village was burned by the troops," said Dr. Tolmie. "The grave of his recently departed wife was desecrated by the soldiers. Yes, they fired the first shot. But it was fired in self-defense, and in defense of their homelands."

"Lies, Governor, all lies," said Mason.

"Could be, Charles," said the new Governor. "Still, I'd like to hear these folks out, if you don't mind."

"Thank-you, Governor," said Dr. Tolmie. "I wish to turn matters over to Lieutenant Kautz."

The Lieutenant jumped up, clicked his heels and executed a smart half-bow. "Your excellency," he began, as he unrolled and explained his survey, showing that the "short-cut" Rabbeson testified Leschi took to the scene of the murder, was twice as long as the road followed by the express riders. "It is impossible," concluded Kautz.

Governor McMullen scrutinized the map, rubbing his chin with his left hand. "*Hmmmm,*" was all he said, but he was ducking his neck by the time he looked up.

"Colonel Casey," said Dr. Tolmie.

"Governor, on behalf of the United States Army, with the approval of Colonel Wright and General Wool, it is our strongly-held view that the killing of one combatant by another in time of war cannot constitute murder. We view the precedent which would be set by execution of Chief Leschi to be very dangerous. It could place all soldiers at risk of execution, based on their actions in the field of battle."

Governor McMullen shifted uneasily in his seat, took a pull at his whiskey. "Yes, Colonel, I can see the difficulty," he said.

"Mr. Meeker?" said Dr. Tolmie.

The scrawny young pioneer rose, hat in hand. "Mr. Gov'nor, Sir," he said, "it was my duty to serve on the jury in Leschi's first trial."

"First trial?" exclaimed the Governor, obviously surprised.

"Yes, Sir, first trial. That one ended in a hung jury, 'cause we didn't think a soldier could be guilty of murder for shootin' a soldier from the other side."

"That didn't persuade the second jury?" pressed the Governor.

"The court wouldn't let the jury consider that," said Charlie. "But to tell the truth, Governor, I don't think it would have made any difference to that jury what they were instructed. You've heard of a hanging judge? That was a hanging jury, every last man."

"Well, if that is all," said Mason, and he began to rise. Governor McMullen didn't rise with him.

"Not quite," said Dr. Tolmie. "Charlie?"

Charlie stepped forward, hand extended, a golden boy with an open and winning smile. "Governor," he said, and of course the Governor shook it, and smiled his big-toothed smile. "As Leschi's son-in-law, I have seen a side of Leschi other white folks don't get to see. He is the best-respected Indian leader this side of the Cascades. He never counsels violence if it can be avoided. So, as I see it, your choice is this: execute an innocent man, and incur the wrath of his people just when we're trying to heal the wounds of war; or spare his life, obtain the good will of all the Indians, and many white folks to boot.

Plus, with Leschi around, you'll have the strongest ally, who will help keep peace with the tribes."

Charlie paused, gauging the effect of his words. He could see the wheels turning in the politician's mind. Then he pressed further. "That, Governor, is the practical side of the matter. Of course, there is another side to it; the side of the angels. That's the side every Christian is duty-bound to heed. I'm talking about your immortal soul, Governor. Are you willing to stand at the gates of heaven with the blood of an innocent man on your hands? As the Bible says, 'Blessed are the merciful: for they shall obtain mercy.'"

The Governor stood before Charlie, head bowed in prayer. For a long time, no one said a word. Then Mason touched his shoulder, wordlessly signaling that they should go.

"Doctor," said McMullen, "you and your friends have made a powerful case for clemency. I think I can safely say that I am moved to a very different view of this matter. I'll get you a decision by Thursday, as obviously time is short."

"There is still one more man to hear from, Governor," said Tolmie. He nodded at Lieutenant Kautz, who opened a door to the hallway and beckoned to a guard. A moment later in walked Leschi himself, looking strong, despite the shackles at his wrists and ankles that chafed his skin.

The new Governor and Chief Leschi stood eye-to-eye, not three feet apart. McMullen appeared uncomfortable. Leschi broke the ice, with Dr. Tolmie interpreting.

"I would shake your hand, Governor, but as you can see ..." he said, smiling as he shook his chains and shrugged. McMullen merely nodded. "I know my good friends have made a far stronger case for me than I could ever make," said Leschi, "so I won't repeat it. I only wanted to ask, do you have any questions that need to be answered by me, personally?"

"Did you kill Mr. Moses?" McMullen's eyes bore straight into Leschi's.

"No, Governor, I did not. I have sworn this before God, and I swear it before you. However," added Leschi, "if I had been on that spot in the swamp, I would have tried to kill the express riders, just as Lieutenant Kautz here tried to kill me during his valiant charge at White River. We were at war with your people, fighting to defend our home. If that is murder, then many brave soldiers on both sides must be condemned."

The Governor held Leschi's gaze a moment longer, then ducked his neck. "Manfully said, my friend," he replied, and patted Leschi on the shoulder.

3

On the Wednesday and Thursday before the scheduled hanging, Leschi had a steady stream of visitors. Even Chief Se-alth came down from Seattle. "We have used different means, great *Tyee*," he said to Leschi, "but our hearts are as one."

"Your tribesman, Nelson, told me you would join us in our fight," replied Leschi. "When you did not, I was angry. Now, I see that you were wise."

"You are too gracious to call it wisdom," said Se-alth, hanging his head. "I miss Nelson; he was a friend."

"I miss him too," said Leschi. "Perhaps I will see him soon."

With Se-alth was Mary's father, John Hiton, who clasped Leschi firmly to his chest, pounding his back with his three-fingered hand. "Among all our people, all the tribes of *Whulge*, you are now a legend," he whispered.

"I don't like the sound of that," laughed Leschi. "Legends are all dead, and as you can see, I am still very much alive. Speaking of which, what has become of that pretty daughter of yours? Wasn't she my *klootchman*? Why do I never see her?"

John Hiton shook his head in disapproval. "She has taken up with a Boston man, a saloon-keeper in Seattle. I have scolded her, but she will not listen to me. She likes the fancy clothes that he buys for her. Do you know that she has three pairs of shoes, all of which hurt her feet? I am sorry."

"Do not be," said Leschi. "She and I were not meant for each other. Tell Mary that I wish her well."

"Thank-you, my friend, I will do so."

"One more thing," added Leschi.

"Yes?" asked John.

"I have heard it said that you played some part in helping the Boston children who fled from White River."

"Yes."

"You know that I was once a rich man. Most of that is now gone – most, but not everything. Dr. Tolmie is holding a credit for me. I want it to go to those children when they come of age. Will you see to it?"

John Hiton nodded. "With pleasure, *Tyee*."

Leschi's next visitor was the *klale t'kope tillicum*, Washington Bush. "My friend," cried Leschi, and the two embraced as if no years stood between them. "It has been too long!"

"Too long," echoed Washington, giving Leschi such a look of sadness as would stop all but the stoutest heart.

"I know," said Leschi, reading his old friend's mind. "You warned me; I did not listen."

"I'm not here to go over all that," said Washington. "I'm here to pay respects. To thank you. There are some white men who still remember what you did for our people, and not just the black white men." They were silent a minute. Then Washington gave voice to what he'd long wondered. "Do you regret it?"

"No," replied Leschi. "How can I regret anything? We are all in God's hands."

Washington nodded. "I have a gift," he said, "from Isobel, with love." From out of a hat box he'd carefully carried up on the steamer, Washington lifted a rich chocolate cake with thick butter-cream frosting. "She says don't worry about getting fat." Together they dug in, happily eating four big pieces with their fingers, which they licked clean. The ache in Washington's belly as he took his leave was not from too much cake.

Leschi was surprised beyond all measure by the next visitor, an elegant native Chief in top hat and tails, wearing white gloves and a sad expression. "I do not like this way of killing," confessed Patkanim to his old enemy. "It takes away all the honor."

"It is much prized by your allies," said Leschi, pointedly.

"I will not apologize, Leschi. You know I was right when I first said to wipe out the white devils, and I was right again when the time came to join them. If things change, and a chance comes to exterminate them, I will gladly do it, but I will need a gun bigger than the sun itself."

"You always changed sides too easily."

"I have never changed sides, Leschi. I have always been on the side of the Snoqualmie. We have a good reservation, on our own lands."

The two rivals fell to silence. At length, Leschi said, "Thank-you for coming, Chief. I hold no ill will."

"Your sister sends her love."

"Thank-you. Please care for her."

"I will, Chief." Patkanim stood to go. There could be no embrace, but the two men exchanged a nod of understanding. Patkanim turned to go, then paused. "To have been killed by you on that day by the Green River, when you held my life in your hands – that would have been honorable," he said. Then he was gone.

Later, Winyea arrived with a hooded stranger called "Yelm Jim," bearing presents of dried oysters and smoked salmon. "When spring comes, we will return with fresh berries," promised Winyea.

"I don't think I'll see spring," said Leschi. "I doubt that I will even see the next full moon."

"You must, *Tyee*, for it measures fifty seasons of your life," said the stranger, who threw back his hood to reveal the hawk face of Wahoolit. Leschi whooped with joy as the two men embraced.

"Dr. Tolmie said that the meeting with the new Governor went very well," said Winyea. "He expects the Governor to spare your life."

Leschi smiled. "We shall see," he said. "White men prefer their justice to mercy."

They were silent, watching dust rise through an errant sunbeam that had fallen unimaginable distances, only to land in the prison shed. "Do you remember, when we charged together down into the sawdust piles by Yesler's mill?" asked Leschi.

"How could we ever forget that day?" said Winyea.

"It is written in my hand," said Wahoolit, holding up his shriveled left stump.

"One of you who fought by my side that day, would make a good Chief for our people," said Leschi.

Winyea went down on his knees before Leschi. "No!" he cried. "You are our one and only Chief. After you, there shall be no other Chiefs."

"No other Chiefs?" asked Leschi. "Think it over, my friend. I am not sure I want to be remembered as the last Chief of the Nisquallies."

Soon it was late on Thursday, with the hanging set for the very next day. No word had yet come from the Governor's office. The little prison shed was crowded with Ann, Moonya, George, Betsy, Wahoolit, Winyea, and Charlie Eden. The men had their faces painted in red stripes. Both men and women beat their carved and decorated *tamanous* sticks on the floor in a circle around Leschi, as Charlie beat a drum. They sang songs to summon the spirits of gentle deer and chipmunk to intercede on Leschi's behalf, to move Governor McMullen's heart, to soften it, to make it merciful.

"The white man's heart is like stone," explained Ann to Charlie. "The Native's heart is like mud. Our medicine men can draw the bad *tamanous* out of the heart of a stricken Native, or even shoot a bad spell into the heart of a tribesman in a neighboring village. But they can neither afflict, nor cure, the white man. His heart cannot be penetrated."

"It is true," added Betsy. "Were it otherwise, your *Tyee* Stevens would have died from heart curse long ago."

"It is not true," replied Charlie. "My white man's heart is pierced and broken."

4

The new Governor's heart had been softened by their words. When Governor McMullen returned to Olympia, he instructed Mason to draw an order of clemency. Instead, Mason handed the Governor a sealed letter from former Governor Stevens, entrusted to him for just such an emergency.

"Inasmuch as you did not live through the deprivations and massacres inflicted upon our people by this black-hearted savage," began Stevens' letter, "please take a moment to heed the words of one who bore the very heavy responsibility of leading the Territory through those dark days." The letter proceeded to detail the broken treaty, the ambush of McAllister, and the White River massacre. "This barbarous stroke struck terror into the whole community, paralyzing farming and commerce, and reversing the efforts of hundreds of pioneers over a decade of back-breaking labor." Stevens pointed out that Leschi's guilt had been adjudged by twenty-two of the twenty-four jurors to hear the case, and by the Territorial Supreme Court. Stevens charged that the other two jurors had likely been bribed by Frank Clark, "who is well known for such crimes." Then Stevens urged upon the new Governor his own political interests, asserting that passage through Congress of the bill to fund Territorial war scrip was dependent on Leschi's execution. "If that is accomplished during your administration, you will have many friends who can well afford to show their gratitude."

Finally, Stevens pressed what he called "the moral aspect of the case." According to Stevens:

The cold-blooded murders of members of the dominant race must be punished swiftly and certainly. Even now, as I write this letter just a few days after submitting my formal resignation as Governor, we are stunned by the news of the beheading of our countryman, Captain Isaac Ebey, at the hands of savages from the North. Nothing other than swift and certain punishment will impress upon the savage tribes a respect for our authority, and deter them from the commission of similar outrages in the future. The situation is parallel to that which you face in your native Virginia, in handling the slave population. I am sure you understand.

Closing with the words, "Clemency, however attractive to your honorable spirit, is in truth the path of cowardice, not honor," the Governor's letter had a powerful effect.

As Governor McMullen perused the words of his predecessor, supporters of the judgment against Leschi circulated word that the Governor was contemplating clemency. Dozens of copies of petitions protesting executive clemency in the strongest possible terms poured into the Governor's office all day Wednesday and Thursday. According to Mr. Mason's count, there were over seven hundred signatures submitted, which was remarkable considering there were only fifteen hundred votes cast at the recent Congressional election, and the petitions had only two days to circulate and make their way back across the muddy roads to Olympia.

Meanwhile, Mason gathered Martha McAllister, Mike Simmons, Mary Slaughter, and Johnny King, to the Governor's office, for personal appeals. McMullen was cajoled by Simmons and threatened by Mrs. McAllister. He had his heart broken by doe-eyed Mrs. Slaughter, and little fatherless Will, Jr. He felt the prick of anger after hearing from motherless Johnny King, who told him he "warn't scairt of nothin'," but whose stepparents confided that he awoke screaming in the middle of the night at least once a week.

Finally, the new Governor sent everyone away and called in a minister, with whom he knelt in prayer as night fell. Then, looking out the window of his office, he saw a sight fit to freeze any politician's heart. It was himself, hanging in effigy, as a jeering mob danced around the gibbet. Mason approached from behind so silently that the Governor jumped when his hand touched his shoulder. "They'll have their hanging one way or the other, Governor," he whispered.

5

After the *tamanous* ceremony, many others from Fort Steilacoom and beyond jammed the tiny prison shed to bursting. It was a raucous living wake, filled with laughter and tears, as the celebrants indulged in pipes of *kinnikinnick* and cups of kalse, the native liquor distilled from the sunflower root.

The waxing half moon rose until it was framed perfectly by the high window of Leschi's cell. "A toast," proposed Frank Clark, holding his cup aloft. "To mercy."

"To mercy," they echoed raising their cups. The libation was interrupted by a sharp rap at the door. It was Colonel Casey.

"I am sorry, Leschi," he said. "The Governor has denied clemency."

Kautz translated to stunned silence. "Please," said Leschi to the Colonel, "join me in a drink." The Colonel nodded, squeezed into the crowded room, and took a cup. Leschi held his up. "To the full moon," he said, and they drank.

6

Based on the Supreme Court's mandate, the Clerk of the Second District Court issued the death warrant to Pierce County Sheriff George Williams of Steilacoom, with instructions "to cause execution upon Leschi on Friday, the 22nd day of January next ensuing, between the hours of ten o'clock in the forenoon and two o'clock in the afternoon of the same day." Sheriff Williams promptly deputized Charles McDaniel to serve as hangman, his qualification being a working knowledge of knots gained at sea. McDaniel asked Colonel Casey if he could use the scaffold at Fort Steilacoom, and was politely declined. He found a suitable plot of ground in a field a mile to the east, where he built a scaffold of cedar, the Nisqually tree of life.

As soon as word of the denial of clemency reached Fort Steilacoom, Frank Clark whisked Winyea from Leschi's cell, handed him a bottle of whiskey, and sent him into town with Charlie Eden. Their mission was to present Winyea as Exhibit A to James Bachelor, United States Commissioner. Then Clark staggered around the fort with his chest stuck out, wagering anyone with a sawbuck that Leschi would not be executed the next day, regardless of the "chicken-shit" Governor.

Mr. Bachelor, a happily married deacon of the Methodist Church, had an inordinate fondness for young women, which Frank Clark was only too pleased to feed. In exchange, Mr. Bachelor could be counted on to do certain favors for Mr. Clark. When he smelled the whiskey on Winyea's breath, and heard the shocking news of who was responsible for the crime of selling liquor to an Indian, Mr. Bachelor did not hesitate to issue the arrest warrant requested by Captain Eden on behalf of Mr. Clark.

Friday, January 22, 1858, dawned clear and cool; perfect weather for a hanging. After a good breakfast of hash and rashers, Sheriff Williams and the hangman, McDaniel, mounted and headed down the road towards the fort. They had not gotten a quarter mile, however, when two men trotted out of the forest and planted themselves squarely across the highway. McDaniel recognized Lieutenant Kautz's brother Fred, and the gruff Scottsman, Lieutenant Angus McKibben.

"George Williams, Charles McDaniel?" cried Lieutenant McKibben.

"Yes, Sir," replied the Sheriff, seemingly unconcerned.

"Gentlemen, you are under arrest on the charge of selling liquor to an Indian. You will please accompany me back into Steilacoom town."

McDaniel could not believe his ears. When the Sheriff did not protest, however, McDaniel went along. They were taken to a snug room in the back of the tavern, warmed by a big fire in a stone hearth. There they were held in comfort, even given a deck of cards and all the beer they could drink, to help them pass the time. The Sheriff seemed grateful, but McDaniel merely feigned interest in the beer and cards. Meanwhile, the big clock on the wall ticked off the minutes permitted for lawful execution under the warrant.

A large and restless crowd had gathered by the gallows in the big field east of the Fort. The McAllisters were there, along with many others who lost loved ones in the war. Gentle Mary Slaughter chose to be elsewhere. Off in the distance, the waters of Steilacoom Lake sparkled in morning sunshine. As the adults huddled, wrapped in coats, children ran and played beneath the cedar posts supporting the gallows. Men furtively nipped at flasks, as they watched the tree line to the west for the first signs of the condemned man approaching from Fort Steilacoom. A few white supporters of Leschi drew near, but no Natives dared show their faces, for fear of violence. The sun reached its zenith, poised to journey towards the Fort, where the condemned man on whom it had already set for the last time, awaited the dreadful knock at the door.

It was just past noon when a messenger from Steilacoom town arrived, bearing the intelligence that the Sheriff and hangman had last been seen under guard at the tavern. Charles Mason, official Territorial witness to the execution, summoned Jack Blunt. Together they rode to the Fort, and demanded an immediate audience with Colonel Casey. The Colonel emerged from his quarters in his undershirt, his big craggy face lathered in shaving cream, his well-muscled torso glinting in the noonday sun.

"Colonel," said Mason, barely restraining the anger in his voice, "I understand that the Sheriff of Pierce County has been arrested. Is that by your order?"

"No, Sir."

"Do you know where the Sheriff is?"

"No, Sir." The Colonel would cooperate – barely.

"Are you cognizant of the fact that the Sheriff is under arrest?"

"I have heard it said he is under arrest by civil authority."

"Please provide me with a detachment to aid in his rescue."

"We're kinda busy here, Mr. Secretary. As the prostitute said to the preacher, I can fit you in Sunday mornin'."

"Damn you to hell," snapped Mason as he pulled the reins away.

It was nearly one o'clock when Mason and Blunt burst into the tavern at Steilacoom. The captives and their captors all jumped to their feet. McKibben wore his service revolver, and Fred Kautz picked up a rifle. Blunt's rifle was lowered to the floor, but that could change quickly.

"Gentlemen, what is the meaning of this?" demanded Mr. Mason.

"These men are under arrest by order of Commissioner Bachelor," said Kautz.

"On what charge?"

"Selling liquor to an Indian."

"Hasn't it occurred to you," spat Mason, "that any Indian in the Territory would so swear, if he thought there'd be a Boston stupid or treacherous enough to believe it?"

The hangman, McDaniel, turned to the Sheriff. "George," he said, "this fool thing has gone far enough. Now give me that warrant."

"Aw, you're just mad 'cause I'm winnin'," said the Sheriff, laying his cards face down on the table between them.

"You are under arrest, Sir," warned Kautz, lifting the rifle towards the hangman.

"You gonna shoot me, Fred?" asked McDaniel, standing. Fred's eyes darted about. "You always were a lousy poker player," said McDaniel. "Now, George, gimme that dang warrant."

"No, Sir," replied the Sheriff. "I'm under arrest, and I for one am a law-abiding citizen. What would people say if the Sheriff himself defied an arrest warrant?"

"You're a law-abiding snake, is what you are, Sheriff," said McDaniel. He turned and began walking across the no-man's land between the captives and their rescuers, when he heard the click of a hammer being cocked. He stopped, raised his hands, and said real softly, "You wouldn't shoot a man in the back, now would you, Fred?" He turned slowly to face the gun.

It wasn't Fred Kautz, or even Lieutenant McKibben, who'd cocked the weapon. It was Sheriff Williams himself, holding McKibben's revolver. Simultaneously, Blunt's rifle zeroed in on the Sheriff's heart, leaving the two sides locked in a tense stand-off.

"Don't think Frank Clark can protect you this time, Williams," said Mason. "If you don't drop that gun and hand over the death warrant I'll have your job, your farm, and I'll run you right out of the Territory."

Few things are more sobering than the wrong end of a loaded rifle at close range. "Not worth it, George," whispered Kautz. Slowly, Williams lowered the pistol, uncocked it and laid it on the table next to the playing cards. Pulling back his frock coat to show that there was no concealed weapon, he reached in to produce the warrant. Then, with a flick of his hand, he sent it flying into the fire.

Leschi would live to greet the full moon that marked his fiftieth season.

7

As the shadows began to lengthen, angry murmurings filled the meadow. Rumors of a plot to foul the pure stream of justice had been circulating ever since Mason's departure, and now the truth was irrefutable. Leschi's few supporters drifted away to celebrate in hidden enclaves.

"To Olympia!" cried the mass of men, and they rode hard, sounding the alarm as they went. "Anarchy! Injustice! Leschi lives!"

By eight o'clock that night, two hundred citizens were assembled at the public school house in Olympia, to hear the evidence and determine what course to follow. Colonel Jack Blunt, esteemed for his service in the late war, was elected Chairman of the assembly. He called Charles Mason before the meeting to tell what he knew. Based on his testimony, a resolution was quickly adopted condemning the conspirators, along with everyone else who'd ever supported Leschi. The resolution, subscribed to by many of the same men who had supported martial law and the arrest of Chief Judge Lander, strongly condemned "interference with the lawful processes of the courts of justice." The resolution noted that the conspiracy "exhibits a most unnatural and unreasonable sympathy for the Indian, who was known to have been engaged in the fiendish massacre of helpless women and children on White River in the fall of 1855." On behalf of the committee, it was signed by Jack Blunt, architect of the Mashel River massacre.

Governor McMullen, cowering before the political hurricane roaring outside his window, appeared before the assembly to express his dismay at this "affront to the rule of law." The Territorial Legislature met the next morning in emergency joint session to enact a measure calling upon the Supreme Court to immediately re-sentence any prisoner whose sentence had gone unexecuted. There was only one prisoner who fit the bill – Leschi.

On Thursday, February 4, 1858, Leschi stood before Judge Chenoweth, and received his sentence for the third time. This time, Frank Clark did not stand by his side. His name had been stricken from the rolls of attorneys by order of the Supreme Court.

"Prisoner at the Bar," thundered Judge Chenoweth, his eyes flashing anger. "For reasons which may not be understood by this Court, the sentence pronounced by the Supreme Court in December last has not been carried into effect. You yet live, and again appear at the bar for sentence." Chenoweth looked up from his paper, as if to confirm the outlandish truth of this. Scowling, he returned to the task of deciphering his handwritten scrawl. "You have had much time to prepare for death, unlike those of our own race with whose murder you are charged." The Judge was breathing heavily now, sweating though the chamber was chilly. The murder of his friend and neighbor Captain Ebey had hardened his heart. He removed a handkerchief and mopped his brow before continuing. "It is therefore considered by the Court that you be deemed and adjudged a murderer, and that you be hanged by the neck until you are dead. That the Sheriff of *Thurston* County," and he emphasized the county, to be sure it was understood that there would be no more evasions, "or his deputy shall cause execution to be done upon you on Friday the nineteenth day of February, 1858, at or near Steilacoom in Pierce County, between the hours of ten o'clock in the forenoon and two o'clock in the afternoon – no, make that four o'clock in the afternoon of said day – such that you be hanged by the neck until you are dead. And may God have mercy on your soul."

After sentence was passed, the weather turned uncharacteristically cold. Killing frost followed killing frost. The early forsythia froze in their beds; the winter kale turned brown and withered. Four inches of snow fell in Olympia and Steilacoom on the 14th, followed by fifteen inches the next day, blanketing a land that was accustomed to no more than a dusting.

The weather did not break until the morning of the hanging, when melting snow turned dirt roads into swamps that devoured wagon wheels up to their hubs. Nonetheless, over two hundred hardy, angry souls, managed to reach the hanging ground, there to ensure with their own eyes that the demon who had haunted them for so long had truly been eradicated. Ann, Moonya, and Charlie, waited quietly by the wagon, which was to return Leschi's remains to the reservation. Leschi arrived on horseback promptly at 10:05 a.m., his hands bound before him. A priest, Abbe Rossi, administered last rites to him at the base of the steps to the gallows.

Leschi's face was radiant. He climbed the twelve steps to the gallows platform without assistance or hesitancy. Charles Grainger, the new hangman, placed the thick rope around Leschi's neck, and tightened the knot with trembling hands. Leschi recognized Grainger as the deputy at his second trial, who had loosened his shackles to permit him to stretch and eat in relative comfort. With the noose around his neck, Leschi thanked him in a voice so clear and calm, that suddenly Grainger knew he was about to hang an innocent man.

The Thurston County Sheriff read the death warrant, as Dr. Tolmie interpreted, tears streaming down his face. "Have you any final words?" asked the Sheriff.

Leschi looked past the crowd to the distant waters of Steilacoom Lake, once the pristine home of *Weatchee*, a goddess who lived beneath the surface and ate unwary fishermen. Now the lake was choked with the backup from Andrew Byrd's sawmill. "Forgiveness," he said in startlingly clear English. "I go now, to *Tenalquot*. Goodbye, my friends."

> *Spirit dances in the rain, in the wave, in the wind,*
> *Spirit dances in rock and tree, you and me,*
> *Our hearts drum the dance.*

Afterword

On January 26, 2005, I found myself driving on the reservation road behind a big yellow Chief Leschi School District bus, on my way to the Nisqually Tribal Center to meet with Cynthia Iyall, a direct descendent of one of Leschi's sisters. It was a misty Pacific Northwest day, but I sped effortlessly in climate-controlled comfort through the bulldozed, clear-cut stubble of an ancient forest, into the thin line of firs guarding the center like verdant arrows.

Cynthia, a bright-eyed sprite wearing a black sweatshirt emblazoned with the pink logo, "My Boyfriend's Cuter than Your Boyfriend," was friendly and open with this Boston stranger from Seattle. Of course, in a sense, we're all "Bostons" now. Cynthia's cluttered office with the 1996 hockey tournament poster, GE digital clock, and framed family snapshots, attest that she and the other members of the Nisqually Nation are as plugged into the mono-culture as anyone. And yet, there is another side to that story – those Nisquallies who have made the effort to reconnect with their tribe, are rooted to the Pacific Northwest in a way we transient Bostons aspire to, but rarely achieve.

Cynthia explained that the campaign to rehabilitate Leschi's name began in June, 2001, in the living room of Sherman Leschi. Sherman, a direct descendent of Quiemuth through his son George, told Cynthia that the time had come to clear Leschi's name. A few days later, Cynthia received a call on the same subject from the Nisqually tribal historian, Cecelia Svinth Carpenter. No, she had not spoken with Sherman; she'd been contacted by the Thurston County Historical Society, in response to a moving presentation made by Jan Stevenson. It was a sign that Leschi's spirit could wait no longer for justice.

Justice does not come overnight, and it never comes easy. Through the efforts of more people than could be named, including Melissa Parr, Sharon and Carl Hultman, John Ladenburg, Bill Tobin, and the Washington State Legislature, a special Historical Court of Inquiry was convened on Friday, December 10, 2004, to re-examine the conviction of Chief Leschi. Chief Justice Gerry Alexander of the Washington Supreme Court presided over a bench composed of jurists from around the State, before a packed auditorium at the Washington State Museum of History in Tacoma. After hearing testimony from historians, tribal members and military lawyers, the Court announced its verdict: the killing of A.B. Moses was an act of war between lawful combatants, and therefore "Chief Leschi should not, as a matter of law, have been tried for the crime of murder." The auditorium erupted in wild applause, the cheers mixed with tears.

In the words of Cynthia Iyall:

I think it finally brought peace and it made so many people happy. Especially for the kids, knowing that the historical icon of our tribe is not the first murderer noted in Washington State, that really makes a big difference for them, going to Chief Leschi High School. Now they know, what was said about him, what happened to him, was wrong. It's been noticed; it's been corrected; and now they can move on. I think it brought a whole new sense of pride to being Nisqually, Puyallup, Medicine Creek.

Still, there is the old saying, justice delayed is justice denied. Sadly, Sherman Leschi, like generations of Nisquallies before him, never lived to witness the exoneration. And regardless of the Historical Court's ruling, the fact remains that Leschi's life was cut short three weeks after his fiftieth birthday.

Isaac Stevens, the "victor" in this war of wills, outlived Leschi's execution by only four and one-half years. For all his intelligence, energy and courage, Stevens was a man whose emptiness could not be filled, so he pushed himself ever harder. As a Union General during the Civil War, Stevens served with courage and distinction, commanding a company known as the Highlanders. On September 1, 1862, near Chantilly, Virginia, Stevens dragged his wounded son, Hazard, from the battlefield, then leaped into the breach, seizing the Highlanders flag from a fallen standard-bearer. Crying "Highlanders, my Highlanders, follow your general!" he led a charge that forced the retreat of the Confederate foe. The tale is told that, just as a bolt of lightning split the sky over the battlefield, a ball struck Stevens in the temple, and he fell dead, clutching the colors. Perhaps if he had survived, his iron will and boundless ambition might have carried him to the President's Mansion. He was only forty-four years old when he died.

❉❉❉

The Puget Sound Coastal Salish are not gone. More than ever, as we Bostons choke on the detritus of our material success, we see the wisdom of their ways. This is not a call for naive worship of an idealized harmonious native society that never existed, but simply a suggestion that the people we defeated and so ruthlessly "civilized" had, and still have, as much to teach us, as we ever had to teach them.

When I interviewed Cynthia Iyall and others, I had in mind writing a magazine article. Obviously, things got away from me. Although this is a work of fiction, there were times when I felt moved by forces outside myself that needed to tell their story. While I have embellished and created some characters and scenes entirely, I have stuck to the historical record of what actually occurred in both broad outline, and in most particulars. More than that, I have aimed at capturing the emotional truth of these turbulent times, to the best of my ability.

How can a Boston channel Leschi's story? He cannot. I firmly believe, however, that this is not just Leschi's story. This is our story. It is the story of all Americans, the story of what happened again and again when different cultures collided on one achingly beautiful and rich land. It is a story that is still unfolding – how fear of the unknown "other" warps the will to goodness. Ultimately, it is the story of our own hearts, which beat and bleed the same, regardless of our Gods or our skin.

On the same day that I visited with Cynthia Iyall, I pulled off the freeway at an exit near the city of Tacoma, into the huge parking lot of the Puyallup Tribe's Emerald Queen Casino. Way down at the far end of the parking lot there is a high chain-link fence. Beyond the fence, on a thinly wooded knoll overlooking what's left of the Army Corps of Engineers' straightened and dredged Puyallup River, and a four-lane highway choked with whizzing automobiles, there is an Indian Cemetery.[1] The day I was there, two days before the 197th anniversary of his birth, Leschi's dark granite tombstone was festooned with chains of flowers and gaily-colored bits of cloth. On one side, the stone says:

CHIEF LESCHI

1808-1858

AN ARBITRATOR OF HIS PEOPLE

On the other side, this version of the truth is cut in stone:

LESCHI

JUDICIALLY MURDERED FEB. 19, 1858, OWING TO MISUNDERSTANDING GROWING OUT OF TREATY OF 1854-5 AND WAR OF 1855 AND 1856. SERVING HIS PEOPLE BY HIS DEATH, SACRIFICED TO A PRINCIPLE. A MARTYR TO LIBERTY, HONOR AND THE RIGHTS OF PEOPLE AND HIS NATIVE LAND. ERECTED BY THOSE HE DIED TO SERVE 1929.

Standing there in the chill by Chief Leschi's grave, I cried tears no different than any other man's.

---

[1] Out of respect, please obtain permission from the Puyallup Tribe if you wish to visit.

Glossary of Native & Chinook Terms

Alala	Nettle
Alki	By & by, eventually
Alta	Now
And	Pe
Chahko	Come
Chuck	River
Cǝbid	Douglas fir
Cultus	Bad, inferior
Doquebulth	Powerful god who can transform matter, a spirit of light or goodness
Elita	Slave
Enumclaw and Kapoonis	Brothers, thunder and lightning
Halo	No
Hama-hama	Rotting fish that washes up on shore
Highas	Here
Huloima	Another
Hyak	Quick
Hyak cooley	Run
Hyas papa	Great Father
Illahee	Land
Iskum	Get
Kahpho	Sister
Kapswalla klootchman	Rape
Kimta	Rear end
Klahowya	How are you?
Klale	Black
Klootchman	Wife, woman
Kloshe	Good
Kloshe tillicum	Good friend
Kopa	With
Kopet	Stop, Surrender
Kopet noise	Silence
Kumtux	Understand
Kwahnesum	Forever
Kwass	Afraid
Laliad	Spirit of the wind
Mahkook	Bargain

Mahsie	Thank-you
Mamook	Do
Mesachie	Evil
Mesika	You (plural)
Mika	You (singular)
Mimoluse	Die
Mitlite tumtum	Remember
Mitwhit	Stand up
Mox-poo	Explode
Muck-a-muck	Eat; feast
Naha	Momma
Nawitka	Yes
Nesika	Our
Nika	Me, I
Nisqually	The river grass; also, the People of the River Grass
Ohanapecosh	Looking down on something wonderful
Otlas-Skio	Land of the dead
Pelton	Crazy
Pight	Battle, war
Pil chikamin	Gold
Polaklie illahee	Land of perpetual darkness
Puyallup	More than enough
Sah-hah-lee Tyee	Great Spirit
Schut-whud	Bear
Seatco	Demon of dark forests who enslaves children and others who stray off the established paths
She-nah-nam	Medicine Creek
Siwash	Savages; derogatory term for Coastal Salish people
S'kookum	Strong, power, demon
S'kookum Chuck	Rough or fast water
Tacobet	"Nourishing breast"; Mt. Rainier. Also known as "Takhoma", meaning "great snowy peak".
Tamanous	Spirit; spirit guide
Tenalquot	Happy Land; generally, the land promised to the Nisquallies by Sah-hah-lee Tyee."

Tenas man	Boy, young man
Tillicum	Friend
Tikegh	Love, sex
T'kope	White
T'kope tillicum	White Man
Tobcadad	War spirit
Tootosh	Breast
Tsiatko	A large, hairy giant, who lives in mountainside caves, and smells terrible.
Tumtum	Heart
Tumtum kunamokst	Agree
Tupso	Rose
Wake	No (something)
Wikiup	Temporary 3-sided shelter made from available materials
Whulge	Puget Sound
Whulshootseed	The South Puget Sound dialect of Salish spoken by the Nisqually tribe
Wollochet	Squirting Clam (geoduck)
Ya-hoh!	Lift together
Zach-ad	Swamp spirit, whose cry portends death
Zug-wa	Demon beneath the lake

Character List

"INDIANS" (Natives)

Alala: Cowlitz wife of Sandy Smith.

Ann: Nisqually, Second Wife of Leschi.

Betsy Edgar: Puyallup, wife of John Edgar, old friend of Sara.

Charlie Salitat: Duwamish, latter-day Paul Revere.

Clipwalen: Similkameen rescued and raised by Jim McAllister.

Curly (Su-quardle): Duwamish Chief, father in law of Henry Yesler.

Elikuka: Nisqually, son of Yokwa Village medicine man, friend of Sluggia.

George: Nisqually, Quiemuth's son.

John Hiton: Nisqually, from Tenino, father of Mary.

Kwahnesum: Nisqually, Leschi's daughter.

Kamiakan: Great Yakama Chief, father of Owhi.

Kanasket: Chief of Klickitat, Leschi's cousin.

Kitsap: Suquamish, Leschi's fellow war chief.

Kiya: Nisqually, little daughter of Quiemuth & Moonya.

Kul-sass: Medicine man of Puyallup village, Wollochet.

Leschi: Nisqually Chief. Son of a Klickitat-Yakama mother, and Sennatco, a Nisqually father. Brother of Quiemuth, Skai-ki. Father of Kwahnesum.

Mary: Nisqually, John Hiton's daughter, Leschi's third wife.

Moonya: Nisqually, Quiemuth's first and only wife.

Moshell: Yakama, Kamiakan's younger son.

Mrs. Mommacdish: Skykomish, McAllisters' cook.

Nelson: Klickitat.

Owhi: Yakama, Kamiakan's elder son.

Patkanim: Chief of Snoqualmies, brother-in-law to Leschi through marriage to Skai-ki.

Quiemuth: Nisqually, elder brother of Leschi.

Sara: Puyallup, First Wife of Leschi.

Se-alth: Duwamish Chief, often called "Chief Seattle" by the White Man.

Sennatco: Nisqually, Leschi's father.

Skai-ki: Nisqually, Leschi's younger sister, wife of Patkanim.

Sluggia: Nisqually, Leschi's nephew, son of Leschi's elder sister who died in birthing him.

Stahi: Puyallup, brother-in-law to Leschi through marriage to his deceased elder sister; father of Sluggia.

Wahoolit ("Yelm Jim"): Nisqually, head man of Yelm village, Leschi's good friend and strongest supporter on the tribal council.

Winyea: Haida slave freed by Leschi who joins with the Nisqually.

Wyamooch: Nisqually, son of old Chief Laghlet.

"BOSTONS" (Americans)

Jack Blunt: Former Hudson's Bay employee who becomes Colonel Blunt, commander of the Territorial Volunteers.

Andrew Bolon: Indian Agent.

Joseph Bunting: Ainsley McAllister's husband.

Washington Bush: "Free Negro" who was co-leader of the first American pioneer party to settle in what became Washington Territory.

Isobel Bush: German-born wife of Washington Bush.

Col. Silas Casey: Commander at Fort Steilacoom.

John M. Chapman: Clerk of the Federal Court in Steilacoom.

Francis Chenoweth: Federal Judge.

Frank Clark: Tacoma lawyer.

Mary Ann Conklin ("Mother Damnable"): Madam of a Seattle brothel.

Michael Connell: Soldier in Territorial Volunteers.

Enos Cooper: Hired man for the Jones family, White River settlers.

Caleb Cushing: Attorney General to President Franklin Pierce.

Arthur Armstrong Denny: Leader of the first pioneers to settle Seattle.

Charlie Eden: Pioneer settler, later Captain of the Territorial Volunteers, and husband of Kwahnesum.

Elwood Evans: Secretary of the Territorial Legislature.

Capt. Guert Gansevoort: Commander of *Decatur*.

George Gibbs: Treaty Commissioner and surveyor.

Hugh Goldsborough: Olympia lawyer.

Charles Grainger: Deputy Sheriff and hangman for Thurston County.

Mrs. Eliza Jones: Pioneer settler on the White River; mother of Johnny King by her deceased husband. Remarried to Mr. Harvey Jones.

Lieutenant Augustus V. Kautz: German-American regular Army; Adjutant to Colonel Casey.

Frederick Kautz: Lieutenant Kautz's brother.

Captain Erasmus Darwin Keyes: Regular army.

Johnny King: 7-year old son of Eliza Jones; White River settler.

George King: 5-year old neighbor of Johnny, but not related.

Edward Lander: Chief Federal Judge for Washington Territory, and a Lieutenant Colonel in the Territorial Volunteers.

Andrew Laws: Territorial Volunteer.

William L. Marcy: Secretary of State under President Franklin Pierce.

Charles Mason: Secretary of Washington Territory; Governor Stevens' right-hand man.

David Swinton Maynard (Doc): Early Seattle settler.

Jim McAllister: Part of the first group of Americans to settle in what would become Washington Territory; later, a Lieutenant in Territorial Volunteers.

Martha McAllister: Jim's wife.

Jimmy McAllister: Jim & Martha's son, also in Territorial Volunteers.

Lila Sue McAllister: Jim & Martha's son younger daughter.

Ainsley McAlister: Jim & Martha's elder daughter, later married to Joseph Bunting.

Charles McDaniel: Hangman for Pierce County.

Ezra Meeker: Puyallup pioneer; served on jury at first trial.

Joseph Miles: Nervous lawyer from Olympia

Abram Benton Moses ("Ben"): Jewish settler and Territorial Volunteer.

Jackson Moses: Brother of Abram, and later, a Territorial Volunteer.

Corporal William Northcraft: Territorial Volunteer.

Lieutenant Thomas S. Phelps: U.S. Marine stationed on the *Decatur*, and sketch artist.

Franklin B. Pierce: 14th President of the United States.

Dandy Pritchard: Governor Stevens' lawyer.

A.B. "Tony" Rabbeson: Governor's right-hand man and Captain in the Territorial Volunteers; one of the express riders and key witness against Leschi.

Benjamin Frank Shaw ("Ben"): Interpreter for the Medicine Creek Treaty council; Major in the Territorial Volunteers.

Mike Simmons: Co-leader of the Simmons-Bush party of first American settlers in Washington Territory; Treaty Commissioner.

Lizzie Simmons: Mike's wife.

Lieutenant Will Slaughter: Young US Army Lieutenant stationed at Fort Steilacoom.

Mary Slaughter: The Lieutenant's wife.

Amy Stevens: Isaac Stevens' stepmother.

Hannah Cummings Stevens: Isaac Stevens' mother.

Isaac Stevens, Sr.: Isaac Stevens' father.

Isaac I. Stevens: first Governor of Washington Territory, and Territorial Superintendant of Indian Affairs.

Margaret Lyman Hazard Stevens ("Meg"): Wife of Isaac I. Stevens.

Hazard Stevens: Son of Isaac & Meg.

Sue, Maude, Kate & Virginia Stevens: Daughters of Isaac & Meg Stevens.

William Tidd: Express rider for the US Army.

Edwin H. Van Decor: Noble Grand Humbug of E. Clampus Vitus Society, San Francisco.

William H. Wallace: Law partner with Frank Clark; Captain in Territorial Volunteers; Prominent Republican member of the Territorial Legislature.

Sidney Webster: President Pierce's private secretary.

J.W. Wiley: Pro-Stevens Publisher of *Pioneer & Democrat.*

George Williams: Pierce County Sheriff.

Henry Wren: One of the Muck Creek "traitors"

Colonel George Wright: Vermonter in charge of U.S. Army operating east of the Cascades.

Henry Yesler: Early Seattle settler and proprietor of the big Seattle sawmill.

KING GEORGE MEN (British) & OTHER WHITE MEN

Dr. Matthew P. Burns: British surgeon who was part of the group of express riders that rode into Connell's Prairie.

John Edgar: British Hudson's Bay Company employee; husband of Puyallup Betsy; guide for Territorial Volunteers; one of the Muck Creek settlers.

John McLeod: Half Algonquin - half Scottish former Hudson's Bay employee; ex-husband of a deceased Nisqually woman; one of the Muck Creek settlers.

Sandy Smith: British ex-Hudson's Bay employee, with Cowlitz wife Alala. One of the Muck Creek settlers.

Dr. William F. Tolmie: Scottish-born British Chief Factor for the Hudson's Bay Company.

Jane Tolmie: Dr. Tolmie's wife.

A Note On Sources

Although a work of fiction, much of this story is based on actual history. Some of the sources I consulted are listed below.

Beck, Mary Giraudo, *Potlach: Native Ceremony and Myth on the Northwest Coast* (Alaska Northwest Books 1993)

Carpenter, Cecelia Svinth, *Leschi: Last Chief of the Nisquallies* (Heritage Quest 1986)

Carpenter, Cecelia Svinth, *The Nisqually, My People* (Heritage Quest 2002)

Carpenter, Cecelia Svinth, *Where the Waters Begin: the Traditional Nisqually Indian History of Mount Rainier* (Northwest Interpretive Ass'n, Seattle 1994)

Clark, Ella E., *Indian Legends of the Pacific Northwest* (U. Cal. Press 1953)

Egan, Timothy, *The Good Rain* (Knopf 1990)

Eckrom, J.A., *Remembered Drums: A History of the Puget Sound Indian War* (Pioneer Press Walla Walla 1989)

Emmons, Della Gould, *Leschi of the Nisquallies* (T.S. Denison & Co., Inc. Minneapolis 1965)

Gunther, Erna, *Ethnobotany of Western Washington: The Knowledge and use of Indigenous Plants by Native Americans* (rev. ed. U.Wash. Press (1973)

Hancock, Samuel, *The Narrative of Samuel Hancock 1845-1860* (Robert M. McBride & Co. 1926)

History and Ritual of E Clampus Vitus, www.phoenixmasonry.org/masonicmuseum/fraternalism/e_clampus_vitus.htm

Jones, Nard, *Seattle* (Doubleday & Co., Inc., Garden City NY 1972)

Leschi v. Washington Territory, 1 Wash.Terr. 13 (1857)

Lotchin, Roger W., *San Francisco, 1846-1856: From Hamlet to City* (U. Illinois 1997)

Meeker, Ezra, *Pioneer Reminiscences of Puget Sound* (The Printers, Everett 1905, new material 1980)

Meeker, Ezra, *The Tragedy of Leschi* (1905 & 1980 The Printers, Everett WA)

Richards, Kent D., *Isaac I. Stevens: Young Man in a Hurry* (Brigham Young University Press 1979)

Underhill, Ruth, *Indians of the Pacific Northwest* (Sherman Institute Press – Riverside CA 1945)

University of Washington, Special Collections, Papers of Isaac I. Stevens, William H. Wallace, Sarah McAllister Hartman

vulcan.wr.usgs.gov/Volcanoes/Rainier/description_rainier.html

Watt, Roberta Frye, *Four Wagons West* (Binsford & Mort, Portland OR 1934)

Winthrop, Theodore, *Saddle and Canoe* (Long Riders' Guild Press) (originally published 1863)

washingtonhistory.org/wshm/education/prototype/leschi/leschitrial.htm

web.bryant/edu/~history/h364material/musket/rev_gun5/htm

www.halcyon.com/arborhts/chiefsea.html - for Chief Se-alth's speech. There is some dispute as to the authenticity of this speech. Chief Se-alth attended the treaty talks at Point Elliott, not Medicine Creek.

www.historylink.org

www.phoenixmasonry.org/masonicmuseum/fraternalism/e_clampus_vitus. htm

www.synaptic.bc.ca/ejournal/smith.htm

www.usregulars.com/drill_history.html

A source I did not consult, because it came out long after this manuscript was finished, but which the reader might find interesting: Kluger, Richard, *The Bitter Waters of Medicine Creek* (Knopf 2011)

Acknowledgements

I wish to thank my dear friend John Sessions for supporting me in the writing of this book. Without your generosity, John, it might not have happened, and it certainly wouldn't have been as much fun. I would also like to thank Leschi's descendent and Nisqually Tribal Chairwoman, Cynthia Iyall, for speaking with me about her remarkable ancestor. Many thanks to Nisqually tribal attorney, Bill Tobin, for providing me with valuable documents pertaining to Leschi's trials. Gladys LaFlamme Colburn was my high school creative writing teacher who inspired in me a lifelong love affair with words – Gladys, you are always in my heart. Thanks are due to John Ladenburg, who spoke with me about the effort to bring a measure of belated justice to Leschi's case. I appreciate the assistance of the special collections reference librarians at the University of Washington library, and Washington State Historical Society. My editor, Yona Zeldis McDonough, holds a special place in my esteem for her astute notes balanced by kind words of encouragement. Greg Watson generously shared with me his broad knowledge of the language and traditions of Puget Sound Native Americans. I attended a very informative lecture by Lorraine McConaghy, whose book, *Warship Under Sail: the USS Decatur in the Pacific West*, has since been released. Doug Honig of the ACLU-Washington shared his perceptive insights about an earlier draft of the manuscript, as did my shirt-tail cousin Gary Tepfer, who is a fine naturalist and photographer. Celeste Bennett did a marvelous job editing the galleys. Wendy Marcus saved me from myself, inspiring me to unpack my heavy sentences. My elder daughter Ava read the galley through and caught last-minute typos. Then my friends Garth Dennis and Bob Jensen read the ARC and uncovered a few more glitches. Thank-you, keen-eyed readers! Kisses to my wife Carol, my first, last and best editor, and to my daughters Ava and Nellie, who inspire and amaze me. All of you helped me improve the manuscript; the mistakes that linger are mine.

About the Author

Michael Schein is a Seattle writer, poet, playwright, teacher and lawyer. His first novel, *Just Deceits: A Historical Legal Mystery* (Bennett & Hastings 2008), tells the gripping tale of a 1793 infanticide trial defended by John Marshall and Patrick Henry. His co-authored play based on *Just Deceits* is currently heading towards production. His poetry is widely published, and has been nominated for the Pushcart Prize twice. He is founder and director of the LiTFUSE Poets' Workshop, held annually in Tieton, Washington, and director of Burning Word at Icicle Creek, a poetry performance festival. Michael has taught poetry and fiction at Port Townsend Writers Conference. Michael runs Rubric LLC, a company that provides seminars for attorneys on legal history, legal ethics and current events. Previously, Michael taught American Legal History at Seattle University Law School, and served on the speakers' bureau of the ACLU of Washington. Michael is married and has two daughters..